Death's Domain

The Sixth Cassidy McCabe Mystery

ALEX MATTHEWS

INTRIGUE PRESS

Philadelphia

ISBN 1-890768-37-5

First Printing, October 2001

This book is a work of fiction. Names, characters, places and incidents are either the product of the author's imagination or are used fictitiously. Any resemblance to actual events or locales or persons, living or dead, is entirely coincidental. Although the author and publisher have made every effort to ensure the accuracy and completeness of information contained in this book, we assume no responsibility for errors, inaccuracies, omissions, or any inconsistency herein. Any slights of people, places or organizations are unintentional.

Library of Congress Cataloging-in-Publication Data

Matthews, Alex.
    Death's Domain / Alex Matthews.
        p. cm.-- (The sixth Cassidy McCabe mystery)
    ISBN 1-890768-37-5 (alk. paper)
        1. McCabe, Cassidy (Fictitious character)--Fiction.
        2. Women psychotherapists--Fiction. 3. Women cat owners--Fiction. 4. Chicago (Ill.)--Fiction. 5. Cats-- Fiction. I. Title.

PS3563.A83958 D43 2001
813'.54--dc21

                                                    2001024763

10 9 8 7 6 5 4 3 2 1

For my husband Allen, who makes all things possible.

Many thanks to all the people who helped in the birthing of this book: my husband, Allen Matthews, whose fourth career has become book promotion; my editor, Chris Roerden, who would not accept less than my best; my fellow critique group members, Nancy Carleton, Cecelia Comito, and Ginny Skweres, who faithfully refused to let me get away with anything; my publicist Barbara Young, who applied her vast energy and enthusiasm to book promotion; Intrigue Press Editor Robert Hermesch, who guided me in preparing the final manuscript; Chicago Police Detective Anne Chambers and Oak Park Police Detective Art Borcher, who educated me on the police response to email threats; Dan Haley, Publisher of the Oak Park Wednesday Journal, who explained the workings of a suburban newspaper; Lucy Zahray, who informed me about drugs; and fellow DorothyL member Charles Ormiston, who provided the words, *Death's Domain*, when my brain refused to generate the right title.

Everyone gave freely of their time and expertise. Where errors exist, they are mine.

1.

Deathless in Oak Park

A paw bapped her nose. Gripped by her dream, Cassidy McCabe burrowed deeper into the covers. Starshine, not easily discouraged, dug her way under the blankets, touched her damp nose to Cassidy's forehead, and purred louder.

Swimming upward from the depths of an unnerving nocturnal vision, Cassidy dragged herself into a sitting position and blinked groggily at the calico cat. Starshine moved to the end of the bed to stare pointedly into the hall. The clock on the bureau said eight A.M., and the pillow to Cassidy's right was empty.

"If Zach's up, I know you're not starving, no matter how much you insist that you are."

She felt edgy and disoriented, a residue from her dream. Staring into space, she tried to recapture it. A multitude of chalky-faced high school girls in flouncy white dresses standing on a rolling green meadow, all gazing east. Although it seemed as if she were observing from a distance, she knew that she was really somewhere among them, indistinguishable on the outside but emotionally set apart, the other girls hating her.

You've had this dream before.

When? What brings it up?

Anniversaries you don't want to remember. Days that

hearken back to bad things from the past.

She looked through her north window at gnarly bare branches against a pale blue sky. November. The only unpleasant anniversaries she could think of were the wedding and divorce dates from her first marriage, and neither of those had taken place in the eleventh month of the year.

Thoughts of the bad old times caused her to shift her gaze to the photo montage on the wall opposite the bed, her eyes fastening on a picture taken at the backyard reception for her second marriage. The print showed Cassidy in the middle, Zach and his teenaged son on either side. *A talisman. A reminder that the past is the past and the present—this week at least—is golden.* She decided everything was fine, she had nothing to worry about, the dream was irrelevant.

"Oh well," she said to the cat, now pouncing on her blanket-covered toes. "Just goes to show that the unconscious really *isn't* infallible, much as I like to delude myself to the contrary."

The phone rang but she let the answering machine on her desk take it, the sound turned down so she couldn't hear the caller.

Starshine succeeded in penetrating the blanket and digging her fangs into Cassidy's big toe. "Ouch!" She jerked her foot away. "Okay, you win. You can have a second breakfast."

Dressing in jeans and a purple sweatshirt, she went into the bathroom to brush her cinnamon-colored hair, thick curls straggling around her neck and shoulders. *Why didn't you get your hair cut two weeks ago, when you first thought of it? And why don't you own a single barrette or clip or scrunchie so you could get this mess off your neck? You're so inept with hair, you wouldn't know how to use those things if you had them. Your girl training was obviously deficient.*

Perhaps she should get rid of all her hair, go bald like Michael Jordan. Trying to picture the results, all she could envision was a light bulb. *Besides, you'd have to shave it every day, and daily is definitely not your strong point.* Sometimes getting herself into the shower on a once-every-twenty-four-hour basis was almost more than she could manage.

Heading down the stairs, she caught a whiff of toast and coffee in the living room, evidence that Zach had eaten earlier. On her way past the dining room table, she picked up a note and carried it into the kitchen, its scuffed cabinets, worn-out countertops, and curling-seam linoleum in dire need of rehabbing. She leaned against the sink to read the brief message.

CASS,
LEFT EARLY TO WRITE UP LAST NIGHT'S SHOOTING. SHOULD BE DONE BY AFTERNOON. LET'S GO TO THE DESERT CAFÉ FOR DINNER. LOVE, ZACH.

He didn't usually work on Saturdays, but he'd received a call late the previous night with news of an alderman's murder and had decided to go into the *Post* this morning to write the story.

Starshine nipped her knee, a reminder that food should always come first. As Cassidy spooned wet smelly glop into the cat bowl on the counter, the calico jumped up to bury her face in it.

Starting fresh coffee, Cassidy stared through the window at sunlight washing over her neighbor's backyard, then glanced into the kitchen window directly opposite hers where Dorothy Stein presided over a gang of adopted teenagers, no two with quite the same racial background.

While the coffeemaker gurgled, she mentally reviewed her

day. Two clients, starting at noon: Joanne, whom she'd been seeing six months to discuss her affair with a married man, and Troy, who'd been coming a little longer to work on his lack of success with women.

She looked out the window again. The unseasonably mild weather beckoned to her, made her want to work outdoors so she could look up into the clear blue sky, feel the warmth of the sun on her face. *You could wash your office windows inside and out. Give Zach a major shock. Make your clients think they'd walked into the wrong place when they saw all that sparkling glass.*

The odds of you carrying soapy water up a ladder are about as great as Dr. Laura acquiring empathy.

Cassidy marveled at how bright the light seemed even so early in the day. *Bet it's warm enough you could drink coffee on the porch one last time.* Porch sitting in November was a rarity.

She filled her mug, then spoke to the cat, who sat on the counter washing her face, a dainty triangle with one black ear, one orange ear, and a small pink nose. "You want to go outside? There might even be a fly left for you to eat." Flies appeared to be as much of a treat for Starshine as peanut butter cups were for Cassidy.

Running ahead of Cassidy through the house and out onto the enclosed porch—its row of dirty windows facing west—the calico disappeared through the one they routinely left open for her. The air felt brisk. The wind chimes jangled from the eaves. Cassidy picked up the *Register* from the top step, then glanced at the yard next door, where Dorothy's husband and three dark-skinned kids were raking crinkly brown leaves from their lawn out to a huge mound at the curb.

She smiled to herself. *You are such a slug. Here they are doing physical labor, and your plan for the morning is to bask in this great air and read the Oak Park paper.*

Even though Zach worked for the *Post*, she disapproved of the media on principle and refused to look at any part of the paper other than the cartoons, which she collected, and the stories written by her husband. But she enjoyed keeping abreast of village controversies through the local weekly. *So what's the issue of the week? Racial balance in the schools? The gay festival? Library staff changes?* Oak Parkers could get up in arms about almost anything.

As she settled on the wicker couch's old floral cushion, the date at the top of the paper caught her eye. November fourth. The words seemed to jiggle something loose from deep down in her unconscious, bringing back that edgy feeling from her dream.

Did something bad happen on November four? Or is it just your imagination going berserk, trying to concoct something out of nothing, dredging up a wisp of bad memory because the past few months have been so trouble-free you've exceeded your tolerance for peaceful, orderly existence.

She flipped through the front section, sipped coffee, breathed in the earthy smells of damp ground and decaying leaves. Gazing out at the street, she noticed that even though the parkway elms were bare, the smaller maples still held a thatch of bright yellow. *Village always looks so serene. Easy to forget your back door window was broken just two months ago. Yeah, but that could happen anywhere and it seemed like the guy didn't even come inside.*

Returning to the porch, Starshine jumped onto her window ledge and said *mrup*. Cassidy moved on to sports, then obituaries. These were sections she seldom opened, but her mug wasn't empty yet and she didn't want to give up the outside air.

She turned another page and stopped abruptly, eyes glued

to a grainy photo of a face identical to hers. A narrow face with deep set eyes, high cheekbones, and pointed chin, curly shoulder-length hair nestling around it. She felt a tingling in her scalp. Her chest tightened.

There was her name, CASSIDY MCCABE, in big bold letters centered above the brief obituary. *How could the paper make a mistake like that? Mixing me up with somebody else. And why a picture? No photos with any of the others.*

November fourth. What happened on November fourth? Oh no, oh no! This is not something you ever want to remember.

She skimmed the two short paragraphs.

CASSIDY MCCABE, 24, DIED NOV. 4 IN AN AUTOMOBILE ACCIDENT. SHE WAS A GRADUATE OF THE UNIVERSITY OF ILLINOIS AT CHAMPAIGN.

SHE IS SURVIVED BY HER MOTHER AND FATHER, MR. AND MRS. DONALD SEGEL, HER SISTER ELAINE AND BROTHER PETER. FUNERAL SERVICES TOOK PLACE NOV. 9 AT FOSTER-HARRIS FUNERAL HOME.

It doesn't say she had a .12 blood alcohol level. Or that she could have gone home safely in a taxi if her friend hadn't forced her to leave. Or that what happened turned out in the long run to be irrelevant, nothing to have hysterics over, no reason at all for a vibrant young woman to die.

The voice in her head faded out. Her surroundings became less real, as if she were floating overhead watching her zombie-self stare out at the street. She saw Starshine leap down from the window ledge, prance over to the wicker couch, jump up on the seat, and bump her head against the figure sitting there. The zombie person let the newspaper slide to the floor, reached out to scratch behind the cat's ear. But Cassidy, observing from above, could feel neither the movement of the hands nor the sensation of skin against fur.

The cat climbed into her lap, kneaded her chest, seemed to be trying to pull her back, but she stubbornly remained outside, not wanting to remember. When the zombie person didn't respond, Starshine left through her window again.

Some time later a gray Nissan pulled up in front of the house. *Oh shit! Don't want him here. He won't let you stay a zombie.* Zach, dark-haired, wide-shouldered, moved rapidly toward the porch, coming inside to stand over her.

"You've seen it."

If you go back, you'll have to remember. You'll have to tell him.

Her zombie-self continued staring at the street.

Sitting next to her, Zach took both her hands in his. "Cass, look at me."

You might as well give up. He's not going away.

The overhead observer slid back inside Cassidy's skin. A deep shudder ran through her. She sighed heavily, blinked, then gazed into Zach's troubled blue-gray eyes.

"Are you okay?" he asked.

"I saw the picture, read the obituary, then just sort of went off somewhere. And wherever it was I went, I really wanted to stay there." She grimaced. "For an instant, I didn't even want to see *you.*" She laid her hand on his arm. "But now that I've regained my senses, I'm really glad you're here." She felt a rush of affection for her husband, who had come running to the rescue the minute he learned something was wrong.

He folded the paper so the fake obituary faced outward. "You have any idea what this is about?"

You have to tell him.

Not yet.

2.

Skeletons and a Vandal

"Maybe this is one of those movies about people who've died but don't know they're dead. Maybe I'm an official ghost only neither of us has figured it out yet." She shook her head. "Sorry, I don't mean to make bad jokes."

He had smooth dark hair above a bronze-skinned face, high forehead, hawkish nose, and jagged scar running across his left cheek. Studying the paper, he said, "Shit. You know where this picture came from?"

She peered at the familiar image. "Oh god. It was taken from the wedding picture on the wall." She met his eyes. "Somebody removed my face from that photo with you, me and Bryce in it? But how would they do that? By sticking a camera up close and taking a picture of a picture?"

"That's what they'd have to do unless they got their hands on a reprint."

"How could they get something like this past the editor?"

"The way copy's transmitted electronically, anybody with the right password could wait until the edition's finished, then delete an existing obit and replace it with this." He paused. "But why? Why fake an obituary of you?"

She stared at him helplessly.

"Okay, let's put the who and the why on hold for now and

concentrate on the one concrete piece of information we have, which is the picture. How many copies are floating around?"

Biting her lip, she pulled up her memory of the month she'd spent organizing and distributing wedding pictures. "I think I gave duplicates to Gran, Mom, and Bryce."

"We'll have to check with them, but since nobody else'd know where the copies are, the most likely scenario is that somebody photographed the picture on our wall." He paused. "Since you keep the door unlocked when you're doing therapy, if one of your daytime clients sat outside the house and watched another client arrive an hour prior to their own session, they could come in early and be fairly certain you'd be locked in your office until the hour was up. Considering I'm usually gone during the day, they could wander through the house to their heart's content without fear of being caught."

How could it be a client? A client wouldn't know what happened on November fourth. Cassidy stared out at the street where a bunch of grade school children were playing soccer. A mother and a toddler in a blue neon sweater watched the game from the sidewalk.

"You have any deranged clients pissed off at you?"

"You know none of my clients are deranged. They're just nice, ordinary people with garden-variety problems like depression and bad marriages."

"Okay, so they're not deranged. How 'bout pissed off?"

"I don't think so." She reflected on the thirty or so people she was currently seeing for therapy. "It's hard to be sure. I undoubtedly say things on occasion that make some of them angry, but the majority wouldn't be assertive enough to tell me." She shook her head. "I just can't believe one of my clients would do this."

His shaggy brows drew together. "I suppose it's possible

somebody walked in off the street."

"What about that break-in where the guy set off the alarm, then disappeared before the police got here?"

Zach cocked his head in thought. "The ADT records showed an eight-minute gap between the window being broken and the police arriving. That'd be time enough to take a picture." He stared into space. "The cop said a similar incident happened at another house in the neighborhood. Maybe our intruder staged a trial run at some other ADT place, then waited outside to see what the response time'd be."

"The other question is how would anybody know the photo was there?" She paused. "Well, I guess it's obvious. He either went in blind, assuming he'd find something, or he's been in our bedroom before."

Smiling, Zach leaned back against the threadbare cushion. "Well, that narrows it down. Either somebody we know, or somebody we don't know." He gave her a long look. "Can you think of anyone who might want to do something like this?"

"Nobody." She put her hand on his leg. "How'd you find out so soon? It's just sort of an accident I saw it myself. I usually don't even look in that part of the paper."

"The editor got hold of me. He discovered it a couple of hours ago. When he couldn't raise anybody here at the house, he called me at the *Post*. He's phoning everybody on the staff trying to track down how it happened." He shook his head. "Bob's trying to pass it off as a hoax, but it reads more like a threat to me."

"A threat?" Her mind was running way behind, so focused on the past she had not yet put any thought into the purpose behind it. *The only person with a reason to hurt you is dead.*

"Well, here's hoping Bob Huske is able to identify the guy who put this trash in the paper so we can back him into a cor-

ner and make him tell us what he's up to. And then, when
we're through with him, he can get busy thinking up a new
career 'cause no newspaper's going to touch him after this."
She glanced at her watch. Nearly ten. "Thank goodness I
only have two clients, a noon and a one o'clock. We have time
to visit Huske before I get started." She gazed at the blue-
sweatered toddler who, having spied Starshine in the yard,
went running after her, arms flapping, voice chattering. The
calico disappeared.

Zach's eyes deepened with concern. "Don't you think it
might be better to cancel? When I first got here, it looked to
me like you were half in shock."

"Well, I was." *You have to tell him.*
Later. I'll do it later. "There's a story behind these two paragraphs. A not-very-nice story. And whoever snuck this obit
into the paper has obviously heard it." She gritted her teeth,
hating the thought that she would have to face someone who
knew about November fourth. "Anyway, that's why I had such
a strong reaction."

"So—you have skeletons too. Except you know all of
mine." His eyes narrowed. "Aren't you the one who always says
secrets are verboten?"

She took his hand. "I should've told you. I don't know why
I didn't."

"Sure you do." His voice amused. "You like to set it up so
the men in your life are the ones with the problems and you
get to be the good woman who stands by her man."

"Zach, that's not true." She pulled her hand away. "Who
was it that got reported for violating confidentiality? Who had
anxiety attacks every time she got in a car, and who had a psychopath referring clients to her? When it comes to problems,
I'd say we're pretty even up." *However, I am the one who most*

frequently gets disapproving and huffy. "Well, all right." She looked up from under her brow. "I guess I have been guilty of adopting a morally superior stance on occasion."

"That's okay. The role of morally challenged jerk suits me." He put his hand on her knee. "So what's this not-very-nice story you've been keeping to yourself?"

She got a sick feeling in her stomach. "I don't think I can talk about it just yet."

"You don't expect me to give you a hard time, do you?" She shook her head. "Whatever it is, I presume it happened before we met?" She nodded. "So what's there to worry about?"

"I know you'll be fine with it. It may not even seem like such a big deal to you. It's just hard for me to talk about is all."

"Okay, I can understand that." There'd been one episode from his past that he had been able to relate only in bits and pieces. "So, when will you feel up to telling me?"

"How about later tonight? We can go out for dinner, then sit in the waterbed and cuddle. I'll tell you then." She gave him a weak smile.

"That'll work."

"Are you home for the day? Don't you have to finish your story on the murdered alderman?"

"Hearing that my wife'd secretly died broke my train of thought."

It wasn't me who died. "Yes, but here I am deathless or undead or something, and you still need to get your story written."

"I'll work on it at home while you see clients. Right now, my top priority is talking to Bob to see if he found out who did it."

"I'm impressed he remembered my name and knew to call you." She'd met Bob Huske only once. Zach and Huske had appeared together on a panel discussion of media ethics. At the time, the *Register's* editor had struck her as a good deal more conservative than her sometimes too-freewheeling husband. "As I recall, you introduced me after the panel was over, we chatted for thirty seconds, and that was it."

Zach gave her an ironic smile. "Have you forgotten that our names've turned up together in a couple of major news stories? How could the local editor not know that you and I are married and living inside his coverage area?" He sat forward, hands on knees. "Let's take a drive over to his office and see what he has to say."

"We probably ought to check the answering machine first. I'm sure people are calling already." She sighed. "The downside of living in a community where half the population either knows you or knows of you."

They went upstairs into the dusty rose bedroom, two executive desks at the north end, a waterbed sporting a burgundy comforter with several fluffy mauve pillows in the middle, a bureau with a TV on top at the south end. Plunking down in her swivel chair, Cassidy gazed at the answering machine's frantically blinking light. Zach sat at his desk a few feet from hers and prepared to jot notes on a legal pad. She pushed PLAY.

The first two messages were from Bob Huske alerting her to the "unfortunate misprint" and promising to publish a correction in next week's paper. Hearing the heartiness in his voice, she drew an overbearing cartoon face on an envelope she pulled from the pile on her desk.

The next two calls were from her friend Maggie and a client, both wanting to make sure the obituary was wrong.

Just as the final beep sounded, the phone next to the machine rang. Gran's voice demanded, "So, what are you doing in the obituaries ahead of me? I oughta have a good fifty years' lead time on you."

Cassidy mouthed to Zach, "It's Gran." Then, speaking into the mouthpiece, she said "We were just on our way out to have a discussion with the editor on that very topic."

Zach crossed the hall into his office and picked up the extension. "Hi Mary. I'm here too."

"So what's up?"

"Damned if I know," Zach said. "But we'll be happy to give you a call as soon as we find out."

Cassidy tapped her pen against the envelope. "I haven't heard from Mom, so I guess that means she hasn't seen it yet."

"I took your mother out to breakfast, then dropped her off at her beauty parlor. She won't know about it till she gets home." Gran paused. "Tell you what. I'll leave a message on her machine asking her to call me as soon as she gets in. Then I'll break the news and convince her not to bug you." She let out a cackling laugh. "But only if you promise to let me in on it if it turns out to be some big mystery."

"You have my word," Cassidy said.

As she hung up, Zach returned to stand in the doorway, his broad-chested, just under six-foot body nearly filling it. His mouth widened in a grin. "If we ever split, you can have the house. I want your grandmother." Crossing to where she sat, he laid a hand on her shoulder. "Let's go see what Bob has to say."

Do you really want to track down the guy who did this? Whoever he is, he's not your friend and talking to him isn't going to make you feel any better. A jittery feeling started in her stomach at the thought of confronting someone who knew about November fourth.

Picking up a black plastic letter opener, she ran her thumb over the sharp edge. "Maybe we should just leave it alone."

"Huh?" Zach gave her a hard look. "Who am I talking to?

You've never left anything alone in your life."

"If somebody's trying to make trouble, why dignify their efforts with a response? Besides, this is connected with something that happened a long time ago and I'd just as soon leave it in the past."

"Aren't you doing a role reversal here? It's me who likes to forget about things. You're the one who always insists on dragging out the dirty laundry."

"Yeah, but if somebody's playing practical jokes, they won't get any payoff unless I react."

"You really think this is just a prank?"

Twisting her head to look up at him, she asked, "Why would anybody want to threaten me?"

"That's the problem. We don't know *why* anything. But I intend to find out." He paused, then said more gently, "Look, maybe you should let me handle it."

"No, I'll go." She sighed and got to her feet. "You know I can never stand to miss out on things."

He rested his hands on her shoulders. "The idea that you might let me take care of anything *is* pretty ridiculous."

"Do you mind that I have this urge to always be involved?"

"Now and then it might be nice to do something entirely on my own." He smiled. "But most of the time, together is better."

3.

A Good Little Puppet

They were headed through the kitchen toward the back door when the ringing started again. Cassidy lifted the receiver from the phone hanging on the wall next to the dining room doorway.

"Cass, I'm so glad you're there . . . something awful's happened . . . I don't know what to do." Her mother's voice, gasping and hysterical.

Oh no, not something with Mom too.

"Take a deep breath," Cassidy said, speaking in a slow, cadenced voice. "That's right. Don't try to talk till you're ready." She paused. "Just keep breathing."

She heard her mother inhale, exhale, the sounds gradually deepening. Zach leaned against the counter to watch.

"The L-O-L Vandal hit my apartment."

Oh shit. The guy who targets little old ladies. Makes a huge mess and steals their underwear.

"Everything's all torn up. Drawers dumped out, my nice clothes just tossed on the floor." She let out a guttural moan.

"Oh Mom, how terrible." The twitchiness in Cassidy's stomach got worse. "Have you contacted the police yet?"

"Wanted to call you first." Cassidy could hear Helen's teeth chattering. "I'm so upset, not sure I could even talk straight."

"I'll call 911, then we'll be right over."

Zach pulled the receiver out of her hand.

"What're you doing?" Cassidy tried to grab it back but she was short and slender and he was almost a foot taller with long burly arms.

"You've got enough to deal with," he said, his palm over the mouthpiece. Then, speaking into it, "What's going on over there, Helen?"

There he goes, taking over again. Being his usual overprotective self. "Give me that phone!" She punched his arm.

Stepping through the kitchen doorway, he leaned close to the dining room wall so she couldn't get her hands on the receiver. "Have you called Gran yet?" A pause. "We've got a problem over here. Cass is in the middle of a major client crisis. Somebody hanging by a thread. She didn't mention it 'cause she doesn't want to let you down. But right now, she really needs to put all her attention into this client of hers. So how 'bout I call Mary, have her be there with you when you talk to the police. We'll come over later." Another pause. "I know you're really upset, but we'll get everything straightened out as soon as we can." Hanging up, he turned toward Cassidy.

"You had no right to do that. I'm going to Mom's. You can talk to the damn editor by yourself." She tried to walk away but he gripped her upper arms to hold her in place.

"Remember when I had the police on my ass and you made me promise not to do anything without telling you first? I was mad as hell but I agreed because I knew I couldn't trust my own judgment."

She frowned fiercely. "This isn't the same at all."

"When I first came home, you were in some kind of weird disoriented state. I don't understand all that's going on with you, but I do know this obituary has you reeling. If you go diving headfirst into your mother's crisis on top of your own, it might just bring on one of those attacks you've had before." A couple of years earlier, she'd had anxiety attacks for a short period following a traumatic experience.

"I'm fine."

"Cass, you're not. When I had all that trouble with the police, you kept telling me I was too close to the situation to be objective. Now you're the one who's too close."

"I admit the obituary caught me off guard. But I'm fine now and I need to be there for Mom." Planting her feet widely, she hooked her thumbs in her jeans waistband. Behind Zach the white phone hung tantalizingly on the wall, just waiting for her to grab it up and call the police.

"What is it you always say to clients? Don't you tell them they have to take care of themselves or they won't be of any use to anybody else?"

She tossed her head. "Will you just get out of my way? I can handle it."

His eyes narrowed. "Why are you acting like this? You know your grandmother'll do fine."

"My grandmother's in her eighties!'

"She's one of the most capable people I know." He paused. "What's making you so frantic to go rescue your mother, anyway?"

She turned away, crossed her arms, paced halfway across the kitchen, then spun to face him. "All right, dammit. I'll be a good little puppet and do what you say."

"You didn't answer the question."

She bit off the words. "Why do you think I'm a therapist?"

"You tell me. Why are you?"

Her voice shrill with anger, she said, "Because fixing other people's problems means I don't have to face my own. Because it makes me feel smart and competent instead of stupid, insecure, and guilty."

Moving closer, he gently grasped her arms again. "Look at all the times you've stepped in when I wasn't thinking clearly. I didn't like it but I needed it. Now it's my turn. Let me be the one to steer us clear of the rocks." *You can't just hand this over to Zach like some mindless little airhead. Yeah, but look at all the times you made him do what you thought was best. And how can you be sure you're not headed for a meltdown?* She realized her stomach was churning, her breath coming too fast. *You are pretty shaky. And you might not be thinking entirely straight either.*

Twisting away from him, she stared through the dining room window at a blue sky dotted with puffy clouds. After a long moment, she turned back to meet his eyes. "Okay, you can take over. But just for today."

Zach phoned Gran and filled her in. She said she'd be at Helen's in five minutes. After a second call to the police, they left for the *Oak Park Register.*

"This isn't the way any of us expected to spend our Saturday morning, is it?" Closing his office door, Huske seated himself behind a battered walnut desk. A wide window to their right filled the room with light, although its view of the backside of a brick building across the alley was less than scenic.

"It hardly ever happens that anyone opens their local paper and *expects* to find themselves in the obituaries," Cassidy replied from one of the two wooden armchairs facing the desk. A dozen neat piles rose from the scarred walnut surface in front of her. In the corner behind the editor's chair, two tabloid-sized metal plates were propped against a heap of other suburban papers.

"You couldn't've been any more surprised than I was," Huske said. "When I realized someone had replaced the original copy with that phony obit, I was mad as hell. Still am, as a matter of fact." The editor was short and paunchy, with a white ruff encircling his head and a round, rosy, jolly-elf face.

"You're not trying to claim that your pain and suffering were greater than Cass's, now are you, Bob?" Zach planted his elbows on the arms of his chair.

"Pain and suffering?" Huske gave them a puckish grin. "What's that supposed to mean? That's not an implication you're planning to get litigious on me, is it?"

"My only plan at the moment is to find out who did it."

Huske voice hardened. "Then you better come up with a different plan."

This is definitely not going the way I'd hoped. Huske is doing his damdest to blow smoke over the fact that I'm the injured party here, not him. This is his domain. He's in control. And Zach's status as reporter for a major daily makes him one part colleague, two parts rival.

Zach asked mildly, "Why would I need a different plan?"

Huske stared out the window at the age-darkened brick structure on the other side of the alley. Returning his gaze to Zach, he said, "To begin with, I don't know who did it."

Zach's eyes narrowed. "You're just going to shrug your shoulders, print a correction, and forget about it?"

"No, of course not. Somebody on my staff broke the most basic rule of journalism and I won't rest till I find out who the son-of-a-bitch is. But we don't have fingerprints or DNA. It may take some time."

Cassidy tapped her fingers against the armrest. "You said 'to begin with.' Does that mean you wouldn't tell us even if you did know?"

"I don't see any reason not to handle this internally."

Zach shifted in his chair. "Somebody deliberately published Cass's obituary. Don't you think she has the right to find out who did it and why?"

"You're making mountains out of molehills, Zach. Somebody got his jollies out of taking a dig at your wife. I *will* find out who did it and he *will* be punished. End of story."

With that white hair, pink skin, and crinkly eyes, looks like he should be dandling a grandchild on his knee. Instead, he's telling Zach to go to hell.

Her jaw tightening, Cassidy said, "So your response to this whole thing is—what's the matter with you, you can't take a joke?"

"Basically, yes."

Zach folded his hands across his chest. "What if this guy turns out not to be entirely harmless?"

"Then I may have to rethink it."

"You publish what?" Zach asked. "Three separate papers out of this office? So you have a fairly large staff."

Huske nodded.

"Would you please explain exactly where an obituary goes from the time the reporter writes the copy till it shows up in the paper?" Cassidy asked, resting her cheek against her open hand.

"The information usually gets called in from a relative or the funeral home. When I first saw your picture, I thought some jokester had brought it in along with a phony story. But then I noticed the date of death was today, and I realized it couldn't've gotten past a reporter with that kind of error. So that means it must have originated inside the office."

Cassidy prompted, "What happens after the reporter takes it down?"

"He types it into the computer, then transfers the file to a design person. These are the guys who do the layout. When the page is finished, it gets sent to an editor, who looks it over and initials it. Then it sits in a box with all the other pages until the courier hauls it to the printer."

"They carry the pages over?" Zach asked. "They don't send it on a disc?"

Huske pulled his head up straight. "This isn't the *Post.*"

"These design people—how many are there?"

"Four."

"And they'd be fairly low level?" Zach asked.

"I know where you're headed. My first thought too. But I've talked with each of them at length—got three out of bed, as a matter of fact—and I'm convinced they didn't do it." He paused. "They're not stupid, but I don't think they've got what it takes to fool a polygraph."

"Or you?"

"Or me." Pressing his fingertips together, Huske grinned maliciously at Zach. "You know, I've been in the business since before you could talk. I put out a good, solid newspaper every week. You may have noticed the certificates on the wall outside—awards the paper's won over the years." He paused. "And you know, in all this time I've never felt the need to create a little action on my own in order to spice up the news. Call me old fashioned, but I still believe a good reporter restricts himself to covering the news instead of making it."

"So you're telling me," Zach drawled, "that because I ended up in a story or two, I should assume your judgment's better than mine and not concern myself with this obituary you published on Cass?"

"You *are* fairly fast on the uptake, aren't you?"

He's not an elf—he's a gremlin. Can't stand the fact that he's at fault so he goes grasping at straws for something to use against Zach.

Cassidy cleared her throat. "Getting back to the editors, they're the last stop before the pages go in the box, isn't that right?"

"My editors have all been with me for years. They'd no more print a bullshit obituary than steal pennies from children."

Sliding lower in his chair, Zach tented his fingers in front of his mouth. "Who'd have the password to the editors' files?"

Huske's gaze moved to a spot on the wall behind Zach's head. His mouth flattened. "We don't need passwords."

Huske may be the boss. He may have all the power. But Zach's got him now.

Zach raised his brows. "And that would be because nobody on your staff would ever print anything that wasn't true?"

"We never needed them before."

"So if you don't use passwords, anybody could have done it."

Huske's shoulders gradually slumped forward, as if the air were leaking out of him. "That's about it."

4.

Affair Gone Wrong

Helen McCabe lived in a three-story greystone with turrets on the corners and carved friezes above the arched windows. When Cassidy and Zach arrived, three squads and an Evidence Technician vehicle were parked in front.

Cassidy raced up the stairs toward Helen's apartment, with Zach close behind. Reaching the second-floor landing, she found her mother's door standing open, a cop leaning against the wall, her mother and grandmother huddled together across from the doorway.

Cassidy took a quick look into the apartment where two plainclothes officers were at work. Her scalp prickled at the sight of upended furniture and heaps of clothing and bedding strewn across the floor. Sucking in air, she turned her back on the devastation and pulled her mother into a close hug. "How you doing?"

"This is the worst thing that's ever happened to me." Helen ran the stubby fingers of both hands through her gray perm, making the hair stand up in short tufts around her moon-shaped face. She was slightly shorter than Cassidy's five-two, her plump body garbed in a sage-colored knit pantsuit that strained across her apple-shaped stomach.

Hard as Mom is to put up with, this time I really feel sorry for her. Having your place torn apart'd be a major violation for any-body.

Gran said briskly, "We'll get this taken care of in no time. I called my cleaning service and they'll be here first thing Monday morning." Gran was thin and sprightly, her tiny face nearly eclipsed by the two black shafts of hair falling from her helmet-like Cleopatra wig.

"I'm sorry I couldn't come right away." Cassidy offered, clasping her hands together in front of her chest.

"Well, I know you always have more important things to do," Helen said, finishing on a sigh.

Cassidy gritted her teeth. *I'm trying to be nice. I really am.*

Zach turned toward the cop, a young black man with a flat-featured face and alert brown eyes. "How'd he get in?"

Pushing away from the wall, the cop answered respectfully, "Came up the back steps and broke the window in the door."

Zach said to Helen, "I'll need to burglar-proof your apart-ment. You can stay with Gran till I get it taken care of."

"I just wish you'd thought of it sooner. All us senior women've been scared to death ever since those stories start-ed coming out about the L-O-L Vandal."

"Helen," Gran said, "you got no business complaining to Zach 'cause he didn't think of everything ahead of time and fix it for you."

Cassidy smiled inwardly. *Half the time Mom's happy as a puppy on a playground to have a man in the family. The other half she's yapping at his heels. Which he never notices anyway.*

Stepping closer, Helen looked up at Zach. "I suppose you're sending me off to Gran's 'cause you don't want to be bothered having a mother-in-law around. It doesn't matter that I've just had the worst shock of my life. What I want doesn't count."

A heavy lump of guilt settled in Cassidy's chest. "Of course you can stay with us if that's what you'd like."

Zach shot Cassidy an irritated look, then responded to Helen in a firm voice. "I'm sorry we can't accommodate you on this, but I'm going to have to say no. Cass is ignoring the fact that she's had a very rough morning and still has two clients to see. As soon as she finishes, I plan to make sure she gets some absolute downtime."

Cassidy pressed her lips in a tight line, one part of her annoyed at Zach for interfering, the other relieved that he was forcing her to do what she knew was really best.

Gran laid an arm around her daughter's shoulders. "There's no reason in the world you shouldn't stay with me. Us girls'll have a slumber party. We can get popcorn and movies and make it a real fun time."

A wounded look came over Helen's face, an expression that never failed to trigger Cassidy's old bad-daughter feelings. *She does that so well. Could teach classes in how to implant guilt, lay blame, and generally keep your adult child jumping through hoops forever.*

"Oh, Helen, come off it," Gran admonished.

Cassidy noted that her mother hadn't said a word about the obituary. *Obviously doesn't know yet. I'll just let Gran take care of that little detail later.*

Zach turned back to the cop. "I'd like a word with one of the detectives."

"Sure thing." The cop disappeared into the apartment.

Stepping into the doorway, Cassidy gaped at the damage, her stomach knotting as she gradually comprehended the viciousness of it. Sheets, blankets, and clothing rippled across the floor, clumps of feathers gathering in the hollows. One lace curtain had been torn from its rod, a ragged edge showing above the window, the length of it crumpled in a swirly mound on the sofa. A flattened Rice Krispies box rested on the coffee table, its contents scattered in all directions. A chair had been turned over, its pole legs sticking up at an odd angle. Photographs and broken knickknacks were tangled amongst the clothing.

A few feet from the door lay a picture in a heavy gold frame, its glass cracked. Beneath the glass was a studio portrait of Cassidy from her college graduation. For the second time that day, she encountered her own face staring up at her from a place it shouldn't have been.

"What did the detective say?" Cassidy asked, buckling herself into the Nissan. "Was there anything to connect this with the obituary?"

Zach hesitated. "I don't think so."

"What are you not telling me?"

He pulled away from the curb. "The word 'bitch' was written in red marker on the bathroom mirror. This is the first instance of a message showing up at any of the scenes. The detective sees it as an escalation."

"You think it might not be the Little Old Lady Vandal? That it could be the same person who did the obit?" She pressed her thumb and middle finger against her forehead. "Now that'd be scary."

"I don't see any reason to make that leap. The vandal's hit at least ten other women around your mother's age. We even talked about beefing up Helen's security and once again, I didn't get on it." He gave her an apologetic smile. "It's nice of you not to yell at me about my procrastinating ways."

Considering he puts up with your touchy-feely therapist questions, it's the least you can do. Especially since it'd be a case of the pot calling the kettle black.

She rested her chin on the back of her curled fingers. "Did you mention the obituary?"

"I decided not to. I doubt that they're connected, and I didn't exactly relish the idea of us having to go down and give statements."

As they approached their corner two-story, driving east on Briar, Cassidy noticed a white Porsche sitting next to her back gate. *Bet that's Joanne.* When the Nissan, on its way to the garage at the far end of the lot, passed the sedan, Cassidy verified that it was indeed her noon client. She waved at the dark-haired woman behind the wheel, then glanced at her watch. *Still plenty of time. I can park her in the waiting room while I run upstairs and put on therapist-clothes.* Zach left the car on the apron and they hastened toward the gate.

Joanne got out to meet them on the sidewalk. "Guess I'm early," she said, ducking her head in apology. She was tall and shapely, with short, stylishly cut ebony hair. *Looks like a non-anorexic model, if there is such a thing.*

"Sorry you had to wait in the car." Cassidy observed that her client's eyes were faded and moist, her lids puffy. *Affairs'll do that to you.*

"Oh, that's okay. I don't mind." Blinking rapidly, Joanne slanted her head away.

Cassidy turned toward Zach. "This is my husband, Zach Moran." *Clients bumping into husbands, always awkward. You can speak his name but not hers.*

He nodded amiably.

Taking a deep breath, Joanne stood straighter and returned the nod. "Didn't you have a garage band back in high school?"

Zach gave her his lazy smile. "Don't tell me you're a groupie from my ancient past."

She shook her head. "It was my brother. He had aspirations to join your band. He always talked as if he wanted to follow in your footsteps or something. My mother absolutely refused but they used to argue about it all the time."

"Your mother was a wise woman. I wouldn't want any son of mine following in my footsteps either."

Cassidy was aware that she, Joanne, and Zach had all attended the village high school at around the same time, although she hadn't known Zach or Joanne and she doubted they had known each other. *Hardly surprising, what with over three thousand students, Zach a druggie, you an egghead, and Joanne probably a cheerleader.*

Zach unlocked the back door and they all paraded into the waiting room, a bright, airy space with filmy mauve fabric draped around the large south window and two fan-backed wicker chairs standing in front of it.

Cassidy said to her client, "Since it isn't noon yet, I'll leave you here while I go upstairs."

"Sure." Joanne sank into one of the chairs, pulling out a tissue to dab at her nose.

As Cassidy and Zach started up the stairs near the front door, he said, "I'd much rather be called out to a grisly murder than have to mop up tears the way you do."

What is it with men that a crying woman seems more of an ordeal than a bloody body?

Guilt. Whenever a woman cries, the guy thinks he caused it. Even though he almost never knows how or why.

At the top of the stairs, Zach veered off into his office on the right and Cassidy turned into the bedroom on the left. Stepping into the closet, she grabbed the first outfit she saw, a magenta blouse with a small stain on the sleeve and black leggings, its dusting of white cat hair within acceptable limits.

A few minutes later Cassidy led Joanne into her corner office, a paneled room with a sand and rose-colored sectional curving around the exterior walls, and in front of the sectional, a low wicker table holding a limp-leafed coleus, a tissue box, and a black plastic pen-holder. Two wide windows flooded the space with light. Joanne perched on the sectional's flat cushion, knees locked together, elbows close to her sides. Her classic face was smoothly made up, her well-contoured body sleekly attired in a black short-skirted dress. But despite the meticulous facade, it was obvious she could barely hold herself together.

"What is it?" Cassidy asked, easing into her director's chair. *You already know. The married lover isn't following her script.*

"Cass, I'm so scared. I don't know what to do." Joanne held the tissue beneath one eye, then the other, attempting to catch the tears before they brimmed over and ran down her face. "KC tried to break it off last night." She always referred to her lover by his initials to make sure Cassidy didn't recognize his name.

"That must've come as a terrible shock." *Almost as bad for Joanne as it would've been for the wife if he'd decided to dump the marriage instead of the affair.*

Joanne covered her mouth with her hand and squeezed her eyes shut. Grabbing a fresh tissue from the box on the table, she wiped her face and gulped air. "I just don't understand it. He's happier with me than he's ever been with anybody else. He says so all the time."

And you know, of course, that every word out of his mouth is the god's own truth. "You said you were scared. What is it you're scared of?"

"I don't think he really means it. I think he's just feeling guilty. Feeling like he ought to put more effort into his marriage. But there's no way he could ever make it work—not when he's in love with me. He's got to come to his senses. Got to see that we belong together."

"But you're afraid he won't."

Joanne's brown eyes were wide and frightened. She pressed her hand against the base of her throat, a gold ring with a blood-red ruby encircling her middle finger. "If this really is the end, there won't be anything to live for."

"Losing someone you love hurts terribly. It's awful. No one ever wants to go through it." Cassidy remembered wanting to die when her ex-husband walked out on her. "But people do get through it, and with enough time, they even manage to enjoy life again." *And they find new things, new people to live for. But she doesn't want to hear it. All she wants is to cling to the hope that KC won't really leave.*

"What can I do to make him understand that he should be with me, not her?"

"There's nothing you can do. He has to make up his own mind." *And whomever he decides to stay with—Joanne or the wife—that's the one with the real problem.*

An angry light flared in Joanne's teary eyes. "You think I should have kept my distance, don't you? Even though we both felt this incredible attraction right from the beginning. You're on the wife's side."

"No, I'm on your side. It's my job to help you do what's best for you, and if KC isn't willing to leave his wife, then loving him may be too painful." *Why bother? You've said the same thing twenty times over and it never gets through.*

"I'm sorry, Cass." She ducked her head again. "I know you're trying to help. I'm just all raw nerves right now."

"Have you had any thoughts of hurting yourself?" *She's not suicidal now 'cause she still thinks he'll be back. But the minute she stops hoping, watch out.*

"Sometimes I wish I could just go to sleep and not wake up . . . but I wouldn't do anything to make it happen."

Forty-five minutes later the clock on the window ledge chimed, signaling the end of the session. Joanne pulled a checkbook out of her soft leather bag. As owner of a trendy boutique on the north side, she presented an exterior as stylish and sophisticated as her interior was chaotic and confused.

Looking directly at Cassidy, she said, "I've been having mixed feelings about therapy. I come here every week and I don't seem to be getting any better."

Maybe that's because you don't listen to anything I say.

"I feel like somehow you ought to be helping me more." She sighed. "But at the same time, I really do need to talk and with the way things are now, I know I won't be able to go a whole week without seeing you." She looked up from under her brows. "So would it be okay if we scheduled an extra session?"

Cassidy picked up her calendar from the wicker table. "How's Wednesday?"

"Do you have a nine o'clock?"

"That's already booked. Could you do ten?"

Joanne said she could, then stepped out into the waiting room where Cassidy's next client, Troy, waited in a fan-backed chair.

"Hey, Joanne, how you doing?" Having passed each other coming and going for months, the two had reached the point of exchanging greetings.

"Okay," Joanne responded listlessly.

You better get him in the office or she'll start crying on his shoulder, the next thing you know they'll be dating, then they'll each come to therapy and tell stories on the other.

Cassidy beckoned Troy into her office and he settled in front of the east window directly across from her chair.

"So how's it going?"

"Well, it happened again," Troy said, his face sullen. In his mid-thirties, he was on the verge of chunkiness, with a hairline creeping up toward his crown. Although he had bright blue, intelligent eyes, the rest of his features were just slightly on the coarse side of handsome. He'd been coming to see her ever since a painful breakup had propelled him into therapy eight months ago.

"What happened again?" Cassidy clasped her hands loosely in her lap.

"There's this new woman at the ski club, Cynthia. She's just my type, exactly what I'm looking for." He sighed. "And of course it didn't go anywhere." Leaning back against the cushion, he slid lower on his spine and rested his hands on his thighs.

Just his type. Thin, gorgeous, and pulling down a six-figure income. "You asked her out?"

"Not right away. I tried to do what you suggested—not come on too strong, chat her up a few times first." He sent Cassidy a rueful smile. "Not an easy task with guys stacked up three deep around her."

"But eventually you asked her for a date?"

"Yep. And she said yes. So last night we went out to dinner."

"And where'd you take her?"

"Oh, this hamburger place in my neighborhood. The atmosphere's not so hot but the food's great."

Cassidy said gently, "We've talked before about the kind of impression you need to make at the beginning."

He glared. "You want me to go into debt taking girls out to dinner?"

No, I want you to date the kind of girl who'd be happy to go to a burger joint instead of the beauty-queen type who naturally expects red carpet treatment.

Sitting straighter, he propped his left ankle on his right knee. "Besides, relationships shouldn't be about money. I don't want some chick who's only interested in five-star restaurants. Bev was just using me. You said so yourself. I don't want to end up with somebody like her again. I need to find a woman who's going to appreciate me for who I am."

Bev, thin and gorgeous but without the income, had briefly been the love of Troy's life. In financial straits when they met, she'd promptly accepted his offer to move in with him, then had run off with another man three months later.

"Okay," Cassidy said, "we've been through this before. You want Julia-Roberts lookalikes to go out with you, but you don't want to take them to the kind of places they're accustomed to going." He started to protest but she raised a hand to stop him. "Tell me about Cynthia."

"I thought everything was going great. She seemed interested in what I was saying, laughed at my jokes. But when I asked if she'd like to do it again, she said we didn't have enough in common." His petulant face darkened; his mouth went tight with anger. "What is it with these chicks, anyway? Why do they just write guys off like that? They ought to go out a few times, get to know me. I hear women all the time complaining about what jerks men are, and here I am, a decent human being, a nice guy, and they won't even give me the time of day."

Cassidy visualized Troy with his developing paunch, disappearing hairline, and irregular features holding hands with Michelle Pfeiffer. *And how he looks isn't half as bad as how he thinks and what he says.*

"Troy," Cassidy said softly, "you always want to date the prom queens. Women who are beautiful, polished, successful in their careers. What do you have to offer in return?"

He drew his brows together fiercely. "There's nothing wrong with me. I've got a good job. Everybody says I'm doing great with the magazine."

Editor of an obscure trade journal.

"I can't help it if I don't feel any chemistry with run-of-the-mill types." He darted a look at Cassidy, no doubt realizing that his comment might not be taken kindly by a female therapist who was no pageant winner herself. "I'm a good person. I deserve to get what I want. I shouldn't have to settle."

All those books on low self-esteem, but I don't know a single thing about people who think they're way better than they are. As much as his exaggerated sense of entitlement irritated her, she could not help but feel sorry for a person so relentlessly determined to be his own worst enemy.

5.

Anticipatory Torture

After Troy left, Cassidy went to the sink to start another pot of coffee. While pouring water into the machine, she heard a familiar *whap*. The cat-door. It whapped soundly every time Starshine went through it. Zach had recently installed it in a window above the basement stairs, located at the far end of the kitchen.

An instant later Starshine sprang onto the counter, washed her orange ear, and said *mrup*. She delicately sniffed her food-encrusted bowl, then pawed the counter to communicate that this dish was so foul it ought to be buried.

Cassidy soaked the offending bowl in the sink. She'd been a little iffy about giving the calico her own private entrance. *We're way too permissive, letting her come and go as she pleases. If she were a kid, we'd have a monster in the making.*

So what if we overindulge her? It's not like she wouldn't be a princess anyway. All cats consider themselves the center of the universe whether they have humans catering to their every whim or not.

Starshine jumped down, trotted over to the back door, leaned against it, and howled.

Following after her, Cassidy said, "The cat-door is fine for coming in but not for going out? This is a show-the-human-who's-boss game, isn't it?"

Cassidy opened the back door and waited as Starshine minced her way over the threshold. *She'll be back in thirty seconds.* The calico's new trick was to come in the cat-door, then demand doorwoman service at the back, repeating the cycle till Cassidy was ready to scream.

Hastily filling two mugs, she left the kitchen before Starshine had time to return. The only way to avoid feline harassment was to vacate the premises.

Upstairs she went into Zach's office where he sat working at his computer. He had installed a fully extended, fifties-style chrome and Formica dinette table as a workspace, with matching chairs in front of the monitor where the two of them sat side by side for her computer lessons. Although she had now mastered word processing and email, much of technology still eluded her.

She put Zach's mug down on the geometrically patterned, pink and green Formica. "How's it going?"

"The cops are still at the 'no comment' stage, so there's not much of a story." He raised his mug and smiled. "Thanks for the coffee." Swallowing, he handed her a sheet of paper. "You've got mail."

Patting his shoulder, she took the paper into the bedroom to read. She had recently sent out a marketing brochure with her email address on it, and a trickle of responses was coming in. Zach routinely printed up her messages since she seldom logged on.

The email was from a former client: CASS, THOUGHT YOU'D LIKE TO KNOW, DAVID AND I JUST ANNOUNCED OUR ENGAGEMENT. YOUR WISE COUNSEL REALLY DID WORK WONDERS. Cassidy grinned, remembering the shy young girl who, when she first started therapy, had never been on a date. *Here's the real reward for what you do.*

Sliding into her desk chair, she dialed Gran's number and asked to speak to her mother.

Helen said, "I still don't see why I can't stay with you, considering you have that extra bedroom and all."

"Gran has plenty of space. And since I've got so much going on right now, I probably wouldn't be able to give you the attention you need."

"But I wanted to spend time with *you*. We hardly ever get together any more. And I'd feel so much safer with a man in the house." She paused. "Zach doesn't like me, does he? That's the real reason he wouldn't let me come over."

How could anybody not like you when you make yourself so delightful to be around?

"Mom, why can't you simply accept what he said? After I spent the morning dealing with a client crisis, Zach thought I needed a break. That's all there is to it."

After listening to Helen moan about the vandalism for several more minutes, Cassidy brought the conversation to a close. *As much as you've always hated giving up control, having Zach turn dictatorial on you isn't all bad. Mom can be mad at him. You don't even have to feel guilty.*

Standing at the west window, she looked down at Hazel, the street in front of her house. A couple of women surrounded by a flock of small children stood talking on the opposite sidewalk. A flat, slate-colored cloud covered the sun, turning the crystalline light gray. A new crop of leaves had blown over the lawn since she and Zach raked a couple of days earlier.

You need to look at the album.

Why would you want to do that to yourself?

To desensitize. To prepare. Anticipatory torture, like anticipatory grieving, so you can talk about it tonight without totally falling apart.

She opened the door to her nightstand and took out three albums, each labeled according to its time frame: GRADE SCHOOL, HIGH SCHOOL, and COLLEGE. Her mother had put the albums together and presented them to her on her thirtieth birthday. Although touched by Helen's thoughtfulness, Cassidy was not particularly thrilled at the prospect of reviewing a childhood she remembered as less than wonderful.

That day she and Helen had sat together on her living room sofa to leaf through the grade school album. A few pages in, Barbara's picture had jumped out at her. Her breath had caught, her hands turned cold. Putting the book aside, she'd hugged her mother and said she wanted to hear every detail of the effort that had gone into compiling the photos.

As soon as Helen left, Cassidy had deposited all three in her nightstand. She'd never opened any of them again, even though she knew she would find Barbara's pictures in only the first. Their friendship had tapered off when they started high school, then picked up again after college.

She sat at her desk, opened the grade school album, and skipped ahead to the first series of pictures featuring Barbara and her family. *C'mon, you can do this.* Making herself breathe deeply, she gazed at half a dozen snapshots of herself and Barbara, both about ten-years-old, at Gran's house, where Cassidy and her mother had lived during much of her childhood.

The girls were dancing, feet off the floor, arms flung wide. Barbara, always the wilder of the two, looked free and unrestrained, green eyes flashing, dark hair flying out around her pert face. *So pretty and high spirited.* Cassidy, the serious one, appeared clearly more earthbound than her friend.

The next page held three pictures of the nightgown-clad girls making faces at each other in Barbara's bedroom, a place where they had talked late into the night, giggled together, told secrets. *Barbara was the most important person in the world to you back then. The two of you clung together in the best-friends-forever way that young girls cherish and adore each other.*

Her throat constricting, she remembered how they had plotted out their futures together. Barbara would be an actress, Cassidy a teacher, and they would share a glitzy, lakeshore high-rise, not marrying until their declining years, not until the ripe old age of thirty at the least.

Turning the page, she came across a posed shot of herself with Barbara and her family, Mr. and Mrs. Segel seated on the sofa, the brother and sister to either side, Barbara and Cassidy on the floor in the middle. Cassidy's father had left when she was five, and her life with her disapproving mother and sup-portive-but-often-absent grandmother had been a lonely one.

Her reprieve had been to escape to Barbara's house, where she was welcomed as part of the family. Mrs. Segel had often urged her to stay for dinner, and after dinner, for reading-aloud time. Mr. Segel had tried to teach her basketball and never grown impatient, even though as far as she could remember, no balls had ever left her hands to go through any hoops.

Gazing at the group clustered in the Segel living room, knowing what had happened to this family she once loved so much, she felt her heart shrivel in her chest.

This is enough. You don't have to do this to yourself anymore. So what if you go on a crying jag tonight? Zach will just have to deal with it even if tears aren't his favorite thing.

As she put away the albums, it occurred to her that physical exertion might help relieve the sadness. Planning to pedal around the neighborhood on her ancient bike, she went out the back door, then stopped to stare at a gimpy old tom strolling across Briar. Milton, the only remaining stray from a colony of feral cats she had rescued the previous summer.

Her spirits lifting, she gripped the stoop's wrought iron railing and watched as Milton disappeared into the bushes in front of her house. Seeing that the elderly cat was still alive always gave her hope. *If Milton can keep going, so can I.*

That evening they went to dinner at the Desert Café, a restaurant that faced Oak Park from the Chicago side of North Avenue. A waitress who looked to be in her mid-twenties, her hair pulled into a ponytail, her dress short and swirly, seated them.

Zach turned his attention to the menu. Cassidy glanced at the list of specials, then allowed her gaze to wander over a rough-textured Native American rug hanging from the exposed brick wall a few feet off to the side. The rug depicted a black coyote howling at a round orange moon.

Tapping her fingers on the burgundy tablecloth, Cassidy was aware of a sense of urgency, a desire to get the dinner over with as soon as possible. *Zach was right about the anxiety. Here you are all itchy and agitated, wishing you could jump up and run back to the house. But as soon you're home, you won't want to be there either.*

The waitress returned and asked for their orders in a high-pitched, sing-songy voice. They both wanted the salmon filet and a glass of pinot noir. Cassidy noticed that the woman kept her eyes primarily on Zach, casting only meager glances in Cassidy's direction.

"What about an appetizer?" the waitress asked Zach, her tone more playful than Cassidy liked. "Maybe something to share."

"We're sort of in a hurry," Cassidy said. "So please, just bring the entrees as soon as you can." The waitress threw

Cassidy a pouty look and flounced away.

Zach, sitting kitty-corner from her, laid his hand over hers. "You're right, this isn't the time for a leisurely dinner."

"You're fairly convinced this isn't going to end with the obit, aren't you?" She caught her lip between her teeth.

"Why would anybody go to all the trouble of sneaking into our bedroom, photographing a picture on the wall, and changing a newspaper page for the sole purpose of spoiling your day? Whatever his reason, I can't see this guy just dropping it."

"What else do you think he might do?"

"I have no idea." The lines running between his nose and jaw deepened. "That's what bothers me."

The waitress set a plate in front of Cassidy, an artful presentation of grilled salmon in champagne sauce, green and orange vegetables, and a twice-baked potato. She nibbled the tip of a bean, swirled her fork in the golden sauce, took a large swallow of wine. "Can we change the subject?"

Zach stared in the direction of a bleached cow skull hanging above the door. "Did I tell you I invited Bryce for dinner tomorrow night?"

Bryce was the eighteen-year-old son Zach had not known existed until the boy rang their doorbell the summer before last. He'd announced to Zach that his mother insisted he stay with them for a few days, even though Bryce himself wanted nothing to do with a father he believed had deserted him before he was born.

During his brief tenure at their house, Bryce had come to learn that his mother's stories about Zach were untrue, but the new information failed to dislodge the grudge the boy had carried for so long. After his mother was murdered, Bryce had moved in with a former nanny who was suffering from MS and needed his help.

"Bryce is coming?" Cassidy parroted. "That's right, you did tell me. My mind's about as sharp as Jell-O tonight."

"At least he said he'd be over. Remember, he canceled out on us last week...." Zach stared at the skull again. "I had to apply pressure to get a promise out of him for tomorrow night."

Cassidy's brow creased. "That's odd. He's usually pissed when you *don't* call." She drank more wine. "In fact, I can't remember him ever begging off before last week."

"He's in college now. That's when kids typically don't want anything to do with their families." He paused. "Not that Bryce'd ever be likely to consider us family."

"I thought things were looking up between you two." She took a square of pumpernickel from the breadbasket, broke off a tiny corner, and put it in her mouth.

During the period when the boy was at their house, Cassidy had done her best to bring Zach and Bryce together, but the process of creating a father-son bond had not gone smoothly. Zach, who frequently declared himself not to be father material, was less reliable and committed than she thought he should be. And even when he did manage to see Bryce on a regular basis, the boy's responses were often angry and rejecting.

"Well, I don't think he hates me any more," Zach said. "And there have been a couple of times when we were together and he didn't actually sneer. But I don't know if I'd call that much of a relationship." He shrugged. "It may just be a case of too little too late. Seventeen years of having considered me slime might be too much to overcome." He stared into space, then met her gaze again. "Maybe it'll end up like my mother and me, where we go years without talking."

Cassidy pictured Zach's mother, Mildred, a tall overbearing

woman with sculpted white hair above an aristocratic face. A beautifully molded face with no warmth in it.

"I think you're more important to Bryce than you realize." Cassidy rested her fingers lightly on his arm. "But say you're right. Say the two of you did drift completely apart. How would you feel about that?"

"You're always asking about my feelings and I never know." He squinted in thought. "I guess I wouldn't be too happy if he just disappeared. I think I've finally got the hang of talking to him, and I've even begun to harbor fantasies of his coming to me for advice." He grinned. "You know, things like what brand of condom to use or how to lure chicks into bed."

Cracks like that used to drive you up the wall. But now you know it's all a façade, behind which lurks a highly devoted husband whose chick-chasing days are long gone.

He looked pointedly at her barely touched plate. "Is that all you're going to eat?"

"I finished my wine."

He beckoned to their waitress. A moment later she came to stand between them, her body angled toward Zach.

"I'll bet you're ready for coffee and dessert," she said in her squeaky, Minnie Mouse voice. "Everything here's homemade and it's all really yummy."

"Just the check," Cassidy said sharply.

The woman gave Cassidy a quick frown, then slanted herself toward Zach again. "Oh, but at least you have to let me tell you what we've got. I won't be doing my job unless I can tempt you into trying something."

The furrows between Zach's eyebrows deepened. "Did you *not* hear what the lady said?"

I don't believe he finds cutesy any more appealing than you do.

As they came in the back door, Starshine leading the way, Zach said, "You want something to drink while we talk?"

You really ought to be able to face hard things without needing alcohol to do it.

Taking the edge off now and then is not necessarily a character defect.

"Yes, definitely a drink."

"You go on upstairs. I'll be there in a minute." He reached into the cabinet for a bottle of Jack Daniel's.

In the bedroom she changed into a long lavender tee, a red rose emblazoned on the front. She was sitting in bed when Zach and Starshine came through the doorway. Climbing onto her chest, the calico greeted her with a nosekiss. Zach handed her a glass, then changed into his blue terry robe and turned off the overhead, leaving the room illuminated by the soft light from her nightstand lamp. He sat on the bed, his knees drawn up, and she came around to rest her back against his legs.

Rubbing the tense muscles in her neck, he said, "So what's this not-very-nice story you've been working yourself up to tell me?"

She closed her eyes, drew in a breath, and allowed the memory of November fourth to wash over her.

6.

Bad Things from the Past

She was twenty-four, married to Kevin for nearly two years and living in an apartment on Austin Boulevard. It was a Saturday night, and she had reluctantly agreed to accompany her mother to a second cousin's birthday party in Crystal Lake, an hour and a half's drive from Oak Park. While dressing for the party, she grumbled to Kevin about being stuck for so many unremitting hours in her mother's company.

Kevin, who never spent time with Helen himself, was philosophical. "It's only one night, darlin'. You'll earn stars for your crown in heaven." Blue eyes dancing, he gave her his adorable lopsided grin. "Not that you should have to wait for the afterlife to enjoy a little celestial delight."

Looping her arms around his waist, she asked, "So how long should I have to wait?"

He nuzzled her neck. "Umm. Wake me when you get in."

His voice flowed over her like warm oil. Stepping back, she gave him a lingering smile. He was astonishingly handsome, with loose bronze curls, crinkly blue eyes, and an irresistible sideways smile. *He should be in the movies. He should be with Meg Ryan. He definitely should not be with a plain Jane like moi.*

Cassidy left to pick up her mother.

Five minutes into the ride, Helen said, "You know, dear, I

won't be able to eat anything at the party tonight. I've had this upset stomach all day long."

Maybe you can get out of this boring-as-vanilla-pudding event after all. "If you're not feeling well, wouldn't it be better to go home?"

"Oh no, I couldn't disappoint Lou. I'll put on a happy face and no one will even know I have this little tummy ache."

Cassidy gritted her teeth and kept driving.

An hour later Helen gripped the door handle and said in a strangled voice, "Oh, dear, I don't think I'm going to make it." She swallowed hard. "Maybe we should just go home."

Retracing her route to Helen's apartment, Cassidy walked her mother upstairs, supported her head over the toilet bowl, then helped her into bed.

At ten thirty she opened her own front door. *Something's wrong.* Tiny needles prickled in her chest. Stepping inside, she caught a whiff of a familiar fragrance. The coffee table was pushed out at an odd angle. A pair of women's flats, one shoe upside down, lay beneath it.

Oh no, oh no, oh no!

Her breath started coming in shallow gasps. Kevin's voice, 'Wake me when you get in,' repeated in her mind. Pushing through a wall of dread, she forced herself to take slow, halting steps down the hall to the bedroom door, put her hand on the knob, open it.

The lamp on her side of the bed spilled light over the back of Kevin's naked half-raised body. Beneath him lay Barbara.

For one instant no one moved. Then Kevin rolled to the side, pulling the sheet up over both of them, and hauled himself into a sitting position. He stared at Cassidy. "Oh shit."

Barbara struggled to prop herself next to him, brushing vaguely at a mass of dark curls with one hand, fumbling to hold the sheet over her breasts with the other. Her triangular face, the cheekbones high and widely spaced, the chin pointed, gaped in surprise. Her blurry green eyes were huge.

Some detached part of Cassidy, like a television voiceover, ticked off details. A nearly empty Gallo jug on the nightstand. Barbara's jeans and red tee on the floor, her white bikini underpants and bra tangled in with the pile of clothes.

Rage flashed through her. "Get out of my bed!"

Barbara staggered to her feet, dragging the sheet with her, leaving Kevin's gleaming, muscular body exposed. She held a thin band of fabric over her breasts, the rest of the sheet stretching back toward the bed.

Kevin said, "Cass, darlin', this is all a mistake. I can explain everything."

"Explain?" Cassidy let out a sharp laugh. Her voice rose and words started flying out of her mouth in a high-pitched scream. "How could you do this to me? How could you? You filthy bitch! You slut! I thought you were my friend!" Her voice reverberated in her ears, shrill and scary. She sucked in air, then clamped her lips together to stop the outpouring of words that didn't even seem like her own.

"Cass, I'm sorry, I'm so sorry," Barbara stammered. "I didn't mean it. I'd never do anything like this on purpose." Breaking into tears, she dropped the sheet and buried her face in her hands.

In some back corner of her mind, Cassidy registered that Barbara was slurring heavily, but at that moment in time her friend's degree of intoxication was of no interest to her at all.

She yelled at Kevin, "Get her out of here. Get her out. I want her out of my house."

"I don't know, Cass." He stared at her in confusion, shook his head, then said in a stronger tone, "You know, darlin', she's had herself a bit too much to drink. I think maybe we should call a taxi." He picked up the phone on the nightstand and asked for the Village Cab number.

Struggling to remain upright, Barbara pulled on her jeans and shirt, leaving two crumpled pieces of white silk on the floor. Her large eyes brimmed with tears. "You're my best friend, Cass. I love you. I can't tell you how sorry I am."

Cassidy moved closer, raised her hand, and brought it down hard across Barbara's face. Barbara stumbled backward. Cassidy's palm burned.

Oh my god! What am I doing? Shocked at her own behavior, she made an effort to get herself under control. "Just leave."

She heard Kevin's voice reciting their address. Barbara started down the hallway, steadying herself with a hand against the wall. Cassidy followed behind her. Watching her friend stumble, Cassidy was aware of a small voice telling her Barbara shouldn't be allowed to drive. That voice was drowned out instantly by a louder one: *She slept with him. She fucking slept with my husband.*

Barbara went through the door and down the stairs.

Cassidy didn't try to stop her.

She paced back and forth for a long time, shivering, her arms clutched beneath her breasts, refusing to listen to a word from Kevin. Finally, exhausted, she sank down at the kitchen table and allowed him to have his say.

Kevin told her that Barbara had shown up at their door, drunk and extremely upset over a fight she'd had with her mother. "It was you she came to see, darlin'. It wasn't me at all. When I explained to her that you weren't home, she didn't know what to do. So I said she should stay here and settle herself down instead of driving around as tipsy as she was."

Letting go with a long sigh, he gazed at the floor. "She

poured herself a big glass of wine, then plopped down on the couch beside me. Next thing I know, she was asking me to hold her." He paused. "Neither of us meant for this to happen. She was so drunk she didn't know what she was doing, and I was just trying to calm her down. Things got out of control."

As he described the night's events, Cassidy could hear a deep sense of regret in his voice. She could picture it occurring just the way he said. Understanding how it had happened did not eradicate her anger but it softened her; it took away some of the brittleness she had begun to feel the instant she walked in the door.

At three P.M. the next day the phone rang. The voice on the other end was thick and hoarse, but Cassidy recognized it as belonging to her friend's younger brother, Peter.

"Barbara didn't make it home last night. Her car crashed into an embankment."

Cassidy stopped breathing. After a long silence she forced herself to ask, knowing what the answer would be, knowing she could not bear to hear it, "Is she going to be all right?"

"She died on impact."

"Oh Lord." Zach's hand tightened on her neck. "What a miserable thing to happen. For Barbara and her family, but almost as miserable for you."

Cassidy blinked back tears. "Even for Kevin. That was the first time he cheated on me, you know. He felt nearly as bad as I did, only he bounced back faster. That's one of his great talents, bouncing back."

Zach asked in a skeptical tone, "He said it was the first time and you believed him?"

"I'm pretty sure there weren't any others before Barbara. Up until that night, we were a happy couple. It wasn't until several months later that I began to notice evidence of his transgressions. And then, when he did start having affairs, he wasn't careful at all. There were hints and clues all over the place."

"So what happened after that night? Did you tell anybody?"

"Not at first. I was desperate to see Barbara's family, even though being around them made me feel so guilty I almost couldn't stand it. But I couldn't stay away either." She swallowed, trying not to cry. "That evening I went to their house and they pulled me inside, hugged me, treated me like I belonged right there with them." She swallowed again. "I remember her dad taking me into Barbara's bedroom and talking about all the things she and I used to do together."

"And I suppose you thought it was all your fault."

She took a long pull at her drink. "The hardest part was the funeral. They had a graveside service and dozens of girls from high school were there. The whole time I kept thinking how much they'd all hate me if they knew what I'd done."

"You know, it's not as if you murdered her or anything. Most women would've reacted the same way you did."

"Don't start rationalizing for me. I just can't take it right now." She drew in air. "That night after the funeral I couldn't sleep. I went for nearly a week without sleeping at all. Then I sat down and wrote a letter to the family telling them that Barbara and I'd had a fight and that I'd made her leave even though I knew she shouldn't be driving. For obvious reasons I left out the part about her sleeping with Kevin." Cassidy gulped at her drink. "Two days later her mother called and said she never wanted to see me again."

Zach stroked her hair. "You're always so hard on yourself."

"That's my line," she said weakly. "What I say to clients."

"So that's it? That's the story?"

"There's one other thing." Her chest grew so tight she could barely breathe. Wrapping both hands around her glass, she raised it shakily to her mouth, only to find it empty, the ice cubes clinking coldly against her teeth. Zach took the glass from her hands and replaced it with his own. She chugged the rest of his drink.

"Two months later Maggie called to tell me that Barbara's father had shot himself. That's the last I heard. I don't know what happened to any of them after that."

"Jesus," Zach said under his breath.

She rested her forehead against his chest and let herself cry. Wrapping his arms around her, he dropped his chin so that it brushed the top of her head and held her close. After a long while she got up, blew her nose, and went into the bathroom to splash water on her face. Settling in beside him again, she said, "Sorry 'bout that."

"Nothing to be sorry about."

"I thought you didn't like mopping up tears."

"Only other people's. When it comes to you, I'm happy to offer a shoulder or chest or any other body part you might want to lean on."

Running a hand down his arm, she whispered, "I'm so glad I have you."

"Whoever put that obit in the paper has got to be one sick son-of-a-bitch. You just wait till I get my hands on him. He's going be sorry he ever thought of it."

Not all bad having somebody who wants to go out and smite your enemies.

He began massaging the back of her neck again. "How 'bout I fix you another drink?"

"No, I've had enough." She gazed in the direction of her

desk, its satiny surface cluttered with papers, standing files, a Rolodex, a gallon wine bottle half filled with coins. "It's sort of ironic, you know. Barbara died from drunk driving and I can't even tell the story without gulping bourbon."

"A little painkiller now and then doesn't hurt anything."

They sat in silence for a moment, then he said, "The person who wrote the obit must be somebody close to Barbara. Did she have a boyfriend? Maybe some guy who used to be in love with her got himself a job at the *Register* and couldn't resist the opportunity."

"Yeah, I think there was a boyfriend." Cassidy made an effort to focus on the obituary, but her mind, still locked in the past, fuzzed out when she tried to entertain thoughts of boyfriends and newspaper tampering. "I'm sorry, I just can't think about it now."

He patted her leg. "We'll put it on hold till tomorrow."

There was another silence. Then she said, "When I was twenty-four, the fact that my husband and best friend slept together seemed like this huge, major betrayal. But then, ten affairs later, I realized how insignificant it really was. That's what makes the whole thing such a waste. I had this big fit and sent my friend off to die over something that didn't even matter."

"I don't know." Zach shook his head. "The first time Kevin cheated, catching them in the act, how could it not matter?" He paused. "You and I have had some rough times of our own. I've done things that brought us right up to the brink. Even though we got through it and we're fine now, I could never say it didn't matter. Knowing that it *does* matter is what keeps me very careful never to do anything like that again."

She knew he was referring to an episode from the previous summer when he'd taken on the undercover persona of a thuggish drug dealer and gotten so caught up in his role he'd started behaving like an abusive creep. But the investigation had been short term, and afterward he'd clearly been sorry and gone out of his way to make up for it.

She folded her hand around his, thinking how much she loved him and how close they were now to a happily-ever-after kind of marriage. *Except you know nothing ever stays in place.*

She said, "There's something I want to ask."

"This going be one of those questions I'd rather not answer?"

"Kevin was twenty-nine, and he sort of implied that the situation was irresistible. That it'd be next to impossible for any red-blooded male not to end up in bed under those circumstances. So I've always wondered if I was being unreasonable. Whether it was asking too much to expect him not to succumb."

"You're a therapist, Cass. You're supposed to know things like that."

"Well, I do. Intellectually, that is. I know that any generalization about a group of people is bound to be untrue. I also know that most guys have powerful sexual urges at least through their thirties. And that in order not to act on them, they need to have damned good impulse control. Which Kevin obviously didn't." She bit her lip. "I guess the real question is, what would you have done?"

"Questions like that have no redeeming value and they also tend to cause trouble. Besides, my circumstances were entirely different from Kevin's. He was married and I was making an all-out effort to avoid entanglements."

"Well, but what do you think you would've done?"

He gave her an annoyed look, then gazed into space for about three beats. "Most guys that age are horny as hell and want to do it any chance they get. During my early twenties, when I was still drugging, I never missed an opportunity. But by the time I hit twenty-nine, I did have some impulse control and I pretty much made it a point not to cheat on whatever woman I was currently with."

What a difference a second husband makes.

"I also never felt right about sleeping with anybody too drunk to know what she was doing." He cocked his head thoughtfully. "But then, I wasn't tied down the way Kevin was. Anytime I wanted a little variety, I had the option of breaking up with the girlfriend of the moment and moving on to someone else."

"You certainly were competent at sidestepping commitment." She smiled. "And a good thing, too, or you wouldn't have been available when I came back on the market."

"A very good thing," he said, drawing her face close and planting a deep, warm kiss on her mouth. "Just look what I would have missed out on if I hadn't waited for you."

"More coffee?" Cassidy watched over Zach's shoulder as he signed on to check her email.

"Sure."

Their usual Sunday routine was to laze around until noon, Zach with the paper, Cassidy with a mystery. But today they'd both been too restless to stay in bed. Neither had mentioned the obituary. Cassidy suspected that Zach was waiting for her to bring it up although she knew he would not hold off much longer. One part of her wanted to dig into finding the person who'd done it, but another part wanted to shove it back into the locked closet in her mind where bad memories were stored.

And you a therapist. What is it you always say to clients about facing their monsters?

"Cass, I think you better look at this." Zach's words caught her just as she was making the turn at the L in the stairway.

Trotting back upstairs, she slid into the dinette chair next to his and read the message on the screen: YOU HAVE RECEIVED AN E-CARD. CLICK HERE TO GO TO THE SITE. THE CARD WILL BE AVAILABLE FOR VIEWING UNTIL MIDNIGHT NOVEMBER 6.

"Another card?" Gran, who loved to tinker with her computer, had sent her a number of them. *Nice but certainly not urgent.* She turned in her chair, draping an arm over the pink and green backrest. "Why is this more important than coffee?"

"It's a little strange is all."

7.

Your Everyday Friendly E-card

Cassidy peered at the screen again. "It doesn't say who it's from. Or the name of the company."

"Plus the time frame's off. Cards are usually available for ninety days or so." He frowned. "I don't like how this looks. Maybe I should've let you make coffee after all."

"Wouldn't've done any good. I'd have to see it eventually. And I just get pissed when you try to shield me from things. You know how I hate it when you act like I'm made of glass."

"I'll try to restrain myself." He moved his chair to the side, making room for her to sit directly in front of the screen.

If this isn't your everyday friendly e-card, then it's something to do with the obit. Something about Barbara. Cassidy's neck and shoulders tightened. She moved the cursor into position and clicked. The screen turned violet and an animated figure appeared. A photographic image of Barbara's face jumped out at her.

"Oh shit." Her voice barely above a whisper.

The screen displayed a cartoon drawing of a woman with Barbara's head pasted on at the neck. The figure was shown in profile, one arm visible, the hand holding a wineglass. The forearm moved up and down, raising the glass from a waist-high position to her mouth. A bottle, suspended in space, refilled the glass each time it reached its lowest point.

The word CLICK hung beneath the picture.

"The person who did this knows I made her drive off drunk. He blames me for what happened."

Reaching across the keyboard, Zach gave the print command. "That's nuts. You're no more responsible than Kevin or Barbara herself."

"I wonder if Kevin's getting e-cards too."

"We'll have to ask him."

Cassidy sighed. "Well, I've had enough of this screen." She clicked again.

The background color changed to gray. Two lines of print, black with silver highlighting, came into focus, another CLICK at the bottom.

LOVING IS THE MOST CREATIVE FORCE OF THE UNIVERSE
THE MEMORY OF LOVING THE MOST DESTRUCTIVE

"I know that quote. I've seen it before." Creasing her brow, she stared at the words as Zach repeated the print command. "Where do I know it from?"

"We can work on that later." Zach nodded toward the monitor. "Why don't you move on?"

She clicked the mouse and the color changed to deep red. A black cross inside a circle emerged on the screen. The absence of a click instruction indicated that this was the final page.

She glanced at Zach. "That's a cross-hair, isn't it? As in, an implied threat that the card sender plans to kill me?"

"It's a cross-hair, all right." He cocked his head. "But it's too much of a leap to say he's planning to kill you."

The letter Z formed behind the cross, filling the circle.

"Oh god." Goosebumps rose on her arm. "It's not me they're threatening to kill. It's you."

"Now don't go running ahead of yourself. It could be a threat, but since the nutcase who designed this trash failed to send us our decoder ring, we can't be certain of anything." He printed the page.

"I think we do have a decoder ring: Psychology 101." She picked up a bright pink pen, jiggled it between her fingers. "Our nutcase was deeply attached to Barbara. Why else center his campaign around her? He experienced severe pain at her death. That shows up in the two-line quote." She gazed at the words Zach had printed, trying again to remember where she'd encountered them before.

"He sees me as the cause of his pain. That comes from the drinking scene. Since I precipitated a major loss for him, he wants to retaliate by taking away the person I love most." A cold, shaky feeling crept over her. "And if what he's after is extreme retribution, he's not so far off the mark. The thought of him killing you strikes a much deeper nerve than the thought of him merely sending a bullet off in my direction."

What if he did murder Zach? Sackcloth and ashes forever. A life sentence in purgatory. The end of the world.

Zach gave her a long, somber look. "Yeah, I know what you mean."

Remembering what it was like for him when you nearly got yourself killed by a psychopath. Why do those damn things that go around keep coming back at you?

"However," he continued, "there's no need to panic as of yet. This guy could be more of an obscene-caller type than an assassin. A lot of weirdoes who get off on scaring people never take it any further than that."

"We've flipped again. Yesterday I was trying to ignore it, you were telling me it wasn't going to go away. Today I'm starting to get really nervous, you're playing it down."

He reached for the mouse, clicked back to the original email, and printed it.

As the printer, located on her end of the table, began whirring, she stood to retrieve the paper it cranked out. She glanced at it, saw nothing out of the ordinary, sat down again, and handed it to Zach.

He studied the gibberish at the end of the message. "This went through a remailer."

"Huh?"

"Remailers are providers that hide the identity of the person sending the email. If I were to threaten anybody online, the recipient could go to the police, the police would subpoena AOL for my name and address, and AOL would send them to my door."

"And well they should, if you were doing anything as creepy as sending threats."

"If the cops had an actual threat in hand, they could arrest me for assault. But since our little missive came through a remailer, I'm not sure it's traceable. Even if it is, the cops wouldn't do anything at this point because the e-card doesn't come close to an overt threat."

"We can't get any help from the police?"

"Not unless a crime's been committed. A threat so obvious nobody could miss it or an attempt to harm you or me. Here's hoping those criteria don't get met."

She clicked the pen repetitively. "So we're on our own here?"

"On our own and out of our depth." He gazed at the screen. "I don't have any experience with remailers. I don't even know if we can send a reply." He tilted his head slightly. "What do you think? Should we try?"

She reflected a moment. "Whatever a person does, they're after some kind of payoff. We want to avoid giving him any reinforcement whatsoever, so that means we ignore him."

"We are, of course, going to find this guy and stop the

harassment. And if the law won't hand down any punishment, I may do it myself."

"No you won't. You're strictly nonviolent except when under attack."

"I may have to make an exception for this asshole." He put his hand on her knee. "Let's go sit at the dining room table and strategize."

She gazed at him blankly, realizing how jumbled she felt. *Well, of course you're reacting. Who wouldn't be all topsy turvy after receiving an anonymous threat against her husband?*

"I think I need a little time to take this in."

"Why don't you go make coffee and then we can talk." He looked at his watch. "When do you think you might be ready?"

"Ten minutes?" *You're going to be calm in ten minutes? I may not be calm till it's over, but we have to get started.*

Downstairs, Cassidy turned the dial on the grinder and poured water. *Why now? Why start a revenge campaign fifteen years after the fact?* As the coffeemaker burbled, she stared out the window at a gray, rainy day.

The cat-door whapped. Cassidy glanced down to see a damp Starshine, head lowered, race into the kitchen. Cassidy's gaze drifted back to the slow, steady drizzle outside. She clutched her arms across her chest to ward off the room's damp chill.

Claws skittered on the floor. She looked down. A limp brown mouse lay on the mottled linoleum a few inches from her tennis shoes.

"Yuck!" Shuddering, Cassidy scrambled around the perimeter of the room to stand in the passage between the kitchen and the client waiting area. Starshine pounced on the creature, carried it over to Cassidy, and placed it at her feet again. Clearly expecting approval, the cat gazed up at her out of wild dark eyes.

"Bad kitty!" Cassidy said sternly.

Never tell children they're bad. Not that Starshine would notice. This cat's bursting with pride, every ounce of instinct telling her she's just done something wonderful.

Performing a gleeful little dance, the calico swatted the mouse into the waiting room, then turned her back and pranced away, a move Cassidy recognized as part of the ritualized stalking game.

Gotta get that dead thing out of here before she knocks it under the refrigerator, way she's done with half her toys.

Cassidy felt a strong urge to run upstairs and tell Zach he had to save her from a dead mouse. *You just told him how pissed you get when he comes on all protective. Talk about double messages.*

An oak cabinet stood perpendicular to the south wall, serving as a room divider between the kitchen and the client waiting area. Clamping her mouth in a tight line, she opened one of the cabinet doors and removed a broom and dustpan. As she knelt beside the rodent, Starshine came streaking up in a last-ditch attempt to regain possession of her trophy. Cassidy grabbed the disgruntled calico and shut her in the basement, then returned to her task, forcing herself not to avert her eyes as she positioned the dustpan next to the corpse. The tiny creature looked entirely harmless.

Poor mouse.

God, you are ridiculous. Feeling sorry for mice is carrying this compassion thing way too far. Better you should reserve your pity for the Bosnians.

Yeah, but I'm not sweeping any dead Bosnians off my floor.

She pulled a jacket from the cabinet and marched out through the misty rain to the trashcan in the alley behind her house.

Coming back inside, she hung her jacket on a hook by the door and dried her face with the sleeve of her sweatshirt. Zach stood on the kitchen side of the room divider, his gaze fixed on Starshine. The cat was intently sniffing the patch of floor where she had last seen her prey. The basement door was open.

"She brought in a mouse."

Squatting next to the calico, Zach scratched behind her ear. "Well, aren't you the clever one?"

"What?"

"That's what cats are supposed to do."

"Not in my house they aren't."

"The only way to stop her is to keep her inside. We try doing that, we'll have one pissed-off cat on our hands."

"We could lock up the cat-door."

"That door's made her the happiest cat on the block."

Cassidy planted her hands on her hips. "If we had kids, I suppose you'd grab up the good-cop role, make me play bad cop."

"As much as we both tend to forget it, Starshine is a cat, not a child." He went to the counter and poured coffee. "Now I suggest we put the cat-door and other parenting issues on hold and settle down to business." He added cream and sugar to the purple mug, then handed it to her.

They sat kitty-corner at the teak dining room table, the email printouts and a yellow pad in front of Zach. At the table's center stood a large bowl of fruit. Cassidy had put it there in hopes that Zach would snack on apples instead of potato chips, but the bowl was just as full now as when she'd first set it out.

He folded his arms on the table. "I thought we should start by listing everything we know or can guess about our E-Stalker."

"I've been thinking about that." She glanced at the cartoon

of Barbara drinking wine, then quickly looked away. "Whenever something changes, therapists ask 'why now?' The E-Stalker must have experienced some triggering event that sent him off on his campaign at this particular time."

Zach gazed at her speculatively. "I guess people who do this sort of thing plan it out in advance."

"Yep." She nodded. "This is definitely not impulsive. He's probably spent years developing and refining the fantasy. Now something's tipped the balance and he's started acting it out."

"What sort of thing would set him off?"

"Two possibilities I can think of: One, he couldn't do it before because of some external constraint but now the constraint's been lifted. Something like—he just got released from prison, or he was living somewhere else and now he's moved back to the area."

"What's the other?"

"He's had some major stressor that's pushed him over the edge. Maybe another loss." She paused. "Now this would make sense. Whenever people experience a new loss, it brings back all the old ones. Say this person was in his twenties when Barbara died. He suffered intensely at the time, nursed a grudge over the years, fantasized about revenge. Then another loss turns his world upside down, he starts reliving Barbara's death, gets enraged over every loss he's ever had, and focuses it all on me."

Zach shook his head. "I know people like that exist, but I can never understand why they don't just get over things like the rest of us do."

"I don't think anybody knows for sure. Some day we're probably going to find out it's all brain chemistry." She sighed. "These are people who *can't* let go no matter how much they might want to. Their whole lives they're besieged by ghosts from the past."

"Okay." He started writing. "So we're looking for a guy who recently got out of the slam or whose mother just died. Or some such other big loss." He glanced up. "We're also looking for somebody who's a techno whiz himself or can afford to hire one. And, of course, somebody who has access to your email address. But that doesn't narrow it down much since you just mailed out those brochures." His forehead furrowed. "Tell me again who you sent them to?"

"Current and former clients. Ministers, doctors, and lawyers." Cassidy noticed a black coffee ground floating on top of the creamy brew in her mug. She picked it out with a burgundy fingernail. "What else can we put on the list?"

Starshine jumped onto the table and began bapping at the pen in Zach's hand. "Somebody who knew about your involvement in Barbara's death. That'd be Kevin, her family, or anyone they told."

It wouldn't be Kevin. Barbara's family then? Amanda or Pete or Lany? Heaviness settled in Cassidy's stomach. She pressed her thumb and middle finger to her forehead.

Zach said in a low voice, "You don't like the idea it could be Kevin or a family member."

"I hate thinking it could be somebody I used to be close to." Leaning sideways to face Zach, she propped her elbow on the table and laid her cheek against her palm. Her hair fell nearly to the tabletop, luring Starshine over to swipe at it.

Cassidy jerked back quickly, removing body and hair from striking range. She added, "It also has to be someone deeply affected by her death."

"It could be somebody outside the family. Somebody who was crazy about her and heard about your letter." He laced his fingers on top of his head. "You said there was a boyfriend. An obsessive boyfriend would fit very nicely."

"I think she had a boyfriend." Cassidy nibbled her bottom lip. "I'm afraid I don't know as much about her personal life as I should."

"I thought you two were best friends."

"That was in grade school. Once we started high school, I hit the honors track and Barbara got a little boy crazy. We just sort of drifted apart. She went to Champaign and I went to the U of I at Chicago. We didn't start seeing each other again until a few months before she died."

"How'd you get back together?"

"Her mother intervened. Let's see, when was it?" Cassidy closed her eyes. "January, that same year Barbara died. I was really surprised to hear from Mrs. Segel. But happy too. She'd always been like a second mom to me. Anyway, she said Barbara was having a hard time and asked if I'd talk to her. And this was before I ever even thought of being a therapist." *You should've done more. If only you'd tried harder, maybe she wouldn't've been so distraught or so desperate or so drunk.*

"What was the problem?"

"She'd been out of school a year and a half and all she was doing was temping. She couldn't seem to take hold." Cassidy ran her finger around the rim of her mug. "I didn't know what to make of it at the time, but looking back, I'd have to say she was depressed."

"What about the boyfriend?" Starshine pounced on Zach's pen, knocking it to the floor. As he bent to retrieve it, the calico jumped down and sauntered out of the room.

Cassidy shook her head. "I don't remember this clearly at all. I believe she said she was in love with somebody she'd met at school, but I couldn't pin her down on any details." Cassidy stared out the window at a vacant bungalow across the street. "I thought she might've been envious of the fact that I was married and she wasn't."

Everything got turned around. She was the pretty one. You were the intellectual. Then you captured the gorgeous Kevin, she was alone, neither of you knew how to deal with it. "It even crossed my mind to wonder if she might've manufactured a mysterious boyfriend from out of town just so it'd seem like she had something going for her."

"But who better than a boyfriend to be carrying around a vendetta all these years?" Zach tapped his pen against the pad. "Anything else we need to add?"

"Nothing I can think of."

"Well, then, I propose we begin by interviewing her family. And Kevin of course."

"Kevin? But he wouldn't know anything about Barbara's boyfriend. And he wouldn't have any reason to send a nasty e-card either."

"Yes, but Kevin's one of the few people who knew how Barbara died. And you can't be certain he didn't have some kind of crush on her before that night. Or some other screwy reason to wish you harm."

She clamped her lips in irritation. *This digging up the past is about as much fun as electric shock therapy.*

"So," Zach leveled his gaze at her, "where do you want to start?"

Nowhere. I don't want to talk to anybody.

Somebody's threatening Zach's life. You have to take this seriously.

"Her mother, I guess. Amanda Segel. The woman who said she never wanted to see me again." Cassidy let out a long sigh. "I have no idea whether she's even still living in the same house."

"I'll check the phone book." Zach went through the kitchen doorway to fish a directory out of the cabinet beneath the wall phone. "She isn't listed but that doesn't mean anything. Since the house is here in Oak Park, let's go knock on the door."

8.

Oreos and Dirty Socks

Zach parked the Nissan in front of a white frame two-story with a small, canopied porch. Staring out the side window, Cassidy pictured two young girls sitting on the top step. She remembered Barbara wearing designer jeans and Reeboks, her hair stylishly cut, gold studs adorning her earlobes. Cassidy, on the other hand, never wore anything better than Penny's jeans, generic shoes, and a cheap Dutch-girl haircut. Her appearance throughout her childhood was a tribute to Helen's dedication to plainness.

Zach said from behind her, "You know, I handle investigations on my own all the time. I really could do this without you."

She turned to face him. "I changed my mind about you not shielding me. It's okay. Do it all you like." She drew in a breath, then raised her hands palms out. "No wait. Don't shield me after all. I'm liable to switch back any minute and bite your head off." She took in another deep breath. "Okay, I'm ready. Let's go ring the bell."

They stood huddled against the rain under the porch canopy, Cassidy stabbing at the button for the third time, when a car pulled up in front of the bungalow to their right. A woman in a black raincoat and hat got out and started for the door, several plastic grocery bags suspended from her hands.

"That's Ms. Riley," Cassidy said. "We can ask her whether Amanda still lives here." *Here's hoping she didn't see the obituary.*

Cassidy and Zach crossed to the neighboring house, feet squishing in the wet grass. "Remember me, Ms. Riley? Cass McCabe?"

The other woman turned to peer from under the brim of her rain hat, her face breaking into a broad smile. "Little Cassie. Of course I do."

She's not looking like she's just seen a ghost so I guess she doesn't know I officially died yesterday.

"That was back in the days when I used to bake cookies." Ms. Riley glanced at Zach. "Never wanted kids of my own but every so often I'd take it in mind to steal the neighbor's. I'd cook up a batch of snickerdoodles and in no time at all I'd have all the little Segels, plus Cassie here, crowded around my kitchen table. It was like becoming an instant grandmother."

Opening the door, Ms. Riley called over her shoulder, "You come on in now so we can catch up on all those years since you last ate cookies at my house." She took them into a kitchen with white cabinets and cherry-colored counters, plunked her bags down near the sink, and hung her coat and hat on a hook by the back door.

"So why were you standing on that porch over there? You knew Amanda and the kids left years ago, didn't you?" Her gray hair formed a smooth cap above her round, jovial face. About the same height as Cassidy, her cushiony body was garbed in a loose striped shirt that hung out over her baggy pants.

Cassidy looked down at the floor. "I haven't talked to any of the Segels since Barbara's funeral."

"You haven't?" Ms. Riley's sharp, gray eyes caught Cassidy's.

"Oh, that's right. I remember Amanda telling me she blamed you for the accident. Which I thought was just plain ridiculous."

The older woman's gaze shifted to Zach. "Guess I'm going to have to introduce myself, since I haven't shut up long enough to give Cassie a chance to do it." She paused. "I'm Tess Riley. Who're you?"

"Zach Moran, Cass's husband." He reached out to shake her hand.

Cassidy watched Zach hang his jacket on one of the pegs and decided to do the same.

Tess carried two bags over to a six-foot tall pantry that stood against the south wall. Atop the pantry sat a collection of baskets, some of them old and shabby, with cobwebs running between them. The refrigerator, a long counter and sink lined the opposite wall, with a square oak table off to the side.

Turning her back, Tess began stuffing groceries into the pantry. "I thought you had a different husband."

"This is my second marriage." Cassidy took up a post in the middle of the kitchen, her arms folded beneath her breasts.

"Didn't learn your lesson the first time, huh?" Snorting, Tess turned around to face them. "I lived with a guy once. Then one day it occurred to me that I wasn't any better off with him than without him, and on top of that he left his dirty socks all over the house. So I told him to take a hike."

This woman's obviously not as fond of sex as you are.

Tess added, "I'm a believer in not making the same mistake twice, myself."

"I agree." Zach rested his hands on his belt. "I prefer each mistake to be unique."

Tess crossed the room to lean against the counter, her big shirt floating out around her, her steps surprisingly light for a woman of such girth. She said to Cassidy, "Well, at least you kept your own name. You get points for that. These new kids coming up, some of 'em have taken ten steps backward."

"Yep," Zach said, his face deadpan. "You and Gloria Steinem did a hell of a job. Must be hard to see these young chicks going back on the revolution."

Tess frowned. "Is he kidding?"

Cassidy cocked her head. "Only partly. He likes to take pot-shots at feminism but he does do more than his share around the house. And he pretty much supports anything I want to do. However, he is awfully male about driving, paying for things, and bailing me out when I get in trouble."

"Oh well," Tess chuckled. "I never did mind having it both ways myself." She carried several more bags over to the pantry. Handing Zach a roll of paper towels, she pointed at the top shelf. "Stick it up there, will you? Your arms are longer than mine."

Zach complied.

Cassidy pulled several soup cans out of a bag and gave them to Tess. "So what happened to Amanda and the kids?"

Tess deposited the cans on a shelf, stood upright, and placed a hand on the small of her back. "You hear about Donald shooting himself?"

Cassidy nodded.

"Now I grant you suicide is a pretty nasty business. And losing their father like that certainly took its toll on the kids. But in the long run, Amanda was better off without him." Tess's lips tightened. "I swear, that man had a black cloud hanging over his head. All he ever did was drag her down."

Tess approves of suicide as a way to dispose of gloomy husbands? Good thing this woman isn't practicing therapy.

"Amanda turned out to be a real powerhouse once she

escaped her hausfrau role. Went scrambling right up that old success ladder, she did, and with no male persons standing by to hold her hand, either."

"What line of work is she in?" Pulling a straight-backed chair away from the oak table, Zach straddled it backward.

"The restaurant business." Tess carried the last plastic bag over to the refrigerator and began putting vegetables away. "She used the proceeds from the house to buy a diner on the far north side. Once that first place got rolling, she turned it over for a tidy profit and moved up to some cutesy little lunchroom in Evanston." Tess closed the refrigerator and leaned her ample body against it.

"You two stayed in touch?" Cassidy picked up the empty bags and handed them to Tess, who stuffed them into a box under the sink.

"Oh, we get together now and then. Anyway, the last restaurant she owned before she retired was this elegant bistro in Wilmette. She invited me up to have dinner with her, and this place turned out to be so upscale and gourmet I didn't even recognize half the items on the menu." Tess chuckled. "Thank god I never had to see the bill."

Running a beefy hand over her chin, she added, "But it's been a while since I've seen her. She's too busy changing everything in her life to visit old friends."

"Changing everything?"

"Talk about making the same mistake twice." Tess grinned. "You're not the only one."

"Amanda got married again?" Zach rested his hands on the top rail of the chair back.

"Yep. She went out and found herself another husband." Tess shrugged her round shoulders. "But maybe you and Amanda've come up with a better use for males than I ever did.

Far as I could tell, the only thing they were any good for was reaching the top shelf and unscrewing jars. 'Course I realize a lot of women like to keep 'em around for stud service, but most of the guys I tried it with weren't so hot in that department either."

Cassidy kept her face carefully neutral but could not refrain from stealing a glance at Zach. Their eyes met, a message passing between them: Little does she know what she's missing.

Zach said, "Maybe your survey wasn't extensive enough."

"Maybe not. But I'm not sure I'd be willing to spend my life picking up dirty socks even for a world class stud."

Stud service in exchange for maid service? What a dismal way to look at love.

Yeah, but Tess doesn't want love in her life any more than your mother does. If you don't get it right, love is a pain in the butt. She remembered the problems she'd had the previous summer with Zach. *Sometimes, even when you do get it right, it's still a pain in the butt.*

Zach asked, "Are you saying Amanda considers her second marriage a mistake?"

"If she did, she wouldn't tell me. Amanda's not a woman who likes to admit mistakes." Poking in one of the cabinets, Tess emerged with a package of Oreos. "You guys want any cookies? I don't bake anymore so this is the best I can do."

Cassidy and Zach spoke simultaneously: "No thanks" from Cassidy and "Sure" from Zach.

Opening the bag, Tess placed it in the center of the table and Zach turned himself around to face it. The two women pulled out chairs and joined him.

Tess asked, "You want coffee or anything?"

"No thanks," Cassidy said quickly, jumping in before Zach could accept. "We can't stay much longer." She rubbed a finger across her ring. "But if Amanda didn't say her marriage was a mistake, what makes you think it is?"

"That's just my anti-marriage bias talking."

Cassidy smiled, liking Tess's honesty. "You said you haven't heard from her lately. Maybe she figured you'd give her a hard time for getting married again."

There's this tightly knit band of single women and they always hate it when anyone leaves the club.

"I never shared my views on marriage with Amanda. Didn't think she'd appreciate 'em. Now with you guys, I get the impression I can say anything I want and neither of you'd be likely to take offense."

Of course she'd think that. Zach's always unflappable and you have your therapist-mask firmly in place.

Zach reached for a handful of Oreos. "You mentioned that she'd retired. Was that because of the marriage?"

"She had a heart attack about a year ago, a few months after they tied the knot. That's what put a stop to her being such a workaholic."

"If you haven't seen her lately, how'd you find all this out?" Zach stuffed an Oreo in his mouth. Regarding the cookies with disfavor, Cassidy wished they'd picked up a bag of peanut butter cups on the way over.

"Peter relays the news. He's the baby of the family. Always was my favorite. Anyway, first he told me about the heart attack, then maybe six months ago he took me out to dinner and said she'd sold the restaurant and retired." Tess shook her head. "Amanda's always been such a go-getter. I just can't see her as a lady of leisure."

"That reminds me," Cassidy said. "I really do need to get in touch with her. Could you give me Amanda's phone number and address?"

"I've been gabbing so much I didn't even shut up long enough to find out why you were standing on that porch over there."

Cassidy took a deep breath. *This is thinking-on-your-feet, here's-hoping-you-don't-spout-gibberish time.* "Several years ago I went back to school to become a therapist, and as a therapist I'm always telling clients they shouldn't leave things unfinished. Well, yesterday was the anniversary of Barbara's death, and that made me realize how bad I felt about never having seen Barbara's family after the funeral. That's why I want to talk to Amanda. I'm hoping she'll accept my apology and we can establish some sort of relationship again."

"That's the ticket," Tess said approvingly. "Much better to get things cleared up than just stop speaking the way you two did. Let me go get her address for you. I've never seen her new place, but Pete tells me she's living in a Northbrook mansion." Tess left the kitchen, returning a moment later to hand Cassidy a slip of paper.

"So how's Peter doing? And Lany, what about her?" Cassidy bit into an Oreo. *Why are you eating this? You don't even like them.*

"Nobody ever mentions Lany. Pete's doing great. At least in his career he is. He's got some high mucky-muck job doing research over at Escovar Lab." She tilted her head. "I just wish his social life was going as well."

"There's a problem with his social life?" Zach asked, biting into another cookie.

"Well, he seems like such a loner." Tess went to one of the cabinets, took out a pile of napkins, laid them on the table, then sat down again. "I can see how it happened, too. Here he was in his senior year of high school, then Amanda sells the house and she's just gone. Of course he didn't want to leave Oak Park with graduation just a few months away, so he found some friend to take him in. But what with his sister and dad both dying, then his mother moving away, he was just this poor, lost soul."

"Everybody just abandoned him?" Cassidy swished Zach's cookie crumbs onto a napkin.

Tess nodded. "He even admitted to getting into some trouble at school after his mother left. Can't recall what it was, but I do remember being shocked that a good kid like Pete would ever do anything to get the principal on his case. Although I guess a little acting out was par for the course after what the kid'd been through."

"Such loss." Cassidy shook her head. "I'd be surprised if he *didn't* have problems." *Serious enough to turn him into a threatening E-Stalker?*

"Well, I'm no therapist, but it seemed to me he just gave up on people and escaped into his books. Although now that I think of it. . . ." She squinted, peering off into the past, "I seem to remember that not too long after Amanda left, he did perk up quite a bit. Maybe it was just getting out of that depressed household that did it for him, but all of a sudden he seemed happier than he'd been in a long time."

Zach brushed his hands together. "What's wrong with being a loner? You think he ought to get married?"

"Of course he should." Tess slapped her palm against the table. "I never said marriage was a problem for men. Everybody knows men are better off married. It's the women who should avoid it."

Zach pulled away from the curb and drove toward Austin Boulevard. "We really hit the jackpot with Tess. I haven't had so much fun on an interview in a long time. Not only did she blab her little heart out, she even gave us Oreos."

"Not little, big. Tess's got one of the biggest hearts of any-one I know. She's also one of the few radical feminists I've ever run across who can make flagrantly anti-male comments and not offend every guy in sight."

"Personally, I don't have a problem with women bad mouthing men. The truth is, a lot of us guys *are* self-centered and insensitive. That's why we need women in our lives to straighten us out. And if Tess doesn't want to be bothered, why should I care? Fortunately, you don't seem to be so up in arms about socks. Which I confess to occasionally leaving on the bedroom floor, although I do eventually get around to picking them up myself."

"I thought you were going to make some comment about how much I enjoy the stud service."

"No you don't. You're not getting away with that one." He reached for her hand. "You and I are never going to refer to our mutual pleasuring of each other as any kind of service."

Warmth flowed through her. Looking across at Zach, she said, "You've come a long way."

"You too."

He's right. We've both come about a light year from where we started.

They drove north on Austin, zigzagged through the city, then continued north on the Edens Expressway, heading toward an elite suburb so far from Cassidy's home base she'd seldom had occasion to go there. Stopping for a quick lunch, they discussed over sandwiches what excuse Cassidy would use to delve into the topic of Barbara's boyfriend.

Twenty minutes later they pulled up in front of a large brick

Tudor with three gables and stucco trim around the arched windows and door. They walked through the rain toward the porch, Cassidy mentally replaying Amanda's last words to her: "I would prefer that you not contact any of us again."

They wiped their feet on the mat, then Cassidy willed her arm, stiff with tension, to reach for the bell. Zach moved closer to her side. Pushing the button, she listened to the faint echoing of chimes from within. Several seconds later, the door was opened by a tall blond woman. Amanda stood in the entryway and stared at her.

9.

Creepy Little Toad

"Mrs. Segel? It's me, Cassidy. And this is my husband, Zach Moran."

Amanda's dark-lashed, brown-flecked eyes moved briefly to Zach, then returned to Cassidy. Her skin paled, her face contracted in a sudden look of pain. She shook herself slightly, took a deep breath, then stood straighter. "I'm so glad you've come."

"You mean . . . it's okay that I'm here?" Cassidy asked, her voice turning young and small on her. "I was so afraid you wouldn't want to see me." She felt Zach take her hand.

"I've thought about calling for years. I just didn't know what to say." Amanda wore a cream-colored silk blouse, a gold chain, and a long knit skirt. Opening the door wide, she added, "Come in, come in, both of you."

They congregated in a vaulted foyer, one wall covered with art, an oriental carpet on the hardwood floor, a sweeping staircase to their right. The air smelled fresh and lemony.

"Here, give me your coats." Amanda hung their jackets in a nearby closet, then held Cassidy at arms' length. "You look wonderful. You must be happy. You couldn't look this good unless you were happy."

Happy? What with phony obits and cross-hair e-cards you're more on the verge of panic. "I've changed husbands and changed careers since last I saw you, and both are a definite improvement." Cassidy rubbed one hand inside the other. "I got your address from Tess. She said you'd remarried also."

"I have a new husband, I've moved into retirement, and this is the best it's ever been." She looked at Zach. "I'm glad Cass found you. Having the right man in your life makes all the difference."

Amanda and Tess are about as opposite as you can get in their opinions of men.

Zach ran a hand over his head. "After avoiding marriage for a lot of years I've come around to a more enlightened point of view."

"I've tried it different ways myself." Amanda coiled the chain around her fingers. "And I can see now that life is better when you have a good marriage. I tried staying in a bad marriage because I thought divorce would be worse. I tried going it alone. And now, at last, I have the good fortune to be with a man who thinks I walk on water."

That blows away Tess's theory about second mistakes.

Taking a step back, Amanda clasped her hands in front of her. "What can I get you to drink? Coffee? Wine? I have a nice little Australian cab I can recommend."

"Make that coffee," Zach said.

Cassidy glanced at him in surprise. *Coffee over alcohol? Even a recommended Australian cabernet? He may turn out to be the kind of man who grows tomatoes in the backyard after all.*

"Come on into the kitchen while I put on the pot." Amanda moved briskly down the hall and into a top-of-the-line kitchen, a long marble counter to the right, a window facing the garden to the left. Open shelving displayed colorful china and glassware. Baskets and old pots hung from the beamed ceiling. She filled the coffeemaker, took out a couple of lacquered trays, and began slicing cheese on an island in the center of the room.

Studying her hostess, Cassidy was amazed at how youthful she appeared. Amanda was slender and graceful, her dark blond hair pulled into a French twist, her skin smooth, her brown eyes large and velvety.

Said I look good but she's the one from the Dorian Gray School of Aging. Must be nearly as old as my mother but could pass for my prettier, richer sister.

Looking this good takes more than just a good husband. It takes a good personal trainer and plastic surgeon as well.

When everything was assembled, Amanda handed the snack tray to Zach, then picked up a second tray holding cream, sugar, and coffee in small porcelain cups. Her long golden skirt swirling around her ankles, she led them into a banquet-hall sized living room where gas flames flickered cozily inside a massive stone fireplace.

"Please make yourselves comfortable." Amanda waited while Zach settled on the sofa in front of the fire and Cassidy sat in a wingback chair to the right of the hearth. Their hostess served coffee, then took a matching chair on the opposite side of the fireplace. "I'm curious to hear what brought you to my door this afternoon."

"All day yesterday I couldn't stop thinking about Barbara's death," Cassidy began. She went on to reiterate the resolving-old-issues speech she'd delivered to Tess. *It's almost the truth. Could be the truth. Only a few omission-type sins short of the truth.*

Amanda responded with a bright, slightly false smile. *Wants to be helpful. But uneasy about it. Not quite sure what I'm up to.*

"What I'd like to do is talk about Barbara's death." She saw Amanda's face tighten. "If that's not too painful. I think going over some of the details might help put it to rest."

"I can do that." Amanda stared toward the window behind Zach's head. "For a long time I couldn't bring myself to even think about that night, but I can talk about it now."

Cassidy sipped coffee from the rosebud-adorned cup, then returned it to its saucer on the round antique table next to her chair. "Before we get into Barbara's death, I just want you to know how much I loved going to your house when I was a kid. I never got the chance to tell you what it meant to me, feeling like I was part of such a warm, close family."

She paused, noting the sudden look of bitterness that flashed across Amanda's face. "You mentioned staying in a bad marriage. Well, I never would've guessed there was anything wrong."

"We were very good at covering up." Amanda's gaze drifted back to the window. "Don just wasn't a happy person. I suppose he must've been depressed most of his life. I was the strong one, the one who always had to make everything work. The enforcer—that's what he used to call me. He'd say it right in front of the kids."

Cassidy winced. "Well, you did make things work. Even with Don pulling against you."

Amanda gave her a small grateful smile. "Up until Barbara died, I put everything I had into the family. I had this vision of what it would be like when my kids grew up and had children of their own. I pictured all three coming to grandma's house for Sunday dinner. I was so certain they'd look terrific and have great jobs and reminisce about what a wonderful childhood they'd had." She went to the cherry wood table in front of the sofa and filled a small plate with snacks.

"Oh, Amanda, I'm so sorry." Cassidy closed her eyes briefly. "If only I'd put her in a taxi."

"It's not your fault. I understand that now." Amanda ran a finger around the rim of her delicate cup. "After the accident, I just went sort of nuts. Don was drowning in grief and I started running around like a madwoman, staying so busy I didn't know what I was feeling. I was afraid to even let myself grieve, afraid I'd get as overwhelmed and helpless as he was. Then Don killed himself, and I abandoned ship."

"Is that when you sold the house?"

Amanda nodded. "I took all the money and bought a restaurant in Chicago. Something Lany's never forgiven me for. I couldn't bear to stay in the same house or even the same suburb. So I threw myself into learning the restaurant business. I just kept moving as fast as I could for about three years, and then I came down with pneumonia. So there I was, flat on my back, with no way to keep the feelings at bay any longer."

You tried to do the same thing. Shoved it in the closet. Refused to think about it. But nobody escapes forever.

Amanda looked down at the plate in her lap, where her fingers were crumbling a cracker. "So I went into therapy and came to discover that either no one was to blame for Barbara's death, or we all were, and it really doesn't matter which we choose to believe."

"That must have been such a terrible time," Cassidy said softly.

Amanda shifted in her chair. "I went from always putting the family first to being totally selfish."

"Grief does that to people. It makes you feel so stripped down and empty that the most you can hope for is to survive." *And Don couldn't even do that.*

"Pete understands. He had a friend who took him in when I left, so I don't think it was as hard on him as it was on Lany." Amanda frowned. "But she's never gotten over it. It ruined her life."

Zach clinked his saucer down on the coffee table. "How was her life ruined?"

"I used all the money to buy the restaurant and there was nothing left for her college expenses. She felt like I didn't care so she dropped out of school." Amanda's mouth compressed in a thin line. "Since then, she's lived with a couple of sleazy guys and had some long periods of unemployment. And if anybody asks her why her life is such a mess, she's very quick to say it's all my fault." Amanda tugged at her gold chain. "However, the problem's solved for the time being. Don's mother died last year and left both kids a nice inheritance, so now Lany will be able to pay her bills for a while."

"Your mother-in-law died too?" Cassidy asked. "Tess told us you got married, had a heart attack, then retired. What a lot to happen all at once."

"It's been a tough year."

"I guess so." Zach said, reaching for a piece of cheese.

No one spoke for a moment. Cassidy allowed her eyes to sweep over the striking mix of antique and contemporary furnishings. The sofa and drapes were done in a matching fabric, satiny and modern, with feathery pink and aqua swirls. Scattered around the room were vintage tables and shelves holding an assortment of old books, shoes, dishes, hats, and dolls. *This is so Amanda. She can take a bunch of stuff I'd consider junk and render it all striking and coherent. She has such a talent for making things work.*

Cassidy brought her gaze back to her hostess. "There's something I'd like to ask. Maybe I shouldn't. Maybe this is too painful. But it's something I really need to know." She moistened her upper lip. "The reason Barbara came to my house— she said it was because of a fight with you. But she didn't say what the fight was about. So . . . would you mind telling me what happened between the two of you that night?"

"Barbara said that?" Amanda put a cracker in her mouth, chewed slowly, swallowed. "Whatever it was must've been pretty insignificant because I really can't recall."

Nobody can't recall a fight they had with their daughter the last time they saw her—a daughter who left the house angry and died in a car crash.

There was a long silence, then Cassidy continued. "Speaking of fights, I wanted to explain why I told her to leave that night." *God, I hate lying to Amanda.* Taking a sip of coffee, Cassidy forced herself to go on. "Barbara said she'd heard rumors that Kevin was sleeping with another woman. Of course later on I found out they were true. But when Barbara told me, I didn't want to hear it. I got angry and turned it against her."

Cassidy sighed. "She'd been telling me about this boyfriend from college, and I went so far as to say I didn't believe he existed. That I thought she was making up stories just to get attention." Noticing that her hands had started to shake, Cassidy put her cup and saucer down with a slight rattle. "But I must have been wrong. Barbara wouldn't have lied about a thing like that, would she?"

Amanda looked away. "I'm not sure. I seem to remember having a few doubts myself."

"I suppose this must seem trivial but I just can't put those awful things I said to her out of my mind. I know it hurt her a lot when I accused her of lying, and I won't be able to let go of it until I find out for sure whether or not I was wrong."

Zach bent forward. "Could you give us the names of some of her friends from college? They'd probably know."

Amanda drew her finely arched brows together. "I can't really see the point of bothering her friends. I understand that it's good to talk, but maybe we should just keep this among ourselves."

This is one of the flimsiest scams you've ever tried to run. "I realize this may sound crazy, but I won't be able to get over these feelings of guilt until I'm certain about her boyfriend."

Cassidy laced her fingers tightly together. "You really don't know whether or not this guy actually existed?"

Looking down at her lap, Amanda shook her head.

Don't believe her. But why lie about the boyfriend? "You'd be doing me a huge favor if you could give me the names of some of her friends."

"There's only one person I've maintained any contact with—Gloria Edmunds, Barbara's roommate during her first three years."

"I'd really appreciate a phone number."

Amanda gazed out the window, then met Cassidy's eyes. "Since you had the courage to make the first move, I guess it's the least I can do." She stood. "Let me go upstairs and get it."

"As long as you're digging up the roommate's number, could you get me Lany and Peter's addresses as well? Today's my day for making amends, and I'd just as soon get all the groveling over at once."

"I don't think there's any need to grovel, but I can see why you'd want to finish up as quickly as possible. Getting back in touch after all this time—it can't be easy." She stood. "I'll be right back." Her tall, graceful figure disappeared in the direction of the stairs.

No harder than diving into a piranha tank. But you should've known Amanda wouldn't draw blood. It was just your own self-blame making you expect the worst.

Returning ten minutes later, Amanda handed Cassidy a sheet of paper. "I called the kids to let them know you're coming." She smiled. "I thought it might be easier if you didn't have to explain yourself at their door."

Bless you, Amanda. Making bullshit excuses is one of my least favorite things to do.

"Lany wasn't home so I left a message on her machine.

Pete's at his condo." She hesitated. "He said it'd be okay for you to stop over."

Cassidy offered a wide smile. "I'm so glad I finally did this. I'd just love to add three Segels to my Christmas card list this year." She paused. "Or maybe you aren't a Segel anymore. Did you change your name when you got married?" *That'd really give Tess something to snort over.*

"I've been a professional woman too long for that."

"What's your husband's name? I'd like to have him on my list, too."

"George Constantine. Here, I'll write it out for you."

As soon as the car door was closed, Cassidy leaned her head against the backrest and blew out air. "I feel like such a creep. Such a furtive, sneaky, creepy little toad."

"Creep or not, you did a great job. You made that 'need to come to terms with it' crap sound so convincing I almost believed it myself."

She turned toward Zach. "Amanda was so warm and gracious. Just the way I remember her. Lying about Barbara's death is one of the slimiest things I've ever done." She shook her head. "After this is over, I'd really like for us to be friends. But I don't see how I could ever face her after what I did today."

"You won't want to be friends if it turns out she's the E-Stalker."

"How could it be Amanda? I can't imagine her doing a thing like that."

He glanced over at her, his brow furrowed. "You've been sounding extremely naive ever since this whole thing started."

He's right. Your denial's running rampant and your objectivity's totally blown. All those warm childhood memories have completely fuzzed out your brain.

10.

What More Could Anyone Ask?

She sighed. "I suppose it is somewhat less than savvy to assume Amanda couldn't possibly be our E-Stalker on the grounds that she was such a nice lady when I was a kid."

"Especially since she fits our criteria very nicely in a couple of regards." Zach stopped at a light behind a minivan full of children. "Where we headed, anyway?"

"Hyde Park." She gave Zach the paper with Peter's address on it.

The light changed. Zach switched to the right lane and passed the slow-moving family van.

Cassidy tried for several seconds to avoid thinking about how Amanda might meet their criteria, then said grudgingly, "I suppose you mean the fact that she's had a couple of significant losses what with her heart attack and retirement."

"I particularly like the retirement. That would've given her the time she needed to work out the details of her fantasy."

Sliding lower on her spine, Cassidy stared out the side window. *I don't want it to be Amanda. What about Kevin? Or maybe Amanda's kids? No, not them either. I can't stand to have it be anybody I know.*

Zach, ignoring the sullen, leave-me-alone message her body was sending, continued. "She'd also be likely to have the required technical skills, since today's restaurants are highly computerized. And if she isn't quite up to snuff on the graphics side, there's always the chance that this new husband of hers who thinks she walks on water is."

Just because you can't stand the idea doesn't mean you can overlook the possibility. Zach's life may be in danger. You can't afford an attack of guilt-induced stupidity.

"Okay, you're right. Amanda's name has to go on the suspect list." She made herself sit straighter. "Especially since I think she lied about not remembering the fight with Barb. Of course it's possible there wasn't any fight, that Kevin just made it up. But the way Amanda suddenly got evasive, I'd have to guess that she's the one who's lying. And I also suspect she lied about the boyfriend."

Zach offered an encouraging smile. "Okay, now that I've knocked down your resistance to looking at Amanda as a suspect, tell me about this guy we're on our way to visit."

"Peter." Cassidy shook her head. "He was six years younger than Barbara, way too little for us older women to bother with. A quiet kid, always in the background. Now Lany, on the other hand, had no problem getting her share of attention. Even though she was four years younger, she always expected to be included, and I seem to remember Amanda backing her up. Barbara used to complain that Lany was the favorite." Cassidy ran her tongue across her upper lip, trying to bring back details.

"Isn't it unusual for the middle child to get special attention like that?"

"I just remembered why. Lany was sickly during her early years, so I guess that led to Amanda's being extra protective."

"Interesting how things turn out. Lany was the favorite as a kid. Now she's the black sheep."

"Sort of the reverse of how it went for you." Cassidy touched his leg. "You were the black sheep kid who turned out to be a pretty outstanding adult."

His blue-gray eyes regarded her warmly. "Not that my mother would agree, but I'm glad you think so."

They drove a while in silence. She watched a shiny new Mercedes on their left roll along nose to nose with the Nissan, the expensive car reminding her that the real Chicago aristocracy inhabited the North Shore and that the moneyed people who lived in Oak Park mansions—people like Zach's family— were pikers compared to the Lords and Ladies of the Land along the Lake.

She brought her errant mind back to Peter. *The funeral. Last time you saw any of them.* She'd hidden out after the graveside service, losing herself in the crowd, afraid that if Amanda or Don had noticed her they would have drawn her into the family circle, something she simply couldn't have handled. But she'd kept a watch on them, peeking out from behind the people in front of her. She could see the family in her mind's eye: Amanda, sleek and sophisticated even in her grief; Don in disarray, the husband and wife turned away from each other; Lany clinging to her mother.

Peter stood apart from the others. As Cassidy's mental camera focused in on him, she noticed how thin and gangly he looked, and that he stood next to an older girl, the two engaged in what appeared to be intense conversation.

Zach drove east to Lake Shore Drive, then turned right for the long trek from the far north side to Hyde Park, the University of Chicago neighborhood that existed like a walled city in the midst of the infamous, gang-ridden, drug-infested south side. People sometimes compared Hyde Park to Oak Park because both were integrated and both were adjacent to ghettos, but Cassidy viewed the U. of C. enclave as far less interesting than her autonomous hometown suburb. She saw Oak Park as a contentious, rabble-rousing, grassroots kind of place and Hyde Park as an intellectual, elitist community where the university ruled.

Zach parked in front of a three-story brownstone with Peter's number above the door. The rain had finally stopped, but as Cassidy stepped out of the car, damp air besieged her. Standing on the sidewalk to wait for Zach, she felt drops splatter down from a nearby elm. She trotted hastily onto the building's porch and punched the button next to Peter's name.

He buzzed them in. One flight up, they found him waiting in an open doorway. He was a large man, tall and muscular, with a shaggy overgrown crewcut above a strong-featured face. *Wow! What a change. He didn't just grow up, he went from the skinny kid that got sand kicked in his face to the kind of guy who throws bullies off the beach!*

Both Peter and Barbara had inherited their father's dark hair and olive skin, while Lany favored her golden-haired mother. Peter's green eyes behind black-framed glasses regarded her coolly.

"Well, Cassidy. I feel like saying 'What a surprise,' but I'd hate to sound so trite." His voice clipped along at a fast, impatient pace. His palm tapped out a rapid rhythm against his right thigh.

Doesn't seem exactly pleased at this reunion. We're interrupting his Sunday football? He's still mad over Barb's death? He's our E-Stalker and he doesn't want us snooping around?

"It's good to see you, Pete." She waved toward Zach. "This is my husband, Zach Moran."

"Peter." Zach leaned forward to shake his hand.

"I guess your mother told you why we're here."

"She said something about talking things through." He frowned. "But I don't understand why you need to see *me*. I wasn't involved in anything that went on between you and Mom back then."

Stepping away from the door, Peter gestured them into a high-ceilinged room, white walls with lots of dark, polished woodwork, books and papers everywhere.

Cassidy shifted her weight. "I forced Barbara to leave my apartment drunk the night she died, and all these years it's haunted me that I never talked about it to any of you, or even said I was sorry. Now I want to make up for it, and that means I need to speak to each of you personally."

His body stiffened; his face closed off from her. "This isn't something I like to get into."

Tilting her head, she said in a begging tone, "Please? As a favor to me? I promise not to drag it out any longer than necessary."

Amanda was wrong—you do have to grovel. Hate doing it but it usually works. The guy'd have to be a real jerk to say no after you've debased yourself like this.

Peter looked away, then brought his gaze back to her. "All right, I can take a little time. Here, why don't you give me your coats?"

As he hung up their jackets, Cassidy and Zach sank onto the cushiony seat of a nondescript blue-checked sofa. A glass coffee table covered with printouts stood in front of it. The furnishings looked sturdy and well made, but the pieces had not been assembled with any eye to design. *Probably spent a bundle. And ended up with the whole less than the sum of its parts.*

Zach asked, "We catch you at a bad time?"

Dropping into an easy chair across from them, Peter said, "There's never a good time. That's the downside of having a job you love. Even when I lecture myself on the importance of having some balance in my life, I can't break away."

Cassidy noted that the room was almost entirely devoid of personality, the walls bare except for one large print, a picture of a dark-haired, leotard-clad woman crouched on the floor, dejection visible in every line of her body.

Zach smiled his lazy smile. "What kind of work is it that's got you so hooked you can't take a Sunday off?"

Pete's expression brightened. "You don't want to get me talking about my job. I can go on for hours. I'm at Escovar Lab, part of a research team that's developing a new Alzheimer's drug. If this Alzar works the way we think it will, it could slow, maybe even stop the progression of the disease. Do you realize people are reaching the point where their fear of Alzheimer's is almost greater than their fear of cancer? Given our aging population, the number of people affected—either as patients or caregivers—is enormous. If this drug makes it through the trials and we can get it to market, it'll literally transform tens of thousands of lives."

He paused, looking from one to the other. "Why am I saying *if*? This team we've put together won't quit till we get it to do what we want it to." His left knee maintained a slight, constant dance. "Do you have any idea how exciting it is to be part of a project that has the potential for dramatically improving the quality of life for a large segment of the world's population?"

Cassidy responded, "A few years from now, we'll be very happy to know your drug's out there waiting for us."

"Well, I could go on and on." His voice shifted from enthusiastic to wary. "But that's not what you're here for, is it?"

A silence ensued, which quickly grew awkward. *Remember how you felt yesterday when Zach tried to get you to talk about the decimation of the Segel family? Now here's Peter, not wanting to talk about it either, but you're going to make him do it anyway.*

Cassidy said in a soft voice, "About Barbara."

"I don't know what to say." He shrugged helplessly. "I crunch numbers and analyze data. I don't discuss things like that."

"I know what you mean." Zach rested his outspread hands on his thighs. "I never used to myself. Put it behind you and don't look back, that's always been my motto."

"Right."

"But Cass is relentless. You won't get her out of here till she's hashed out every detail."

Cassidy shot Zach an irritated look. *There he goes, making me be the bad cop again.* To Peter she said, "Did your mother tell you why Barbara was driving with all that alcohol in her?"

"Yeah, I know about the letter you sent Mom."

Cassidy launched into her fictitious account of the argument she'd had with Barbara over the existence of Barbara's boyfriend. "What do you think? Did the family ever meet him?"

"Not that I heard about." Peter rested his right ankle on his left knee and jiggled his foot. "But I was pretty tuned out to what was going on at home. It was my last year of high school and I was working my rear off to get a scholarship to the U. of C. My family was so benighted they didn't even own a computer. I figured they were all living in the Dark Ages and I didn't want anything to do with them." He drummed his large fist on the chair's arm. "So I spent every waking moment at my buddy Jeff's. The one thing I do remember is Mom and Barb fighting all the time. Another reason I wanted to be at Jeff's."

"What were they fighting about?"

He shook his head. "I didn't know. I didn't want to know. I just wanted to get away from it."

Cassidy hunched forward. "After Barbara died, I went through one of the worst periods of my life." Zach laid his hand on top of hers. "It must've been twice as bad for you."

"I don't know. I probably was in shock more than anything." He stared into the middle distance. "Barbara and I were never close. What happened to her didn't seem nearly as bad as what Dad did." He glanced at Cassidy. "I guess I was kind of mad at him for giving up like that."

Shifting in his chair, he went on. "But you know, seeing the family fall apart the way it did—it taught me an important lesson. The lesson I learned was, you can never count on anything." His voice turned bleak. "No matter how secure your life may seem—your career, your health, your bank account—it can all be gone in the blink of an eye." He rubbed his fingertips back and forth across his thumb.

Never stops moving. Can't tell if he's nervous about us being here or just a type-A fidgeter.

"Right now I have everything in place," Peter added. "But I could walk out the door tomorrow, get run over by a truck, and end up like Christopher Reeve." His green eyes met hers. "The one positive that came out of the family debacle for me is, I never take anything for granted."

"So you're doing okay?" Cassidy felt her throat thicken. "My sending Barbara off to have an accident didn't ruin your life?"

"Look, I've got the greatest job in the world. What more could anyone ask?"

Some of us want a person to love, a cat to pet, friends to care about as well.

"And your mother?" Cassidy asked. "She okay too? That heart attack must've given you all quite a scare."

"Yeah, George and I were pretty worried at the time. But now that all the stress from the restaurant is gone, her health seems better."

Zach leaned slightly forward. "George? Her new husband? He in the restaurant business too?"

"It's turned out that George is really good for Mom. First time in her life she ever had anybody taking care of *her*."

Interesting how he dodged the restaurant question.

Peter pushed his black-framed glasses farther back on his nose. "George doesn't have a lot of formal education but he's amazingly sharp. One of the few people outside of Escovar I can discuss work with." He gestured toward the printouts on the coffee table. "The guy actually listens when I go on about things like statistical analysis."

"More than I could do," Zach said.

The mumblings of street corner schizophrenics make more sense to me than statistics ever would.

"Here I go, sliding off into talking about work again." He glanced at his watch, his brow furrowing. "I can appreciate your feeling a need to apologize but it really isn't necessary. I never thought of the accident as your fault. To me it was just something that happened, like a natural disaster. A hurricane hit our house and blew the family apart."

"Well, thanks for taking the time." She realized that her bladder was making a bid for her attention. "You mind if I use the bathroom before we leave?"

"Go right ahead." Peter stood, his bulky figure looming over her, and pointed in the direction of a hall leading off to the left of the living room.

The bathroom was white also. Another print hung on the

wall, a twin to the one she'd seen in the living room. In this picture the same woman in the same black leotard sat cross-legged on the floor, her face a portrait of hopelessness. *A dark-haired woman. Subliminal reminder of Barbara?*

After using the facilities, Cassidy washed her hands at the sink. On the counter next to the soap dish stood a porcelain container holding two toothbrushes. *Well, what do you know? Maybe Pete gets a little starburst delight from sources other than his job after all.*

11.

Clichés and Correspondence

As Zach pulled away from the curb, he said, "That paper you gave me with names and addresses on it? It says the roommate lives in Hinsdale. How 'bout we make a circle and stop by her house before calling it a day?"

"I feel like such an idiot every time I reel off that bogus reason for needing to find the boyfriend."

"But you do it so well. You get this sincere look on your face that adds to your credibility. Which is why I'd rather do it in person than over the phone."

"What's happening to me?" She pressed a hand to her cheek. "Not only have I become a skilled liar, I've even developed facial expressions to support the deceit. I was an honest person before I hooked up with you."

"Ah, but see how I've expanded your repertoire?"

"Now there's an understatement. Since you entered my life, I've become a highly competent manipulator, shot two people, and acquired a surly stepson." She checked her watch. Four-thirty. "Speaking of which, you said Bryce was coming for dinner. Is there enough time to get to Hinsdale and back before he arrives?"

"He's not due till seven."

Zach headed onto the outer drive, this time traveling north

on the lanes adjacent to the lake. The overcast sky had rendered everything colorless and dull, pavement, sand and water a nearly uniform shade of gray. Cassidy stared out over the lake, its flat emptiness matching her mood.

Zach glanced across at her. "So, you going to fight me over adding Pete's name to the list the way you did with Amanda?"

She shook her head. "This is no time to lose my grip on reality. And the reality is, any one of these people could be a borderline, which is undoubtedly what we're dealing with here."

"Borderline? Isn't that what you said Ryan was?" Zach's brother, Ryan, had once been Cassidy's client. It was his apparent suicide that had brought Cassidy and Zach together.

"Borderlines make the best candidates for any activity involving rage, obsessiveness, and revenge. But they're usually smart enough to hide their weirdness, so unless you're their therapist or you live with them, they can be pretty hard to detect." She looked down at her hands. "I had Ryan in therapy for over a year and didn't get his diagnosis right."

"Even therapists are entitled to an occasional mistake." They passed a green sign announcing the entrance to I-55. Zach merged onto the interstate, sliding in behind a battered old Cadillac with a grizzled black man at the wheel.

"So," Cassidy continued, "unless I see evidence of borderline behavior, there's no way to know which, if any, of these people is the type to be driven by the desire for revenge."

"Okay, skipping the professional diagnosis, what do you think of Pete?"

"Well, there's no question he has the computer skills we're looking for, but he didn't seem unhappy enough. The

E-Stalker sees himself as still suffering in the present because of this terrible thing I did in the past. He's probably a martyr, a person who feels he's sustained lifelong emotional injury because of me."

Zach accelerated to pass both the Cadillac and an ancient, rusted-out station wagon. "I can't quite picture anybody being so gung-ho about his career and at the same time centering all this attention on revenge."

"I agree. The person we're looking for is going to be more focused on the past than the present." She stared straight ahead. Drops were splattering against the windshield again, the wipers swishing back and forth, clearing the glass in front of her.

Stroking her jawline, she said, "I may be getting too analytical here, but I noticed Pete had only two pictures in his house, both women in poses of despair. Taking into account those pictures along with his statement about never feeling secure with anything, I'd have to guess there's some underlying depression he's not even aware of."

"You're getting too analytical. Depression he's not aware of? Are you saying he's deluding himself about being happy? He's really depressed—he just doesn't know it?"

She lowered her brow in a mock frown. "Why can't you accept that I'm the expert on psychology and just take my word for it the way everybody else does?"

"You'd get bored if I never challenged you. You wouldn't like it if I let you be the expert any more than I'd like it if you let me be right all the time."

Don't mind being challenged as long as I get to win, which I usually do. "Underlying depression means a person is carrying around great amounts of pain they've never worked through, and they organize their life around fending it off. Maybe the reason Pete works so hard is to avoid facing all those losses from the past."

Zach looked at her again, his face thoughtful. "I'm not sure I buy the analytical crap, but if what you said is true, it'd rule Pete out as the E-Stalker, wouldn't it? This business of avoiding things—that's what I do. To avoid things you have to not think about them. And if you're not thinking about them, you can't seek revenge."

"You're right. We're not looking for someone who uses avoidance or sees himself as a happy person. We're looking for someone who obsesses about the past and enjoys a good wallow. And that doesn't seem to fit either Amanda or Pete. If you stay on the surface and leave the underlying stuff alone, they both seem pretty satisfied with their lives."

"Yeah, but the person who sent the e-card is not about to lay out his problems for us. You said it yourself—he's going to hide his weirdness." He gave her a stern look. "You are not allowed to remove anybody's name from the list because of apparent normalcy."

"Okay, okay." She replayed the interview with Pete to see if there was anything she'd missed. "This is probably completely unrelated to the case, but it looks like Pete isn't quite the loner Tess thinks he is. At least, not unless he uses a separate toothbrush for morning and evening brushing."

"Two toothbrushes, huh? So old Pete does have somebody in his life after all. Well, I'm glad to hear it." Zach put his hand on her knee. "I agree with Tess. Men *are* better off when they have a woman around."

A warm feeling rose in Cassidy's chest. *Tess had it right on the topic of marriage being good for men. But boy, am I glad I don't share her perspective on second-time-around events for women.*

Cassidy pushed a button in the center of a brass medallion to the left of a carved walnut door. They stood on a narrow porch in front of a tall, Italianate house, a row of windows with decorative shutters stretching across the first and second stories.

The door was opened by a thin woman with straight blond shoulder length hair. Gazing at them out of wide set, hazel eyes, she said, "Let me guess. Jehovah's Witnesses putting in your obligatory door-knocking time? Fund-raisers begging money to send inner city kids to camp? Befuddled visitors who got lost and ended up at the wrong door?"

"None of the above," Zach retorted.

"You're Gloria Edmunds?" Cassidy asked.

The woman nodded.

"I'm Cassidy McCabe. I got your name from Amanda Segel. Barbara and I were best friends in grade school."

Gloria's pale eyebrows rose. She blinked, then stared off into space, looking as if she'd suddenly been thrown back in time. She wore a paint-splattered plaid flannel shirt and sported a small red dot on the left cheek of her delicate oval face.

Returning to the present, she met Cassidy's eyes. "Barbara. I haven't thought about her in a long time." The furrows between her brows deepened. "Wasn't it around this time of year the accident happened?"

"November fourth. Yesterday was the fifteenth anniversary. Which is what sparked this odyssey I'm on to resolve some lingering feelings about her death." Cassidy offered a small smile. "I'm a therapist. That's why I fall into this awful clichéd jargon. I try not to but sometimes it just slips out."

"It's also why she can never leave things in the past the way I think she should." Stepping forward, Zach extended his hand. "Zach Moran, Cassidy's husband. I'm here mostly for moral support."

"Glad to meet you," the blonde responded. She looked at Cassidy. "So the reason you came to see me has to do with some therapist-type cliché?"

"I'm afraid it does."

"Well, that sounds interesting." Gloria looked from Cassidy to Zach. "Come on inside. I'm so starved for company, I'd probably ask you in even if you *were* Jehovah's Witnesses."

They followed Gloria through the foyer into a sleek, contemporary living room. A metallic gray sofa stood in front of the exterior wall, two small upholstered chairs facing it. A deep red area rug graced the hardwood floor between the sofa and chairs. In the center of the rug stood a kidney-shaped glass table supported by a steel boomerang pedestal. Atop the table sat two art books and an arrangement of yellow and red mums. A dull gray light filtered through the windows.

Gloria stood in the center of the room, her right elbow cupped in her left hand. "I've got some paints I need to put away. Why don't you make yourselves comfortable while I take care of it?"

Zach lowered himself onto the sofa. "You painting a picture or a room?"

"A picture. In search of my creative side, don't you know." She wrinkled her nose. "Talk about clichés. I feel like I've been turning into one ever since Ameritech cut me loose." She tucked a strand of hair behind her ear. "Would you like coffee, tea, soft drinks?"

"We're fine," Zach replied, falling into his old habit of answering for Cassidy.

"Okay, I'll be back in a jiff." Gloria turned and flitted toward the rear of the house.

Minutes later she settled in one of the small chairs. "So, what are these old feelings you want to resolve?"

Cassidy told the story about accusing Barbara of lying and needing to find out whether or not the boyfriend really existed. *Feel like an actor who's been reciting the same speech all day. Just wind me up and hear me spout dialogue so bad it'd be an embarrassment on your worst soap.*

Gloria said to Zach, "You know, I think you're right. She should put all this behind her." Her slender hands moved rapidly as she talked, painting pictures in the air. "When I invited you in, I thought it'd be a kick to hear a therapist discuss," her voice went melodramatic, "her *issues*." Giving Cassidy a direct look, she continued more seriously. "But listening to you talk about Barbara's accident has got me sad all over again."

"You two were close?" Crossing her legs, Cassidy rested her hands in her lap.

"Barbara and I met the first day of college. We roomed together in the dorm, both joined Alpha Theta and then roomed together there. Well, you know what it's like right at the beginning of school. Scary, exhilarating, overwhelming. We went through all that stuff together. Told each other everything. Got each other over all the big humps." She blinked, her eyes glistening. "I think Barbara was about the last real friend I had."

Cassidy said in a soft voice, "No real friends since Barbara?"

"Mom came down with cancer so I had to drop out just before my senior year. Then, after she died, there wasn't much money, which meant I had to work part time and get my degree here in Chicago. When I finally started at Ameritech, I was in a big hurry to move up, and relationships just got sort of back-burnered. So here I sit on a generous package with no job, no friends, and no idea what I want to do with the rest of my life." Cassidy noticed a shift in Gloria's hazel eyes: a dip into bitterness.

Gloria grimaced. "I'm a damned poster girl for the burned-out workaholic."

"Can't find what you want?" Zach asked.

She shrugged, the angry lines in her pretty face deepening. "How do you find what you want when you haven't a clue what that is? For the past ten years I put everything else on hold so I could work sixteen-hour days, and now I'm downsized, with no life to fall back on. I read the want ads, and take painting, French and swimming lessons, and try to fill my time. So, if you have any ideas on how I can match my Ameritech salary without getting back into the corporate rat-race, I'm all ears."

"You must be feeling pretty stuck."

"Well, you are a therapist, aren't you? Here you've been in my living room all of five minutes and I've told you my life story." She gave them a feeble smile. "Now that you've listened to me whine, what can I do for you?"

Cassidy rubbed her garnet ring. "I'm trying to make sense out of Barbara's death, trying to understand what might have led to her getting drunk and coming to my house that night. All I know is, when she came home from college, she seemed subdued, depressed, not the person I remembered at all. What do you suppose might've caused these changes?"

"I haven't thought about this in so long." Gloria raked her fingers through her hair and stared into space. "She certainly wasn't subdued when we roomed together. A major partyer, that's what she was. Boys always buzzing around her. I used to worry. Lectured her sometimes about pregnancy, STDs, that sort of thing."

"So what do you think could have made her so . . . I don't

know, listless, unmotivated after graduation?"

"That last year when I was home taking care of my mother, Barb and I corresponded. Doesn't that sound Victorian? But neither of us could afford to run up the phone bill and we didn't have email then, so we actually sat at our computers and typed out letters. As I think back about it, I remember a couple of things. First, there was a long period when I didn't hear from her, and then after she started writing again, she didn't seem quite herself. I think I called a couple of times to see if she was okay. She said everything was fine but I wasn't convinced."

Zach shifted on the sofa next to Cassidy. He was leaning back, hands on his thighs, expression alert but not too eager. *Got it down exactly right. Here for me. Just wants to be helpful.*

He said, "Maybe a fight with her boyfriend?"

Cassidy bent forward. "Did she mention the boyfriend in her letters?"

Gloria's forehead contracted into deep grooves. "I seem to recall that in one of her letters she announced that she'd met the man of her dreams. Well, as soon as I heard the news, I got on the phone and tried to dig out all the details. But I guess I didn't find out very much. Which, now that I think about it, is fairly odd in itself. Girls in love usually want to talk your ears off about the light of their life."

"So there *was* a boyfriend from college." Cassidy tilted her head reflectively. "Maybe it was on-again, off-again, and that's why she didn't say much." *You certainly didn't want to go into any blow-by-blows when Zach was playing that game with you.*

"Now you've got me curious." Gloria's face tightened in concentration, then eased off into a smile. "I do believe I'll make this into a project. Trying to piece together what was going on with Barb that last year of college should be way more fun than painting still lifes or memorizing French verbs.

Fortunately, I'm a pack rat so I've still got all her letters. I'll read through them, then call around to some of the old gang from Champaign."

"You have the letters? That's wonderful."

"I doubt that there's much there. But if anything happened to Barbara, our dear old Alpha Theta sisters will know what it was. You put a bunch of girls in the same house together, there's no such thing as a secret."

Cassidy dug out a business card and handed it to Gloria. "You'll let me know what you come up with?"

"Sure, why not?" A bright smile lit the blond woman's face. "I not only got a mini therapy session out of the deal, I now have a new project to throw myself into."

12.

Broken Windows

"Well," Zach said, parking next to their back gate, "I'd say we accomplished a lot. Gloria's a godsend. Tess fed us Oreos. Amanda's given us at least one viable suspect. You even managed to drag a little info out of old let's-forget-it-ever-happened Pete."

Cassidy opened the Nissan door. "So where do we go from here?"

Zach joined her on the sidewalk. "We order pizza and hope Bryce is in a decent mood."

Only six-thirty and the daylight was completely gone, although the street lamps and the peach-colored city glow maintained a constant, low-level visibility. Cassidy gripped the neck of her jacket to keep out the cold as they walked through the gate, past the yellow and russet-leaved tree behind her office, and up the steps of the concrete stoop at the rear of the house.

Zach poked his key at the lock but it wouldn't go in. He tried a second time without success.

Her chest tightened. "What's wrong?"

"There's something in the lock."

"Oh shit. Does this mean what I think it means?"

Zach's bronze face went a shade darker. "There goes my

somewhat delusional hope that our nutcase would restrict himself to long distance emails."

"I knew this was going to be bad. I just knew it." Little jolts of anxiety started in her stomach.

Zach peered into the keyhole. "It's full of some kind of transparent gunk. Could be glue."

"Let me see." She lined her left eye up with the hole. It was just as Zach had said. Straightening, she examined the door. Beneath the lock a drip adhered to the weathered oak panel. She picked at it but it held fast. "Yep, I'll bet it's glue." She clutched her arms across her chest. "At least he didn't break in. If he'd breached any of the openings, the alarm would've gone off and the police would have called your cell phone."

"Yeah, at least there's that." Zach started down the steps. "Odds are he hit the front door too, but let's go check it out."

After a couple of attempts to insert the key in the front door lock, Zach unclipped his phone from his belt. "Time to call the cops."

She placed her hand on his arm. "If we sic the police on the Segels, there's not much chance any of them'll ever speak to us again, and I haven't even had my shot at Lany yet. Are you sure we want to turn everything over to the cops so early on?"

"Maybe not." He returned the phone to his belt. "We better think through exactly what we want to say before we call in the cavalry. But the first thing is to get inside the house."

"You're going in the side door?" The side entrance was secured by a deadbolt that could be easily reached by breaking the window.

"Yep. I'll have to get the tire iron out of the car. Why don't you go wait by the door?"

As Zach trotted back to the Nissan, Cassidy went around to the south side of the house to stand in front of the door that opened onto the landing in the middle of the basement stairs. An image came to mind of a jagged hole in their back door window, the hole the person who'd broken into their house two months earlier had made. And just inside, shattered glass on the waiting room floor. That was the second time her back door window had been broken. Then yesterday her mother's window, and now their own again. A shiver ran down her arms. *Broken windows, a recurrent theme. Symbol for what? Broken hearts, broken dreams, broken lives?*

Zach came toward her, the tire iron in hand.

"We've had too many broken windows," she said. "Everybody has to sweep up glass sometimes, but we've had more than our share."

"You have a better suggestion?"

"Get in the car and drive to some other part of the country?"

"Your clients would object to the commute."

Letting out a heavy sigh, she said, "Okay, do it."

She squeezed her eyes shut and gritted her teeth as he raised the tire iron. The sound of iron striking glass exploded in her ears. Sucking in air, she heard the jingle-jangle of glass falling to the floor within. Zach, his face grim, pulled shards out of the frame, then thrust his arm inside.

When the door was open, he hurried toward the rear entrance to turn off the security alarm. Picking her way through the glass on the landing, Cassidy followed him up the half flight of stairs and across the kitchen to fetch a broom and dustpan from the room-divider cabinet.

Standing near the door, Zach said, "Why don't we sit down and talk about what we're going to tell the cops first?"

"Because I can't think with glass all over my floor." Her voice was shrill, her skin crawly.

Zach's steady blue-gray eyes appraised her. "This is really getting to you, isn't it?"

"Of course it's getting to me. A phony obit, my mother's apartment vandalized, an email threatening you. And now our locks jammed? Anybody who's the least in touch with reality ought to be panicking. What's wrong with you that you're not?"

"Actually, I'm fairly freaked. I just hide things better than you." He took the cleaning implements out of her hands. "You go have a glass of wine or do deep breathing or whatever and I'll sweep up." He headed for the basement stairs.

Opening the refrigerator, she gazed longingly at a bottle of Chardonnay. *Wouldn't you love to chug down a big glass of that nice white wine? But you know perfectly well that'd be the exact wrong thing to do.* She went into the living room and plopped down in one of the two small armchairs that lined up at a right angle to the blue paisley sofa. Behind the sofa a picture window looked out onto the enclosed porch.

You should've stopped for peanut butter cups. Here you are, an emergency on your hands, not a crumb of chocolate in the house. She closed her eyes and focused on taking long slow breaths.

Twenty minutes later Zach came and sat beside her. "We need to get the cops involved, but I'm starting to think we should keep the whole Barbara situation to ourselves for a while. Eventually we'll have to give up everything, but we could postpone it a couple of days. Talk to the Segels a little more before we do."

"You mean, lie to the police?" She frowned. "Show them the obit and the email and say 'Gee, officer, I haven't a clue what this is all about?'"

"Something like that, yeah."

"But then we'd have to go back later and tell them we lied."

As if you haven't withheld information plenty of times.

Yeah, but I never deliberately put myself in a position where I knew I'd have to admit it.

"So?" He shrugged. "What can they do? They may rant and rave a little but they won't put us in jail."

"I hate having the police yell at me." She pressed her fingertips to her cheek. "I always end up with the sense that they're right and I'm just this stupid little person messing in their case."

"Both times it happened, it turned out that your instincts were on target and the cops were wrong."

"Doesn't matter. I hate being lectured at by authority figures. It puts me in a one-down position, something I work strenuously to avoid."

He looked her in the eye. "We either don't tell the police about Barbara or we very likely lose access to Amanda, Pete, and Lany."

"Would that be so bad? Maybe we should just let the police handle it. It's not as if lying my head off to the Segels is my favorite thing to do."

"Yeah, but people clam up in front of cops. The two Segels we've talked to so far seem to like you. I'd prefer to see you do one more round of interviews—Amanda, Pete, and Lany— then we can go back to the cops and acknowledge our lack of forthrightness."

Biting her lip, she stared at a large raku pot, aswirl with shades of rose, blue and teal, sitting on a round marble table at the far end of the sofa. The pot had been a birthday present from Zach.

"And the reason we need the police is so they can trace the email?"

"Two things: First, I want the doors dusted for prints. I

don't expect any to turn up but we can't just leave it undone. However, that's minor compared to finding out if the email can be traced. If the police are able to locate the sender, our problem's solved."

"I really wish we didn't have to do this." She sighed again. "But you're right—we need to bring the police in and we don't want to cut ourselves off from the Segels." She drew her brows together. "Why is it we're so often faced with no good options?"

"Look, pissing off the police doesn't bother me nearly as much as it does you. I'll do the talking, you stay in the background. Then, when they come down on us, I'll be the primary target."

"What? Be the mousy little woman who stays out of the way?" She shook her head. "I'd rather be yelled at."

"There's no pleasing you." He smiled. "We probably won't get your detective friend this time unless he's the computer geek."

"Manny?" Detective Manny Perez had reamed her out thoroughly the last time she'd interfered in a murder investigation. "I'd prefer to face the shark from *Jaws* than tell Manny I'd been meddling again."

They went up to the bedroom to make the call. A message from Helen complaining about the bad day she'd had awaited them on the answering machine.

What Mom'd really like is for me to forget everybody else and devote myself to her.

Stop being a brat. This time her whining is valid and you should be nice to her. But not until you've dealt with the police.

Zach sat in his desk chair and pulled out a pad.

Starshine moved from the bed to the nightstand, fastened her large green eyes on Cassidy, and gave a coaxing *mwat*, the sound she used to entice her human into petting her. Cassidy, a well-trained cat owner, started to sit on the bed, then suddenly noticed a tiny dead mouse tucked into the fold where the comforter encased the pillow.

"Oh god!" She took a quick step backward.

Zach looked up. "What is it?"

This is too much. I think I'm going to scream.

You scream at the sight of a dead mouse, you've forever compromised your claim to equal toughness.

Zach came up next to her to stare at the mouse.

Cassidy giggled.

"Are you all right?"

"I was just debating the feminist correctness of screaming."

"You feel like screaming, go right ahead and do it. After the past two days, you're entitled."

She scowled, first at him, then at the mouse. "I hate it that I'm not as strong as you. I go around ranting about how I don't want you treating me like a lesser being, but the only reason I make so much noise about it is, deep down inside I know I have all these weaknesses. I seem to spend half my life fending off anxiety, while you sail through the worst situations without breaking a sweat."

"Cass, I never see you as a lesser being." He tried to pull her into a hug. She resisted at first, then allowed herself to lean into him.

"We just handle stress differently," he continued. "And I'm not so sure your way isn't better. You get emotional, sometimes you have to stop and calm yourself down, while I'm more like Pete. I go into denial and tell myself it's not so bad. But sometimes it is and then I'm apt to misjudge it. And if my denial breaks down, I'm liable to drink myself stupid at a time when I absolutely need to be clear-headed." He dropped a kiss on her forehead. "I don't see it as a weakness that you get anxious in threatening situations."

Leaning back to gaze up at him, she said skeptically, "You really wouldn't look down on me if I screamed?"

His mouth tilted at one corner. "I think it'd be great. Give me a chance to play he-man for once."

"What about the looking-down-on-me part?"

His brow creased. "Okay, I might be dumb enough to feel superior for some brief period. But you'd slap me out of it fast enough."

She pulled away, crossed her arms, went to stand in front of the window. *What a lousy thing to say. This is a husband who needs to be sent to sensitivity school.*

He said from behind her, "Hey, I thought the deal was, we always have to tell the truth."

She turned to face him. "I'll just have to make sure never to scream when you're around then."

"Look, there's no way I'd ever think of you as weak for more than thirty seconds. And I'm sure you've spent a lot longer than that thinking of me as a jerk." He laid his arm across her shoulders. "Well, it must be my turn to dispose of the corpse."

"I'll take the comforter down to the laundry," she said as Zach picked up the mouse with a paper towel. "And while I'm in the basement, I'm setting the lock on the cat-door so our little princess here doesn't bring us any more trophies." She frowned. "And don't you dare try to convince me that Starshine's happiness is worth a few dead mice."

Heading down the basement stairs with the comforter in her arms, she saw that Zach had already boarded up the hole. She started the washing machine, then halted in front of a basement window a few feet to the right of the side door. Half the window was taken up by a wooden panel that held a swing-ing flap. Beside the flap was a control knob that could be used to lock the door in place. Cassidy turned the knob to OFF.

She sat in her chair a few feet from Zach's desk to listen as he talked to an Oak Park detective. Finishing, he swiveled to face her. "Their computer guy said he'd be over in half an hour."

She looked at the clock on the bureau. Nearly eight. "Wasn't Bryce due at seven?"

"Shit. I forgot about Bryce." Zach blew out air. "Well, I guess that tells us where we stand with him."

Last summer the kid was furious because Zach went a few weeks without calling. Now he's just blowing us off? Something's wrong here.

"What're we going to do about it?'

"Nothing we can do. If he doesn't want to see us, we can't force him."

"We may have to force him. Or at least crank up the pres-sure high enough that he can't get out of it." She laid her hand on Zach's arm. "This is a sudden, fairly extreme change in behavior. It could be a warning sign. The beginning of college is a time when a lot of kids get in trouble."

"Crank up the pressure?" Zach said, his voice ironic. "We don't have any pressure to crank. May I remind you that his trust fund exceeds our total assets, he's living with that old lady who used to be his nanny, and he considers his genetic con-nection to me mostly irrelevant." Zach shook his head. "Besides, I don't see any reason to assume a sudden change means anything. Isn't that what adolescents do? Swing from one extreme to another?"

She leaned back, crossed her legs, jiggled a pen between her fingers. "Zach, you're his only living relative. As much as he tries to hide it, I know he looks up to you."

"Yeah, but he's in college now. When I started college, the older generation ceased to exist. He's probably fallen in love and lost all interest in anything that happens outside of bed."

What's the matter with him, he's just brushing it off? Bryce needs a father, and half the time Zach fails the test.

Generalizing from his own experience, that's what he's doing. Zach cut himself off from his family, screwed up all over the place, and came out okay. Probably thinks the best thing he can do for Bryce is leave him alone.

"Bryce is not the same kid you were. By the time you hit college, you were tough and strong and you'd been running your own life for years. Bryce went to boarding school, hardly made any of his own decisions, then all of a sudden his world exploded and he lost everything. This is a high risk kid."

"I don't buy it." Zach drew his brows together. "He went through that rough period, picked himself up, and he's been fine ever since. Why would he have problems now?"

"Because people have delayed reactions all the time. Post traumatic stress can show up years after the precipitating event."

"Anytime you can't win with logic, you throw psychology at me." He paused. "Okay, you're worried. You want some kind of reassurance. I guess that's reasonable—except I don't know how you think you're going to get it."

"We have to make him talk. Bribery won't work so I guess it'll have to be threats. The overt, un-anonymous kind."

"Make him talk?" Zach snorted. "The way you do it with me is you threaten to cut me off."

"I do not." She pushed out of her chair and went to stand

in front of the wedding photo from which her image had been lifted. Zach's face was round and smooth, with straight shaggy brows, a broad nose and strong chin. Bryce's face was narrow and craggy, with peaked brows, a thin nose and pointed chin. They stood with arms across each other's shoulders, Cassidy in the middle, a goofy smile on all three countenances.

"C'mon," she said, "help me out here. You're better at bullying than I am."

"You're just more subtle." He pressed his fingertips together. "I suppose you could tell him if he doesn't get his butt over here, we'll go to his house and interrogate the nanny."

Cassidy gave Zach a direct look. "You have to do it."

Zach's voice turned growly. "You're the one who wants to make him talk. Besides, you're always better with him than I am."

"He needs to know you're concerned—even if you aren't."

"You want to drag him over here, you make the call." The line between the base of Zach's nose and jaw deepened, an expression Cassidy read as stubbornness.

"Why are you digging in your heels like this? I can usually talk you into almost anything."

"I don't pursue people."

So that's what's going on. Zach's mother didn't like him, he didn't like her more. Nobody gets to reject Zach. He's gone before they even think of it.

Returning to her chair, she rolled it around so they were face to face, reached over, and placed her hands on his knees. "I understand that you don't want to put yourself in a position where Bryce can thumb his nose at you one more time. You've tolerated plenty of insolence and hostility from him already, and it's probably been harder on you than I ever realized." *Not that Zach'd let me know if anything bothered him.* "But he's still so young. And there are so many pits out there for kids to fall into." She tilted her head. "Please make the call. Don't let him get away with thinking you don't care."

He gave her a sardonic smile. "And if I don't you'll cut me off?"

She stood and punched his shoulder.

Zach picked up the desk phone and Cassidy scrambled into his office to listen in on the extension.

"Sorry, I forgot about tonight," Bryce said in the same listless tone Cassidy often heard from depressed clients.

"You're not getting out of this," Zach said firmly. "I want you over here some night this week."

"Uh, how 'bout Tuesday?"

"If you're not here by seven, Cass and I are going to arrive at your door and have a long talk with Ellie."

Cassidy smiled inwardly. *There've been plenty of times you thought of him as a jerk. But in the long run—given sufficient nudging—he usually does come through for you.*

13.

Nobody Knew

An hour later, after the evidence technician had dusted for prints and gone, Detective Wharton sat in front of their computer screen. Zach was seated to his left; Cassidy stood behind Zach's chair. The black cop clicked the mouse and the cartoon figure with Barbara's head appeared on the screen.

"Who's the woman?" Wharton asked in a smooth cultivated voice.

Cassidy bit her lip. As adept as she'd become at improvising, she still tended to choke up over a direct lie.

"No idea." Zach looked straight at the cop. "Nothing about the obituary or the card makes sense to either one of us."

He does that so well. He ever starts lying to you, you're in big trouble.

Wharton clicked through the card's three pages. In his early thirties, he had short hair above a smoothly molded face. A high forehead, challenging eyes behind wire-rimmed glasses, and a wide full mouth. When she'd first seen the techy cop, Cassidy had been surprised to find him rugged and handsome, no sign of nerdiness at all.

As much as you rail against stereotypes, you frequently embarrass yourself by stumbling over them in your own head.

Arriving at the last page, the detective shoved his glasses up to the top of his head, then twisted around to look at Cassidy. She responded to his unspoken question by spreading her palms wide and shaking her head. *Maybe I will play little mouse in the corner after all.*

Wharton gazed from Cassidy to Zach, his eyes narrowing. "Why do I get the impression that the person behind this has something on one of you? Some nasty little secret you don't want to tell."

Uneasiness rippled through Cassidy's stomach.

"Beats me," Zach said.

Wharton gave him a long look, then turned his skeptical gaze on Cassidy. She gritted her teeth and held his eyes.

"If you say so," he remarked in a tight voice. "I assume you won't mind if I forward a copy to my computer."

"Be my guest."

Wharton pulled his glasses down, tapped keys, then said, "I've got a couple more questions."

Zach stood. "Let's go downstairs to talk."

The detective, his wire-rims on top of his head again, settled in one of the two small armchairs in the living room and pulled out a pad. "Know of anybody who might have a grudge against either one of you?"

Cassidy and Zach sat on the sofa. "Everybody I ever made look bad in a news story," he said. "It's a pretty long list."

Not anyone from Zach's list. Somebody who hates me. It made her feel small and shivery and scared to be hated so much.

"What about you, Ma'am?"

"I can't think of anyone."

Zach leaned forward, propping his elbows on his knees. "Can you trace email that goes through a remailer?"

"Not if the remailer's outside the US. People who traffic in kiddie porn route it through an IP in some other country so we can't subpoena the records."

Curling her fingers beneath her chin, Cassidy asked, "What if the remailer's here in the states?"

"Depends. If they keep records of every message that goes in and out, we could probably track down the sender."

"What else will you do?" Now that they were past the lying-in-the-cop's-face part, Cassidy wanted to assert herself.

"Canvass the neighbors. Talk to the *Register's* editor."

"And if nothing pans out?" Zach asked.

"Tell you what." His voice snide. "You come up with more information, I'll develop some additional avenues."

As she closed the door behind the detective, Cassidy said to Zach, "You're probably ready for food, but I need to call my mother first."

Upstairs Cassidy picked up her desk phone while Zach sat in his swivel chair, the newspaper spread out in front of him.

"It's been hours and hours since I left that message," Helen said plaintively. "What took you so long?"

A death threat against your husband does make returning phone calls seem less of a priority.

"I'm sorry, Mom. We were out all day."

"In this miserable weather? Where'd you go?"

Oops! Wrong excuse. A moment of silence. "We spent the afternoon at Navy Pier."

"I hope you enjoyed yourselves." Sarcasm heavy in her voice.

One good thing about self-absorbed people, they often fail to notice your long pauses and little slips. "Well, I'm here now. So, what was it you called about?"

"I need you to come with me tomorrow morning at nine

when I open up the apartment for the cleaning service. Going back alone is just too much for me."

"Tomorrow morning?" *What if there's another e-card?* "Won't Gran be with you?"

"First you wouldn't let me stay at your house. Now you don't even want to help me with my apartment."

Another pause. Starshine jumped onto the desk, picked up a catnip-filled toy, and bounced off to play with it. "It's not that I don't want to help." She glanced at Zach, who'd turned to face her. "It's just that I thought as long as you were already there with Gran. . . ." *God, does that sound feeble.*

Helen lowered her voice. "I've been stuck here almost two days now and she's really getting on my nerves."

Gran getting on Mom's nerves?

"Please, Cass, I need your help."

Starshine returned to the desk and fastened her large green eyes on Cassidy's face, an I'm-ready-to-be-adored-now look.

Cassidy frowned at Zach, remembering how he'd played drill sergeant and refused to let her assist her mother the day before. *Should I get permission from my keeper? No, I should give my mother a little support and if Zach doesn't like it, to hell with him.*

"Okay, Mom, I'll pick you up a little before nine. But I have a client at one, so Gran'll have to handle the second shift." Cassidy put the phone down and said in a belligerent tone, "I'm helping Mom tomorrow."

"Good."

"Good?" She scratched behind the calico's ear. The cat purred rapturously and nuzzled her hand. "How come you're not trying to stop me?"

"The only reason I interfered on Saturday was because you were still reeling from the obit. At this point—a broken window and dead mouse not withstanding—you seem fine." He ran a hand over the top of his head, squeezed the back of his neck. "However, I'm not exactly fine myself. What I need about now is a stiff drink, a thick steak, and half a bottle of good, red wine." He stood. "Let's go get dinner."

Garbed in a long tee, not yet fully awake, Cassidy sat up in bed, hands clutched around a mug of steaming coffee. Starshine, eager for her morning cuddle, stood on Cassidy's lap and bapped her arm, trying to get closer.

"You don't understand. I need my coffee first."

The cat bumped her head against the mug, causing a drip to slosh out and run down the side. Catching it with her tongue, Cassidy gave up and set the mug atop a stack of paperbacks on her nightstand. Starshine touched her nose to Cassidy's lips, then tucked herself into a neat bundle just beneath Cassidy's chin, ready for a good long pet-in.

The phone rang. Zach, seated at his desk in his robe, picked up the portable, spoke into it, then handed it to her. "It's Gloria."

What's she doing making phone calls before eight A.M.? Ameritech must've turned her into one of those disgusting twenty-four-seven people.

"Hi Gloria," she said, trying to sound alert. "Find anything?"

"Not much." Cassidy heard the other woman chew and swallow. *Probably eating breakfast, talking on the phone, and painting with her toes.*

"But you know," Gloria continued, "that's the interesting part. I called three of my old Alpha Theta buds and as soon as I mentioned Barbara's name, everybody tried to change the subject. They all said the same thing—nothing wrong, no big problems. Only one even remembered Barbara having a major crush on someone her senior year."

Cassidy pulled herself straighter, causing Starshine to go sit at the foot of the bed, her face turned pointedly away. "You think they were hiding something?"

"Well, I don't know." Cassidy heard crunching on the other end. "When you put it that way, it sounds so melodramatic. Maybe they just can't remember. After all, we're talking seventeen years ago. Or maybe I'm just trying to create a big mystery to get my mind off my own problems."

"Anybody else you could talk to?" Cassidy stuffed another pillow behind her back and pulled the burgundy comforter higher on her lap.

"Barbara had one friend who wasn't Greek. An intellectual type, lived off campus. I don't have her number but I'm going to keep calling till I track her down."

"When you do, would you ask her to contact me?"

"No problem."

"You find out anything more about the boyfriend?"

"Just his name, Teddy Wilson. That was in one of the letters. But a name like that's not going to take you very far."

"Any personal information? His major? Anything?"

"It was all very general. She'd met the right guy. Sparks were flying. Talk of marriage in the air." Gloria paused. "Those letters did not sound at all like the blabbermouth Barbara I used to know."

Cassidy looked across at Zach, his chair swiveled to face her. He wore jeans and a black tee that strained across his thick chest, his shirt bearing the orange-lettered slogan:

Hungover and it was worth it.

Still wants to proclaim his drinking prowess, even though he doesn't do so much of it anymore. Males are such an alien breed.

Her gaze shifted to the window between the two desks, hers facing north, his east. Behind the long skeletal fingers of the maple, she could see the gently sloping roof of the bungalow across the street, a house where she'd found a body the previous summer.

And now it's Zach in danger. How can everything be going wrong again? What an excessively rotten person you must have been in a former life to deserve all this.

She took a swallow from her mug. "The boyfriend's name is Teddy Wilson, about as generic as you can get. The only other tidbit is the fact that none of Gloria's pals wanted to talk about Barbara. Which could imply a secret but more likely is simply the result of people not remembering."

"Teddy Wilson, huh? Too bad she didn't do us the favor of falling for a Percival Paderuski."

Starshine, in a forgiving mood, climbed back onto the human's chest and Cassidy obediently began scratching the cat's head and neck. "I keep hearing you can find anybody on the Internet. But how do you conduct a search when you don't even know if the person's first name is Ted or Theodore? Or maybe even Edward?" She shook her head. "I suppose we could tell the computer to spit out all the possibilities from the giant telephone book in the sky, but I'm not sure what we'd do when we got them."

"Well, obviously, call all the Teds and Theodores and ask if they're sending e-threats."

Starshine nipped her chin, a reminder that it was not okay to let her hands fall idle. "How about the alumni association? Assuming he was a fellow student, they might have a current address." She drew her brows together. "But I suppose they wouldn't tell us anything. These privacy laws certainly do get in the way of snooping. Which brings us back to the Web, where I gather everything is totally unprivate."

Cocking his head, Zach gazed into space a moment. "There probably are ways of tracking the boyfriend on the Net, but none of them leap instantly to mind. I'm planning to stay home long enough to get our locks and window fixed. While the repairman's here, I'll set it up for him to install unbreakable plastic in your mother's door as well. After that I'll be going into the office and I can ask around there to see if anybody has tips on cyber people-finding."

"Do you think the university'd tell us anything?"

He scratched his jaw. "I believe enrollment records are public information. Which means we can get attendance dates for all the Teds and Theodores who were there the same time Barbara was. I'll call the registrar's office today."

"Or—another option—we could tell the whole story to the police and they could get his social security number from the university and run him down in no time."

"Actually, they couldn't. With no major crime committed and no probable cause, they wouldn't even try for a subpoena."

"This guy has to kill you before the police'll do anything?"

"You know how the system works. We can use guile and deceit, hack our way into records, do anything we want. The police are hamstrung by having to follow the rules. Which is why I don't want to hand everything over until we've gotten as far as we can on our own."

Nudging Starshine off her lap, Cassidy finished her coffee. "I don't suppose you've checked the email yet."

He shook his head. "I was afraid you'd accuse me of trying to protect you again."

A feeling of dread gathered in her stomach. *This maniac's not done with us. There's bound to be more.* She sighed heavily. *If you were a rational person, you'd dump it all on Zach's big broad shoulders and stay away from the computer till it's over.*

Seated at the dinette table in Zach's office, Cassidy read the message on the monitor. A second e-card announcement. She clicked on the website address and the screen slowly filled with an animated image.

"Oh my god!" Her fingers clutched at the base of her throat.

In front of her was a side view of a bed, the same photograph of Barbara's head, now lying on a pillow. Two figures beneath the covers. The male on top, pumping up and down. A photographic image of Kevin's head on the man's body.

Cassidy stared wide-eyed at Zach. "Nobody knew about the sex. Nobody except Kevin and me."

"Well, what do you know? I'd say we just got lucky."

14.

My Own Personal Avenger

"You think it's Kevin," she said flatly.

"You're sure you didn't tell anybody?"

She took a moment to recheck her memory. "Not even Maggie. It was just too awful." She looked at Zach again. "So then it has to be Kevin or somebody he told."

"I know you don't want it to be Kevin," Zach said, holding her gaze.

She pictured her ex, the way he'd appeared a couple of years earlier when he'd popped up out of nowhere to say he wanted her back, an impulse that had disappeared before the day was out. In his mid-forties, he'd retained much of his youthful attractiveness, with his windblown bronze curls, high-planed face, and chiseled features. She could see him now, his eyes gleaming lustfully as he told her about his latest get-rich-quick scheme.

She shook her head. "It's not Kevin."

"Why not Kevin? You always said the guy's a fuck-up. Why couldn't it be that his life fell apart one too many times and now he's gone over the edge?"

"Because Kevin can't hold a thought. When one plan fails, he drifts on to the next. He'd be the last person to plot revenge."

"Then it has to be somebody he told. Maybe the boyfriend took him out for drinks. Or one of the Segels. We just have to find out who he talked to."

"Maybe," she said doubtfully.

Zach gave her a quizzical look.

"I'm not surprised he told somebody. Maybe several people. Kevin's a big talker. But he's got a lousy memory."

"Let's hope for the best. You know how to get hold of him?"

"He gave me his cell phone number so I should be able to reach him anywhere. I'll call and set up a meeting." She propped an elbow on the Formica tabletop, rested her chin in her hand. "Actually, I'm pretty curious to find out if he's getting e-cards too."

"Let's print this up, then see what other cheery little messages await us in today's missive."

She gave the command, then watched the printer as it started to whir and clank on the table to her right. A stack of loose papers stood between the printer and the keyboard, an amoeba-shaped coffee stain on the top sheet.

She clicked the mouse and the quotation they'd seen the day before came up on the screen: LOVING IS THE MOST CREATIVE FORCE OF THE UNIVERSE. THE MEMORY OF LOVING THE MOST DESTRUCTIVE.

"He's starting to repeat himself."

"Don't talk." She put her hand on Zach's arm. "I need to let my unconscious work on this." She closed her eyes and focused on the slow stream of air going in and out of her lungs, allowing her mind to wander. Images floated up. Kevin's back as he went down the stairs, a suitcase in his hand. Herself as an adult curled into a fetal position in the middle of their bed. Herself as a child in a torn shirt with tears in her eyes. A small book on the nightstand. Zooming in on the cover, she saw black words against a white background, with two overlapping red hearts, one upside down.

Opening her eyes, she said, "*How To Survive the Loss of Love.*"

"Huh?"

"It's a book with comforting little poems and words of wisdom on how to get through a grieving period. I read it over and over after Kevin left, and I've lent it to several clients."

"Anybody you've given it to recently?"

"It's been a while since I handed it out."

"Where do you keep it?"

"I have two copies, actually." She rubbed the garnet in her ring. "I keep one in the waiting room for clients and I've got my own personal copy stashed away in the new bookshelves." Zach had recently filled a wall with wooden shelving in the spare bedroom next to his office.

"If it's in the waiting room, any of your clients could've seen it."

She remembered Zach's speculating that a client might have gone through the house and found the wedding picture on their bedroom wall while she was in session with someone else. "But what's the connection between a client and Barbara?"

"It's possible that—"

She raised her hands to stop him. "I know, I know. Barbara's boyfriend could've come in as a client to scope me out." She bit her lip, shook her head. "But that just doesn't seem likely. I don't think I've had more than five men start therapy in the past year."

"Only five? You've gotta be kidding."

"You know my practice is still pretty small. I don't get that many new clients." She ran a finger across her chin. "I'll look through my records, but at the moment I can't think of anyone who seems the right age."

"Let's finish up here, then go check out your waiting room copy."

The final page of the e-card was also a repetition, a Z emerging from behind a cross-hair. Even though she was prepared this time, it still made her breath catch. She laid an outspread hand on Zach's thigh, reassuring herself of his solid, corporeal presence.

He put his hand over hers. "You have to keep this in perspective. The main reason people make anonymous threats is they don't have the balls to stand up to anybody face to face."

The more he doesn't take it seriously, the more I want to give him a good hard shake. Make him see that a little anxiety is a good thing. I may have too much of it, but here's a guy with an obvious deficit.

"I'd feel a lot better if you were more scared."

"Yeah, but I'd feel worse and I'd also be less effective. Now let's go downstairs and see if that book's still in the waiting room."

It wasn't. They gazed at an open shelf beneath a cartoon-plastered bulletin board on the wall opposite the chairs. On the left end of the shelf lay a stack of magazines, next to that a row of paperbacks, then a mauve-flowered cat figurine.

"Any other place you might've put it?"

"I don't think so. It looks to me like somebody's walked off with it."

"A client."

"Not necessarily. It could be that the E-Stalker broke into our house, went upstairs to photograph the picture, then grabbed the book on his way out."

Zach shot her a skeptical look and she couldn't blame him.

"Besides," she plowed ahead, realizing as she went how lame it sounded, "our guy might've taken his quote from some other copy. This book's all over the place. A lot of therapists use it with clients."

"I'd like to see what it looks like." Zach turned toward the stairs, with Cassidy following after him.

The spare bedroom, which in the past had provided temporary housing for Starshine's kittens, Bryce, and a feral cat, had now become Zach's construction project. Deciding to teach himself carpentry, he'd filled the cracks in the ceiling, put up drywall, and built sturdy wooden shelves. The room was empty except for a stepladder, two sawhorses, and some tools on the floor. When the remodeling was finished, Zach planned to buy new furniture and move his computer in.

Cassidy pulled a slender volume from one of the walnut-stained shelves and handed it to Zach. He flipped through it, stopping to read a page here and there.

"This looks like a chick book."

"You mean *you* wouldn't read it," she said, an edge to her voice.

His mouth crooked up at the corner. "I may misplace things now and then but I have no intention of losing *you.*"

"I've given this to male clients." *Yeah, but you always suspect they just take it to be nice and bring it back unopened.*

Zach's eyes narrowed. "You give it to any of those five guys who started therapy in the past year?"

She screwed up her face in thought. *Troy. You lent it to Troy when he first came in all broken-hearted over his girlfriend's leaving him.* "Actually, there was one."

"Is this somebody who could've been Barbara's boyfriend?"

"I believe he's about five years younger. So no, I don't think that Barbara, at twenty-two, would have fallen for a seventeen-year-old."

"Maybe that's why she was so secretive about it." He studied Cassidy a moment. "If you give me a name, I could have a PI run a background check, see if he was in Champaign the same time Barbara was."

She thought about it, then shook her head. "It's too far fetched. I can't break confidentiality over anything as thin as this." She returned the book to the shelf. "Having you propose a background check on one of my clients gives me a whole new appreciation for due process laws."

"You know I'm a believer in the ends justifying the means."

She frowned disapprovingly. *As if you haven't played fast and loose plenty of times yourself. You just rationalize it more.*

Glancing at her watch, she said, "As much as I'd like to stand around and lecture you on your ethics, I have to get dressed. I'm supposed to pick up my mother in half an hour."

"How 'bout making that call to Kevin first? Your mother should know better than to expect you on time anyway."

She left a message on Kevin's voice mail, then headed for the shower.

As she was passing through the kitchen on her way to the back door, she caught a glimpse of Dorothy Stein through their parallel kitchen windows. Seeing her neighbor reminded Cassidy of Bryce, because the Steins had adopted a teenaged girl, Melissa, who'd also been left alone in the world after the death of her nearest relative, a grandmother. When Melissa first came to live with the Steins, she'd been seriously depressed, but this past summer Dorothy had reported that Melissa was doing much better.

And Bryce is depressed too, whether he knows it or not. Regardless of what Bryce himself might say, regardless of what other difficulties he might be facing, Cassidy knew that no young person could undergo the death of a mother without incurring a deep psychic wound. *And if the wound isn't addressed, if no one helps him with it, it could fester forever.*

She kicked herself for the umpteenth time for her failure at getting Bryce to talk about his loss, even though the boy'd become withdrawn every time she brought the subject up.

He keeps pretending everything's okay. But no kid has his mother murdered, picks up, dusts off, and is fine.

She looked at the clock above the window. Since she was running only a few minutes late, she decided to make a quick call.

Dorothy moved away from the window to answer the phone.

Cassidy said, "You mentioned that Melissa was coming out of her depression. Was there anything in particular that seemed to turn her around?"

"It's the support group. She started attending a group for teens who've had a death in the family, and after she'd been going awhile, we could see a real difference."

Any possible way of getting Bryce to a group? Maybe with a cattle prod.

Cassidy tried to push the key into Helen's lock but the lock was plugged. *Oh no, oh no. Not my mother. Not the E-Stalker coming after her too.*

"What's the matter, dear?" Helen asked from behind her.

"It's, uh, nothing to worry about." Cassidy drew in a breath, then turned to face her mother. "The lock's jammed. We'll have to get somebody out to fix it."

"The lock?" Helen's round face went pale; her hands began

twisting together. "Do you think that vandal came back and did something to the lock?"

"Look, this is just a minor problem. We'll use a neighbor's phone to call a locksmith and have it fixed in no time." She looked at her watch. "You said the cleaning service is due at nine-thirty?"

"We'll have to let them in the back door."

"Mom," Cassidy gently grasped Helen's upper arms, "I don't think we'll be able to get the back door open either."

Her mother's lip trembled. "Then you do think it's the L-O-L vandal. That he came back and jammed the locks."

"I think it's possible you were hit by the same person twice." *But not the guy who targets little old ladies. My own personal avenger.*

Helen's hands clutched at her. "Oh, Cass, what am I going to do? I can't move back in. I'll never feel safe."

"We'll think of something. After we get the doors open, we'll go back to Gran's and figure it out." She gave Helen a hug, then persuaded her to go downstairs and wait for the cleaning service while she called a locksmith.

Having deposited her mother at a friend's apartment, Cassidy watched a heavyset man in work pants and a flannel shirt drill through her mother's lock. *This is weird, Zach at home getting our locks replaced, me here doing the same.*

You could think of it as a competition, a manic voice popped up. *You should call him and see who came in first at getting their doors open. And the prize? Making the other person take out the next dead mouse? Not having to open tomorrow's email? Getting to kill the computer?*

Smiling at her own silly thoughts, she suddenly realized

that the goofy little voice in her head had a hidden agenda: it wanted her to call Zach so they could work out a plan together on how best to protect her mother and grandmother.

During the early stages of their relationship, she'd been overly independent, her hackles rising whenever Zach tried to do anything for her. Now the pendulum had swung, and she found herself wanting to talk through every detail. *It's so tricky, getting the balance right. I love that we can share so much but don't want us sliding off into clonedom. Not that Zach would allow it. But I might be tempted.*

She decided that getting her mother and grandmother out of harm's way was something she could handle on her own. *Be good to practice a little independence. You can take care of the situation yourself, brag about it later to Zach.*

15.

Beware of What You Wish For

When the front and back door locks were repaired, Cassidy and Helen returned to Gran's bungalow. Trudging inside, Helen called out, "I'm home."

"In the kitchen." Gran's voice came from the rear of the house.

They went through swinging Dutch doors into a warm, airy, bacon-smelling room, where Gran sat at a white table with black bentwood chairs, a newspaper spread out in front of her. She gave them her twinkly smile, reminding Cassidy of a bright-eyed squirrel. Above the small wrinkled face, Gran's scalp, with no wig to cover it, sprouted tufts of sparse white hair.

The walls were daffodil yellow, the cabinets white. Well-used copper pans hung from a rack above the table. At the far end of the room, a large window, half covered with sheers, looked out onto trees and grass.

Gran's gaze bounced from one face to the other, her features puckering in concern. "What's wrong?"

Helen began wailing about the locks, the vandal, the lack of safety in her own home.

Cassidy gazed at her mother's contorted features. *Oh god, I hope I'm not as bad as that when I go into* my *panic mode.*

Listening to her makes me want to take stoic lessons.

When Helen stopped to catch her breath, Cassidy sat down and said, "Mom, I know you're having a really hard time with this, but we need to talk."

Her mother, still on her feet, retorted, "You just don't understand how awful this is. I need my own bed. But how can I go home with that vandal still on the loose?"

"For Pete's sake, Helen, will you give it a rest so we can hear what Cassidy has to say?"

Looking deflated, Helen dropped into a chair.

Cassidy caught her grandmother's gaze. "Did you tell her about the obituary?"

"Um, I thought she had enough on her mind already."

Laying a hand on her mother's arm, Cassidy said, "There are a few things I need to fill you both in on." She proceeded to tell them about the obituary, the e-cards, and the plugged locks at her own house. Not wanting to frighten her mother any more than necessary, she left out Barbara's death and the specific content of the e-cards.

Helen stared wide-eyed at Cassidy for a moment. Then, making a visible effort to calm herself, she awarded Cassidy a look of genuine concern. "You mean, the L-O-L Vandal's harassing you too? I thought he only went after older women."

"It isn't the L-O-L vandal at all." Gran's gnarly face drew into a tight frown. "It's somebody who's got a grudge against Cass and is taking it out on you."

"A copycat crime." Cassidy folded her arms on the table. "The E-Stalker tried to make it look like the vandal's work. Although he had to know we'd figure it out as soon as both houses turned up with plugged locks."

Helen went to the sink, filled a glass with water, sat back down, and gulped half of it. "You mean, we're both in danger?

Somebody's out to get both of us?"

"That's what it sounds like." Gran banged her fist softly on the table. "'Course he won't succeed. Cass and Zach will figure it out and stop him. But there's one thing I don't understand. If this guy's making such a big deal out of trying to scare you, why would he want to give any of the credit to the vandal?"

"That's a good question." Cassidy gazed at a refrigerator covered with snapshots, notes, and magnets. "Wait—I've got it. He wanted to trick us. He's saying, 'Aha! Gotcha! See how clever I am?'" *You should've figured it out. The vandalism and obituary on the same day. The word "bitch" on the mirror. Your college graduation photo on the floor.* She shivered slightly. *So far this guy's running circles around us.*

"Now don't you worry," Gran said, as if reading her mind. "We'll catch him."

"We're not going to do anything." Helen thumped her glass sharply on the table. "We're going to leave it to the police and just concern ourselves with making sure nobody gets hurt."

"Exactly!" *Bless you, Mom, for once you said the right thing.* Cassidy took her mother's hand. "I know you're already scared, and I hate to make this sound any worse, but we're dealing with a very disturbed person here. Somebody who seems to be lashing out at everyone close to me. The two of you," she nodded at Helen and Gran, "are both at risk, and I can't put my full attention into tracking this wacko down unless I know you're safe."

"You shouldn't be tracking anybody down," Helen insisted.

"'Course she will. You oughta know by now that Cass and Zach never let anything stop them. And I want to pitch in and do everything I can, too."

Cassidy looked Gran in the eye. "I *do* need your help. What I need is for you to take Mom and go someplace safe." She laced her hands together. "If you do that, it'll free up my mind so I don't have to worry about the people I love getting hurt." *Except Zach, of course, who's going to drive me crazy not taking precautions.*

"But where can we go?" Helen pressed her fist against her cheek. "I don't want to have to stay at a hotel or anything. And I can't think of anybody with room enough for both of us."

Gran waved her hand in the air. "We can pick a relative we want to spend some time with, then get a hotel nearby and go back and forth."

"You're not going to argue with me?" Cassidy asked in surprise.

"I wouldn't want you worrying."

She narrowed her eyes at Gran, who looked back at her out of a face filled with innocence.

After some discussion, they agreed on the Crystal Lake cousin. Helen called to make arrangements, and Gran promised they'd be on the road by mid-afternoon.

Cassidy opened her rear door to find Starshine in one of the waiting room chairs. The cat twisted her ears backward and let out an aggrieved *mror*. Jumping down, she stalked toward the basement stairs at the opposite end of the kitchen.

Cassidy followed her to the locked cat flap. Starshine sat on the ledge beneath it, stared at her human out of angry yellow eyes and uttered a second *mror*, which clearly translated to: Open this door right now!

"You did this to yourself," Cassidy said, trying to reason with her. "I told you no more dead mice and you didn't listen."

Mrorr!

"Look, when it gets a little colder and the mice are gone, we can open it up again. And besides, you still can go in and out the back door." *Where I can make sure she doesn't have any little animals in her mouth.*

The cat glared balefully.

Cassidy had to clench her hands together to keep them from flying to the switch and turning it back on. *You're just like all those ridiculous parents who cater to their children because they're afraid the kids won't love them if they say no.*

"You've misbehaved and the consequences are you've lost your cat-door privileges. I don't care if you don't speak to me for a month." *Yes you do.* "I'm not giving in."

She turned and marched upstairs, where she attempted to place two phone calls and in both cases had to leave messages. The first was to Zach. The second was to Detective Wharton, who needed to know about her mother's jammed locks. She then hastened to get ready for her one o'clock client.

After the session she pushed PLAY on her answering machine and listened to Kevin's voice, then Zach's. Sliding into her desk chair, she picked up the phone. *Current husbands first, exes second.*

Zach said, "I've found a hacker who's willing to put in some billable hours, and I've got a plan for locating the boyfriend. This is something of a long shot, but if everything goes our way, it might work."

"Everything never goes our way. Or anybody else's, for that matter." Swiveling her chair toward the window, she propped her heels on the radiator. The weather had turned sunny again, a cold bright light glinting off the remaining gold and wine-colored leaves in her maple. The leaves moved continuously in the breeze, rippling and waving like tiny flags.

"So what's the plan?"

"First, I should tell you I called the university and there were three Ted Wilsons, one Theodore and one Theobald enrolled during Barbara's senior year."

"Five?" she said in dismay. "How could there be so many?"

"That's counting everybody from freshmen year on up to Ph.D."

Really necessary to include all the grade levels? Yeah, I guess it is. "So what's this hacker going to do? Break into student records?"

"Exactly. If this guy I've found is able to get social securities and dates of birth on each of the Wilsons, I'll run credit checks and we can track their movements, see who's currently in the area, see if anybody disappeared, then resurfaced. Or if somebody's recently moved here from some other part of the country."

This is beyond flimsy. I bet Zach just wanted an excuse to hack into the university records. One of those male challenge things.

"You think your computer guy has much chance of breaking in?"

Aren't you going to lodge even a token protest? This is way over the line in terms of legality.

No point fighting battles you're sure to lose. Especially since there are bound to be other, more winnable battles you'll need to fight later.

"This hacker was a student at Champaign himself a while back and he used to know his way around the system. 'Course everything's changed in the interim, but that still might give him an edge."

"How'd you find him?" Propping her right elbow on the chair's arm, she leaned her ear against the phone.

"One of the reporters here said he'd call around for me, then a couple of hours later this Charles Maxal gave me a ring.

His wife and kid are off visiting relatives, he's stuck in town without a car, so he was more than happy at the offer of a little diversion. We're going to work at our house because he's installing upgrades and his computer is currently in pieces on the floor."

"When's he coming?"

"I'm bringing him home tonight. We'll grab a quick dinner, then hit the computer."

"I've got only one client this evening—eight P.M.—so I'll get to meet your hacker. Now what was that you said about dinner?"

"I said—what kind of carryout would you like tonight, my love?"

"Oh, anything. I don't care." She watched a man on a ladder cleaning gutters on the Victorian across the street. "Now I've got news too and it's not good." She went on to tell him about finding her mother's locks plugged and sending Helen and Gran off to Crystal Lake.

"An attack against your mother? How come you didn't you call me?"

"Because my brain will atrophy if I don't do some thinking for myself."

"Does that mean I get to make an occasional decision on my own too?"

"You can decide about the carryout." She sucked in one cheek. "As long as we're discussing not being joined at the hip, would it be okay if I paid Lany a visit this afternoon? I realize you like to get a look at all the suspects yourself, but we've got a lot of territory to cover and who knows how long it'll be before the E-Stalker makes his next move." During past investigations, they'd both tended to get snarly when the other person acted unilaterally.

"Lany." He paused. "I can live with Lany, but don't try to sneak off and visit Kevin on your own."

Since Zach had never shown the least sign of jealousy, his comment surprised her. "Why not?"

"I want to see what the son-of-a-bitch looks like. And I also don't trust your judgment where Kevin's concerned. I think you're too quick to jump to his defense."

Zach's got it wrong this time. It's not that I'm harboring any soft spots. It's just that I know Kev too well to think him capable of anything this elaborate.

"When would you like to schedule our visit?"

"Make it first thing tomorrow. I'd like to meet with Kevin, then get into work as early as I can. If I wrap up a few stories, I can take some days off later this week. But who knows? Maybe Kevin will send us straight to our nutcase. Then I won't need any time off and our hacking will be for naught."

"But you still want to do the hacking."

"I wouldn't mind picking up a few pointers."

When she finished with Zach, she searched for her calendar, which turned up under a book on her nightstand. Normally she was able to keep track of all her sessions, but this week she was too distracted to trust her memory. Tuesday morning, the time Zach wanted to schedule with Kevin, was free, but Tuesday night, the time Bryce had said he'd come for dinner, was filled with clients.

So what's more important? Your clients or Bryce? Except for Joanne, her clients were all stable, long-term people who would not be disturbed at missing a week.

Bryce may be in worse shape than any of them. You have to be available to see what's going on with him.

Looking further, she discovered that Wednesday and Thursday nights were booked also. She bit her lip. She wouldn't be able to run all over interviewing people with Zach if she were stuck in her office doing therapy. *Your job is becoming a definite interference.*

She didn't like letting her clients down, and she also didn't like losing the income, which was all too low already, but stopping the threats against Zach felt much more urgent than maintaining her usual routine for the rest of the week. Pulling her dog-eared Rolodex to the front of the desk, she began rescheduling clients, none of whom objected to the change.

Next she punched in Kevin's number.

"Cass, darlin', you can't imagine what a surprise it was to hear your bonnie voice on my machine this morning." He tried to inject a note of heartiness but couldn't quite pull it off.

"I need to see you first thing tomorrow morning." Cassidy could tell by his voice he wasn't eager for this reunion. *But you will make him do it.* She grinned, thinking how good it felt to jerk him around a little after all the years he'd done the same to her.

"Now that you've caught yourself this new hotshot reporter- husband, what could you possibly want with the old one? A little liaison, perhaps? But Cass, baby-cakes, I thought you were the one who always walked the straight and narrow."

"I'll tell you about it in the morning." She ran her fingernail along a small scar on the satiny, inlaid surface of her desk, an elegant piece of furniture Kevin had acquired, then left behind when he moved out with only his suitcases.

"You know I'll always love you, babe. But it'd be a trifle inconvenient for me to see you now. As it happens, I'm living with someone myself."

"Since when did that stop you?" *This is not the Kevin I ever knew.*

"This woman I'm involved with, she's a lovely girl—well,

actually, she left her girlhood behind a few years back. But you see, she has this wee problem with jealousy. I'm sure you'll understand, since you used to feel the same. And she's let it be known, if she ever catches me with any of my old flames—or new ones either—it's my walking papers she'll be handing me. It's not that easy to slip out, either. Whenever I leave the house, she always likes to know where I'm off to."

"So this woman of a certain age has you on a short leash, does she?" Cassidy's grin widened. "I take it she has money?"

"Her deceased husband did leave her a tidy sum."

So dreams really do come true. Here's Kevin, who always wanted to be a kept man, and now he's achieved it. Beware of what you wish for, Kev.

"I'm so happy for you," she said sweetly. "But I still need to set up a meeting. You can tell your girlfriend not to worry—I'm bringing my husband along. So the choices are—we can meet in a restaurant, or Zach and I will ring your doorbell at nine A.M. tomorrow."

Kevin opted for The Java Joint, a coffeehouse near Clark and Diversey.

After Kevin, she phoned Lany, who said she'd be happy to have Cassidy drop by her apartment that afternoon.

16.

Entrapment

Cassidy zigzagged through Chicago in a northeasterly direction toward Andersonville, a one-time Swedish neighborhood that now was as ethnically diverse as any area in the city. She rang the bell at the entrance to Lany's gray limestone building and was buzzed in. As she trudged up three flights of poorly lit stairs, her stomach winced at the mingled smells of smoke and urine.

On the third floor landing, the door was opened by a young woman who had inherited Amanda's height, face, and bone structure but who clearly had not been the beneficiary of her mother's neatness gene. Lany's dark blond hair, drawn up in a style vaguely resembling her mother's French twist, had a greasy look to it. Her low cut sweater, straining across her full bosom, was missing a button. The loose hem of her long skirt draggled on the floor.

Lany blinked thick dark lashes and smiled slyly. "I've been looking forward to this little visit ever since Pete told me what you were up to."

Cassidy drew back slightly. "Pete thought I was up to something?" *As in, interrupting his work? Or as in, using a bullshit excuse to connive my way inside his house and interrogate him against his will?*

Lany let out a musical, let's-be-friends sort of laugh. "Come on in. We have a lot of catching up to do."

Cassidy went through the doorway into a cavelike interior, the drapes across the window shutting out all but a diffuse gray light. Beneath the window sat a stained, pumpkin-colored sofa, and across from the sofa, a state-of-the-art entertainment center dominated by a giant screen TV, picture running, sound off. Two threadbare easy chairs faced the television. A faint sour smell hung in the air.

"Take the sofa. That's the most comfortable." Lany gestured toward it. "What would you like to drink? Juice? Water? Or maybe some herbal tea? I've got a dozen different flavors."

"Just water, thanks." Cassidy settled on the orange upholstery as Lany whisked around the corner to the right. On the floor next to one of the chairs stood a glass with an inch of what looked like very old milk and a plate with a slice of dried pizza. The skeletal remains of a tall plant rose from a pot near the door.

How could a woman as pristine as Amanda ever have produced this messy creature?

Who're you to talk? Your mother's penchant for cleaning certainly didn't rub off on you.

Yeah, but I only have cat hair and dead mice on my floor—no glasses of sour milk.

Lany returned with water for Cassidy, a cup of tea for herself. As Cassidy accepted the glass, she noticed that it was not entirely clean, either. Taking the chair that did not have used dishes next to it, Lany turned it around to face the sofa.

Cassidy observed that Lany was sipping from a thin-shelled porcelain vessel not unlike Amanda's coffee service. *The hairstyle, the cup. There's some part of her that does want to emulate her mother.*

"Well," Lany fingered a button on her tight sweater, "what brought on this sudden urge to talk to everybody?"

Cassidy delivered her canned unresolved-issues speech. "So the reason I'm here," she finished, "is to try and understand why it happened and to tell you how sorry I am about making Barbara leave that night."

"Why it happened?" Lany gave her sly smile again. "I'll bet you didn't have much luck getting Amanda to talk about *that*."

Wants to play deep throat. Be the one with the insider information. She's so eager to tell all, it almost makes me not want to hear it.

Leaning back against the cushion, Cassidy asked, "Do you know what led to Barbara's coming to my house that night?"

"Of course I do," she said in a playful tone. "We all do. But Amanda won't talk because she always has to be perfect and Pete won't talk because he has to be loyal to Amanda."

"So what did happen?"

Lany raised her delicate cup. "Barbara was headed for trouble from the day she got home from college. There was some guy at school she wanted to marry but Amanda just wouldn't have it. She always regretted getting married and having kids instead of going on for a career, and she was absolutely determined to stop Barbara from making the same mistake."

Back to not reiterating mistakes.

"Are you saying it was Amanda's pressuring Barbara not to get married that made her so upset that night?"

"Well, the pressure'd been building for a long time, and then that night they had another one of their fights." Crossing her knees, Lany spent several moments arranging her faded floral-print skirt over her lap.

She added, "I always felt sorry for Barbara, her being the oldest and all. She could never live up to Amanda's expectations so she finally just quit trying. There was no way any of us—even Dad—could ever be good enough."

"Barbara said there was a fight but she didn't go into any of the details. Do you know what it was about?"

"I was home that weekend so I saw some of it. A letter came for Barbara while she was out and Amanda opened it. I don't know what was in that letter, but whatever it was, she just went postal. Barbara came home later and Amanda lit into her like you wouldn't believe. I'd heard them shout at each other before but this was the worst. I was dying to find out what'd set Amanda off like that but she never would say a word about it."

"Do you know anything about the boyfriend? Any idea what happened to him after Barb died?"

Frowning, Lany waved a hand as if brushing off the query. *Isn't interested in questions she doesn't have answers to. Or questions that don't lead to heaping blame on her mother.*

Lany said, "All I know is, Barbara told me this guy loved her more than anybody else ever had." She touched a finger to her lips. "Except for that, he was a big mystery. I figured the reason she didn't talk about him was she didn't want to give Amanda any more ammunition to use against him."

Think I've had about all I can stomach of this anti-Amanda rap. "Well, this has been very helpful—"

"Did Amanda tell you about the inheritance Pete and I got from Grandma Segel?"

Interesting curve. First the bad stuff about Amanda, then the good stuff about her. "I think she mentioned it."

"She left the house on Fox Lake to Peter and the cash to me." Lany's mouth curved craftily. "A quarter of a mil."

"How wonderful for you." *She knows good and well how tasteless it is to talk dollar amounts. Wants to be the bad girl. I'm getting an uneasy feeling in my gut. And what the feeling's telling me is—I've found my borderline.*

"Mom can't understand why I haven't moved up in the world. Why I didn't rush out and buy a fancy condo in an upscale part of town and fill it with beautiful things. She just doesn't get it that I don't want to be her."

Now why would anybody want to be lovely, impeccable, and gracious when they could be slovenly instead? Cassidy stared down at the smudged glass in her lap.

Lany tucked a loose strand of blond hair back from her face. "I'll bet Amanda and Pete made it sound like I'm the only one who never got over the family breakup. They love to take the attitude that their lives are wonderful and mine's all screwed up." Her brow creased. Her voice turned bitter.

"But they're not as perfect as they pretend. Pete, the boy genius. I'll bet he didn't tell you he got himself suspended from school for a whole week shortly after Amanda ran out on us. And Amanda—she loves to go on about this fantastic new husband of hers, except if you look real close, you might see the clay feet."

"Clay feet?"

"You'll have to ask Amanda about that," Lany replied in a sugary tone.

"And Pete. What did he do to get suspended?"

Lany waved her hand dismissively again. "Oh I don't know. Probably hacked his way into the Pentagon."

Something to do with computers? We should check this out.

"Well," Cassidy slid forward on the sofa, "I've really enjoyed our visit but I have to get home in time for my client." *No need to mention he isn't due till eight.*

"So soon? I was expecting a nice long girl talk. I thought you wanted us to be friends again."

Again? I don't recall that we ever were. "I'm sorry, but I have a client to see." Cassidy stood up.

"But didn't you say you were here to apologize?" Lany came around to stand in front of Cassidy, her tall figure looming several inches above Cassidy's head.

"Oh, I'm sorry. Of course that's what I meant to do." She took a deep breath, her mouth suddenly going dry. "I can't begin to tell you how much I regret forcing Barbara to leave my house that night. And how sorry I am about all the terrible things that happened to you and your family afterward."

Lany's body stiffened. Her face turned stony.

Cassidy raised her hands slightly, palms out. "Can you ever find it in your heart to forgive me?"

Lany took a step back, her cheeks reddening, her brown eyes flashing. "Why should I? You think you can come here and pretend to like me when you really don't, then just apologize and that's supposed to wipe the slate clean? Well, that's not good enough. My sister died, my father died, and my family fell apart because of what you did. It wasn't the greatest family in the world. Amanda was always hard to deal with. But at least we were a family. And we would have stayed a family if you hadn't sent Barbara off to her death that night."

Turning on her heel, Cassidy marched out of the apartment, closed the door behind her, and fled down the stairs. She slid behind the wheel of her car and sucked in air. Hands shaking, she turned the key in the ignition and pulled away from the curb.

She could tell you were disgusted. That you weren't buying her let's-dump-it-all-on-Amanda spin. You're a therapist. You should be able to keep your feelings from leaking through.

Yeah, but this girl's mission in life is to make people disgusted, then attack them because they are. What, you're disgusted because I don't wash my hair and I behave in rude, inappropriate ways?

How could you be so judgmental? Poor little me, nobody likes me. It's entrapment. A set-up. She has her life's script at work here, and no one can come near her without getting caught in it.

Cassidy drove three more blocks. Stopping at a red light, she stared absently out the window at a restaurant, the name ANN SATHERS on the sign, a Swedish eatery that featured huge, gooey cinnamon buns. Her hands were steadier now, her breathing less ragged.

One thing you and Lany have in common. You both set out to invent identities the opposite of your mothers'. When you're intent on being different-from, it's oh so easy to go too far.

And what about you? Could you be taking your own rebellion against your mother's cleanliness-next-to-godliness ethos a little further than you should?

I think I will go home and sweep my floor.

Cassidy was at her desk at six-thirty when the doorbell rang, a signal from Zach that he'd come in the back door with dinner in a bag. In the kitchen she found him removing salad and lasagna from Styrofoam containers and arranging the food on three plates. Beside him stood a man in his mid-forties, leaner than Zach but about the same height, with dark curly hair above a round face. He carried a wine bottle in a paper bag.

"This is Charles Maxal, the guy I told you about." He nodded toward Charles. "This is my wife, Cassidy." Zach kissed her on the cheek.

Charles handed her the wine, which proved to be a white zinfandel. "I hope it's all right," he said. "Ask me anything about computers and I'm fine, but send me shopping for wine and I'm completely lost."

"Good choice," Zach said, although she knew he'd prefer to take his alcohol in almost any form other than a blush wine, which he considered one step up from Shirley Temples.

She set the table, putting out stemware for the men, water for herself. "I've got a client later so I'll have to pass on the wine."

As they took their places, the men at opposite ends of the table, Cassidy between them, Charles said, "So you're not going to sit in with us tonight?"

"I'm a computer illiterate. The most I can do is email."

He gave her a sweet, rather shy smile. "Email puts you ahead of a lot of people."

"Computers make my head hurt. I do my damndest to stay away from them but Zach keeps making me learn things."

"Not true." Zach waved his fork as he talked. "I don't *make* you do anything. I entice you. I lure you. I create temptation by explaining how much faster and easier it is to do things electronically than the old, out-of-date ways you used to do them before I enlightened you."

Looking at Charles, Zach asked, "So how many megabytes does your new computer have?"

Charles produced a string of words she didn't understand. *There they go, off and running. Two males checking each other out to see who's got the biggest hard drive.*

17.

A Crash in the Night

For the next five minutes Charles and Zach conducted a conversation that was totally incomprehensible to Cassidy, who chewed and swallowed, chewed and swallowed as her eyes slowly glazed over. *I don't get it. Everybody knows how rude it'd be to jabber Polish in front of a non-Polish-speaking person, but nobody thinks twice about spouting Computerese in front of a Luddite like me.*

Finally there came a moment when both men had their mouths full simultaneously. Cassidy jumped in. "So, I understand your wife and child are out of town."

Charles nodded.

"Boy or girl?"

"A boy, Tommy. Just turned four." Again the shy smile. "I don't suppose you'd like to see some pictures?"

Not really but it beats computer talk. "Sure I would."

He took snapshots out of his wallet and handed them to her. One was of a small boy on a trike, his face screwed up against the sun. Another showed a slender woman in a tank top, a ginger-colored pageboy, headband across her forehead, one thin arm slung over the boy's shoulder.

"Great looking family." Cassidy passed the photos to Zach, who she knew would not be interested in the least.

"How long will they be gone?"

A faint flush rose on Charles' cheeks. His eyes moved away from her. "I'm not, um, exactly sure. We haven't set a date yet for when she'll be back."

With her body twisted toward Charles, she couldn't see Zach but could hear him stir behind her. She picked up the thought he was telegraphing: *Leave it alone.*

Resting her chin in her hand, she gazed at Charles. "I know this is none of my business and I hope you don't mind my asking . . . but are you and your wife having problems?"

Zach said in a wry tone, "I believe I mentioned she's a shrink."

Charles' skin went a shade darker. "She's staying with her parents. This is sort of . . . well, it's a trial separation." His soft brown eyes deepened with pain.

"I'm so sorry," Cassidy responded. "This kind of thing is always very hard."

Charles stared into the darkness outside the wide dining room window. "It's my fault, really. She's been after me to go to counseling with her for the past year. I kept telling her I would, but then at the last minute I'd break the appointment." He shook his head, his face perplexed. "I don't know what's wrong with me. Here I am, practically a genius when it comes to computers, I couldn't make myself go in for counseling."

"A lot of people find it threatening." *Zach wouldn't go unless he saw me packing my bags. But fortunately, I can run a do-it-yourself operation at home.*

"But why? Why is it that even though I knew she was planning to leave, I couldn't get myself to follow through?"

You were afraid of what you'd hear. Afraid of finding out you were defective and wrong and had to change. Or afraid that you wouldn't be able to change, that you'd fail therapy.

"If I'd just done what she asked, if I'd just gone to counseling with her, maybe I would've been able to figure out how to make her happy."

Or maybe not. Ann Landers always tells couples to go to therapy. What she doesn't tell them is how often it doesn't work.

"What's your wife unhappy about?"

"She wants me to talk more. I try. I start telling her about my day but then I go rambling off about computers and she's bored. I don't know what she wants from me."

Zach reached across the table to refill Charles' glass. "Yeah, most of us really hate it when our wives tell us we have to talk."

A look of understanding passed between the two men.

"How do you do it?" Charles asked Zach.

"I'm fortunate enough to have a master interrogator who drags things out of me even when I try to avoid it." Tugging on Cassidy's arm, he said to her, "However, I think it would behoove you to remember that Charles is neither your husband nor your client and lay off him."

"Okay." She smiled sweetly. "Since my stomach's full and I'm sure you two would prefer not to be interrupted with mundane, non-techy conversation, how 'bout I go get ready for my client and leave you to finish by yourselves?"

After her eight o'clock client, Cassidy glanced in at Charles and Zach huddled in front of the computer, then went searching for Starshine. At the back door, she looked through the glass to see the cat on the stoop watching over her domain. Beyond the stoop the dusky yard stretched out to the garage, a squat building topped by a pyramid-shaped roof. Past the garage lay the alley, and on the other side of the alley, a long line of tall houses silhouetted against the rose-colored glow from the city.

Pulling the door wide, Cassidy waited for the calico to come in, assuming she would follow her normal procedure of passing through any portal that became open to her.

To Cassidy's surprise, Starshine went down the porch steps, sat on the apron at the bottom, and looked coldly up at her human.

"It's getting late. You should come inside."

The cat didn't move.

Cassidy thought of the threats against Zach, the vandalism at her mother's apartment. She shivered slightly, realizing there was no reason to assume the E-Stalker wouldn't hurt her cat. And Starshine, who routinely greeted clients at the door, was particularly vulnerable. She had no fear of strangers. Saw them, in fact, as serving a useful function, personal valets who let her in and out.

Have to get her inside. Cassidy strolled down the porch steps, keeping her face averted, acting as if the calico were the last thing on her mind. Out of the corner of her eye, she watched the cat back off a few paces. Cassidy sidled in Starshine's direction, then turned abruptly and swooped down in an attempt to catch her. The cat leapt easily out of reach, moved a short distance away, sat down again and glared. Cassidy knew that in trying to grab Starshine against her will, she had committed a severe breach of catly etiquette. *Now I'm really in trouble. She won't have anything to do with me for hours. Not until the next time her food or cuddle alarm goes off.*

Without much hope of feline forgiveness, Cassidy sat on the bottom step and said, "Kitty, kitty," in a begging tone. Sometimes it happened that if Cassidy remained still long enough the cat would come to her.

This time Starshine stalked to the far end of the yard, her tail erect and twitching.

Cassidy suddenly realized what tonight's game was about. *Wants her cat-door open. Refusing to come inside until I unlock it. Well, this is one time* I'm *going to win.*

She would unlock the cat-door and leave it open until Starshine was safely in the house, then relock it. After that the trick would be to keep her quarantined until the threat was over. When they'd tried in the past to prevent the cat from going outside, she'd always found ways around them: clients would open doors for her, or she would wait until someone went out and streak through their legs. *But with a psycho trying to get at me through everyone I care about, we have to do it.*

Sitting in bed with a book at eleven-thirty, Cassidy waited for both her cat and her husband to come home. Starshine was still in the yard. Zach was driving Charles back to his city condo.

Five minutes later Zach came through the doorway carrying two glasses of bourbon and soda. He handed one to Cassidy, then sat in his desk chair facing her.

"Did you see Starshine?" Cassidy asked.

"She was on the stoop but she ran away when I came up. What do you suppose is going on with her, anyway?"

"She's reading my mind. Somehow she's figured out that I plan on keeping her locked up until the E-Stalker's taken care of." A deep frown came over Cassidy's face. "Damn! I don't intend to stay up all night waiting for her, but I sure hate going to bed without knowing she's safe in the house."

"I guess that's how parents of teenagers feel." He took a swallow of his drink. "Starshine's holding out on us and the university's refusing to give up any of its data. Although I have to say, it certainly was fun learning a few tricks of the trade from a master hacker." His mouth tilted at the corners. "I'm almost hoping Kevin doesn't remember who he talked to so I'll have an excuse to set up another session with Charles. If you haven't scared him off, that is."

She made a face at Zach. "Just what we need. One more way for you to break the law."

Removing his black tennis shoes, he added them to the pile under his desk. "How'd it go with Lany?"

She described their visit, then added, "Remember when I said the person behind this has to be a borderline? Well, Lany showed all the classic signs. She was overly eager to see me at first, then flipped into an attack mode. She's hypersensitive to rejection. She sees herself as the perpetual victim. She has a distorted perception of Amanda as the bad mother who caused the family downfall." Cassidy tapped the ice cubes in her glass. "And she considers me almost as much to blame as Amanda."

"Sounds perfect." He cocked his head. "So why am I picking up this little note of doubt in your voice?"

"It doesn't feel right." She creased her brow, trying to pinpoint why a voice in her head was saying: *Not Lany.* "I think she has the kind of rage it takes to develop a revenge fantasy, but I'm not sure she's organized enough to pull it off. Some borderlines are extremely high functioning. They often perform wonders on the job. But Lany's just a mess. I can't imagine her being able to mastermind a scheme like this."

"Yeah, but look at the inheritance. She could've been lusting after revenge all these years, then suddenly enough money falls in her lap to make it happen. With two hundred and fifty grand, she could hire out everything."

Fingering one of the many cat-tears in the burgundy comforter, Cassidy said, "But why me instead of Amanda? In Lany's scheme of things, her mother gets top billing for the role of villain."

"Maybe it's the mother *and* you. For all we know, Amanda's getting e-cards too."

Cassidy shook her head. "As much as Lany's an obvious borderline, she just doesn't seem right. Too helpless. Too victimy."

"Nobody seems right. You've got this strong resistance to having it be anybody you know. The only thing that'd make you happy is if it turns out to be a complete stranger." He swiveled around to face his desk. "I'm going to sort the mail. I need to get my mind on something simple like paying the Visa bill so I can turn everything off and go to sleep."

Zach can switch mental channels as easily as clicking a button on the remote. He'll be asleep in no time, and you'll spend an hour listening to the chatter in your head.

Cassidy brushed her teeth, then decided to make one more pass through the house to see if Starshine had come inside. She was near the bottom of the stairs when she heard a loud crash. Zach had been sitting in his swivel chair directly in front of the window when she'd left the bedroom. A picture flashed into her mind of her husband crumpled over his desk, blood splattered all around him.

18.

Shared History

Shaking her head, she threw the image off. *Sound came from down here, not upstairs.* She heard Zach's footsteps in the hall above. She hesitated, feeling an urge to let him go first. *No you don't. Making Zach take the lead is almost as bad as screaming at a dead mouse.* She forced herself to keep moving.

It was dark in the living room but a spill of golden light was visible from the dining room on the other side of the L. Zach had once again left bulbs burning in his wake.

As she rounded the corner of the L, she spotted Starshine hunkered beneath the table, her ears pricked forward. The cat was staring at something directly in front of her. A large, irregularly shaped rock rested up against the wall near the doorway into the kitchen. Glass lay on all sides of the cat. In the corners. On top of the table and credenza. Just above the credenza, a wide window stretched across the north wall. In the center of the window, a jagged hole.

Breathing through her mouth in shallow gasps, she heard Zach coming up behind her but couldn't tear her eyes away from the sharp-edged opening in the glass. Their shelter was breached. The thin shell separating their secure world from the chaos outside had a hole in it. Night was leaking in, bringing with it the terror of a disturbed mind bent on doing them harm. Nothing was safe.

"Oh shit!" Zach put an arm around her shoulders. "You okay?"

She felt brittle, on the verge of shattering herself. "No, I'm not okay!" Her voice high and thin. "Everything is wrong. Everything's breaking down, breaking apart, coming to pieces."

He turned her around so that her back was to the window, held her tightly, and spoke into her hair. "*We're* not breaking down. You and I are in this together and we're not going to break apart or go to pieces."

Zach called Detective Wharton, who came to their house and took a report on the latest acts of vandalism at Helen's house and their own. After he left, Zach taped cardboard over the window and then they spent a long time cleaning up glass. She couldn't believe how much there was of it, how one hole could have produced enough chunks and splinters and shards to travel across every inch of the dining room and on into the kitchen as far as the sink on the opposite side.

When they finally got to bed, Cassidy lay with her head on Zach's shoulder, her body pressed against his. Then she rolled over and fell instantly asleep, so tired that even her voices were silent.

The next thing she knew, Starshine was purring in her face. Eyes closed, Cassidy reached out and scratched fur, then snuggled up against Zach in an attempt to ward off the cat's get-the-humans-out-of-bed attack. Starshine purred louder, played in her hair, nibbled her ear.

Zach said, "She's pawing my nose. I guess I better go down and feed her."

"Thank god she's reached the point where she usually holds off till seven. I really hated when she used to do this at three A.M."

By the time Zach returned with coffee, Cassidy was sitting up in bed in her long tee.

He handed her the cat mug. "I screwed up. I was so fuzzy-headed when I first went downstairs, I forgot that we're trying to keep her in."

"She got outside?"

"She gobbled her breakfast and was gone before I even thought of locking her door."

"Shit." Cassidy glared at him briefly. "I'd like very much to be mad about this. In fact, I'm so infuriated at everything that's happened in the last few days, I'd love nothing more than to yell and scream and take it all out on you. But I know you're not the one I'm really angry at. And besides, it's hard to yell at somebody who just brought you coffee."

"The price of self-awareness. It takes all the fun out of being pissed."

They parked in a lot on Diversey and walked a block through a cold drizzle to The Java Joint, the coffeehouse Kevin had designated. Inside they picked a table near the front, draped their raincoats over chairs, and went to stand in line at the counter along the south wall.

The room was long and narrow, the tables widely spaced, about half of them occupied. All the patrons were professionally attired except one man in the corner who wore a dirty plaid shirt, his hair sticking out at odd angles, his hands rubbing his bleary face. The noise level was low, the decor subdued. Between gurgling outbursts from the espresso machine, Cassidy could hear soft jazz in the background.

Zach paid at the register, collected his black coffee, and went to sit at their table. Cassidy moved to the far end of the counter to wait for her latte.

Earlier that morning they had read the third e-card, this one only two pages in length. As Cassidy stood staring at the shiny brass machine on the other side of the counter, she realized that, even though this morning's card had been more threatening than the previous ones, she had not reacted as intensely. Not to the first page: a car crashing into a wall and bursting into flames. Not even to the more ominous second page: a coffin inscribed with the letter Z, the words LET THE GAMES BEGIN hanging above it. She had calmly discussed the message with Zach, her stomach quiet, no twitchiness anywhere, even when they'd agreed it probably meant the sender was about to make some kind of move against Zach.

She wondered if a daily threat was becoming commonplace, like her morning coffee, or if she'd simply gone numb from overload. *Whatever the reason, I hope the numbness lasts.*

The girl behind the counter handed Cassidy a steaming paper cup. Carrying it across to where Zach sat, she plunked down in a ladder-backed chair, put her elbows on the table, and breathed in the fresh brewed aroma. In the middle of the slate tabletop stood a green bottle holding sprigs of poinsettia.

Zach took a notepad and pen out of his raincoat pocket, folded his arms on the table, and stared at the door.

Smiling to herself, Cassidy realized how much she was anticipating the meeting ahead. *You just want to show off, don't you? Let Kevin see how much you've advanced yourself in terms of marital attainment.*

After Kevin had discarded her, she'd wasted far too much time pining over him. Then Zach had entered the picture, and she'd come to see that while Kevin was nothing more than a pretty face, Zach was a man who did things, a person of substance. *It's not just that Zach's such a prize. Sometimes he isn't. It's that he loved you enough to make substantial changes in his lifestyle so you could be together.* Now Kevin had a rich woman who, in exchange for paying his bills, had apparently gained title to his life, and Cassidy had Zach, a man she could be proud of. *Even Kevin, as full of himself as he is, can't fail to notice which of us has come out ahead in the new S.O. department.*

A horrified voice popped up inside her head: *Are you using the fact that Zach married you to validate yourself?*

So what if I am? We validate ourselves with everything we do, including who we marry. Besides, this is mostly competition. There's nothing quite like the thrill of beating out the guy who dumped you.

Laying his hand on her arm, Zach asked, "What are you looking so pleased with yourself about?"

She sent him a warm smile. "You."

A few minutes later Kevin, wearing a top-of-the-line trench coat, came strutting through the door and over to their table. He held out his hand to Zach, who rose and shook it. "Well, and you must be Zach Moran, the new husband. I hope you realize what a treasure you've got here." He leaned down to place an ostentatious kiss on her cheek.

As Kevin settled in his chair, Cassidy noticed a bemused smile on Zach's face. *Poor Kevin. It's never dawned on him that the hammier he gets, the more he makes a laughing stock of himself.*

"Well, Kev," she said, "let's get down to it."

"So now do I get to hear what the big mystery is?" He tugged at the sleeves of his cashmere sweater. "I have to admit, babe, you've got my curiosity going."

She moved the poinsettia off to the side so she could watch him. The bronze curls, though receding, held a luster Cassidy thought must have come from a bottle. His crinkly blue eyes were not as bright as they used to be and his face had grown fleshier, but he was still handsome enough to qualify as a trophy boyfriend.

She caught his gaze. "Have you been getting e-cards from somebody who knew Barbara?"

"Barbara?" The wide smile disappeared. He cleared his throat. "Why do you ask?"

"How 'bout you answer the question first," Zach said in a mild tone.

"Not e-cards. Regular greeting cards. I have no idea who sent them but they both had Barbara's name at the bottom."

"Barbara's name?" Cassidy blinked in surprise. "What kind of cards?"

"Well, they're. . . ." He cleared his throat again. "What they are is romantic. Little love notes with lots of innuendo. It's causing no end of trouble at home. Miriam was there when the first one arrived and then yesterday, when the second one came, she made sure to get to the mail before I did. Hard as I try, I can't convince her there is no Barbara. That Miriam's the only woman in my life."

Yeah, right. Until he can figure a way to sneak around her.

Zach tapped his pen against the pad. "I'd like to see the cards."

"There's no way I'd be fool enough to hang on to them with Miriam slamming things around the way she was. The both of them went straight down the garbage chute."

"When did the first show up?"

"November fourth. It was this lovely, expensive card with no return address, just the name Barbara. At first I couldn't even think which of all the lasses it might've been. Then I remembered what'd happened on November fourth."

"We've been getting e-cards." Cassidy twisted her cup in slow circles. "From somebody who wants revenge for Barbara's death. This person is making threats against Zach. The second one showed you and Barbara in bed together." She gave Kevin a direct look. "I never told a soul about the sex."

He stared across the room, his skin turning gray. Cassidy saw a confused, slightly helpless expression come over his face. She had to stop herself from feeling sorry for him.

Looking down at his hands, he said in a low, husky voice, "Then I must have told someone."

"So who was it? Who did you tell?"

He gazed at her, his sky blue eyes full of regret. "Oh, Cassie, those were bad days, darlin'. Don't you remember what bad days they were? You were in such a terrible funk, blaming yourself for Barbara's death. And I felt so awful that my bonnie young wife who used to be all smiles could barely stand to look at me."

An image flashed into her mind, sepia-toned, like an old photograph: Kevin at the kitchen table, shoulders slumped; herself at the sink, back turned, shutting him out.

"I got laid off, don't you remember?" Kevin's fingers brushed at his temples. "And I started spending my days at the bars. You were so lost to me, I don't think you even noticed. I was drinking too much, and then I got to sleeping around. And I talked. I talked to anybody I could get to listen. Sometimes it was all my great plans for the future. Other times it was the bad things that had happened. A lot of it was Barbara. But don't ask me who I talked to, because I can't remember any of it."

Cassidy's eyes moistened. *Here you were, ready to gloat. Now you're all caught up in this shared history, feeling like there's a connection between you you'll never be free of.*

She looked away from him at a collection of old black and

white photos on the wall: children, families, two old men with full white beards on a park bench.

"Oh Cass, I loved you so much back then." He reached across the table to finger her hair.

She shuddered slightly but didn't push him away.

"It broke my heart to see you so sad."

Leaning back in his chair, Zach watched closely. *Curious to see how I handle this onslaught of ex-husbandly affection.*

She removed Kevin's hand, laid it on the table and folded hers over it. "Those were hard times for both of us."

He pulled his hand away, sat straighter, gave a large shrug. "Well, but the past is the past, and now somebody's out to make trouble, and there's no way for me to help." His voice returned to its robust level. He shrugged again and said, "But you know I'd do anything for you, babe."

Zach shifted in his chair. "Did you ever meet a man named Teddy Wilson?"

Kevin stared into space. "Not that I recall."

"Have you talked to Amanda or Pete Segel since Barbara's death?"

"I don't believe so."

"What about Lany?"

"No, not Lany either."

Heading west on Diversey, Zach said, "So Kevin denies having told anyone on our suspect list, but I'm assuming we shouldn't take his denials any more seriously than we take anything else he said."

"I agree. I don't think we can eliminate anybody on the basis of Kevin's faulty memory."

Zach leveled his eyes at her. "We also can't eliminate Kevin.

He's the only one we're certain knew about the sex. Even though he appears to be genuinely fond of you, he's still the most logical suspect."

She frowned. *Hate it when I know I'm right and Zach won't listen.* "Kevin lives from moment to moment. Right now the only thing on his mind is appeasing Miriam so he doesn't lose his toehold on this current affluent lifestyle of his. How could he be throwing rocks through our window at midnight when he can't leave the house without permission?"

"So he says." Zach glanced over his shoulder, then switched into the left hand lane.

"The E-Stalker is just the opposite of Kevin—extremely focused and in a position to put all his attention into harassing us."

"Somebody not involved in a job or in hanging onto a relationship." Zach paused. "Lany and Amanda come to mind."

Except that neither of them—nobody so far—seems right. Cassidy stared at a string of yuppie stores jammed together up against the narrow sidewalk. The car ahead of them, a BMW, bore a rainbow-flag sticker on its bumper. A tall woman with closely cropped hair, a long fur coat, and three-inch heels strode across the street in front of the Nissan, moving dynamically it was as if sparks were flying off her.

"We've already talked to everyone we can think of," Cassidy said. "Where do we go from here?"

"What the police do is reinterview. That's not so easy for us since we don't have any legitimate reason to grill these people. The other thing is to keep searching for the boyfriend. Which means, I need to set up another session with Charles." He scratched his jaw. "We've got Bryce coming tonight so I'll see if Charles can make it tomorrow."

With everything else dead ending on you, this illegal hacking gig is looking better by the minute.

"Reinterview, huh? Okay, what I'm going to do is take another crack at Amanda because I really want to know what that fight was about." Cassidy tilted her head one way, then the other. "I can't think of a single lie that would induce her to tell me something she's kept secret all these years. So why don't I get really radical and tell her the truth? I can throw myself on her mercy and ask for help in finding the E-Stalker. Then, after I've dug out everything possible, we can go to the police and unload the whole story."

"I always think of the truth as a last resort." He paused. "But okay, we'll do it your way."

He turned south on Ashland, a wide street that took them through a Hispanic neighborhood. They drove in silence for a few blocks, then he turned to her and said, "You know, I never did understand how you and Kevin ended up together. After meeting him, I understand it even less."

"Are you asking why Kevin picked me or why I picked him?"

"Both."

Bristling, she said, "You mean, you can't understand why gorgeous Kevin would be interested in plain-vanilla me?"

He glanced across at her, his face amused. "Considering you've had your way with me about almost everything from the day we first met, that comment's not worth a response."

Get off your high horse. Coming from a man who adores you, the question is not an insult. "Why did I pick Kevin? Because I was always the serious, responsible one, and here was this wild, impulsive guy without a serious, responsible bone in his body. Kevin taught me how to laugh and play." Her throat constricted briefly over the loss of that dazzling first year they'd had together. "And the other part was, I'd never received much male attention. Then all of a sudden here was this great looking guy coming on to me. I took it to mean that somehow I'd finally achieved desirable-woman status."

"Far as I'm concerned, that was never in doubt." He patted her knee. "What about Kevin? Why did he pick you?"

"Because I was serious and responsible. He needed me to be the anchor so he could blow in the wind. He wanted a nice steady wife at home while he went out to play with all the other girls."

The car stopped at a light and Cassidy gazed out the side window at a pushcart parked next to the corner, a small man huddled beside it. She could see unfamiliar food items hanging from racks inside the glass-enclosed top. The Spanish words on the side of the cart failed to enlighten her.

"The other thing I've often wondered," Zach said, "is why you stayed with him after you discovered the cheating. You've always been very clear with me that if I were to even think about it, I'd get sent straight to divorce court without passing 'Go'."

"That's not wanting to make the same mistake twice."

"But why make it in the first place?"

"To some extent it was fear of being alone. The fear that I'd never find anybody else." *Something you have in common with half your clients.* "But that's not all of it." She sighed. "That time Kevin was talking about when I practically wasn't speaking to him. It wasn't just anger. I was so depressed and hurt I could barely make it through the day. We didn't have sex for months. So when I found out he was sleeping with other women, it seemed like I was partly to blame. That it happened because I'd stopped being a wife to him. Then later, when I finally figured out the real reason—that Kevin was constitutionally incapable of keeping his pants zipped—by that point I'd simply gotten used to it."

Zach reached over to squeeze her hand. "Well, Kevin's an ass. And it's my good fortune that he is."

19.

Truth Telling and a Closed Door

As they approached their rear gate where Zach would drop her off, her mind veered back to that morning's e-card, the coffin with the LET THE GAMES BEGIN message above it. *Our nutcase is going to try to hurt Zach. Probably today.* She pictured the cross-hair with the letter Z behind it. *Not hurt, kill.* The jittery feeling started in her stomach again. *Looks like permanent numbness isn't an option.* She knew it was illogical, but having him close at hand gave her the sense of keeping him safe. *You can watch over him like a mother hen, ward off bullets with the power of your love.*

She hated it that he was going to leave and she wouldn't see him again until evening. *If only I could glue myself to his side. Sit on his lap while he writes, follow him into the men's room. Or at least insist he call home every five minutes.* But she couldn't do that. She couldn't even ask for phone calls. If she were the one feeling anxious, it was her job to handle the anxiety. Trying to get Zach to rescue her from her feelings would only cause trouble. It was a basic rule of couplehood, one she frequently explained to clients.

Parking behind an old Ford sedan with a mashed in fender, he turned to meet her eyes. "What's wrong?"

"The meaning of the coffin e-card suddenly hit me."

"You want me to come in with you, make sure everything's okay?"

She shook her head. "With the security system on, I don't think there's any chance he'd get in the house." *It's not the house that's at risk. Or me. It's only Zach.*

"I know it's stupid to say 'Don't worry.'"

"And just as stupid to say 'Be careful.'"

"Short of wearing a bullet-proof vest, there's not much I can do."

"Actually the vest sounds like a really good idea. But I suppose you wouldn't do it."

"Not a high probability."

She reached for the door handle.

"Wait, let me get it." He came around and opened the door for her. When she stepped out, he gathered her into his arms and kissed her soundly, their faces misting over, their raincoats rustling against each other.

"Look, it's going to be all right. I'm not going to let anybody do me any damage." He got back behind the wheel and drove toward the alley, a shortcut to Austin Boulevard.

Watching the Nissan disappear, she gave herself a small shake. *You have to believe him. Zach's been in tough situations plenty of times and he's always come out on top.*

As she started through the gate, she noticed the calico sitting on the stoop. *Starshine's here. The E-Stalker didn't get her. It's a good omen.*

When she opened the door, Starshine raced inside to sit beside her bowl on the counter. Cassidy, moving almost as fast, went straight to the cat-door and locked it.

Dishing up food, she said triumphantly, "I've got you now. You're in for the duration. And if you give me too much trouble, I'll make you spend a time-out in the dungeon."

She taped notes on both the front and back doors request-
ing that the cat not be let out.

Taking her purse upstairs, she fished out the sheet Amanda
had given her, sat at her desk and stared at the Northbrook
phone number. Earlier that morning she'd talked glibly about
throwing herself on Amanda's mercy, but now that she was
faced with the prospect of explaining Sunday's lies, she realized
how unpleasant her encounter with Amanda was likely to be.

A cat toy sat on the corner of her desk: a weighted magenta
ball with a ten-inch rod sticking up from its center, a short cord
attached to the rod, orange and green feathers at the end of the
cord. Flicking the rod, Cassidy watched the ball rock back and
forth, feathers fluttering, until it reached stasis again. *Stasis
would be nice. Getting constantly jerked around the way it's been
since Saturday isn't fun at all.*

Telling herself that the unpleasantness of a difficult conversation was nothing compared to the unpleasantness of threats
against Zach, she picked up the phone.

"Amanda, this is Cassidy."

"What a nice surprise, hearing from you again so soon."
The usual warmth and animation in her voice.

*Amanda's one of the kindest people you know. She couldn't pos-
sibly be sending e-cards.*

Oh yeah? What about good old kindly clown John Gacy?

Cassidy sighed. "There's something I need to tell you. And
I need to do it in person, not on the phone."

"What, more confessions?" Amanda laughed brightly. "You
know, I was so glad to see you on Sunday. You always used to
seem like part of the family. And now, with Lany hating me the
way she does . . . Well, after your visit, I found myself won-

dering if you and I might be able to do some mother-daughter things now and then. But as to unburdening yourself, I don't feel a need to know anything further about what happened between you and Barbara."

"This isn't unburdening exactly, but it is something I need to discuss with you. Could you find the time to see me this afternoon?"

"If it's important to you, of course I will. Come anytime. I'll be here all day."

"I'll leave the house around noon."

Cassidy stuffed the sheet of phone numbers back in her purse. *Just on the off chance I get a brainstorm and need to contact one of the Segels while I'm on the road.*

The front doorbell rang. Looking down from the west window, Cassidy saw a small red Chevy parked in front of her house. Gran's car. *Oh shit. Well, you didn't really expect her to cave that easily, did you? You know how she always has to be in the thick of things.*

At the bottom of the stairs Cassidy found Starshine hovering near the oak door, ready to bolt at the slightest opportunity. Picking the calico up, she brought Gran inside, then dropped the cat to the floor.

The two women settled in the living room while Starshine, offended that her human had grabbed her without permission, marched huffily toward the kitchen. Cassidy fixed her grandmother with an irritated gaze. "You promised to stay in Crystal Lake."

Gran, wearing a short silvery wig, its feathery edges framing her bright-eyed, wrinkly face, said, "All I promised was that I'd drive out there. I never promised to stay. I was very careful in how I said it."

Cassidy heard an indignant howl from the other side of the house. *She just found out she's under house arrest again.* The first howl was followed by several others, the tone increasingly plaintive.

"Gran, I couldn't bear it if something happened to you. Please don't do this to me."

"I wish you wouldn't worry. I've gotten myself in and out of so many scrapes I'm sure one more won't kill me. Besides, I've thought of a way to help."

"You don't think Zach and I, plus the Oak Park PD, can handle this on our own?" She gazed at the tiny figure perched on the edge of the blue paisley sofa, her grandmother's tomato red slacks and white sweater creating a bright spot in the room. Gran sat forward, her stubby hands on her knees.

"What does Mom think about you leaving her at Cousin Lou's?"

"She doesn't exactly know it yet. I just said I had an errand to run. But she'll be fine. Her and Lou are having a ball. Your mother never did like living alone, you know."

Cassidy felt resignation settle on her shoulders. "I suppose there's nothing I can do to talk you into going back."

"It occurred to me after I left that I know this girl, Cindy, who's a reporter at the *Register*. Me and her are real good friends. I used to baby-sit her, seems like just a few years ago. Anyway, I'm sure she'd talk to you and Zach if I asked her to. 'Course she might not know who planted the obituary, but she sure could fill you in on office gossip."

"And you couldn't just call?"

"The phones in Crystal Lake don't work so good."

Cassidy scowled. "Okay, I guess I'm stuck with you. And, as always, you've come up with a great idea. Zach and I've been so focused on the Barbara connection we sort of dropped the ball with the newspaper."

"Well, then, I'll go straight home and give Cindy a call." Gran pounded her fist on her knee. "And if you come up with anything else for me to do, I'll get right on it."

"Gran . . ." Despite the fact that Cassidy had told Zach to be careful earlier that morning, she generally did not go around delivering cautionary advice. She considered it self indulgent and patronizing, as if the other person wasn't able to figure out for themselves what kind of care they ought to take. *Reason people are so fond of telling others to be careful is, it makes them feel powerful. Makes them think they can get the other person to mend their heedless ways.* Cassidy certainly knew that nothing she could say would change her feisty little grandmother's behavior. But she couldn't entirely keep her mouth shut either.

"Gran," she started again, "will you promise to call 911 if you see anything the least bit suspicious?"

"'Course I will. I don't want to miss out on any of the action, but I sure don't plan to let this goofy E-Stalker do me any harm, either."

Closing the door on her grandmother, Cassidy checked her watch. Her eleven o'clock client was due any minute, and after the session, Cassidy would be off for a second visit to Amanda.

Standing on the porch in front of the Tudor, Cassidy wiped her feet carefully on the mat, not wanting to track any of the day's dampness or mud into Amanda's elegant house. The arched door in front of her swung inward.

Cassidy stepped inside the foyer with its oriental rug, curving staircase, and art-filled wall. Amanda, garbed in a black-embroidered sweater and matching pants, took her coat.

"The coffee's all made. Come on into the kitchen and we can pour ourselves a cup." Her blond hair pulled loosely back from her smooth-skinned youthful face, Amanda gave Cassidy a welcoming smile.

They settled in the same wingback chairs on either side of the hearth, a small gas fire once again flickering inside the large stone construction.

"You know, I really enjoyed meeting your husband. He works for the *Post*, doesn't he? It wasn't until later that I realized I see his byline all the time. Wasn't it just last summer he was involved in some risky undercover operation? It must make you crazy, seeing him put himself in dangerous situations like that."

Why is she talking about Zach and danger and making me crazy? Just casual conversation? Or wanting to see me squirm?

"It's funny you should mention Zach being in danger because that's exactly the reason I'm here."

Amanda's warm brown eyes regarded Cassidy curiously. "Your husband's news stories? How could that have anything to do with me?"

Cassidy's chest tightened. *Now comes the part where you admit that all the warm, mushy sentiments you expressed Sunday were for the purpose of getting her to talk. Except the sad thing is, they really were true. Only now she'll never believe it.*

"Somebody who was very attached to Barbara blames me for her death and is threatening Zach's life as a way to get even. We've received three e-cards depicting details of the night Barbara died. Details only a few people knew."

Amanda abruptly moved her gaze away from Cassidy. A vein pulsed at her temple. "Why are you here?"

"I need your help. I need to find out who might've been so deeply hurt by Barbara's death that they'd be driven to do a thing like this. We thought her boyfriend might be behind it. That's what we were trying to find out on Sunday—who the boyfriend was."

"No, it wasn't." She returned her gaze to Cassidy's face, her eyes flat and cold. "If the boyfriend was your primary interest, you would have brought up the e-cards then. What you really wanted was to find out everything you could about me and my children. You think it's one of us."

"Honestly, Amanda, I don't know what to think. I've always liked and admired you, and I still wish we could be friends." *I'd love to do mother-daughter things. Fat chance now.*

"Why would you come snooping around here instead of taking it to the police? I'm not even sure I believe the threats are real. Maybe *you're* the crazy one." Amanda went to stand in front of the window, her arms clutching her chest, her back to Cassidy.

Cassidy positioned herself so that she faced Amanda's profile. "Lany said you opened a letter addressed to Barbara, then you and Barbara had a big fight over it. What was that about, Amanda?"

"Lany makes up stories."

"Barbara told me she'd come to my house because of the fight she had with you." *Or at least that's what Kevin said.*

"I have nothing more to say on the subject."

Cassidy went out the front door, then turned to watch Amanda as she closed it. The older woman looked at her out of a face completely devoid of emotion.

She definitely knows something. If only I could read her mind. Where are my psychic powers when I need them most?

20.

Meeting a Tipster

Cassidy had just thrust her key into the ignition when it hit her that she'd made a tactical error in picking Amanda as the best family member to disclose the truth to. The one she should have talked to was Pete, the guy who spent all his time working. He was the least likely suspect. And, she suddenly realized, she had an approach available to her that might elicit his help.

She stared at the stately brick Tudor, certain that if she possessed X-ray vision, she would see Amanda on the phone to Pete that very moment.

Any chance Pete'll talk to you if Amanda gets to him first? Probably not, but you won't know unless you try.

The first hurdle would be finding him. He'd mentioned the name of his company but the corporate title was unfamiliar to her and had failed to lodge itself in her memory. Zach, however, would have it written down. Fishing her cell phone and a spiral pad out of her tote, she called him.

"Yeah, I can get it," he said. "Just give me a minute." She sat on hold for a while. "Escovar is the name you're looking for. I've got the address right here on the screen in front of me. Fortunately, there are only two buildings. The lab is the one you'd want." He reeled off an address.

"What neighborhood is that?"

"Goose Island."

"Okay, I'm off. Here's hoping the Segels haven't raised their collective drawbridge."

Cassidy parked in front of a block-wide, one-story industrial building. Inside was a small, gray-toned lobby. The security guard, a short plump older woman with a weathered hard-as-nails visage, sat behind a metal desk near the entrance. Cassidy gave her name and asked for Peter Segel. The marine-sergeant woman talked on the phone, then reported in a soft, rather sweet voice that Mr. Segel would be out shortly.

Much better than "Mr. Segel said to throw your butt out"—which is what you more than half expected. Cassidy pulled the straps of her tote higher on her shoulder, shoved her hands in her pockets, and stood beside the desk wishing the lobby provided the option of sitting or leaning or doing something with her body other than standing like a soldier on alert.

Ten minutes later Pete's large figure came through a door in the opposite wall. Cassidy crossed to meet him in the middle of the lobby. "You shouldn't have come here," he said in a voice just above a whisper, his gaze darting toward the security guard.

Cassidy appraised the green eyes behind the black plastic frames, noticing that they seemed dull and blurry, as if he hadn't been sleeping. The fingers of his right hand raked through his dark untidy crewcut. *This guy's looking pretty haggard. Just overworked? Or something else?*

"Have you talked to Amanda?"

Shifting his weight, he nodded.

"So you know about the threats."

He turned his head away, then brought his gaze back to Cassidy and nodded again.

"I've got one more thing I need to add to what I told Amanda. Just let me say my piece and then I'll leave."

"I can't take you inside. Security's too tight."

"In my car then. It's right outside the door."

When they were seated in the Toyota, she said, "Pete, there's a good chance these e-cards are being sent by either Lany or your mother. The first card showed Barbara drinking wine. I told your mother in the letter about Barbara being drunk. I didn't tell anybody else." *What you're not saying is even the Segels didn't know about the sex. Not unless Kevin told them.*

"Why can't the police just trace the email?" He rubbed one fist inside his other palm.

"They're being sent through a remailer. This person definitely knows his way around the net."

"Then it isn't Lany or Mom. I'd be a much likelier suspect than either of them."

"Except you don't seem particularly interested in the past." She paused. "If it's Lany or your mother, they've probably got somebody else doing the techy stuff. Your mother's new husband, maybe."

"George?" He sounded surprised at the idea. "Look, this whole thing is ridiculous." He glanced at his watch. "I've got a lot of work to do, so if you'll excuse me . . ."

"I'm not quite done." She took a deep breath. "Pete, we're dealing with someone who really needs help. So far, the E-Stalker hasn't done any serious damage. But this person is escalating. The last card we received indicated that the next step'll be an attempt on Zach's life."

His face turned skeptical. He ran his fingers through his hair again.

"Pete, I wouldn't be here begging for your help if I didn't absolutely believe that the E-Stalker is going to make an attempt on my husband's life. If you have any reason to think it might be Lany or your mother, you need to do everything in your power to stop them. You need to get them into a hospital. Or, if they won't go, take your suspicions to the police. Don't let someone you care about commit a crime that could ruin their life." *And mine as well.*

Lowering his head, he shook it repetitively. "It isn't Mom or Lany."

She didn't believe him. Or, more accurately, didn't believe he was as certain as he sounded. Driving home, she mentally reviewed his body language. *Could be he's just a natural born fidgeter, but it seemed more like agitation to me. Like I'd caught him at something. Caught him suspecting that his mother or sister might've gone over the edge?*

Amanda and Pete had both acted strangely. They knew or suspected something. Or one of them was guilty. *So, if it is a Segel, which one would you pick?*

She envisioned the three adult Segels seated in a circle on the floor. Cassidy, in the middle, had a Coke bottle in her hand. Giving the bottle a mighty twist, she watched as it continued to spin and spin and spin, refusing to settle on any of the three.

Pete was too caught up in the present, Lany too disorganized, Amanda too healthy.

The image of Amanda's blank-screened face as she'd closed the door suddenly came back to Cassidy. *Is Amanda really who I think she is? Or am I idealizing her because, when I was ten, she seemed like the perfect mom?* Cassidy remembered wishing she and Barbara could change places so she could have Barbara's mother instead of her own. But now, looking at it from an adult perspective, Cassidy realized that Amanda could have a hidden, narcissistic side that Cassidy would never have seen as the visiting friend.

When it came to personality disorders, a narcissist would make as good a candidate for revenge-seeker as a borderline. Narcissists craved admiration and went to great lengths to appear beautiful, accomplished, and in the right about everything. They tended to be charming and manipulative, and were usually well regarded by the outside world. But within their own families, they were rageful and abusive. Cassidy thought about the fight Lany had described as a shouting match and Amanda had refused to talk about. Was that an instance of Amanda's verbally ripping Barbara to shreds because the daughter refused to kowtow to the mother?

Cassidy shook her head. Which version of Amanda was the real one? *Impossible to tell.*

At four-thirty, Cassidy, in the basement doing laundry, was making her best effort to tune out the aggrieved yowls coming from the direction of the cat-door. Hearing the phone, she trotted upstairs to pick up the handset in the kitchen.

Zach said, "I just got a call from a tipster who claims to have information on the alderman's murder. He wants me to meet him at this northside bar at five-thirty."

"You're not going, are you? Not with that coffin e-card this morning."

"This is a very trendy neighborhood. There'll be people all over the place."

"You think he couldn't shoot you in a crowd? And doesn't it seem strange you'd get a call like this on the same day the cof-

fin appeared?" She leaned her shoulder blade against the doorjamb. Staring out the kitchen window, she noticed that a heavy
rain had started.

"I get calls like this all the time. The majority are cranks but
now and then I break a big story because somebody has information to sell. Besides, I'm still not convinced there's any real
danger. We've got no evidence that the e-card guy's actually
homicidal."

"By the time we have evidence, it'll be too late!" *Shit. There's
no way I'm going to get him to listen. Dammit, Zach, don't go!*

"I realize this could be a set-up. But I promise not to go
anyplace there aren't a lot of people and if he doesn't show on
the dot, I'll come straight home."

"Please don't do this."

"I can't stop living my life. And there's no way this bastard's
going to intimidate me into curtailing my normal activities."

"I'm not asking you to quit your job. Just not to meet a sus-
picious-sounding stranger in a bar."

"Cass, I know this whole e-card thing is making you nuts.
But if anybody ought to understand about not letting some
asshole jerk you around, it should be you."

The problem was, she did understand. She had a history
of behaving recklessly in similar situations herself, and she'd
given Zach more than his share of grief in the process. She let
out a sigh.

Racing into the kitchen, Starshine began leaping wildly,
twisting into odd contortions as she tried to catch her tail.

Zach added, "You know how you're always lecturing me on
not getting overprotective? Well, I'd appreciate a little less hovering myself."

*Yes, but you need me. I have to ward off bullets and not let you
go into dark alleys and call 911 if you get in trouble.*

Oh no you don't. Can't break the basic rule of your marriage. You absolutely have to treat each other like equal adults. And that means granting Zach an equal right to do stupid things.

"Did you remember that Bryce is coming at seven? If he shows, that is."

"I did. But there's no reason I wouldn't be home by then."

At five-twenty-five Zach called again. "Just wanted you to know I arrived safely." She could barely hear him over the background noise. "This place is seriously rocking. Definitely not the kind of place I'd pick if I wanted to kill somebody. Anyway, I thought I'd warn you. The rain's got traffic totally glommed so I may be a little late after all. Oh, and I think I'll stop for a pizza, which means I'll be later yet."

She recalled the opposition Zach had raised to her insistence on making Bryce talk. "You're not doing this just to get out of having to ask the kid hard questions, are you?"

"Possibly."

Bryce arrived at seven-fifteen. Scrutinizing him at the door, she noticed that his knit shirt was badly wrinkled, his khaki pants overdue for the laundry.

"Haven't seen you in a while." Standing on tiptoes in the entryway, she reached up to hug him. The boy touched his hands to her sides, a minimal response.

Except for his bronze-toned skin, Bryce bore no resemblance to his father either physically or temperamentally. He had dark brooding eyes in a rough-hewn, angular face that Cassidy thought might someday turn achingly handsome. He was long and lanky, already a couple of inches taller than Zach. And as for personality, Cassidy would have described him as stormy, a moody adolescent with a dark river of anger running just beneath the surface. *The kind of disposition that's bound to create misery for both himself and anybody who ever dares to love him. Unless he works hard to change it. Which at this point, he's obviously not inclined to do.*

Flopping on the paisley couch beneath the front window, Bryce sprawled out low on his spine. "So, when do we eat?"

"I'm not sure. Zach said he'd pick up pizza but the traffic's slow and that makes the ETA a little fuzzy." She tried to catch Bryce's eye but he was staring fixedly at a rose and blue rug hanging on the opposite wall. "So," she forged ahead, "how do you like Northwestern?"

"School sucks," he said, his voice lethargic.

She studied his face, wondering if he might be high. She'd seen him stoned once before and he'd displayed a similar flatness. But this time it looked more like depression to her, although, having little experience with drugs, she couldn't be sure. Zach was the house expert on substance abuse.

"School sucks? How does it suck?"

He threw her an annoyed look. "I hate it when you ask those shrink questions."

"Then why do you do things that put me in the position of having to assess your mental health?"

"I don't know what you're talking about."

"Oh yes you do." He might not look like Zach, but she was fairly certain he had Zach's quickness of mind, even though his high school grades had failed to bear that out. "You've started avoiding us—a sudden change of behavior. Since there's no one else to keep tabs on you, that means Zach and I are stuck with having to find out what's going on."

"Not Zach. He doesn't care." Bryce gave her a hard stare. "You may've gotten Zach to make the phone call, but I bet it was your idea to drag me over here."

Starshine came into the room and made straight for Bryce's lap. Standing on his chest, she rubbed her face against his. When Bryce had stayed at their house, he'd become the cat's accomplice in dodging the pills Cassidy and Zach were forcing on her. A strong bond had been forged between the boy and the cat, and since then they'd always greeted each other enthusiastically. But today, Cassidy noted, the boy's face did not brighten at the sight of the calico.

One part of her wanted to continue with her questions, to chip away at Bryce's wall until she'd gleaned enough information to get some kind of fix on what had triggered his change in mood. Cassidy had a good grasp of the underlying cause of his depression—the way his mother had raised him, the way she'd lived, the way she'd died—but the treatment couldn't start there. It had to start with what he saw as the problem and move backward. And even if Cassidy knew what the treatment needed to be, she wasn't his therapist and couldn't provide it.

Another part of her, however, did not want to proceed without Zach. It was basic systems theory. If parents did not present a united front, if they polarized the way Amanda and Don had done, the kids suffered. Even though Bryce had already identified that this was Cassidy's agenda and not Zach's, even though Zach had almost as much resistance to her playing shrink with Bryce as the boy did, she knew she could count on Zach to back her up.

If he ever gets here. If he doesn't procrastinate all night because he doesn't want to deal with Bryce's problems. If he isn't lying dead in a northside bar. She shuddered visibly.

"What's wrong?"

"I just wish Zach would hurry up."

Bryce frowned. "Something going on between you two?"

"We're fine," she said, her tone not entirely convincing.

Having decided to hold off on her assessment, she searched for a neutral topic. "How's Ellie?" Ellie, his childhood nanny, was now incapacitated with MS. He had decided to move into her house both because she needed someone with her and because his feelings toward his father were so ambivalent.

Looking relieved at the change in subject, Bryce launched into an account of Ellie's health problems.

Fifteen minutes later the phone rang and Cassidy scurried into the kitchen to pick up, Bryce trailing after her.

"Cass. . . ." She felt an enormous relief at hearing Zach's voice. Bryce stood in the middle of the kitchen, feet spread wide, hands resting on his belt, to listen.

"I'm at the Eighteenth District Police Station. I want you to write down the address." His speech wasn't right, a little slow and mushy. In the background she could hear aggressive male voices.

"Police station?"

"They picked me up for driving erratically. I'm at one-thirteen Chicago Avenue. You got that? I need you—" A shouted argument prominently featuring the word *mother-fucker* drowned out his words.

"You're not drunk, are you?" *No, of course not. It's something the E-Stalker did.* "What's going on?"

"Don't worry, I'm fine." The words came out sluggishly, not sounding fine at all. "I just need you to get down here as soon as you can." Another burst of noise. "This place is a zoo. I'm going to hang up now."

21.

Blond Hair and Big Ugly Glasses

Hanging the receiver back on the wall, she stared at Bryce. *Shit, what do I say to the kid? Here he is depressed already. Not the best time to tell him his father's life's in danger.*

"Zach got picked up on a DUI?"

She shook her head vigorously. "He doesn't get behind the wheel when he's drunk." *At least, I hope he wasn't matching drinks with that tipster. No, he wouldn't do that. He must've been drugged.*

"Zach'd never drive drunk?" Bryce's craggy face turned skeptical. "Then how come you have to pick him up at the police station?"

She felt suddenly frantic to get to Zach. "I'll call you when I find out." She headed toward the coat closet inside the room-divider.

"There's something you're not telling me." Bryce grasped her arm as she reached for her coat. "What is it? You and Zach had a fight and he went out drinking?"

"No, nothing like that." *What're you going to tell him? That a psycho's after Zach?*

Bryce's somber brown eyes fastened on her intently. "You promised not to lie to me, remember?"

"I'm not lying. It's just that there are things going on. . . ."

Things that would not improve your state of mind if you knew them.

"I'm coming with you."

"No, you're not." *Don't want to tell him about the death threats. Can't lie. So what do I say?*

He laughed harshly. "You think I'm too innocent to see the source of my Y chromosome drunk on his ass?"

Innocent? This kid whose mother was a high-priced madam? Whose girlfriend died of an overdose? Not hardly.

"Besides," he added, "if you have to drive him home, you'll need somebody to pick up the Nissan."

If you were Bryce, how would you feel about being sent off with no explanation?

"Okay, you can come." She drew in a breath. "I'm not sure I ought to tell you any of this, but maybe not knowing is worse. I'll explain in the car."

As they drove east on Chicago Avenue, she told Bryce about Barbara's death and the e-card threats. "Look," she said, "Zach's really tough and smart. He's not going to let anything happen to him."

"Tough and smart don't mean shit if there's a hit man on your tail." A long silence. "Sorry, I shouldn't've said that."

"There's nothing you could say I haven't obsessed about already."

"It feels kinda weird admitting this, but if anything did happen, I guess I'd sorta miss him." He ran a hand over his dark crewcut. "Maybe you could tell him I said that."

"Are you saying he's important to you? That you care about him?"

He mumbled, "Something like that."

"Why don't you tell him yourself?"

"Nah, it'd never happen."

"You two are more alike than you realize."

Cassidy parked around the corner from the squat, flat-roofed police station that abutted the sidewalk on the south side of Chicago Avenue. Walking back through the rain with Bryce, she gazed at the two open glass doors flanking the brightly lit entrance. As they turned into the wide doorway, she saw a half flight of stairs leading to a short vestibule, a young guy slumped on the steps, an older guy curled up asleep on the landing, and beyond the vestibule, a second set of closed doors.

This ought to be prime real estate for the homeless. The doors never close and the crime rate is low. Walking past the squatters, Cassidy led Bryce into the long, narrow room on the other side of the interior doors.

They took their place in line behind half a dozen people waiting at a counter along the right side of the room. Officers came and went on the other side of the counter, weaving their way through a maze of desks, computer equipment, and filing cabinets.

Where is he? Cassidy drummed her fingers on the counter's polished wood surface. *I want to see him now.*

"This is kinda cool," Bryce remarked, standing beside her. "You think they've got him locked up in back?"

"No," she snapped, "I don't think he's locked up any-where."

A minute later a black cop asked if he could help her.

"I'm here to see Zach Moran." *To spring him, break him out of here, take him home. I hope.*

"Oh yeah, the guy they brought in to take the breathalyzer. I'll go get him."

The results? Dammit, what were the results? She wanted to grab the cop and demand that he tell her but she made herself wait quietly. *After telling Bryce you're positive Zach isn't drunk, you don't need to let him see that you're not.*

A young white cop came through a doorway in the far wall with Zach behind him. Studying Zach's movements, she detected a slight unsteadiness. *Gotta be drugged. If it turns out he really is drunk, I'll beat the E-Stalker to the punch and kill him myself.*

The cop and Zach stopped on the opposite side of the counter. "Well, " Zach rubbed his face, "I'm starting to pull out of this thing, whatever it is."

"We don't know what's wrong with him," the cop said. "According to the machine, it isn't alcohol."

"A mystery." Bryce rested his forearms on the counter. "Cool."

Zach frowned at the boy. "You shouldn't be here."

"What happened?" Cassidy asked.

"I stopped him on Ashland. He was weaving all over the place. Didn't give us any trouble, though. Seemed to understand he shouldn't be driving. Didn't even hassle us to get his keys back." He handed the key ring to Cassidy.

Punching Zach lightly on the shoulder, he added, "Go home and sleep it off. And if my name ever comes up in any of your news stories, don't forget I did you a favor."

The cop left and Zach joined them on the civilian side of the counter. "What's Bryce doing here?"

"I was at the house when you called," the boy said indignantly. "Besides, I have to drive the Nissan back to Oak Park."

"I'm still not thinking straight." Zach rubbed his face again. "Yeah, you can drive my car home."

The three of them returned to the Toyota. As Cassidy started the engine, Zach told her where the Nissan was parked.

She said, "I assume you were drugged."

"Had to be something in the bourbon. First time I ever

walked off and left half a drink. If I'd gulped it all down, I would've passed out behind the wheel for sure."

"Did you tell that cop your drink was drugged?"

He shook his head. "I wasn't sure how to handle it so I didn't say anything. Guess I ought to tell Wharton tomorrow."

"So what happened at the bar?"

"This waitress took my order, and when the drink arrived I noticed it was stronger than usual. I waited fifteen minutes and the tipster didn't show so I decided to go home. At that point it actually occurred to me I didn't need all that booze on an empty stomach, so I began signaling for the waitress. Eventually this woman came over and gave me the bill, but she said somebody else'd taken the order. Anyway, I started driving and just got groggier and groggier until I was practically asleep at the wheel. When the cop stopped me, I was just as glad to have somebody take my keys away."

"Why didn't you pull over and call me?"

"I didn't know what I was doing. All I could think of was getting home."

Leaning forward from the back seat, Bryce inserted his head between them. "What're we going to do now? Go back to the bar and try to find that waitress?"

"You're going to drive my car home," Zach said. "That waitress wasn't a real waitress and by now she's long gone."

Cassidy said, "We need to find an ER and get your blood tested."

Zach regarded her fuzzily. "You think I need a blood test?" He shook his head. "Sorry, I'm still pretty out of it."

"We need proof an attempt was made on your life. We can take it with us when we go in tomorrow and tell Wharton all the stuff we didn't tell him the first time."

"Yeah, you're right. We'll drop Bryce off, then go find the

nearest ER." He rubbed his face. "I should know what hospital that is. This is my old neighborhood." He paused. "Oh yeah. Northwestern."

Cassidy braked for a pedestrian crossing in the middle of the block. "What was it that cop said about doing you a favor?"

"He didn't ticket me. If he'd gone strictly by the book, I'd have a driving left of center on my record. Only reason he didn't is that I was so cooperative." He twisted around to talk to Bryce. "If you ever get picked up, remember that. Never give cops any shit. They always make you pay."

An hour and a half later they sat in the brightly lit ER reception area awaiting the results of Zach's blood test.

"I think the drug's finally worn off." Zach shook his head slightly. "I believe I can hold an entire thought in my mind at once now."

"Well, good," she said, sitting next to him on a wood and vinyl sofa. "I was getting tired of having to talk slowly and wait for you to catch up."

"Now that my head's clear, I realize I have to get back to that bar tonight and see if I can run down anybody who got a good look at the woman who served me. My guess is, she waited outside till she saw me go in, then walked up to my table with one of those pads in her hand. I seem to remember she stood off to the side, not directly in front of me. I told her I wanted a bourbon and soda, then she probably went off and ordered a double. She mixed in some drugs, put the drink on my table, and disappeared."

"So the E-Stalker must be a woman. Amanda or Lany. Exactly what I was leaning toward myself after seeing how Amanda and Pete reacted this afternoon. Only it can't be

Amanda because you'd have recognized her, so it has to be Lany."

Zach leaned forward, letting his hands dangle between his knees. "Cass, I didn't pay any attention to the woman at all. I was looking around for the tipster. *You* could have taken my order and I wouldn't have noticed." Sitting straighter, he put his hand on her leg. "The only time I look at waitresses is when they're wearing skimpy costumes or have big boobs. And then I don't notice their faces."

"But why would Amanda take a chance like that? I think this rules her out."

"No you don't. People disguise themselves. They wear wigs or do strange things with their makeup. The E-Stalker is clearly unbalanced. We can't say for sure what this person would or wouldn't do."

And if Amanda's a narcissist, she'd be pretty grandiose. Which means she'd expect to do anything she wanted and get away with it. Yep, I can see a narcissist walking up to Zach's table even if he'd seen her before.

Drawing his brows together, Zach stared across the room in the direction of a stringy-haired woman in a tattered coat clutching a baby to her chest. Silent tears ran down the woman's cheeks.

He said, "We still have lots of holes. We can't prove Kevin told any of the Segels about the sex and there's nothing to link either Amanda or Lany to that book in your waiting room." Zach's mouth pulled down at one corner. "We don't even know for sure that the woman who served me *is* the E-Stalker. Our nutcase could have hired somebody. In fact, hiring a stranger would've been a lot smarter than approaching me himself. Or herself."

"Damn!" She scowled at Zach. "Here you are giving me all

these reasons to reject Amanda and Lany just at the point where I'd talked myself into accepting that it probably is one of them."

Barbara's ghost. Who else could lift a picture from your bedroom wall, insert an obit, send untraceable email, know about the sex, steal a book from your waiting room, appear as a waitress and then vanish. She shivered. *You've never been a believer in the occult. But if this keeps on, you may become one.*

"The phone call." Cassidy laid her hand on Zach's arm. "Didn't you say the tipster was male? It seems to me that the person who called is most likely to be our guy."

"All I heard was a husky whisper. I assumed it was a guy at the time, but that might just be because the majority of tipsters are male." The lines between the base of his nose and his jaw deepened. "There's also another possibility."

"What?" She stared into his face, noting that his eyes seemed troubled. "Oh shit. Two people working together. A man and a woman."

"It's just a possibility. Which is all we have—a lot of possibilities, hardly any facts."

Cassidy stared into space, her mind busily pairing people up: Pete and Lany; Amanda and her husband; Lany and the boyfriend. *But Zach's right. We don't know anything.* Her gaze settled on a woman pacing in a small circle on the opposite side of the room.

That woman could be me. I could be waiting to hear the news about Zach. If he'd finished his drink. If the police hadn't stopped him. Fear clamped down on her. *Oh, god, please don't let anything happen.*

Her mouth dry, she said, "You know, it just hit me how close the E-Stalker came to recreating Barbara's death. He or she got you behind the wheel in a state approximating drunkenness and sent you off to have an accident."

"But it didn't happen. I'm not about to let anybody kill me."

Five minutes later a nurse handed them a report. "You tested positive for barbiturates."

The music pounded. The kind of hammering, repetitive, pure-beat music Cassidy hated. Intense pools of light from hanging spots illuminated the centers of the black granite tables. Except for these circles of light, a thick darkness blanketed the room. *Perfect for not being seen. The waitress really could've been me and he wouldn't have noticed.*

Zach spoke to the manager, who directed them to one of the waitresses. Pushing their way through the crowd, they stopped a young woman on her path to the bar.

"I'm Zach Moran from the *Post*. The manager said it'd be okay for you to take a few minutes to talk to me."

Cocking her head, the waitress said in a bright, excited voice, "A reporter? You want to talk to me?" Her brow creased as she studied his face. "Weren't you in here earlier?"

"That's what I want to talk about."

"Um, I have to put these orders in. Let me see, I'm not sure. . . ."

"There's an empty table over in the corner." He nodded toward it. "We'll wait there till you can break yourself loose."

"Um, okay." She started to move away, then turned back. "You won't leave or anything?"

"We'll be there."

They sat kitty-corner in curved chrome chairs. Directly under their table's spotlight stood a crystal vase holding a single red rose.

Leaning close to her ear, Zach said, "You know something?

I don't even want a drink. Feels strange to be sitting in a bar and not have any urge for a bourbon and soda."

"Unfortunately, this aversive drug reaction will probably wear off just like the other one did."

"You know something else? I hardly ever go to bars anymore. Before I moved in with you, I spent half my life in them. How'd you do that, anyway?"

"Did I forget to mention I'm a witch? A white witch, of course."

"So that's how you turned me into a guy who pounds nails instead of drinks."

Five minutes later the waitress plunked down in the chair across from Zach. She had burgundy hair, loose wisps dangling into her face, blue eyeliner and purple nails. "Am I really gonna get my name in the paper?"

"Can't say yet. I'm still at the early stages."

"It's Patsy Sheely." She paused. "Um, shouldn't you write that down? To make sure you get the spelling right, I mean? And could you call me when the story comes out? I don't read the paper that much and I wouldn't want to miss it."

"Sure." Taking out a pad, Zach dutifully asked her to spell her name. "Earlier tonight I had a drink at that table over there." He pointed to a table near the door. "When I was ready to leave, I couldn't find the woman who served me so I had to get somebody else to bring the bill."

"Yeah, that was me. That's why I remembered you. There was some kind of screw-up 'cause this girl I never saw before took my table. I was pretty pissed but it worked out all right 'cause I got the tip." She carefully moved a strand of hair out from in front of her eye. "Um, you were a pretty good tipper, too."

"Did you see the woman who waited on me?"

"Yeah, sort of."

Resting her arms on the table, Cassidy leaned in toward Patsy. "Could you tell us exactly what you saw?"

"I noticed this girl serving you a drink. Well, that was my table and she wasn't supposed to be there, so I started after her to tell her to stay away from my customers. But she just kinda disappeared into the crowd and I never saw her again. At first I thought she was a substitute and she'd just gotten confused, but when she took off like that, I didn't know what to think."

"What did she look like?" Cassidy asked.

"I'm pretty sure she was blond. Yeah, blond with straight hair falling over both sides of her face. And these big ugly glasses. Reason I noticed is, I said to myself—that girl needs to dump those oversized glasses and get herself a new hairstyle. I mean, eyes are really important. You need to be sure you have the right makeup so people notice 'em."

Cassidy stared at Patsy's eyes: blue liner, violet shadow, mascara-thick lashes. *My totally naked orbs must have her itching to send me off to her cosmetologist.*

"How long was her hair?" Cassidy asked. "Was it light or dark blond?"

"Well, it was sorta long. I don't remember the shade."

"What kind of body build?" Zach asked. "Tall, short?"

Patsy shrugged. "Just regular. There wasn't anything special about her except you could hardly see her face."

They talked to several other people but no one else remembered seeing a blonde with big glasses and hair falling over the sides of her face.

22.

Adultery and Affairs

As they walked from the garage to the back door, Cassidy spotted Starshine under the porch light on the stoop. "Now how the hell did she do that? She was locked in the house when I left, I'm sure of it."

"Walking through walls again," Zach said, his voice tired.

Cassidy attempted to slip up close enough to catch the calico but she evaded her human and went to sit in the yard.

"I don't know why I even try. It's impossible to grab her when she doesn't want to be grabbed."

Inside, Cassidy went directly to the cat-door and unlocked it so Starshine would be able to re-enter later. Coming up from the basement, she found Zach in the kitchen, a sheet of paper in his hand.

"A note from Bryce. *SORRY ABOUT STARSHINE. I OPENED THE BACK DOOR TO GO PEE AND SHE CAME STREAKING OUT BEFORE I COULD STOP HER.*" Zach laid a hand on Cassidy's shoulder. "Don't worry. She'll be here tomorrow for breakfast and maybe this time I'll remember to lock the door before I feed her."

Cassidy sighed and ran her fingers through her thick hair. *Your white-witch powers are slipping. You can't ward off barbiturates. You didn't get Bryce to talk. And you're a complete failure at keeping your cat inside.*

"Still not interested in a drink?" Cassidy asked.

"Why? You want one?"

"Well . . . what I really want is for you to make two drinks and bring them upstairs without asking so I can act like you're pushing alcohol on me."

He dropped a kiss on her mouth. "Is that why you married me? Because I allow you to maintain the pretense of innocence?"

Twenty minutes later Zach sat at his desk reading a magazine, his body angled toward her, a bourbon close at hand. Seated on the bed, sipping her own drink, Cassidy kept her eyes glued to his figure. His black hair, just beginning to show threads of silver, was trimmed neatly at the nape of his neck. His black tee, the fabric thin from too many washings, strained across his heavy shoulders. His face appeared remote, the expression that typically came over him in repose. *Gone inside himself to repair the emotional damage of getting drugged and hauled in by the police. Calling me to pick him up probably wasn't the easiest thing either. He hates sending out SOS's even more than I do.*

Keeps saying nothing's going to happen but that's just his usual denial. Neither of us can possibly know where this is going to end. A small ache started in her chest.

She came up behind Zach's chair, looped her arms around his neck, and rubbed her cheek against his. He turned his face toward her and smiled.

Standing back, she asked, "How you feeling?"

"I've been better."

"Zach, I really need for us to make love tonight."

"Look, I'm not going to die on you."

"It's not that exactly. It's just wanting to get as close to you as I can. Feeling like I want to crawl inside your skin."

"You know, I'm not doing so great right now. I'm not sure I'd be able to deliver."

"Well, there are other things we could do."

"Just so long as you don't mind if it isn't up to our usual standard."

Laying on her back, Zach raised on one elbow beside her, she said, "Sex between us is always so good. It doesn't matter what we do. It's always wonderful."

"Not tonight it wasn't."

"Sex is not just about a big hard penis."

"Sure it is."

She opened her mouth to protest but he put a finger across her lips to stop her.

"Just kidding. I know it's not." He stuck the tip of his finger inside her mouth and she nibbled on it.

"Remember when I first told you about Xandra?" he said, referring to Bryce's mother. "I made it sound like that was the best sex I'd ever had. It was only later I realized that what I said wasn't true at all. Sex with you is better than it's ever been with anyone. There's nobody else that even comes close."

A warm glow spread throughout her body.

"It's amazing the difference being in love makes. This is something I never thought I'd be able to feel."

She breathed softly, wanting to hold onto the moment.

"I'd done it with so many women. I thought I knew everything there was to know." He shook his head. "I didn't know anything."

She smiled. *Looks like you haven't lost those good witch powers after all.*

The phone rang. Zach said, "Yeah." Cassidy felt cat foot-steps move toward her, heard Starshine purring in her face. She pulled a pillow over her head as Zach's voice came through distantly. "It's Gloria. Shall I tell her you'll call back?"

Cassidy removed the pillow and opened her eyes. "Gloria? Who's Gloria?"

Zach was sitting up in bed, his hand over the mouthpiece of the portable phone. "The roommate. Why don't I just say you'll call back?"

"Ask her to hang on a minute." *Anybody who calls at seven* A.M. *damn well deserves to be put on hold.*

Cassidy dragged herself into the bathroom, threw cold water on her face, picked up the phone that Zach had left on her nightstand, and sat down on the bed. "Sorry to keep you waiting," she said irritably.

"Did I wake you?" Surprised.

"As a matter of fact, you did." *That was rude. So what? Civility before coffee is too much to ask.*

"Oh, I'm sorry. I just assumed everybody was up by now." *There should be a twelve-step recovery group for former execs.*

"Well, I'm awake now, so what can I do for you?"

"Have lunch?" Gloria asked in a begging tone.

"Lunch? Does that mean you have something new?"

"Nothing I couldn't tell you over the phone. I just want to have lunch. This is friendless Gloria, remember? The ex-corporate executive who would've invited you in even if you had been Jehovah's Witnesses. At first I was going to make up some excuse, say I had business in Oak Park and as long as I was going to be there anyway—yadda, yadda, yadda. But then I thought—Cass is a therapist. She deals with pathetic people all the time." A pause. "So, would you be willing to take on a charity case and have lunch?"

Cassidy thought fast. Two clients in the morning. A meeting with Detective Wharton—which she wouldn't mind putting off as long as possible—in the afternoon. "Do you know where Erik's is?"

"Erik's on Oak Park Avenue?"

"I'll meet you there at noon."

Zach came into the bedroom, two mugs of coffee in his hands and a frown on his face. "She outfoxed me again." He gave Cassidy her purple mug.

"What? You forgot to lock the cat-door this morning too?"

"I was specifically thinking I had to lock her in before I fed her, but she raced ahead of me and went straight outside without even looking at her bowl."

"No breakfast?"

"I left some food out last night. I guess that was enough to hold her." He sat in his swivel chair. "But I don't think there's anything to worry about. She hasn't brought in any mice for at least two days and I suspect at this point the E-Stalker is too involved in hatching plots against me to be bothered with our cat."

"Well, that's reassuring." She tilted her head. "So, you think we should give up on trying to keep her inside?'

"Personally, I hate losing. Especially to a cat. But this looks to me like a battle we can't win." He stood. "You ready to check today's email?"

An image came into her mind of the coffin that had appeared on the final page of yesterday's e-card. *Rather run a marathon on my hands and knees than have to listen one more time to that damned "You've got mail."*

She swallowed and said, "Let's get it over with."

Cassidy's mailbox contained only one message, a note from Gran: I TOLD HELEN THAT YOU AND ME AGREED I SHOULD

STAY IN OP AND SHE WAS FINE WITH IT. I ALSO LEFT A MESSAGE FOR MY REPORTER FRIEND. I'LL LET YOU KNOW WHEN I HEAR FROM HER.

Cassidy propped an elbow on the green and pink Formica table. "So what do you think it means that we didn't get a card this morning?"

Zach shrugged.

"Don't give me that shit. You know as well as I do."

His eyes narrowed. "Was that a trick question?"

"Yes!"

"And just why would you be asking trick questions?"

"I don't know." She looked away, drew in a breath, then looked at him again. "Sitting here at the computer, waiting to see what this psycho's going to do next—it's got me so I don't know what I'm doing."

"I think you were testing me to see if I'd meet the situation head on or play it down the way I've been doing these past few days. Okay, if it'll make you feel any better to hear me say it out loud, I will. The reason we didn't get a card today is that our nutcase has moved from the threat stage into the kill stage."

"You know, strangely enough, that does make me feel better. If I know you're sufficiently concerned, I won't have to worry for both of us." She clicked her fingernails against the Formica. "So, what's your plan for the day?"

"I'm pretty much caught up at work, which means I can take time off as it suits me. But Wharton's shift doesn't start till four, so I think I'll head on in to the office and see what I can dig up on Amanda's husband—one of those loose ends we haven't tied up yet. I'll be back later this afternoon so we can go make our confession to the Oak Park police. Then, after the good detective finishes reaming us out, I'll pick up Charles and we can continue our quest for student data."

Joanne, always prompt, was in the waiting room when Cassidy ushered her nine o'clock client out. The dark-haired woman picked up a small mug of tea from the round oak table between the two chairs and carried it into Cassidy's office, a cloud of cinnamon aroma wafting in with her.

As Joanne took her usual place on the sectional, Cassidy noted that, instead of tearful, her client now looked quite pleased with herself. She was, as usual, well turned out in a taupe jacket and trousers with an ivory silk shell. Joanne's costume was so impeccable it made Cassidy feel a brief sense of inadequacy over the shopworn appearance of her own: a purple sweater dotted with fuzzballs above threadbare black leggings.

Joanne's mouth curved in a small gloating smile, "I was right. He isn't going to be able to walk away from me."

"KC changed his mind about breaking up?"

"He saw me again last night. He's still trying to convince himself that he's going to work on his relationship with his wife, but if he can't stay away from me, what chance does the marriage have?"

"So he wants to continue the affair but he doesn't intend to leave his wife." *Have his cake and eat it too. What most of these jerks do. Certainly what Kevin did.*

Joanne set her mug on the wicker table beneath an arching coleus stem. "Actually, he's still saying we have to end it. But the words and behavior don't match up. And what the behavior's telling me is, he can't let go." She crossed one long leg over the other and smiled smugly.

Cassidy eyed Joanne suspiciously. *He can't let go or she won't let him?* "How did the two of you happen to get together last night?"

"I called him at work and he let it slip that his wife would be stuck at the office until at least midnight. So then I said I could drop by his house and he didn't say no." She smoothed a manicured hand along the side of her short, ebony hair. "He wouldn't have mentioned his wife working late if he didn't want to see me, would he? And he certainly wouldn't have let me come over if he really wanted to break up."

"You went to his house," Cassidy said flatly. Memories rushed back at her: finding Barbara in bed with Kevin; Kevin's staying out till dawn; discovering a love note hidden beneath his socks. *She did it in the wife's house. Fucked him in the wife's bed.* Taking a deep breath, Cassidy worked hard at keeping her face and voice neutral. "Haven't you and K.C. always gone to your place before? Why the change in pattern?"

Joanne's gaze moved toward the north window. "KC was certain she'd be gone till all hours."

"But wasn't it risky? What if she'd come home early?" *This was no accident. Joanne knew exactly what she was doing.*

Joanne's dark, sultry eyes met Cassidy's. "Well, so what if she did?"

Taking another deep breath, Cassidy forced herself to speak in a low, gentle tone. "So you thought maybe his wife would find you together and then she'd divorce him."

Joanne's smugness suddenly slipped away and she ducked her head like a kid caught with her hand in the cookie jar. "Well, but he must want that too or he wouldn't have let me stay. He's been telling me for months how unhappy he is, how much he wants out. And last night it was so obvious that he loves me, not her. What's the point of keeping a marriage together if the passion's gone out of it?"

Having decided that the marriage ought to die, she's attempting euthanasia.

"If KC really wants out, why doesn't he just go ahead with the divorce?"

"He's too kind-hearted," Joanne said in a bitter tone. "His wife's going through a hard time right now. He's afraid she'll fall apart if he leaves."

After Joanne departed, Cassidy stood in front of the kitchen window, opened a fresh bag of peanut butter cups, and gobbled four of them. Another gloomy rainy day. The session with Joanne had stirred up feelings as unpleasant as the weather. *On Saturday she accused me of being on the wife's side. I didn't realize it at the time, but the truth is, she's right. How am I ever going to provide decent therapy given how pissed I am?*

Cassidy recognized that she needed help in dealing with her anger toward her client, and the best person to call would be Maggie, her friend and fellow therapist, the two women having provided peer consultation for each other in the past.

A movement in the kitchen next door caught her eye. Two teenagers were pulling food out of the refrigerator. *Must be one of those days off from school mothers always complain about.* The teens reminded Cassidy that she wanted to talk to Dorothy's daughter about the group for kids who've had a death in the family. But first she needed Maggie's help in getting herself out of the role of cheated-upon-wife and back into the role of Joanne's therapist.

Upstairs she sat in her swivel chair and picked up the phone.

Maggie said, "So, did you ever find out about that weird obituary?"

The obit? That was days ago. We're way past the obituary now. "It's a long story and this isn't a good time to go into it, but I promise you a blow-by-blow as soon as everything settles down." *Assuming I'm not in deep mourning and incapable of speech.*

"Does that mean you've got yourself in some kind of jam again? I don't know anybody who has half the excitement in their life that you do. How do you manage to get yourself in so much trouble, anyway?"

"Let's see, first I married Kevin, then I married Zach." *Except you can't blame any of this on Zach. No, but you could assign it all to Kevin's wandering ways.* "Anyway, the reason I called is, I'm doing major counter transference with one of my clients and I need you to straighten me out." She described the affair and the behavior on Joanne's part that had triggered her sense of outrage.

"I'm feeling pissed and judgmental as hell," Cassidy said, wrapping the phone cord around her fingers. "Now somewhere in the back of my mind, I know the answer to this question but at the moment it eludes me. Why is it okay for therapists to be judgmental about any and all forms of abuse but not about adultery?"

"Adultery?" Maggie laughed. "You forgot. Therapists don't use words like that to talk about affairs. I'm not entirely sure why we don't judge affairs the same way we judge abuse, but I think it's because abuse is always harmful while some affairs have a useful function."

"Oh, that's right." Cassidy retrieved some of the concepts that had been blocked out by her emotions. "Affairs serve as a catalyst to get people to either leave a bad marriage or work to make it better. At least some affairs do. Others are simply messy and painful."

"Just look at you and Kevin. What would've happened if he hadn't run around on you?"

"We might still be together. Oh god, that'd be awful."
Picking up a pen from her desk, she jiggled it between her fingers. "Okay, now I remember why I'm not supposed to judge affairs. But how can I stop feeling disgusted at Joanne's attempt to break up her lover's marriage?"

"What prompted Joanne to start an affair with a married man in the first place?"

"Her husband dumped her about a year ago. He was quite generous with the settlement, but of course that didn't keep her from being devastated. I didn't start seeing her until a few months later, but it's clear her self-esteem was really demolished." Cassidy drew a sad cartoon face with short black hair on the back of an envelope.

"Was her divorce anything like what you went through?"

"Probably a lot—without the settlement of course. But I didn't run out and latch onto a married man in order to make myself feel desirable again."

"What stopped you?"

"Well, I had more self-control . . . I was able to foresee consequences . . . I recognized how pathetic it'd be to base my sense of worth on getting some man to have sex with me." An image suddenly flashed into her mind of a small, bedraggled child: the real Joanne. Seductress on the outside, lost little girl within. Cassidy's anger vanished. "Okay, I get it. I believe my empathy is making a comeback." She stuck the pen in a pink-flowered ceramic mug. "Thanks for coming to the rescue one more time."

"You can repay me by explaining every little detail about the phony obit as soon as you get the chance. My life's so dull compared to yours."

What I wouldn't give for a little boredom.

23.

A Charity Lunch

A mocha-skinned teenaged girl opened the Steins' carved walnut door. "Hey Cass. Mom won't be home till six."

"Actually, I came to see Melissa. Is she here?"

"She's upstairs." The girl pulled the door wide and Cassidy stepped into the foyer. Several pairs of large tennis shoes were piled on a plastic boot mat and the odor of wet socks hung in the air. The girl added, "Why don't you wait in the living room while I go get her?"

The room was occupied by three other teenagers: a chunky boy sprawled across two-thirds of the sofa; a tiny girl curled up in the remaining space; a tall thin boy draped sideways over a matching easy chair. They all said "Hey" to her.

"I'm sorry, I can't remember anybody's name."

"That's okay. Even Mom gets us mixed up sometimes." The tall boy unfolded himself from the chair and stood up. "You can have my place. I was just gonna go watch TV anyway."

All three teens paraded out of the room, leaving behind coats, books, and soda cans on the leather furniture, the beech coffee table, and the oriental rug.

A lovely pecan-colored girl with long wavy hair falling below her shoulders descended the stairs at the south end of the room. "You wanted to see me?"

"You're Melissa?"

She nodded. The girl took the easy chair and Cassidy sat across from her on the sofa.

"I have a stepson." Bending forward, Cassidy folded her arms across her legs. "His mother died and he's never dealt with it."

"Most kids don't. I mean, unless you get in a group or something you'd just ignore it, wouldn't you?" She had thick curved brows, taupe-colored eyes that met Cassidy's straight on, and a full sensuous mouth.

"Your mom told me about the support group you're in. What do you think of it?"

"At first I didn't want to go. I mean, it seemed weird, you know? I thought all the kids'd be mental or something." She offered a friendly smile. "But now my parents don't have to force me any more. I mean, now it's something I do for me. It's like, the kids in the group are the only ones who understand."

Cassidy's mouth tightened in frustration. "The problem is, Bryce doesn't live with us and I can't force him to do anything."

Melissa tugged at the small silver hoop in her right ear. "You want me to talk to him?"

Cassidy gazed at her speculatively, wondering if Bryce would listen to a high school girl. *Yeah, but look how pretty she is. And I bet there's not more than a couple of years' difference in their ages.* "It'd be great if you could do that. He might even pay attention to you." Cassidy rubbed her fingers over her chin. "When would be a good time for us to get him over here?"

"Mmm." She tilted her head one way, then the other. "Could you come Friday after school?"

When Cassidy arrived at Erik's, Gloria had already secured a table in the center of the large dining area. The space was bright and airy, greenery dripping on all sides, a few umbrella tables attempting to create the atmosphere of an alfresco café. Making her way through the congested room, Cassidy greeted Gloria, tossed her jacket over the back of a chair, then went to take her place in the line extending in front of the glass display cases that stood along the north side of the deli.

Near the far end of the counter sat an old-fashioned iron soup kettle, and beyond that, at the very end, a bakery display case: three shelves of goodies including black forest cake, chocolate éclairs, and brownies. Cassidy considered having an all-chocolate lunch, maybe three different desserts, but virtue won out and she kept herself moving in the direction of the taco salad she planned to order at the cash register.

Cassidy placed her order and the teenager behind the counter handed her a tray with a napkin, silverware, and a number on a metal stand that would enable the waiter to deliver the food to the right person. Carrying her tray to the table, she sat across from Gloria. "So, what is this new information you've come up with?"

"Remember I told you Barbara had one close friend, Lupe, who wasn't in a sorority? Well, I talked to her last night and she confirmed what I suspected from the letters—that Barbara did experience some kind of major change around January of her senior year." Gloria pushed one side of her straight blond hair behind her ear and took a sip of cola.

Cassidy leaned in closer. "So what happened?"

"Lupe doesn't know." Gloria shook her head, her wide set hazel eyes puzzled. "She kept asking, but Barbara wouldn't say a word about it."

"So what did Barbara do that made Lupe think something major'd happened?" Cassidy laid out her silverware and napkin, then set her tray aside.

"Up until January Barbara was the same as ever—partied a lot, had a new boyfriend every month." Gloria's hands moved rapidly, drawing pictures in the air. "Then all of a sudden she withdrew. For a few weeks the only time Lupe saw her was in class. Then later, she started hanging out with Lupe again, but she seemed like a different person. She stopped dating, dropped out of all her sorority activities, acted as if Lupe were her only friend."

Cassidy tapped her fingernails against the blond wood table. "Did Lupe say anything about Barbara's boyfriend?"

"Yep, I scored on that one. She didn't tell me anything specific but she thinks she may have a lead for you. She's going to check it out and give you a call." Gloria grinned widely. "Now was that worth a charity lunch or what?"

Cassidy returned the smile. "You're just fishing for reassurance."

"Oooh, never cross swords with a therapist."

"We're not crossing swords. We're getting to know each other. And if we enjoy each other's company, we'll probably do this again."

The food arrived, a colorful salad in a large tortilla bowl for Cassidy, an Erik burger garnished with tiny French-fried onion rings for Gloria. They dug in.

Swallowing the last bite, Gloria dabbed at her mouth with the napkin. "You know, I keep making jokes about being lonely, but going back over all those good times with Barbara has made me aware of just how much I miss having a girlfriend." Gloria's eyes turned misty. "I feel so bad about her dying the way she did."

"Me too."

"And now that I know something bad really did happen, I can't let go of it." Gloria pressed her fingertips against her cheek. "I keep remembering how impulsive she was, how she'd go too far with things and then be devastated when the consequences caught up with her. She got picked up for shoplifting in her freshman year and then absolutely fell apart when the police took her in and booked her. I spent weeks telling her that one arrest does not a criminal make."

Staring into space, Cassidy pictured the vibrant dark-haired child Barbara had been. "I remember her exactly the same way. She had these two urges warring inside her. One part wanted to be wild and rebellious and break all the rules. And then there was this other part that wanted constant approval." Cassidy felt a wave of sadness for her lost friend. "And she never could have it both ways."

Cassidy was at her desk working on a stack of overdue managed care forms when Starshine jumped onto the nightstand and said *mwat.*

Turning to answer, Cassidy said, "I have to finish this up. Some of my clients won't get approval for any more sessions if the paperwork doesn't get in."

The calico fastened her luminous green eyes on Cassidy's face and repeated the scratchy, begging sound.

She needs you. How can you deprive her like this? Besides, you hate forms.

Oh no you don't. You've been procrastinating for days. You have to keep putting words on paper till they're done.

She swiveled back toward her desk. Behind her she heard the tippety-tap of Starshine's footsteps trotting across the radiator board. The cat hopped onto the desk and walked back and forth across the papers, bumping Cassidy's chin with her head, waving her tail in Cassidy's face. Cassidy laid her arm across the form and hunched forward, attempting to fend Starshine off, but the cat flopped down on top of the paper.

"Okay, but five minutes is all you get. Then I have to go back to the damned forms." *If this is the best you can do at saying no, it really is a good thing you didn't have kids.*

Feeling secretly pleased that Starshine had won, Cassidy carried the calico over to the bed and tried to settle in for a petting session, but Starshine squirmed out of her arms and walked a few steps away. She sat tall, fixed her eyes on Cassidy, and said *mwat* again.

Oh, so this mwat *means "play" instead of "pet."*

She's so clever. Cassidy felt herself puff up with pride at her cat's ability to communicate. *Here she got this new toy, then she had to figure out a way to tell me when she wants to play with it. So she makes the same sound she uses for petting but doesn't let me near her. And bingo—process of elimination—I know exactly what she wants.*

Cassidy fetched the toy from the top of a tall cabinet in the hall. It had ended up there because, when she'd left it in more accessible places, Starshine had taken it out for herself and nearly destroyed it. The toy had bright green feathers attached by a string to the end of a stick, and it fluttered through the air like a bird.

Sitting on the bed, Cassidy whipped the feathers high in the air and the cat made incredible leaps in her attempt to catch it. Whenever she succeeded in clamping her jaws around the faux bird, she clawed, chewed, and kicked in her efforts to kill it. *Amazing this bird ever lives to fly another day. And I can certainly see why keeping tigers as pets would be a bad idea.*

Cassidy was back at work on the forms when Zach came in later that afternoon. He sat in his chair facing her.

"Amanda's new husband—this paragon who's made her life so wonderful—has quite a history. He's owned a string of restaurants in the past and currently presides over Gabrielle's Trumpet, that posh new eatery in River North. Seven years ago he lost his license for serving minors, and over the past ten years he's had two restaurants burn down. Buddy of mine in arson tells me they're fairly certain these fires weren't accidental, but no one could prove anything against George."

"So in other words, he's slime." She pictured Amanda with her dark blond hair pulled back, her warm velvety eyes, the welcoming smile on her face. "Why in the world would she marry a creep like that?"

"You married Kevin."

"That was in my misguided youth."

He smiled wryly. "You married me." Zach had been guilty of a few instances of bad behavior that might lead some to call *him* slime.

Cassidy turned to stare out the west window at rain pelting through a thick maze of bare branches, and behind the branches, a deep charcoal sky. *Why* would *Amanda marry a guy like that? Either because she's convinced herself he's innocent or because arson isn't a problem for her.*

Swiveling back toward Zach, she said, "So George torched a couple of buildings. What does that tell us? Nothing except that he's probably not too high-minded to object to a little revenge."

"That's about it." Zach glanced at his watch. "I made a four-thirty appointment with Wharton. Let's go get our truth-telling session over with."

"And what else haven't you told me?" the detective inquired, his dark, challenging eyes pinned on Zach.

"That's all of it."

They sat in the brightly lit interrogation room around a table suspended from the south wall, Wharton in the middle, Cassidy and Zach on either side. She had, in previous investigations, spent far more time in this small room than she ever would have wished. *And with each new visit I like it less.* The walls were cream-colored, bare except for a bench at the back and a small gang-type symbol drawn in the far corner.

"And the reason you didn't spell this out up front?"

"Cass knows all the key players." Zach gestured toward a sheet of paper he'd given Wharton containing numbers and addresses for Kevin and the Segels. "We thought she might be able to dig something useful out of them."

"And did she?" Heavy sarcasm.

"Obviously not," Cassidy said, annoyed that Zach was taking all the heat. *This guy's acting as if Zach's completely in charge, I'm just the little twit being led down the garden path.*

Turning his hard stare on Cassidy, Wharton pulled his wire-rims out of his pocket and settled them on his nose. "So what we have here are three family members with no evidence that any of the three knew about Barbara's sleeping with your ex. And we also have Kevin, whom you've ruled out on the basis of personality type. Seems like you've already determined in your own minds that none of the potential suspects is likely to have done it. So what is it exactly you expect me to do?"

His voice mild, Zach said, "The tipster called my office around four-fifteen yesterday. You might want to check the phone records."

"Well, I'm sure I never would've thought of that on my own."

Cassidy propped her elbows on the table. "I assume you weren't able to trace the email?"

"You withhold information from the police, then you expect me to spell out what we've got?" Wharton drummed his pencil against his notepad for about three beats. Looking from Cassidy to Zach, he asked, "What kind of insurance you two have on each other?"

Zach reared back in surprise. "You think *Cass* is trying to kill me?"

The cop gazed at Zach. "Or maybe vice versa."

In the car she remarked, "I assume he just said that to give us a hard time. He couldn't possibly imagine that either one of us would cook up a crazy scheme like this to kill the other. Could he?"

"If I were in his place, I'd consider the possibility. And then reject it because there's nothing to back it up."

Zach stopped at the Ridgeland-South Boulevard light. Cassidy stared into a boutique on the corner where three dramatic outsized costumes in shades of orange, amber and taupe hung in the window.

Turning toward Zach, she said, "We still have to talk to Bryce."

"Didn't you take care of that yesterday?"

"I was waiting for you."

"I don't feel any need to participate."

"You have to be there. We need to present a united front." The light changed and they drove under the El tracks and past the Ridgeland Commons swimming pool. "I think he's pretty depressed. I want to get him into a group." She told Zach about Melissa's experience and her offer to talk to Bryce.

"So what do you want me to do?"

"Drive us to Bryce's house now, before we pick up Charles

Maxal. Then come inside and help me find out what's wrong."

"You're not going to leave me alone until you get your way on this, are you?"

"No, I'm not."

Zach drew up in front of a small dwelling in the Albany Park neighborhood of Chicago, the house where Bryce lived with Ellie, his former nanny. The boy's yellow Miata was in the drive.

Ellie's house was nondescript, but the neighboring house was an eyecatcher. Above all the windows were aluminum awnings which, in the darkness and rain, gave off a sinister look. But offsetting any hint of menace was the comical wooden bird that stood in the front yard atop a six-foot pole, its windmill wings whirling madly. *Any house with a bird like that cannot be taken seriously.*

She buttoned her raincoat and pulled up her hood, delaying for an instant the moment she would have to leave the car. She felt reluctant to face the weather, reluctant to pry monosyllabic answers out of Bryce, reluctant to engage in the verbal arm wrestling that would be necessary to get him to agree to talk to Melissa.

"You ready?" Zach asked.

"Okay, let's go."

24.

Talking to Bryce

They stood on a concrete porch in front of a battered screen door. Rain blew in Cassidy's face. Zach stabbed the doorbell a third time. "Most people eventually break down and answer if you just keep ringing long enough."

After a couple of minutes, Bryce opened the door. "What're you guys doing here?" he asked in a listless voice.

Cassidy replied, "Remember yesterday I said I had to do an assessment? Well, I never got to finish." She noted the bleariness in his eyes, the rumpled appearance of his clothes. *Only six o'clock and he was in bed asleep, I'd bet on it.*

Bryce frowned, his tone turning belligerent. "I'm not letting you do any assessments on me."

"Can we come in? It's wet out here." Zach opened the screen door and stepped inside, forcing Bryce backward. Cassidy followed Zach into the living room.

"You've got no business coming here. I did what you said. I went to Oak Park." The boy pulled himself up to his full height, about two inches taller than Zach, and squared his narrow shoulders.

"Somebody has to look after you," Zach said. "And we're all you've got." He hung his jacket on a coat tree and lowered himself onto the sagging sofa. Cassidy did the same.

Bryce hooked his thumbs in his pants pockets and shifted his weight. "I'm busy. I don't have time for this."

Busy sleeping. "We're not leaving till we have answers."

"Aw shit." He shifted his weight again. "Well, if I can't get rid of you, I'll have to go tell Ellie who's here. She heard the doorbell and she'll be wondering." Bryce disappeared up a staircase facing the door.

Cassidy scanned the living room. Everything was old and shabby except for a very large TV that stood against the wall across from the sofa. In front of the sofa sat a mahogany coffee table with a half-full bowl of cereal on it. On the left side of the room next to an easy chair, an end table held a porcelain lamp with a dusty pleated shade, a dancing shepherdess adorning its base.

Bryce thumped downstairs and flopped into the chair. "So what do you want?"

"I want to know what it is you don't like about school."

He shrugged. "Everything." A long silence. "I'm not like anybody else. They all come from some different planet than me."

"What kind of planet?"

"The kind where people have normal families." He grinned wickedly. "You know, a mom and stepfather, a dad and stepmother, a bunch of stepsibs." Bryce's mother had operated an escort service and his family had consisted of her driver and the girls.

He's got half the equation—a dad and stepmom, even if he doesn't choose to claim us.

"Have you made any friends?" Cassidy asked.

"Nobody there I want to be friends with." He sat straighter. "I'm tired of this. Will you please go home now?"

Zach laced his hands together on his chest. "Not till we're done."

The boy stared darkly at his father. "This is her gig." He jerked his head at Cassidy. "How'd she suck you into playing along?"

Zach gave him a steady look. "I'm here because I care what happens to you."

Well, what do you know? It might just be possible for Zach to get this father thing right after all.

Cassidy clasped her hands loosely between her knees. "Are you going to classes?"

"Sometimes."

"When was the last class you attended?" Zach queried.

Another long silence. "I dunno."

"Why aren't you going to classes?" Zach asked gently.

"It's boring…. Nobody there I want to see." Bryce's gaze darted to Zach's face. "You know how long it's been since I even had sex?"

Maybe he does want his father's advice on luring chicks into bed.

Zach said, his voice amused, "Would you care to enlighten us?"

"I'm sick of these questions. I'm gonna get a beer." He stood abruptly and went into the kitchen. Cassidy squeezed Zach's hand, her way of saying "You're doing good."

The boy returned with three Buds. He handed them out, then dropped back into his chair, legs spread wide, knees high in the air. Zach and Bryce each took a long swallow, then Zach clinked the can down on the table in front of him. Although Cassidy could see that the mahogany surface already bore several rings, her social training wouldn't allow her to add a new one, so she set her unopened can on the floor.

"Since you're not going to classes," she said, "what are you doing with your time?"

"I don't know," he mumbled.

"I need an answer."

"I play my guitar. Listen to music."

"Are you sleeping quite a bit during the day?"

"No," he said angrily.

Cassidy caught Zach's gaze. She could tell he didn't believe the boy any more than she did.

"I bet you think about a lot of things while you're hanging around the house." She moistened her upper lip. "I bet one of the things you think about is dying."

He looked at her in surprise, his eyes glistening, his face suddenly naked.

"When you think about dying, how do you see yourself doing it?"

He gazed into space. Finally he said, "Sticking a gun down my throat."

Zach shifted on the sofa beside her. His usual look of detachment remained in place, but Cassidy suspected he was not as calm as he appeared.

She drew in a breath. "Do you have a gun?"

After several beats of silence, he mumbled, "No." Again, she didn't believe him.

"I think you do have a gun," Zach said. "You have to give it to us. We're not leaving without it."

Bryce sat for a while just staring into space, then went upstairs and returned with an automatic. He handed it to Zach. "I couldn't use it anyway. I don't have the clip."

Cassidy said, "And the reason you don't have it is, you're afraid of what you might do if the clip were here?"

He didn't answer, just sat back down in his chair.

Zach looked at her, telegraphing: *What do we do now?*

Cassidy sat forward, her hands gripped tightly in her lap. "Bryce, when people get overwhelmed, sometimes it's impossible for them to sort things out for themselves. Sometimes they need to go into a hospital where there are professionals who can help them."

Bryce flung himself out of his chair and stood over her, a

fierce scowl on his face. "Don't you even think about putting me in a hospital. You try anything like that, I'll never speak to either one of you again."

Standing, Zach put a hand on the boy's shoulder. "We'll do whatever we have to to keep you safe. Now back off and give Cass a chance to think."

Suddenly feeling shaky, Cassidy took in a deep breath through her mouth. "I'm going to get some water." She went into the kitchen, filled a glass, sipped slowly. A heap of chipped white dishes filled the sink. A framed needlepoint homily hung on the wall.

If you call the cops, they'll take him into a hospital, a psychiatrist will evaluate him, and the responsibility will be off your shoulders. If you don't, you'll have to live with the fear that at any moment he could get impulsive and just do it. Throw himself in front of an el, whatever.

Yeah, but hospitalization is no guarantee he won't. He could sign himself out after three days, refuse medication, come home and be more depressed than ever. And more ashamed, more stigmatized, more set apart as well.

She couldn't hospitalize him. The risk was too great. *We can't afford to lose him. He cuts himself off from us, he'll be completely alone.*

She returned to the living room. Zach and Bryce sat where they'd been before, not looking at each other. The gun was nowhere in sight, undoubtedly tucked away in Zach's waistband.

Returning to the sofa, she said, "You realize if I call the police, they'll take you to a hospital and a psychiatrist will commit you."

"Fuck!" Bryce shot to his feet and began pacing in front of them. "What a dumb shit I was to let you inside this house."

"But I won't do it if you agree to get help on your own."

"No therapy. Uh uh. No way."

Needs both therapy and a group. But if you insist on therapy, he'll just lie and say he's going when he's not. If you start with the group, you can monitor his attendance through Melissa.

"Okay, I'll compromise on the therapy. There's a group that meets in Oak Park for kids who've had a death in the family." She told him about Melissa's endorsement. "If you promise to talk to Melissa on Friday and then start attending the group, I won't hospitalize you. But you also have to give Melissa permission to let us know if you stop going."

Dropping back into his chair, he grumbled, "I don't wanna be in any groups."

"If you refuse, I'm calling the cops right now." *This is one threat I hope I don't have to make good on.*

Zach unhooked his phone from his belt and handed it to her.

"All right, I'll go to your fucking group."

"And I also need a promise that, if you feel an urge to hurt yourself, you'll talk to me personally—that means, no leaving a message on the machine—before you do *anything*."

"I promise."

She thought she heard a note of relief in his voice. *He's pissed as hell. But also feeling like a burden's been lifted now that somebody's stepped in to protect him from his own impulses.*

"And one more thing. I need you to report in on the phone to either Zach or me every night so we'll know you're still alive."

"Okay." This time Bryce didn't even sound angry.

Sliding behind the wheel, Zach ran a hand over his face, his bronze skin a shade paler than usual. "I was scared shitless when he brought out that gun."

"Me too."

"I can't believe he had a gun."

She kept her mouth firmly closed, not allowing any I-told-you-sos to slip out."

"Cass," he rested his hand on her knee, "I'm so glad you didn't let me squirm out of this."

"Why'd you try so hard to avoid it?"

"I don't know." He shook his head. "I guess because I like to be in charge. I like to know what I'm doing. When we went in there tonight, I had no idea how this thing was going to play itself out."

She laid her hand over his. "You did great. You were calm and firm and supportive. Everything a father should be."

"I have to admit, watching you in action, it's made a believer out of me." Putting the key in the ignition, he started the engine. "I hereby take back all the disparaging remarks I ever made about therapy."

"No more cracks about me playing shrink?"

"You can be a shrink with everyone else." He gave her a stern look. "But not with me."

As if he could stop you.

Zach headed east. "I think I better find some secluded location along the Chicago River before we pick up Charles."

"What? You're going to throw the gun in the river?"

"Don't you think that'd be best?"

"Well. . . .," she sucked in one cheek, "wouldn't this be a good time for you to have a gun?"

He looked at her, apparently considering it, then shook his head. "Wharton's already got me on his radar screen. I don't think I should take the chance of being caught with an illegal weapon."

Seated at the dining room table in front of a Boston Market take-out, Charles said, "My wife called to say she's going ahead with the divorce. She'll be home next week. Wants me to start looking for an apartment." He stared toward the window, his round, even-featured face drawn and tense.

Zach lowered his fork. "Sorry to hear it."

Remembering the same thing almost happened to us. Just a few months ago. Makes it easy for both of us to empathize.

"I've been through a divorce." Cassidy rubbed her thumb across her garnet ring. "It's always difficult. Even when people want out—which you obviously don't—it's still hard."

"I keep telling myself it's for the best. If I can't make her happy, we'll both be better off apart."

That's what he tells himself. But he feels like shit.

"Most people *are* better off in the long run. But the short run can hurt like hell."

Staring down at his plate, Charles fingered the stem of his wineglass. "You're the first people I've told. It's easier with you because you didn't know us as a couple. I'm going to have to say something to my family pretty soon." He shook his head. "I don't know how I'm going to do it."

Bet he does it by email. Oh the wonders of faceless, voiceless communication. Takes the sting out of almost anything.

After dinner the men went to work in the computer room. Cassidy, having canceled her evening clients, didn't know what to do with herself. She tried to read but her mind refused to follow the story: one paragraph after another got sucked into her brain and disappeared. Images kept pushing out the words: Amanda closing the door in her face; Zach at the police station; Bryce handing his father a gun.

Finally she carried her desk chair into the computer room and stationed herself to the right of Charles, who sat in front of the monitor, Zach on his other side. She didn't understand what they were saying, but their words washed over her, drawing her out of her own frightening internal spaces.

A few minutes past eight, Charles' cell phone rang. He conducted a brief conversation, then clicked off and said, "Hey Zach, you think I could borrow your car for about an hour? My sister's kid is sick—she's a single mom—she needs me to pick up a prescription."

Eyes narrowing, Zach gazed at Charles a moment, then pulled out his key ring and jiggled it in his hand. "Okay, sure. I'll just keep plugging away at these files while you're gone."

"Let me get your jacket for you." Leading him downstairs, Cassidy dug his windbreaker out of the room-divider closet and watched as he pulled up the hood and left through the back door.

At nine-thirty Zach came into the bedroom. "I need a drink. How 'bout you?"

Cassidy, who'd been staring through the north window at reflections of her neighbor's porch light on shiny wet concrete, said she'd have one too. She followed him down to the kitchen and watched as he poured hefty shots of bourbon into two glasses.

"It's probably the traffic," he said. "You know how rain jams everything up."

"Zach, I have this terrible feeling."

He turned toward her, his face grim. "Yeah, I'm having the same one."

"What if the E-Stalker was watching the house, waiting for

a chance to catch you alone." She paused, not wanting to say the rest of it.

"He's only half an hour late. It's too soon to be thinking this way."

"If the E-Stalker saw Charles get into the Nissan, there'd be no way he could tell it wasn't you."

"You know, I didn't even think to ask for his cell phone number." Zach shook his head. "I feel so stupid."

"We have to call the police."

"They'll think we're nuts." He added soda, handed her a glass, then slugged down half his drink. "Okay, I'll make the call."

Wharton told Zach he would put out an attempt-to-locate message on the Nissan, which meant the Chicago area police would be watching for the car. If Charles had not been found after a couple of hours, the detective said he would take a missing person's report.

They went to sit in the living room. Gritting her teeth, Cassidy said, "We don't know the sister's name. We don't know what pharmacy he was headed for. I can't think of a single thing we can do."

Zach nursed two more drinks. Cassidy would have liked to drink along with him but knew that tranquilizing herself with alcohol was a bad idea. At eleven-thirty Zach drove the Toyota to the police station and filed the report. At one they gave up and went to bed.

They were all in the Nissan: Zach at the wheel; Cassidy watching in horror from the passenger seat; Charles in back crying; Bryce seated behind Zach holding a gun to his head. An ancient stone wall, something out of a medieval country-side, stood a hundred yards in front of them. Bryce shouted,

"Faster! You have to go faster! We're all going up in flames!"
The car continued to accelerate until Cassidy thought they
would leave the ground and go flying into the air. They
zoomed straight toward the wall. An instant before impact,
Cassidy opened her eyes. Her heart was pounding, her forehead damp with sweat.

A big red 3:15 stared down at her from the bureau clock.
She reached toward Zach's side of the bed, wanting to touch
some part of his body, to ground herself with the solid reality
of his presence. He wasn't there.

Up in the middle of the night? He never does that. Kevin had
been a nighttime brooder. Even when his life was falling apart,
as it did at frequent intervals, Kevin had succeeded in maintaining his delusional optimism during the day. But at night,
when his guard was down, a bitter gloominess would sometimes overtake him, leading him to sit in an old recliner in the
junk room and stare down at the yard below. Cassidy had
always dreaded these nocturnal ruminations, because the more
Kevin acknowledged his troubles, the more he needed to make
them somebody else's fault. And Cassidy was far and away the
handiest scapegoat. His powers of rationalization, his ability to
take something that was solely his doing and find a way to
blame it on her had never ceased to amaze her.

She hadn't thought about Kevin's brooding spells in a long
time. Now, as she remembered them, she wondered if she'd
been too quick to dismiss him as a potential revenge seeker.

You need to stop thinking about the bad old days and go find Zach.
She pictured a huge, ephemeral hand lifting Zach out of
bed and carrying him away.

*Stop that. The E-Stalker does not have supernatural powers
and he didn't snatch Zach away from you. Zach can't sleep for the
same reason you can't, and he has every right to wander around in*

the middle of the night if he wants to.

She put on her long tee and slippers and went down to the living room, where Zach sat on the sofa in the dark, a half-filled glass in his hand. She eased down beside him.

Raising his glass, he rattled the ice cubes. "This is only my second. And I'm stopping here. Right now the idea of drinking myself unconscious is fairly tempting, but then I'd have a pissed-off wife and a hangover to face in the morning."

Three drinks before bed, two more now. Why does he have to handle everything with booze?

Because that's how he handles it. And he drinks way less now than he used to because he knows you don't like it. So leave him alone.

She clamped her mouth shut, trying to stop the words, but they slipped out anyway. "Zach, I really wish you wouldn't—"

The lines in his face deepened. "Don't start."

She sighed. "I'm sorry. I'm just so edgy it's hard to keep from picking at you."

He put his hand on her knee. "I know. I wouldn't be up drinking in the middle of the night if I weren't feeling the same."

"You want company? Or would you rather be alone?"

"It's been a long time since I thought I needed to be alone. It'd be nice to have you sit with me. Just don't try to make me talk."

She said in a small voice, "Talking really does help."

"Not always. And not now."

Snuggling up against him, she remembered Charles asking Zach how he was able to satisfy Cassidy's need for talking and Zach's saying it was because she dragged it out of him. But dragging it out of him, she suddenly realized, was only okay if she knew when not to.

25.

Jealousy Demons

The next morning Zach said, "I need to get into the office and find something to do to take my mind off Charles. You planning to use the Toyota? If you are, I can get a rental."

Cassidy, who normally loved working at home, had one instant of devoutly wishing she had an office to go to instead of three clients and vast stretches of empty time, which she knew would be filled with thoughts of Charles.

"As much as I'd like to get in the car and drive off somewhere, I can't think of a single place to go."

Zach was barely out the door when the phone rang. Picking up at her desk, Cassidy heard Gran's voice on the other end. "I talked to Cindy, that girl who works at the *Register*. It turns out she's not real crazy about her editor. Called him a despotic old fart. After I explained how he acted with you and Zach, she was real sympathetic. She thinks if somebody at the *Register* is making trouble, then that old Bob Huske ought to bend over backward to help you find out who it is."

"Does Cindy know anything?"

"She has her suspicions. You just call her at home and set up a time to get together. She's a single mom, lives with her parents. Anyway, her babysitter had to go to a funeral so Cindy's working out of her house today." Gran rattled off a number.

Could this be an actual break? Nah, nothing in this century's ever going to go right again.

"Gran you're a peach."

"You betcha! I'm a peach of a detective and you should let me do more."

"We can't even come up with anything more to do ourselves." Cassidy picked up a loose pen and stuck it in her flowered-mug pen holder. "By the way, you haven't had your house vandalized or your locks glued, have you?"

"Nary a thing. And Helen's fine too." She paused. "Now I have a favor you can do for me."

"Anything." *Gran's done so much for you, you could spend the rest of your life as her personal slave and it still wouldn't even the score.*

"My VCR's on the fritz. It plays but it won't record. So could you tape *The Simpsons* for me tonight?"

"Sure, I'd be happy to. Are you going out?"

"Nah, I'll be home. But I always watch tapes instead of live TV. I just plain love the remote. I can fast forward through the boring parts and replay the good stuff as much as I want. Plus I can stop and go pee whenever I feel like it."

Cassidy finished talking to her grandmother, then called Cindy.

"I feel like I'm playing deep throat," the young woman said with a laugh. "Which is a real turnaround, considering I'm a reporter. Not that I have any facts, mind you, but I do have some guesses."

"Which Zach and I would love to hear. When would be a good time?"

"Could you come by my house at twelve-thirty today?" She gave Cassidy the address.

Clients at ten, three and four. "Twelve-thirty will be perfect."

Since Cassidy's first client was due soon, she left a message on Zach's voice mail about the meeting with Cindy, then went downstairs to tidy her office.

When her session was over, Cassidy went into the bedroom to set up the VCR. The television with its built-in recorder sat beside the clock on the bureau, which stood against the south wall about three feet from Zach's side of the bed. Putting the tape box behind the clock, she inserted the tape, then went to the opposite side of the bed to do the programming. She checked the listing, pointed the remote at the TV, and began pushing buttons.

Just then Starshine raced into the room, her eyes wild and black, clearly in her playful, jungle-cat mode. She jumped onto the waterbed, pounced on a ripple, then made a flying leap for the bureau, skidding into the clock and knocking the tape box down behind the drawers.

Cassidy finished setting the VCR, then returned to Zach's side of the bed and got down on her hands and knees to retrieve the box. Since the bureau was too low for the vacuum to fit under it, the floor beneath it seldom got cleaned. As she gazed under the piece of furniture, she noticed a small object nestled amid the dustballs near the front of the bureau. She picked it up.

A gold shell-shaped earring. Her stomach lurched. Static buzzed in her brain. She got to her feet and stood staring at the dusty circlet in her palm. *Not mine. Definitely not mine.* She had a sudden flashback from her years with Kevin. She'd taken the sofa cushions off to clean beneath them and come across an unfamiliar lipstick. *Oh no! Not this again. Not Zach.* She squeezed her eyes closed, bit down hard on her lip.

This can't be Zach's doing. It has to be the E-Stalker coming up with a new way to torture you.

But why would the E-Stalker put an earring under your bureau? An earring you might not even find?

She wanted to convince herself that the E-Stalker had done it, but her jealousy demons, instilled in her by Kevin's waywardness, had burst into a full-blown rage at the sight of the earring and were unable to conceive of any explanation other than Zach as philanderer.

Zach wouldn't bring any earrings—or earring-wearers—in here, her voice of reason said, trying to assert itself. *The only way he'd ever have brought a woman into the bedroom is if he were so drunk he didn't know what he was doing. The way Barbara ended up in bed with Kevin. And besides, he couldn't have done it because you're always around.*

You weren't around back in October when you attended that Wisconsin seminar, her jealousy voice whispered back. *Gone four days. Both of you missing each other. Zach said he was fine but you knew he was a little lonely. Remember that night you called late in the evening and he didn't answer?* She pictured Zach in a sleazy dive, a dozen empty glasses on the bar, a slinky woman rubbing up against him.

Zach doesn't do things like that.

Oh yeah? What about that bimbo last summer? Besides, you can never know for sure what anybody else might be capable of. Just look at all the things you've done yourself you would've sworn you'd never do.

She flew to the desk and called Zach's cell phone. When he answered, she said, "Did you get my message about the meeting with Cindy?"

"Yeah, I was planning to leave in about half an hour."

"Could you come home now? There's something I need

to talk to you about."

"What is it? Did something happen?"

"I'll tell you when you get here."

"Are you all right?"

"No, I'm not all right. But I'm not in any physical danger. Just get home now."

"I'll be out the door as soon as I can."

When Zach came into the bedroom, she was staring at the dull gray sky outside the window, the earring in the pocket of her wine-colored slacks. She jumped to her feet and stood facing him.

"Remember when I went to that seminar? There was one night I called after ten and you didn't answer."

"Huh?" He looked at her as if she were nuts.

"Why didn't you answer?" she asked, her voice spiraling higher.

His eyes narrowed; his brows drew together. "What in the hell is going on?"

"Just tell me why you didn't answer the damn call."

"I was asleep."

"Before eleven? You never go to sleep before eleven."

"I got a little sloshed. I fell asleep early."

"And just where did you get sloshed?" *And with whom?*

He said in his on-the-verge-of-walking-out tone, "Cass, I don't like this one bit. I think you better explain yourself."

Taking a deep breath, she forced herself to speak more calmly. "Will you please just humor me? Where did you do your drinking? And when we talked the next day, why didn't you say anything about missing my call?"

Zach's jaw clenched. He took so long to answer she thought he might leave. Finally he said, "I sat here in bed, had a few too many drinks, and fell asleep. I don't get wasted in bars and climb behind the wheel any more. And I didn't mention it because you rag at me about my drinking."

She pulled out the earring and held it in front of him. "I found this under the bureau."

He stared at her, his eyes going dark with outrage. "You think I brought somebody home?"

She studied his reaction. He looked and sounded exactly like a man who'd just been accused of something he'd never do. *Stop this right now!* her voice of reason commanded. *This is your husband. The man who'd lay down his life for you. You have no right to treat him this way.*

She covered her face with her hands. "Oh God, what am I doing? I know you wouldn't bring anybody home."

"So why are you attacking me?"

"Ever since the obituary, I've been feeling like the past is standing right behind me, breathing down my neck. Then I found the earring and it brought back all the things Kevin used to do."

"And you thought I'd do the same?" Planting his hands on his hips, Zach regarded her coldly.

"I didn't think at all. I can't think once the feelings get started." She clutched her arms across her chest. "I don't like myself when I get this way anymore than you do."

"So when's it going to end? You had all that therapy. What's the matter? Didn't it work?"

"Feelings get wired in and it takes a long time to undo the wiring. The therapy helped but it wasn't a magic wand. This jealousy is programmed into my system."

"So you're saying I just have to live with it?" He brushed past her and went to lean his hands on the window frame.

"Zach, I'm sorry." She chewed on the inner lining of her lip. "I'm doing the best I can. Right now it probably doesn't seem nearly good enough. But our only choice is to put up with each other's imperfections or not be married."

He turned to stare at her for several seconds. "Well, since not being married isn't an option, I guess I'll have to work on not taking these flare-ups personally."

Moving closer, he rested his arms on her shoulders. "You know I hate fighting with you."

"It's not my favorite thing either."

"Does that mean we get to kiss and make up?"

Looping her arms around his neck, she pressed her mouth against his. After a long and satisfying kiss, she took a step back, opened her hand, and gazed at the gold shell again. "So this must be a little memento from my personal tormenter."

Zach took the earring and examined it. "Not too hard to figure how it got here. The guy—or woman—probably planted it when he came into the bedroom to photograph our wedding picture."

"But why put it out of sight? It's kind of a fluke I even found it at all."

"Well, first of all, he didn't intend to launch his campaign until November fourth, so he probably didn't want you to find it right away. And second, he may like the idea of creating a minefield. Having something like this show up unexpectedly is certainly a way to keep you off balance." His brow creased. "The part I can't figure is how he'd have such a clear sense of what sets you off. Of all the people we've talked to, Kevin's the only one who'd know your hot buttons so well."

Tilting her head, Cassidy considered the question. "It had to be a woman who thought of the earring. A woman who's been cheated on herself and knows what it's like to go around for years afterward expecting it to happen again. Sort of like a cancer survivor constantly on guard against a recurrence."

Zach wrapped an arm around her shoulders. "What an ass-hole Kevin was for doing this to you."

She picked up the earring and held it between her thumb and forefinger. The gold was thin and lightweight, clearly nothing more than costume jewelry. "I wish it could tell us something about its owner, but it seems too cheap for Amanda and too tailored for Lany."

"The only thing this earring is telling us is that you need to work harder at trusting me and I have to try to understand it when you don't."

Shortly before they were due to leave for their meeting with Cindy the phone rang. Zach was in his office. Cassidy picked up at her desk.

A soft voice introduced herself as Lupe Greer. She said she'd heard from Gloria that Cassidy was trying to locate Barbara's boyfriend and she had a suggestion for how they might find him.

Cindy and Lupe in the same day? Maybe you shouldn't sink into total despair just yet.

"I really appreciate your calling." Cassidy propped her feet on the radiator. She could hear happy, chattery children noises on the other end. "This Teddy Wilson guy is so elusive, it almost seems like we're chasing a ghost. Did you ever actually meet him? Can you verify that he does in fact exist?"

Lupe laughed, a light, musical sound. "I don't think any of Barbara's friends ever got a glimpse of him. But I do know he was a townie."

Not a college student? Then Charles had no reason to even be at our house. His disappearance is just a nasty cosmic joke.

"I guess you've already heard that Barbara went through a

period when she isolated herself," Lupe continued. "Then she started hanging around with me, and she got really clingy, like she needed constant hand-holding. But after she met Teddy, she seemed more at peace. She didn't need me with her all the time anymore."

Cassidy watched a mother in the yard across the street raking leaves into a small pile near the curb. Her two young children, wielding toy rakes, kept dragging them off in the wrong direction.

"What can you tell me about this Teddy Wilson?"

"Only one thing. Where she met him."

"That's all?" *Total despair may be the best choice after all.*

"When Barbara dropped out of her college activities, she started going to one of the local bars. It wasn't my sort of place, but she kept after me to go with her and I did a few times. She said she liked it because it was so different from any of the college hangouts. Just a typical neighborhood bar. All blue collar. Same crowd every night. I couldn't figure it out. Barbara didn't have anything in common with those people."

Cassidy pictured a poorly lit room, paunchy geezers leaning against the bar, all dressed in overalls or pants with wide red suspenders, straw poking out from behind their ears.

"Barbara was so into being cool," Cassidy said. "So quick to pick up on the latest trend. I just can't imagine her in a place like that."

"I always figured the reason she kept Teddy Wilson so completely under wraps is that she was embarrassed about him. You know, the guy was dumb, fat, and old or something."

"You said you had an idea about how we might track him down."

"There's one possibility. These guys all knew each other, so if you call the bar you might be able to locate somebody who can tell you where he is. He might even still be pounding beers there himself."

"You remember the name of the place?"

"I didn't at first. But I went through the Champaign yellow pages on Switchboard Dot Com and was able to recognize it when I saw it. Sort of amazing to find any place still in business under the same name seventeen years later."

Be even more amazing if Ted or any of his buds are still there. But worth a phone call.

Lupe gave Cassidy the name and number.

"It's so nice of you to go to all this trouble to help somebody you don't even know."

"I'm a librarian. I do research all the time. The only thing is, I'm not sure I understand why you want to find him."

There it is again. The question you hate. Cassidy delivered her need-to-make-sense-out-of-Barbara's-death speech.

"Well, um, okay," Lupe said, sounding confused. "If you ever come up with an explanation for all those changes Barbara went through, I'd sure like to hear it."

Cassidy said she'd be happy to report back and wrote down Lupe's number. "One thing I'm sort of curious about is how you and Barbara came to be friends. Gloria gave me the impression you were the only non-Greek in Barbara's life."

"I tutored her in her freshman year and we just hit it off. She called me her token egghead buddy. In fact, she used to say I reminded her of her best friend back in grade school, which I guess would be you." Cassidy heard a shriek of childish laughter in the background from the other end. "She was so popular and I wasn't at all, but she made a real effort to keep the friendship going." Lupe paused. "I sometimes wondered what she saw in me."

Cassidy smiled, feeling a sense of commonality with the

other woman. "I used to ask myself the same question. Looking back, I'd have to say that high fliers like Barbara need somebody with their feet on the ground to hang onto the kite string."

"I never thought of it that way."

Cassidy saw the mother across the way drop her rake and go running after one of the toddlers who was chasing a squirrel into the street. While her back was turned, the other child plopped into the middle of the pile of leaves, scattering them in all directions.

"Barbara had this mission in life to convert me. So every time she'd get ready to dump her boyfriend du jour, she'd try to fix me up with him. She even tricked me a couple of times by dragging her soon-to-be ex along on coffee dates with me in hopes that the boyfriend and I would fall in love."

Cassidy laughed. "That sounds just like her. But you obviously held out. Although from those kid sounds in the background, I'd guess you eventually developed some interest in guys."

"Yep, I have the kids now. But I also have a husband and a job." She sighed. "I just wish Barbara's life had worked out half as well."

Cassidy informed Zach about the bar. Since it was nearly time for their meeting with Cindy, they decided to hold off on contacting the place until later.

26.

A Fed Ex Bill

"I can't believe the boss tried to brush that obit off as a harmless prank," Cindy said. "He may have given you the impression he didn't take it seriously, but when it came to dealing with the staff, I've never seen him so mad." The reporter, wearing a black sweater tucked into khaki pants, sat with her feet curled under her on the sofa. No-nonsense blunt-cut hair, a taut thin-featured face, inquisitive dark eyes. Intense. They were conferring in the living room of her parents' house in west Oak Park.

"Gran said you may be able to tell us who's behind the obituary," Cassidy prompted.

"I understand the obit wasn't all of it." Cindy met Cassidy's eyes briefly, then turned her attention to Zach. "That you received some email threats right after the obituary came out."

Gran told a reporter about the e-cards? You shouldn't have spilled all those juicy details. You know she can never resist the chance to gossip.

Oh, come off it. If Gran trusts Cindy, that ought to be good enough for you.

Seated in an armchair to Cassidy's left, Zach pulled himself straighter. "This is off the record, I presume?"

"I'd much rather it wasn't," Cindy replied with a small

smile. "Don't you think it might be useful to run a story? You know how people come forward when they read about things in the paper."

"I couldn't have said it better myself." Propping his elbows on the chair's arms, he laced his fingers together. "However, now that we're the ones with a problem, I don't want a word of this to get out."

"If you insist." Cindy's narrow mouth pulled down at one corner.

You tend to forget. Reporters have ethics just like therapists do. Even Zach—as fast and loose as he is—would never print anything he'd been told off the record.

A moment of silence, during which Cassidy's gaze skimmed the room. In some ways it matched Cindy: the furniture all sleek and contemporary, each piece constructed in thin fine lines. But the color was wrong. Nearly everything was blue and white: the striped sofa, the flowered chairs, the checkered rug. Cindy was not a blue and white person. She was jet black or flame red.

Cassidy rubbed her fingers against the nubby fabric of her armrest. "Since you're not certain who the guilty party is, that must mean your editor never figured it out."

"Nobody got fired. If Bob had identified the culprit, someone would have been instantly gone."

Zach removed a notepad from his inner jacket pocket. "So who do you think got creative with the obit section?"

"Howard Markowitz. As you undoubtedly know, the pay scale at a suburban paper is pretty pathetic. Well, one of the major themes of Howard's life is how broke he is. He's constantly complaining about not having enough money to pay his bills. But then, last Friday night a bunch of us went out after work, and for the first time in history

Howie bought a couple of rounds. Eventually everybody else left and it was just Howie and me, both of us a little blitzed, and I asked if he'd won the lottery. That's when he made this odd comment." Cindy stared straight ahead, her brows drawn together, apparently trying to recapture it.

This actually is *a break.* Cassidy, who could sit calmly through long stretches of silence in a therapy session, gritted her teeth in impatience. *If only life came with a fast forward button.*

After several seconds, Cindy picked up her story again. "I wish I could remember the words exactly. I think it was, 'How sweet it is. All my life I've been hoping that someday my ship would come in. Well, now it has, and let me tell you it was worth the wait.' Something like that. I tried to get him to explain but he just gave me this Cheshire cat smile and wouldn't say anything."

"How sweet it is," Zach repeated. "You think someone hired him to insert the obituary, and the sweet part was getting his hands on a bunch of money?"

"That's the first time he ever bought drinks." Pulling her legs out from under her, Cindy leaned forward. "But it isn't just the comment. At the time I didn't make anything out of it. Then your grandmother asked what I thought about the obituary. At first I said nobody had a clue. Then it hit me. Out of everybody on the staff, Howie's the only one I could imagine doing such a thing."

Cassidy asked, "What makes him such a likely prospect?"

"Well, it's . . ." Cindy's brow furrowed again. "It's the chip on his shoulder. He's always mad about something, always feeling picked on. One time he wrote an exposé about an affair between two married trustees. Like he thought he was working for the *National Inquirer* or something. Well, of course Bob quashed the story and reamed his ass for even thinking we'd print such a thing. We all knew Howie was nuts for writing it in the first place. But he went around complaining for weeks because he thought the *editor* was out of line."

A grudge bearer. A grievance nurser. This is sounding better and better. "If Howard's such an obvious pick for planting the obituary, why hasn't your editor nailed him?"

"It's certainly possible that Bob's reached the same conclusion I have, but there isn't any evidence. Bob may not be my first choice in editors, but he is fair. He'd never can anybody on the basis of a hunch."

Zach cocked his head. "What else can you tell us about old chip-on-the-shoulder Howie?"

"Not much. He's been at the *Register* less than a year. Says he used to work at a daily in California but he's pretty vague about his past. I wrote out his phone number and address. Let me get it for you."

She went to a small desk in the corner. Beneath the desk, Cassidy spotted a pair of tiny, lace-edged, pink-checkered tennis shoes.

Cindy handed Zach a business card with handwriting on it. "He lives in a coach house. Tiny place, very cheap rent. It faces an alley in back of a mansion. A bunch of us ended up there once after hitting the bars."

"I assume he'd be at work now?"

"Probably. I couldn't say for sure since I haven't been in today."

As they stood to leave, Cassidy held out her hand. "Thanks so much for your help."

"Well, you know I love your grandmother."

Gran and her fan club. How sweet it is.

As he pulled away from the curb, Zach said, "Since we haven't got anything better to do with our time, let's swing by Howie's on the off chance he came home early for an afternoon nap."

Nothing better to do with our time. Our real lives have disappeared and all we have is this big empty space where we run around in circles trying to occupy ourselves as we await the next attack. Without the least clue as to which direction it'll be coming from.

Cassidy gazed out the side window at a corner flower garden filled with ragged salvia, the once-crimson blossoms faded to a dull burgundy.

Zach said, "We've been speculating that the E-Stalker is not just one person but a man and woman working together. So, how's this as a theory? Howard Markowitz is really Teddy Wilson. Before Barbara died, Amanda met Teddy, but since she disapproved of the marriage they weren't exactly pals. But then, after the accident, their shared grief drew them together, which led to Amanda's showing your letter to Teddy so they could sit around the kitchen table and both get off on reviling your name. Teddy even went so far as to hang out in bars with Kevin until he'd dug out all the sordid details about the night Barbara died."

Pressing the back of her fingers under her chin, Cassidy thought through how the situation might have unfolded. "So they gradually went from commiserating with each other to plotting against me."

"But then Don committed suicide, Amanda bought a restaurant, and they both moved on."

"Except they didn't lose touch. They exchanged Christmas cards or something. And Ted never married. Never got over seeing Barbara as his one true love, lost to him forever because of my heartlessness."

Like Zach is to you. Somebody you'd never get over.

He nodded. "Then Amanda has her heart attack. And while she's lying in bed week after week, she has plenty of time to relive the family tragedy and create fantasies of retribution against you."

"And the heart attack brings on a new sense of urgency. She's facing her own mortality. If she's ever going to have her revenge, it has to be now."

Zach stopped behind an ancient, tomato-red beetle with stickers in the window exhorting people to make love not war. "But Amanda can't do it alone. So she feels Teddy out, and Ted, whose life has not been stellar, is ripe for it. And maybe also ripe for the money he can get out of Amanda for doing it."

"Ted has to create a new identity before he can get started." Cassidy nibbled her lower lip. "Maybe Amanda's husband helped with that part. George, the arson expert, would probably know how to set Ted up with all the right papers."

"So Teddy, a.k.a. Howard, moves to Oak Park and gets a job at the *Register*. Then, the night before the obit comes out, he suddenly isn't poor any more, and something in his life is feeling very sweet." Zach stopped in front of a graystone mansion that stood about twenty feet back from the street on a half-block lot. "So, what do you think?"

"I like it."

Cassidy stared at a two-story building with tall arched windows and a recessed entrance flanked by fluted columns. A low hedge in front. Lofty elms overhanging the slate roof.

Zach said, "I should have realized it was this place when

Cindy mentioned the coach house."

"You've been here?"

"A couple of times. The people who used to own it were friends of my mother's."

Cassidy glanced at her husband. With his cheap haircut, nondescript jacket, and faded black tee, no one would ever guess that his family belonged to the mansion set. *Goes out of his way to hide it. As if growing up with money were a dirty little secret.*

"Well, let's drive around back and see if Howie's home."

They parked in the alley in front of a small two-story building standing next to a three-car garage. The coach house had the same graystone, slate-roof construction as the big house but possessed none of its architectural features. The dwelling was quite simple: a low concrete porch, a door in the center, a multipaned window on either side of the door, a row of windows along the second story. Nestled in shrubbery, it reminded her of a cottage in the woods. *If I hadn't grown accustomed to having nine rooms to rattle around in—way more space than we can keep up—I might like a pretty little dollhouse like this.*

Opening the car door, Cassidy said, "He probably parks in that big garage, so the fact that there's no car in sight wouldn't mean anything. But the odds of finding him home at one-thirty on a week day are pretty slim."

Zach punched the bell several times.

Cassidy shifted from one foot to the other. "He's obviously not here. We might as well go home."

"If Howard's the boyfriend, and if he's an obsessive type who never got over Barbara's death, wouldn't he have pictures of her in his house? Wouldn't we find a shrine or something that would link him to Barbara?"

"Are you doing what I think you're doing?"

"What's that?"

"Trying to rationalize breaking in?"

"Yeah, that's what I'm doing."

"This is crazy." Scowling, she backed away from him. "We should give Howard's name to the police and let them handle it. There's absolutely nothing to be gained by going inside. Even if we found something, the police couldn't use it because of our felonious means of entry. Besides, this is Oak Park. Neighbors watch out for each other. The last thing we need right now is for you to get arrested."

Or maybe that would be a good thing. The cops could keep him in jail until the E-Stalker gets bored and goes away.

"Okay, you're right. Trying to break in would be nuts. It's just that I'm so damn frustrated." He started down the porch steps, then turned back toward the house. "Okay, all I'm going to do is take a good look through the front and back door windows just in case he's got pictures of Barbara plastered all over his walls."

Zach opened the screen door and moved up close to the glass. Crowding against him, Cassidy gazed in also. The door opened onto a living room with the kitchen off to the right. She saw several pieces of mismatched furniture, all littered with beer cans, ashtrays, and fast food containers. The walls were bare.

Zach tried the brass doorknob.

"What are you doing?"

"Just checking to make sure Howie locked up properly."

They circled the house to peer in the back door window, which afforded a view of a messy, galley-style kitchen.

He tried the back doorknob. It turned. "Well, what do you know? Looks like our Howard got a mite careless."

"Zach, don't do it." *You know he's going to.* "Somebody's bound to see us."

"This is nothing more than illegal entry." He shrugged. "Trespassing. A low end misdemeanor."

"Wharton doesn't like us already. He'd be so pleased to have a reason to lock us up."

"I want to take a quick look at those upstairs rooms." Zach's mouth lifted at one corner. "Tell you what. You don't try to talk me out of going inside, I won't try to talk you into staying in the car."

"All right," she said through clenched teeth. "Let's get it over with."

The inside air was thick with smoke and beer and something else, something unpleasant she couldn't identify. She closed the door and followed Zach up the open staircase, treading on steps that were dark with wear, just like her steps at home. At the top, a short hallway softly illuminated by a glass sconce on the right-hand wall, two doors standing partway open on either end of the corridor.

Zach went into the room on the left. Cassidy sidled around the other door, a room furnished as an office, the blinds closed, the light dull and gray. The odor she'd picked up downstairs was stronger here and beginning to smell familiar.

At first all she noticed were a number of filing cabinets and two large desks covered with computer equipment. Then she saw the body. It was in a swivel chair in front of the desk against the far wall. The man's head and shoulders were crumpled over a keyboard.

Oh my god! Her stomach lurched. Her hand clutched the base of her throat. Stumbling backward out of the room, she said in a strangled voice, "Howard's in there. He's in that room . . . he's dead."

Zach came through the other doorway.

She started shaking all over. "Why the hell did we have to

come in here? Why did you do this to me? I don't want to find any more dead bodies ever again. I want to go home and lock my doors and make you stay inside with me until this is over." She began pounding on his chest with her fists. "Why can't you ever let the police handle anything?"

"I'm really sorry I brought you in here."

Stepping back, she held her outspread hands rigidly in the air to stop herself. "We have to get out of here."

"You go sit in the car. Just give me five minutes and then we'll call the cops."

"Five minutes? What's the matter with you?" She sucked in air. *Calm down. You have to calm down. Howie's dead. Nothing more is going to happen.*

Zach gave her a long, steady look. "Just wait for me in the car."

He's going to examine the crime scene. You can't stop him any more than he could've stopped you from talking to Bryce.

"Okay, take your five minutes. But I'm not leaving till you do."

Removing a handkerchief from his jeans pocket, he used it to turn on the light in the office, then went to stand over the body. Cassidy stepped inside to watch. "He *is* dead, isn't he?" *You were ready to bolt, didn't even check to see if he's still breathing. Good thing nobody's life depends on you.*

"There's a scissors blade buried deep down inside his rib cage and the blood's dry. So yes, he's dead all right."

Zach stared down at the desk where Howard lay, then went to study the other desk as well. Using his handkerchief, he started removing papers from a wastebasket a couple of feet from the body. He glanced at each one, then set it aside on the floor. Holding up a form, he said, "This is a Fed Ex lading bill." He scanned the room. "I don't see anything that looks like a Fed Ex box or envelope, do you?"

"No, but I'm not getting close enough to tell."

"It's dated yesterday. I wonder where the packaging went?"

"You're not taking it with you?"

"That'd be tampering with a crime scene."

He pulled out two more flat sheets of paper, then one that was wadded into a ball. Careful to touch it only with the handkerchief, he straightened the paper out. "I don't like this."

"What is it?"

He looked at her a moment. She could see he was reluctant to tell her.

"Instructions on how to detonate dynamite. Probably something he took off the Internet."

"The Fed Ex bill." She drew in a breath. "You think that might've been a box of dynamite? But people can't just buy dynamite, can they?"

"I've heard you can buy anything over the Internet."

27.

The Bulldog Inn

Once they were back in the Toyota, Zach pulled out his cell phone, started to dial 911, then clicked it off. "We need to think through how we're going to deal with the police. And what the dynamite means."

He didn't look quite as steady now as he had while standing over the body. *Always calm in a crisis. Hits him afterward. I had my little tantrum upstairs, now I'm okay.*

Zach went on. "Howie was working with Amanda or some other woman. They concocted some scheme involving dynamite."

"Oh shit!" Cassidy gasped, suddenly seeing the implications. "A car bomb."

"That's what I'm thinking." He put a reassuring hand on her knee. "But a car bomb is something we can take precautions against. We can keep the Toyota locked in the garage when we're home. I'll drive if you need to go somewhere. If we have to leave it on the street, we'll park in places with people around." He paused. "I can rig up a mirror on a stick so I can look under the car to see if there's any sign of tampering. This isn't as bad as it sounds."

She wanted to shake him. "There you go again, saying it isn't so bad." She took a deep breath. "I'm sorry. Getting hys-

terical doesn't help. Okay, we'll set it up so the woman—
Amanda, Lany, whoever—can't get at our car."

"Howie's partner in obsession and revenge."

"The blonde who served you that drink. She must have
killed him and taken off with the Fed Ex box. Unless we get
lucky and the police find dynamite somewhere in the house."

*You're not going to get lucky. There's a crazy lady running around
with a load of dynamite just waiting to blow Zach up.*

Cassidy clutched her arms across her chest. "What's going
to happen with the police? I suppose they're going to consider
us suspects, at least until we've told our story ad nauseam."

"Cops always take a close look at whoever reports a murder.
They'll question us separately and we both need to tell the exact
truth so there won't be any inconsistencies. You need to say that
you tried to talk me out of going into the house and that you
watched me take papers out of the wastebasket. All of it."

She put a hand on his arm. "I just remembered. I've got
clients at three and four."

"You'll have to cancel."

"Their cell phone numbers are at the house. Could we go
home, then come back and report the murder?"

He started the engine. "I guess fifteen minutes won't make
any difference to Howie."

"I suppose we have to tell the police we took a side trip
home before calling it in?"

"Yep."

*For someone who hates being yelled at by cops, you certainly set
yourself up for it a lot.*

When they returned, Zach called the emergency number
and several beat officers arrived to situate Cassidy and Zach in
separate cars and secure the scene. A short time later a detective Cassidy hadn't seen before took her preliminary statement.

She spent more time in the squad, then was driven to the station and interrogated at length. After another hour, Wharton came into the small room to take her through her story again.

Pushing his glasses onto the top of his head, the detective gave her a hard look. "So it's your belief Moran hadn't connected Howard Markowitz to the phony obituary before you talked to Cindy, but you don't know that for sure."

"I *do* know for sure because Zach and I always work together. If he'd gotten Howard's name, he would have told me."

Wharton glanced down at his notes. "Now there was a period of about two hours last night when Moran was missing, wasn't there?"

"Missing?"

"You told me you went to bed at one, then woke up at three and found him in the living room."

"What are you thinking? That he waited till I was sound asleep, jumped out of bed, went to Howard's and killed him, then came home, changed into his robe, and settled in the living room with a drink?"

The detective didn't reply.

At six o'clock the police released them. As Cassidy buckled her seat belt, she told Zach about the detective's implication.

"Yeah, they kept hammering at me about whether or not I'd gotten Howard's name from some other source before we talked to Cindy. You can't blame them. If they could prove I'd identified Howie as the person behind the phony obit, they'd have a motive."

"Here's hoping they turn up evidence in the house that'll lead them to a blonde driving around with a box of dynamite in her trunk."

But they won't. You know it's not going to be that easy.

Returning to the house, Cassidy found a message on the machine. She pushed PLAY. "I got a call from Bev," Troy's voice said, sounding agitated. Troy was the client who, although barely a five himself, had set his sights on having a woman who ranked up around an eight or a nine. "You remember, the woman who was living with me, then took off with another guy? Well, it seems like she's come to her senses now 'cause she wants to get back together. I agreed to see her tomorrow night but I thought I'd better have a session with you first. I'm afraid I might do something I'll regret."

As if I could stop him. She gritted her teeth. The thought of listening to Troy agonize over whether or not to take back the woman who'd dumped him made her skin itch. *How will I ever get through an hour of Troy's petty little soap opera when the E-Stalker is out there hunting Zach?*

Don't you dare belittle your client like that. You think your troubles are so much worse than Troy's? At least you have someone to lose. If you ever start trivializing anybody else's problems, you won't be fit to be a therapist.

She called Troy. Paying penance for her spiteful thoughts, she spent extra time on the phone with him, then scheduled an appointment for ten o'clock the following morning.

She heard Starshine thumping up the stairs. *Who's she coming to harass? Zach in the computer room or me in here?*

The cat jumped on the bed, trotted across the radiator board and landed on Cassidy's desk. She brushed her tail in her human's face and reached out for a nosekiss. Bouncing down, she walked purposefully toward the door, then turned to see if Cassidy had gotten the message. Cassidy obediently went downstairs and filled the cat's bowl.

Taking out a bag of Reese's, she bit one in half. "It's not as if I'm eating because I'm hungry," she told Starshine, who'd inhaled her food and now sat erect on the kitchen counter. "I gorged myself with pizza less than an hour ago. But lately I almost never make it through the kitchen without sticking chocolate in my mouth."

Starshine stared at her out of luminous green eyes, the adoring look that followed dinner, then began scrubbing her face with her paw.

"Given how I am with chocolate, it's certainly a good thing I don't have Zach's penchant for alcohol. My track record for giving up bad habits isn't half as good as his." Zach had quit drugs in his twenties, then quit cigarettes a couple of years before they met.

Mwat, Starshine said, holding up her end of the conversation.

"Now that I think about it, my track record for giving up anything is nonexistent. If stuffing my face with chocolate ever gets to be a problem, I'll be in real trouble.

Cassidy went back upstairs, sat at her desk, and stared at the notepad with the name of the Champaign bar on it. The Bulldog Inn. She tried to picture Barbara, green eyes flashing, dark hair springing from her head, standing among the geezers with straw sticking out of their ears. *Why would sophisticated Barbara go to a place like The Bulldog Inn?*

The place she met Teddy Wilson. Teddy, who was town not gown. Earlier that afternoon Zach had speculated that Howard was really the boyfriend, but as Cassidy thought about it now, the theory seemed more a desperate attempt to connect unconnectable dots than an assumption based on logic.

Heading into the computer room, she slid into the chair

next to Zach's and propped her elbow on the green and pink table. "I've been thinking about your Howard-as-boyfriend theory and I don't believe it holds up very well. Lupe told us Teddy wasn't in college, but Howard would've needed a degree to get a job as a reporter. It also seems a bit of a stretch to think he'd get a call from Amanda, drop everything, move to Oak Park, and pick up a job at the *Register* just like that. For the village paper to have an opening at the same time Amanda was ready to launch her revenge scheme seems a tad coincidental."

"When you put it that way, my brainstorm of this afternoon does sound a little lame." He cocked his head. "Okay, let's do a reversal. Let's assume Howard didn't have any connection to Barbara. In that case, his motive would be purely monetary."

"So how did the E-Stalker find Howard? I suppose she must have checked out the staff of the *Register* and arrived at the same conclusion Cindy did—that Howard was the weakest link. Then she would've paid him to insert the obit, call you in the guise of a tipster, and order the dynamite. If we think of it as just a woman and her hired hand, that would eliminate the boyfriend altogether. Maybe we don't even need to call the bar."

Zach's brows drew together. "An obsessive boyfriend just seems so right for this." He paused. "You know, it's possible my theory about the boyfriend and Amanda—or Lany even— forming a partnership isn't wrong after all. Maybe the two of them together hired Howard."

She shook her head vigorously. "I don't like that at all. That would mean we still have two bad guys out there to worry about."

"Yeah, but we can't just rule out the boyfriend. We need to make that phone call and find out if anybody at The Bulldog Inn knows where Teddy Wilson is."

"But what do we say? We think Teddy Wilson is a deranged killer and we'd like you to help us find him?"

"Well, obviously, we need a scam."

They bounced ideas around until they came up with one they liked.

Returning to her desk, Cassidy dialed the number on the notepad. Zach sat in his chair to listen, Starshine prancing over to plop in his lap.

"Yeah," a gruff voice answered. In the background she heard raucous conversation accompanied by the sweet sound of Willy Nelson waxing nostalgic over blue eyes crying in the rain.

"May I speak to the owner?"

"That's me."

"Do you know a man named Teddy Wilson who used to be a patron of yours back in the eighties?"

"Huh?" His voice suspicious. "What're you asking about Teddy for?"

"This is kind of a long story. Do you have time right now?"

"Hey," the owner said, speaking to the customers, "will you bozos pipe down? I got a lady with a story about Teddy Wilson."

"Teddy was engaged to my sister Barbara in the early eighties. In fact, they met at your bar. She was a college student at the time."

"Hey," he said, speaking to his cronies again, "did you guys know Teddy was engaged to some broad from the college?"

And they say women are gossips.

Speaking to Cassidy: "Nobody here knows nothin' about any engagement."

"Well, they kept it kind of a secret. Anyway, Barbara died in a car crash and we never heard anything more from Teddy after that. But I've been cleaning out the house—we had to put my mother in a nursing home, you know—and I found a box of mementos Barbara'd kept, letters from Teddy, pictures, things like that. And I thought Teddy might want to have them."

"After all this time? What would he care?" The owner snickered.

"I'd like to at least ask him. Is he still in Champaign?"

"Nah, he moved to Chicago a while back."

So he's here. Close enough to throw a rock through your window. "Do you know how I could reach him?"

"The wife might have his address. She likes to keep in touch with people. Gimme your number and I'll call you tomorrow."

Clicking down the phone, she gazed at Zach, who was brushing Starshine's fur. "This is amazing. I finally found someone who actually admits to knowing the Phantom of The Bulldog Inn."

When her back doorbell rang at seven-fifteen, Cassidy's first thought was that it was a client arriving for an appointment she'd neglected to record in her calendar. Since the door was locked, she hurried downstairs, not wanting a forgotten client to be left standing on the porch.

"Wonder who that is?" Zach said, coming after her.

As she entered the waiting room, she could see Joanne's face in the back door window. Stopping a few feet behind Cassidy, Zach leaned his shoulder against the oak room divider.

"Hi Joanne," Cassidy said, stepping back to let her client come in. "What's up?"

She studied Joanne's face, checking for signs of distress. Her client appeared a trifle embarrassed but otherwise okay. Her large, almond-shaped eyes were clear, her makeup perfectly applied, her short dark hair smoothly in place.

"Hey Cassidy." She ducked her head. "Sorry to bother you. I was here in Oak Park visiting my mother and I realized my checkbook was missing. The last time I used it was when I paid you yesterday."

The phone rang; they let it go on the machine.

"I didn't see your checkbook but it's possible it slipped down between the cushions." Cassidy started into her office expecting Joanne to follow. Instead, her client approached Zach. "Hey, I was meaning to ask. Do you still play the guitar?"

"I gave it up when I got serious about earning a living."

"That's too bad. I told my brother I'd seen you and he said you had a lot of talent."

What's going on here? Cassidy stood in her office doorway to observe.

Zach retorted, "Your brother was in high school at the time so what would he know?"

She tilted her head and said in a suggestive tone, "I bet you *do* have talent."

Taking a half step back, he folded his arms across his chest. "Sure, but it's for tracking down stories, not twanging a guitar."

Shifting her gaze to Cassidy, Joanne said, "You're probably better off married to a reporter than a musician, anyway."

She's overstepping boundaries all over the place.

"Joanne, why don't you come in here so we can look for your checkbook." Cassidy spoke firmly, making it clear that Joanne did not have permission to chat up either her therapist or her therapist's husband.

They found the checkbook and Joanne went on her way.

When Cassidy returned to the kitchen, Zach stood, his back against the counter, waiting for her.

"Was she flirting with me?"

"I'd say she was."

He shook his head. "Why would your client flirt with me right in front of you?"

If I explain, am I breaking confidentiality? Should be okay as long as I don't reveal any specifics. "She's mad at me. I didn't handle our last session very well. Now for her to show it by making a play for you is pretty immature, but then her lack of emotional development is one of the main reasons she needs to be in therapy."

"When something like this happens, do you talk about it in a session?"

"I'll have to bring it up the next time I see her." Cassidy sighed. "From time to time clients get mad at their therapist and then the therapist has to process the anger. It's always hard. I really have to work at not getting defensive."

He gazed at her, his brow creased, eyes narrowed. She knew that look. It meant he was trying to make sense out of some behavior he didn't understand.

"You don't seem jealous or anything."

"Why would I be jealous? You backed off and crossed your arms. It's not what the woman does, it's what you do. Women could be throwing themselves at you in droves and as long as you don't respond, then it's great. That would mean I have a highly desirable husband who loves only me."

"Well, you do. The second part anyway." He smiled his lazy smile. "A husband who loves only you."

Upstairs they found a message from Bryce assuring them that he was still alive. He did not mention the Friday meeting with Melissa. Cassidy wondered if that meant he was planning to blow it off. *Now that you've convinced yourself hospitalization is a bad idea, what'll you do if he calls your bluff?*

28.

Life Sentence

Leaning back against the sectional, Troy smoothed a hand over his receding hair. "Bev told me this guy she thought she was in love with turned out to be a jerk. So after living with him for eight months, she now realizes how good she had it with me."

"Eight months?" Cassidy rested her elbows on the arms of her director's chair and laced her hands in front of her. "Did she move directly from your apartment to his?" *What choice did she have, considering how much she doesn't like to work?*

Morning sunlight slanted in through the east window, backlighting Troy's head and shoulders, rendering his coarse-featured face a little indistinct. Behind the nearly bare branches of the small tree outside her office, the deep blue sky was dotted with marshmallow clouds.

Troy, his dress shirt pulling in wrinkles across his stomach, looked down at the floor. "Well, yeah, I guess she started living with him right away."

"So if you begin seeing Bev again, what do you think will happen? You think she might want to move back in with you fairly quickly?" *First time around, she had her clothes in his closet in less than three weeks.*

Troy shot Cassidy a defiant look. "Well, why not? It's not

like we have to take time getting to know each other or anything."

It's not like they ever did get to know each other. "Let's see if I remember how the scenario went. You met Bev, she promptly moved in and let you support her, then she met someone else and went to live with him. You were brokenhearted when she dumped you. And also convinced she'd just been using you all along. So . . . why would it be different this time?"

You shouldn't be so hard on him.

But I have to make him see he's on the verge of another Bev-related debacle.

Yeah, but he isn't going to listen so you might as well be nice.

He glared. "People change. I think she's learned her lesson and wouldn't do it again."

The editor of a trade journal, for god's sake. There's no way he could be as dumb as he seems.

Cassidy said in a gentle voice, "When have *you* learned from your mistakes?"

"I have. Plenty of times." His round face twisted into a frown. "Why couldn't it simply be that this other guy swept her off her feet and now she understands I'm the one for her?"

Optimism is not always a good thing.

"I just want this so bad," Troy continued, gazing downward. "I want to rewind the tape, go back to the beginning, and have it come out right this time." He looked up at Cassidy, his blue eyes tinged with sadness. "I don't understand why this is so hard. Other people just fall in love and get married. It's no big deal."

No big deal? You and Zach had to practically turn yourselves inside out to make it work. In fact, most of the people you know had to change themselves before they could succeed in a relationship.

"Look at you," Troy added. "Here you are, happily married, sailing along. You make it look easy."

She suddenly went tense. "What makes you say that?"

"Oh, I don't know. Things you've said."

"I don't believe I've discussed my marriage." *There's no way I'd rave about my wonderful marriage to a client who can't get a second date.*

He gazed at her innocently. "Maybe it's just the way you talk about relationships. You always sound so sure of yourself. I don't see how anybody who isn't happily married themselves could be so confident."

She straightened the tissue box, squaring it up with the corner of the wicker table. "So you're going to start up with Bev again. Given that you've already made up your mind, I wonder why you thought you needed to see me."

"When I called last night, I hadn't decided yet. But now I realize I can't just walk away from this." He glanced out the north window, then down at the floor. "I know you don't agree with me, but I really think it's going to work this time." He cleared his throat. "And since the reason I started therapy was to get into a relationship, and now I am in one, I guess I don't need to continue."

"Well, Troy, I certainly wish you the best of luck."

She felt a certain relief that he was terminating. *Working with people who want you to solve their problems but refuse to change makes you feel useless. And guilty for taking their money.*

Cassidy spent the rest of the hour processing the work they'd done and saying good-bye. Then Troy handed her a check and they started toward the door.

That comment about you being happily married was pretty weird. And don't forget, he's the client you lent the How To Survive *book to.*

She was fairly certain he'd returned it but wanted to see how he'd react to her bringing it up. "Oh, by the way, did you ever return that book I lent you?"

"What book?"

"*How To Survive the Loss of Love.*"

He squinted in thought. "That's funny. I don't remember anything about it. Maybe it was somebody else you loaned it to."

She closed the door behind him, wondering if his marriage comment and his memory loss meant anything. She wished she could tell Zach about it, but a couple of anomalies did not a killer make. *You can't go blabbing confidential information every time a whiff of suspicion passes under your nose.*

Standing in front of the kitchen window, she ate a peanut butter cup and thought about the day ahead. *Friday, no more clients until tomorrow.* Zach had announced earlier that he intended to attach a mirror to a stick for inspecting the underside of the Toyota, then spend the afternoon working from home. Some time after three, Bryce was due to meet Melissa at their house to discuss the teen grief group.

In front of her, the Steins' window, with its fringe of lace curtain at the top, opened onto a cheery red and white room devoid of people. By three, it would be teaming with adolescent bodies.

So what's the best use of my time?

Well, obviously, all the things you haven't done while futilely and uselessly chasing your psycho E-Stalker. The laundry. A trip to the store to restock your empty refrigerator. Housecleaning. Maybe even finish the damn forms.

But start by calling Gran. You need to let her know you talked to Cindy and she sent you straight into the arms of a dead body.

Although maybe not the first body, an uneasy voice whispered. *Charles didn't spontaneously combust or get abducted by aliens. He's out there too, waiting for someone to find him. Or what's left of him.*

Not wanting to think about that, she went upstairs and called from her desk phone. Leaving out the part about the dynamite, she brought her grandmother up to date, making it sound as if discovering Howard's body was no big deal, nothing to hyperventilate over.

"Finding Howard—that's a good thing, isn't it? Shouldn't they be able to track down the woman who's behind it through his phone records or email?"

"I hope so." *But you don't expect it. So far she's been too slick to leave any trace of herself.* "Let's talk about something else. Tell me what you've been up to so I can get my mind off the case."

Gran cackled. "You should see my latest project. It's a doozy. I've been building myself a bird feeder."

Cassidy grinned. "What brought that on?"

"My neighbors hung one in their tree last summer and I just had a ball watching it. Sometimes those bushy-tailed old squirrels'd climb all over it and try to wriggle down inside to get the food. Then, when the squirrels went away, this flock of birds'd come, and they'd fly back and forth between the feeder and the ground. It was more fun than a TV nature show 'cause I didn't have to watch any cute little critters get eaten. So I decided I had to have one of my own."

"But why build it?"

"'Cause I got too much time on my hands. 'Cause I'm an old lady and I can do whatever I want. Mostly 'cause I never tried my hand at carpentry and I wanted to see if I could do it."

"Well, can you?"

"Hah! First of all, the nails were so small I could barely see 'em. And then when it came to hitting things with a hammer, boy am I good at mashing my thumbs. If you saw it, you'd think it was made by a one-armed drunk."

Cassidy laughed. "But you're going to put it up anyway, aren't you?"

"'Course I am. The birds won't care. And anybody who sees it will think it's cute that a little old lady made her own bird feeder. That's the great thing about being old. Now that I'm over eighty, I get credit for just getting out of bed. You wait till you're my age. You'll love it."

Picking up a small onyx cat figurine, Cassidy rubbed the smooth surface with her thumb. "Way my life is going, I'm not sure I'll make it to forty."

"Sure you will. I can just see you and Zach now. Two white-haired, scrunched-up little old people out solving mysteries and giving the cops a hard time. And I'll be sitting up there on a cloud, pulling strings to make sure everything comes out right."

"Gran, you're so good for me. I always feel better when I talk to you."

"Then you should do it more often."

At two-thirty Cassidy was cleaning the upstairs bathroom and feeling quite virtuous about it when Zach came to lean against the doorjamb.

"I'm going to drive over to Bryce's and haul his ass back here just to make sure he doesn't stand Melissa up."

"That's a great idea." Cassidy sat down on the bathtub rim. "You want to come with?"

Picking up Bryce beats scrubbing toilets like a bag of Reese's beats overcooked cabbage.

Yes, but you can't go. This needs to be a father-son gig with no social worker-stepmom getting in the middle.

"I think it'd be better for you and Bryce to have some time alone."

"He's probably going to sulk all the way here."

She tilted her head, considering what Bryce's reaction would be. "He may pretend to sulk, but deep down inside he'll be secretly glad to have his father make him do what's best."

"Yeah, but he'll act like I'm a royal pain."

"And you'll do it anyway." She sent Zach a warm smile. "Isn't that what parenthood's all about?"

He frowned. "I never could figure out why anybody'd want to be one."

29.

A Mass Hypnosis Illusion

Forty minutes later she heard the back doorbell, the signal Zach used to let her know he was home. She reached the bottom of the stairs at the same time Zach and Bryce were coming through the archway into the living room.

Standing in front of her, Bryce rested his hands on his belt and lowered his brow. "This is a huge waste of time," he grumbled. "Talking to that girl, making me go to some stupid group. It's not going to work. So what if I don't like college? You should just leave me alone."

Leave you alone and let you blow your brains out?

"You better hope it works. If it doesn't, Zach and I will personally escort you to a psychiatrist. Every week if necessary."

"So how're we going to do this?" Zach queried.

"I'll call Melissa and ask her to come over. After she gets here, you and I can wait upstairs till they're done."

A few minutes later Cassidy led the pretty teenager into the living room. Bryce looked her up and down, the defiance on his face gradually shifting into an expression that appeared almost welcoming.

"Hey," he stood to greet her, "I'm Bryce."

It was more than an hour later when Cassidy heard Bryce's footsteps on the stairs. She went out into the hall, where the boy stood looking into the computer room at Zach.

Bryce said in a neutral tone, "Okay, I'll go."

"That's it?" Cassidy said. "Just 'I'll go?'"

"What else do you want?"

"How 'bout—Melissa's pretty cool. It's really terrific I'm going to be in a group with her. In fact, the more I think about it, the more the group seems like a totally awesome idea."

Zach laughed.

Catching his father's eye, Bryce said amiably, "You never know what's going to come out of her mouth, do you?"

Zach smiled at his son. "That's half her charm."

Shortly after Zach returned from taking Bryce home, the phone rang. Cassidy picked up at her desk.

"You the lady wanted Teddy Wilson's address?"

She acknowledged that she was.

"The wife had it just like I thought," the bar owner's voice said, reeling off a north Chicago address and phone number.

Cassidy wrote it on a pad, then dashed down to the basement where Zach was sorting through a box of paintbrushes. "I thought as long as we're staying in tonight, I'd get back to work on the extra bedroom."

She told him about the phone call. "This cannot possibly be where the real Teddy Wilson lives. There's no way Barbara's boyfriend is going to turn out to be a flesh and blood person. He's got to be some sort of mass-hypnosis illusion."

"We'll find out soon enough."

Wilson's address led them to a townhouse in a congested northside neighborhood, which meant they had to park several blocks away. Cassidy was uneasy about leaving the Toyota on the street, but Zach assured her that, with the mirror on a stick and a flashlight, he'd be able to tell if anyone had tampered with the car.

They hiked back to the townhouse, then stopped on the sidewalk to look through a picture window into an elegant, softly lit room. Standing on display on the other side of the glass was a large metal sculpture that vaguely resembled the Sphinx.

"This is not what I expected," Cassidy said, shaking her head. "How did Teddy Wilson go from The Bulldog Inn to a pricey Chicago townhouse?"

"Let's ask him," Zach replied, approaching the street-level door. The man who opened it was slim and wiry, with a long face, high forehead, and prominent features. His skin was the color of mahogany.

Cassidy drew in a breath. *Guess who's coming to dinner? Is this Amanda's secret—her daughter wanted to marry a black man? But Barbara died in the eighties, not the fifties.*

"Are you Ted Wilson?" Zach put one foot in front of the other, letting his body go loose.

"What's this in regard to?" the man responded in a soft voice.

Cassidy took a half step forward. "I was a friend of Barbara Segel."

Wilson's head reared back; his eyes widened in surprise. "Barbara Segel? I haven't thought of her in years. What does this have to do with me?"

"Ted?" A slim Asian woman in a long skirt and jacket came

up behind him. "What's this about?"

"Do you remember me telling you about a girl I was involved with before I met you? This woman," he nodded at Cassidy, "claims to be her friend. But so far I have no idea why they're here."

The Asian woman stared at her.

"The reason I'm here is, I'm trying to make sense out of the circumstances surrounding Barbara's death."

"She's dead?" Deep ridges appeared on Wilson's forehead. "When did that happen?"

This guy's play-acting, right? He can't possibly not know.

The woman put her hand on Wilson's arm. "Are you all right?"

Supportive partner right by his side. This does not fit the picture of a man pining for his lost love.

"I'm just surprised to hear it. But Barbara's ancient history. This has nothing to do with me."

"Well," the woman said, "I'm supremely curious to find out what this is about, but I'm already late for the opening." She stood on tiptoes to kiss his cheek. "However, I know I can count on you to fill me in on every single word when I get home." Turning, she disappeared behind him.

Zach said, "You didn't know about the car crash? It was exactly fifteen years ago. We were under the impression you and Barbara were planning to marry at the time."

"Oh my god." Wilson's face registered shock. "Oh my god."

"Can we come in?" Cassidy asked.

He led them into the living room. Dropping onto a sectional, he briefly buried his face in his hands. Zach shook his head at Cassidy, signaling that he didn't think Wilson was their man. She nodded in agreement. They sat across from him on the sectional, a built-in platform that curved around the north-west corner of the room. Circles were a dominant theme in the open, high-ceilinged space. In front of the sectional stood a round, brushed-chrome coffee table with a jagged metal sculpture on top. To their right a circular desktop floated above a carpeted base.

Art was everywhere. Cassidy counted four other pieces of metal sculpture: the large sphinx in front of the window; a flame-shaped piece at the opposite end of the sectional; a sail-shaped piece in the far corner; and an elongated human figure near the entryway. In addition to the sculpture, large abstract paintings and smaller framed textiles hung on every wall.

Wilson straightened his shoulders and gazed at Cassidy. "I'm sorry, I don't know why this hit me so hard. I love my wife. My feelings for Barbara are long gone. It's just that . . ." He shook his head, a dazed expression coming over his face. "God, I can't reorient. All these years I assumed the reason I never heard back from her was that she decided to dump me, and now you're saying she died and I never knew it." He paused, then continued in a grim voice. "There I was, crying in my beer, feeling sorry for myself, and Barbara was dead."

"You sent her a letter." Cassidy touched her fingers to her jaw. "Is that right?"

"Look, I don't mind talking about it. It *is* ancient history. But I don't have a clue why you're asking these questions."

Cassidy looked at Zach. "Should I?"

"Might as well."

She told Wilson about the threats against Zach and the mission she was on to piece together the events leading to Barbara's death.

"Something happened to Barbara in January of her senior year. Something that changed her. Do you know what it was?"

"I may be the only person she ever told." Wilson leaned forward, resting his forearms on his legs. "She made me swear never to say a word to anyone."

Putting her hands together in her lap, Cassidy bit her bottom lip. *Do you really need to hear this? Is there any reasonable justification for getting him to break his promise to your dead friend? Maybe not, but I can't stand not knowing.*

"I wouldn't ask you to disclose Barbara's secret if the end of her life weren't having such a terrible impact on mine. I'm so scared this person who hates me will kill my husband." Zach took her hand in his. "I realize that what happened to Barbara in college probably has nothing to do with what's happening now. But I need to know."

"Well . . . as long as Barbara's dead, I guess it doesn't matter." Leaning back against the cushion, he gave Cassidy an appraising look, then started to talk. "Barbara told me that before we met, she used to be a real flirt. I never saw it, but I'm sure she was."

Zach nodded. "We've heard the same thing from several people."

"From the way she described it, I'd guess it was the thrill of the chase she got off on more than anything. She'd get some guy to like her, then lose interest and go after somebody else." He stroked his chin. "I never saw her in action, but I didn't get the sense of her being predatory or anything. Just young and flighty."

Cassidy smiled sadly. "A kid in a candy store. I don't think she ever meant to hurt anybody." *Certainly didn't mean to hurt me.* "She just never thought about consequences."

"So anyway," Wilson ran a hand over the top of his head, "this thing that happened. It started with her getting a crush on this frat guy. And the fact that he was hot and heavy with one of her friends didn't slow her down at all. So one night she went to a party and it turned out the girlfriend was home sick and the guy was there without her."

"And Barbara probably flirted up a storm."

"She got a little drunk and went too far. Kept coming on to the guy, trying to kiss him, groping him all over until finally he said, 'Okay, if you want it so much, I'll give it to you,' and he just took her right there on the living room floor in front of all her friends." Wilson's eyes misted over. Blinking rapidly, he looked down at his hands. "She tried to stop him, tried to push him off, but she was too drunk. The others watched, some of them cheered him on, some turned away. Then he just left her lying there on the floor with her skirt up and her underpants off." Wilson wiped the corner of his eye.

"Oh god!" Cassidy pressed her fingers around the base of her throat.

"What a shit!" Zach said.

"Yeah, that's what I thought."

Cassidy shook her head. "So that's why her sorority sisters won't say anything."

"I don't imagine anybody's too proud of themselves. When Barbara talked about it to me, I couldn't tell who she hated more—herself or her so-called friends."

"And then she started coming to your bar," Cassidy said. "I suppose she just wanted some place to go where she wouldn't run into anybody she knew."

"The guys there were pretty decent. She made it clear she didn't want to be bothered and they left her alone."

"So she started coming to the bar," Cassidy said, "and then what happened?"

"One night I was standing beside her and she just started talking to me." He rubbed his eyes with his fingertips, then stared into space. "Not flirting or anything, just simple conversation. I think she must've been lonely. So I talked back. But I didn't hit on her or try to buy her drinks. Here she was, this gorgeous white college girl, way out of reach for a black factory worker like me. I had aspirations. I knew I wanted to do metal sculpture. But at that point, I didn't expect to have any money in the near future."

Zach said, "And then you fell in love."

"Not right away. We took it real slow. After we finally started sleeping together, she said that what had attracted her most was how comfortable I was to be with."

Can see how it happened. Teddy was a safe harbor for a bruised and battered Barbara.

"So then after college, the reason she kept you in the closet was because you were poor and black?"

"Not just poor—a factory worker who spent his off-hours playing with a blowtorch. Barbara's mother didn't want her to marry anybody. Can you imagine how she would've reacted if Barbara'd given her any more than the bare-bones information about her boyfriend in Champaign?"

Poor Barbara—torn between needing to live her own life and wanting to keep her mother happy. Cassidy gazed at a large, abstract painting on the wall above the floating desk. Lit from below, the painting had considerable white space broken by thick swirls of black and red.

Cassidy met the sculptor's eyes. "The night she died her mother'd opened a letter addressed to Barbara and they had a big fight about it. I assume the letter was from you."

"So it was my letter that set everything off." He stood and paced, punching his right fist into his left hand. "Barbara'd come down to stay with me the weekend before, and a friend of mine had taken a picture of us together. While she was in Champaign, she told me she wanted to elope as soon as possible.

A couple of days later, I wrote her a letter saying I'd come to Oak Park and pick her up on a certain date, and I included the snapshot." Sitting down again, he let out a heavy sigh. "When she didn't get back to me, I assumed it meant she didn't have the guts to go through with it. And I didn't call because I didn't want to hear her say that she was dumping me."

Cassidy closed her eyes briefly. "There were so many of us that played a part in it. You, her mother, her father for abdicating, Kevin, me." *But mostly it was Barbara. Barbara, who never paid attention to consequences.*

"Well," Wilson said, "that's the story."

"Thanks for telling me. I'm not sure why it matters so much, but I always need to understand things before I can be done with them."

Wilson gave her a sardonic smile. "I'm not sure *I* feel any better. But at least now I know she didn't just walk away."

30.

A Loud Obnoxious Bar

After closely inspecting the Toyota, Zach got inside and turned on the ignition. As soon as it was running, Cassidy left the spot where he'd told her to stand and joined him in the car.

"One more dead end," he said, pressing the pedal a little harder than necessary. "It's been two days since Charles got in my car and drove off into nowhere. Do you realize how spooky that is? Why the hell can't the police find the Nissan? Or uncover a link between Howard and some other screwball woman?"

Cassidy heard the tension in his voice. *Usually so unflappable. You tend to forget–even Zach has his limits.*

She turned toward him. "You feeling guilty about Charles?"

"I'm not big on guilt." He drove another half block. "I just wish to hell I hadn't given him the keys. Or that I'd offered to drive. This shouldn't've happened. I should've done something different."

Sounds like guilt to me.

Reflecting on how often she'd seen people take responsibility for things that were not their fault, she had a sudden realization about herself.

"You know something? I don't feel guilty about Barbara's death anymore."

"Never was any reason for it."

"Yeah, but people like me who received early guilt-training don't need much of a reason. We just figure that whenever bad things happen, it must be our fault."

"So how did you get over it?"

"By telling my story over and over. That's why talking is so good for people. It enables them to put things in perspective." She paused. "I wish you'd do more of it."

"Isn't that what I just did?"

Cassidy, her mind still fuzzy from sleep, sat up in bed watching the back of Zach's terrycloth-clad body leave the room as he headed downstairs on his coffee mission. Her gaze drifted to the north window. A dull morning light, twisted branches, the remnants of scrappy leaves. *Tuesday Zach's drink was drugged. Wednesday Charles disappeared. Thursday we found Howie. Friday our nemesis took the day off. So what's next on her agenda? When and from what direction?*

Zach came into the room and stood near the bed, his face tightly drawn. "The Nissan's here," he said in a gentle voice. "It's parked out front."

"Oh shit." She pressed an outspread hand against her throat.

Zach picked up the portable phone from his desk, stood looking down at the car from the west window, and talked to the 911 operator. Clicking off, he threw his robe on the bed and hastily dressed in his black tee and jeans. "I'm going to go look inside the car."

"You think Charles is in it?" *Not Charles, his body.* Jumping out of bed, she grabbed up her own clothes. "You can't touch the car. It could be wired to explode."

"I'm just going to check out the interior." He started to leave, then turned. "Cass, if there's a body in the back seat, you don't need to see it."

Her mouth went dry at the thought of looking in the car. "I'll let you go first. If he's in there, you can tell me."

Zach nodded and left. Putting on her tennis shoes, she followed him outside into the chilly air.

"It's okay," he called from where he stood a couple of feet behind the car.

She went to stand beside him. They both stared at the trunk. "In there?"

"That's my guess."

A green and white squad skidded around the corner to park behind the Nissan, closely followed by two more beat cars. Three officers congregated around them.

"We have to be careful," Zach said. "There might be a car bomb."

Two of the cops stepped away from the Nissan. The third, a sturdy young woman with broad features and a shiny brown pageboy, introduced herself as Officer Perry and took out her pad.

When Zach finished explaining, she radioed the information in, then said she'd been instructed to rope off the area. As they waited for the sawhorses, neighbors began coming out of their houses, only to be sent back inside by the police. After a truck dropped off the sawhorses, the uniforms began setting them up about twenty feet in front and in back of the car, with yellow tape along both sides. Shivering from the cold, Cassidy fetched jackets for herself and Zach. Shortly after that, a sergeant, Detective Wharton, and a second detective arrived, followed minutes later by two men from the Cook County Bomb Squad. Cassidy and Zach, along with the cops, waited at a considerable distance behind the Nissan while the bomb experts went over the car. An hour later, one of the men told the detectives that the car had checked out as safe and they were ready to open the trunk.

Zach said to Cassidy, "I'm going to stand here and watch. Why don't you go someplace else?"

Not a single part of her felt any urge to argue. She went to wait near the porch steps, her arms folded tightly across her chest.

Zach handed a bomb squad guy his key. The cops crowded up against the sawhorses to the rear of the Nissan as the explosions expert approached the trunk. Cassidy held her breath. The cops fell silent.

He has to stay right there and act like it doesn't bother him even though he's going to be sick about it. Real men can't not look.

The bomb expert popped the trunk, then waved at the men to come closer. Zach and the cops gathered around the open trunk. Some of the officers leaned forward. A young beat cop stumbled back to his car. Zach stood rigidly still.

"Looks like we found your friend," Wharton said.

"Gonna need a lot of aerosol and bleach before you haul groceries in there again," one of the uniforms said, eliciting nervous laughter from the other cops.

Zach came over and stared at her, his face pale and stony. He reached out his arms, she went into them, and they held onto each other for a moment.

Stepping back, he ran a hand over his face. "If only I hadn't given him the fucking key."

"Shot?"

"Two or three times in the head."

Closing her eyes, she pictured how it might have happened. "It was raining really hard that night. The E-Stalker probably followed Charles to the pharmacy, waited till he came out, and had a gun in his face before she ever realized it wasn't you."

"And when she did realize, she didn't want to leave a witness. So she forced him into the trunk and shot him."

Wharton joined them. "We're going to have to take you two down to the station."

Cassidy gritted her teeth. *I can't stand this. Another day of sitting in that awful little room, going over every little detail again and again, then having Wharton act like we're the psychos because somebody keeps putting dead bodies in our path.*

At two P.M. a beat cop drove them to the house. The body had been taken to the morgue and the Nissan towed into the station so the evidence technician could go over every inch of it. Wharton had grilled Cassidy for more than an hour even though she had nothing new to tell him.

Hanging her jacket in the room-divider closet, she said to Zach, "I can't believe Wharton still thinks of us as suspects."

"You and I are right at the center of the storm. We're the only ones with some connection to everybody. He can't dismiss the possibility that we cooked up this whole deal for the purpose of whacking those two dead guys."

"That's absurd."

"But that's at least one of the lines he's pursuing." Zach glanced at her, then away. "I've gotta get out of here. I'm starting to feel all caged up."

"That didn't sound like an invitation."

"I know I said I haven't needed to be alone in a long time, but now I think I do." He tucked his hands into his back pockets. "Would you mind staying home by yourself for a few hours?"

"I certainly would mind. I've got this crazy notion that if I stick like glue to your side I can keep you safe. But since I know that's just magical thinking, I won't try to stop you." She rubbed her garnet ring. "Any place in particular you plan to go?"

"Thought I'd start car shopping. The Nissan doesn't appeal to me much anymore."

Zach left and Cassidy got out a bag of Reese's. As she stood in front of the window munching chocolate, she heard the sound of the cat-door. A moment later Starshine sauntered into the room, no small creatures in her mouth, and jumped onto the counter. Cassidy spooned smelly food into her bowl.

The calico finished eating, then started licking her front paw.

Standing a couple of feet back from the counter, Cassidy hooked her thumbs into her waistband. "How can you just sit there and be so tranquil when I'm going nuts?" She shifted her weight. "The helplessness is the worst of it. Zach's right to go car shopping. Anything'd be better than hanging around the house obsessing."

Starshine twisted her ears back, as if not wanting to be bothered with Cassidy's problems. Bending forward, she washed the base of her tail.

"This is like a serenity-prayer test. The second part—the courage to change the things I can—that's where I excel. When there's anything I can dig into and *change*, I'm happy as a Starshine in catnip."

The calico gazed at Cassidy with indifference, her green eyes turning to slits.

"But the first part—the serenity to accept the things I can't change—that's where I always fail. What am I supposed to do? Just sit back and be serene while our E-Stalker makes one attempt after another to kill my husband? Just wait around until she finally gets it right?"

Starshine rose and picked her way along the edge of the sink to the other side of the counter, where she found the large blue bowl Cassidy had used for fruit and failed to put away. The cat delicately sniffed the bowl's rim, then stepped inside, curled into a ball, and fell asleep.

"Cats, on the other hand, could pass any serenity-prayer test with flying colors. When they want something changed, they just keep at it till they get their way. And when there's nothing to do, they stare at the wall or fall asleep." She sighed. "Why can't I be more like a cat?"

Two hours later she was at work at her desk when she heard Zach's footsteps.

"Did you buy a car?" she asked as he came into the bedroom.

"No, but I made dinner reservations." His voice was slightly defensive, a tone she seldom heard from him. "Mac the Knife's at seven."

Mac's was always packed and rowdy on a Saturday night, with music so loud it was painful to her eardrums. The kind of place she hated. The kind Zach had spent half his life in before he started parking in her garage.

Regressing. Well, of course he is. That's what people do when life gets to be too much.

"Okay, we'll eat at Mac's."

31.

The E-Stalker

Mac's was situated about a mile west of the village on Madison Street, a major east-west thoroughfare. They left the Toyota under a streetlight across from the bar, a location uninviting to car bombers.

She's probably given up on that plan by now and moved on to something even more nefarious. Makes me nervous she hasn't tried anything since Wednesday. What's worse? When she's actively attempting to kill Zach or when she isn't?

The instant Cassidy stepped inside the dark restaurant, she was bombarded by assaulting music, loud voices, bodies crowding in on all sides. Anxiety twitches started in her stomach. *This may be what Zach needs but it's exactly the wrong place for me.*

The host seated them at a table next to the window, which afforded them a view of the Toyota. The room was square, a bar in the center of the opposite wall, tables jammed together. Directly behind Cassidy an overweight man with a booming voice carped about his boss.

Zach, wearing a blue jacket over his black tee, leaned across the table and said, "I'm going to order a couple of drinks before dinner. If you're hungry, you can get an appetizer."

She scowled. "What's going on? You never have drinks

before dinner. We always just order wine."

"It's been a rough week. I want something stronger tonight."

Cassidy's mouth clamped in irritation. She didn't want to spend one minute longer than necessary in this noisy place. She was never happy when Zach exceeded his usual daily quota of alcohol, and she especially wasn't happy now, when someone was out to kill him.

A young woman with short red hair, dark penciled brows, and bright lipstick asked for their drink orders. Zach requested bourbon, Cassidy a Coke. A few minutes later glasses were placed in front of them.

Zach laid his left arm on the table, angled his body toward the room, and drank his way steadily through two bourbons, then asked for a third. Cassidy gritted her teeth and fidgeted in her chair, her anxiety level rising faster than the alcohol in Zach's bloodstream. She heard his voice in her head: *And when my denial breaks down, I'm liable to drink myself stupid at a time when I absolutely need to be clear-headed.*

She stared out the window in an effort to distract herself. A minivan with a caved-in passenger door pulled up in front of a fireplug. Three young guys walked past, the one in the middle giving his buddy a shove toward the street. A white sedan parked behind the Toyota, but she couldn't see the person who got out.

Glancing at Zach, she saw that he was holding up his empty glass and scanning for the waitress.

Cassidy grabbed his arm. "You're not ordering another!"

"One more," he said evenly. "That'll get me where I want to be." His voice wasn't slurred. She knew well enough that he could hold large quantities of alcohol without showing it.

"Don't you dare!" She pounded her fist on the table. "I've

been sitting in this miserable place for over an hour while you guzzled three bourbons. I think that ought to be enough for one night."

"Are you telling me how many drinks I can have?"

"I understand you feel terrible about Charles. So do I. But drinking is not considered a high-level coping device."

He regarded her coldly. "You know, the times I like you least are when you put on your therapist hat and start lecturing me."

She turned her head sharply away. *What a nasty thing to say. Yeah, but you have to admit, you do get a little preachy sometimes.* Forcing herself to take a deep breath, she put her hand on his arm again. "Zach, please, let's just eat and get out of here. If you have to drink, do it at home where it's safe."

He removed her hand. "You'd still be pissed. You always get pissed."

"You're right. I don't like to see you using booze to avoid feelings. But home would be better than here."

"I don't want to sit at home. I need people and noise and distraction."

"Well, I don't. I hate this place."

"Then you go home. You can take the Toyota. I'll catch a cab later. I'd rather not have you sitting across the table glaring at me anyway."

Damn him. How can he even think of such a thing. "You can't imagine I'd leave you in a place like this, can you? Half smashed with that woman out to get you?"

He sat straight and looked her in the eye. "I'm not half anything. I just need to unwind."

"What about what I need? I need for you to get some food in your stomach and sober up, then come on home with me."

Sober up? What are you talking about? You know he isn't any-

where near drunk. You've blown this whole thing out of proportion just because you're so edgy and anxious to get out of here.

Gazing into Zach's rigidly angry face, she reached across the table one more time and folded her hand over his. "I'm sorry. I shouldn't have said any of those things. I'm going to go spend some time in the bathroom and calm myself down."

Slinging her bag over her shoulder, she went into the restroom at the far end of the building. Two young women stood in front of the mirror, one in a neon orange crop top, the other in a miniskirt that barely covered her crotch. The woman in orange took an odd contraption out of her purse and applied it to her mascaraed lashes. The other woman freshened her lipstick and talked nonstop about the guy who was buying her drinks.

Cassidy felt an urge to warn her about the danger of accepting drinks from strangers but realized this woman probably wouldn't appreciate being lectured at any more than Zach.

After spending some time in a stall, Cassidy came out to find the women gone. Staring at her reflection, she noted the tight lines at the corners of her mouth, the weariness in her eyes.

You and Zach both getting close to the edge. And you jumped on him because of it. Demanding that he not have another drink—what a stupid thing to do. When you ask nicely, he often obliges. But you know good and well he doesn't take any more kindly to order-giving than you do.

She washed her hands and fluffed her thick, untrimmed hair. When the jittery feeling in her stomach finally subsided, she left the restroom and threaded her way toward the window.

She was about ten feet from where they'd been sitting when she got her first clear view of the table. She jerked to a stop. Zach wasn't there.

Where is he? The bathroom? Or did our blonde nutcase vaporize him?

Hurrying to the window, Cassidy stared out at the street. The Toyota was gone.

Oh my god! She must have stuck a pistol in his ribs and marched him out at gunpoint! Then she took the Toyota so I'd be stranded!

Noise jumbled Cassidy's brain waves. She pressed the fingertips of both hands to her temples in an effort to focus. One frantic thought raced in her head: *She's going to do it. She's really going to kill him.*

Needing to get away from the uproar, Cassidy put on her jacket and started toward the door, then remembered the drinks. *No idea how much three bourbons and a Coke cost.* She dropped a twenty on the table and dashed out onto the sidewalk.

The air was sharp. Clutching the neck of her jacket, she paced in front of the tinted glass window adorned with cursive gold letters, MAC THE KNIFE, at the top.

Call the cops? She absolutely didn't want to. They would stick her in that tiny room and make her tell her story ten times over while nobody did anything. The police had totally failed them up to now. And once Wharton got his hands on her, she'd be sidelined. Taken out of the game. No longer free to figure out who the killer was and go find Zach.

Yeah, but you've been thrashing around all week and don't know anything. The police have resources you don't. They could put out an APB and have cops all over the state searching for the Toyota.

She strode past the restaurant entrance, reached the end of the building, turned on her heel and retraced her steps. A homeless man pushing a shopping cart shuffled along in the opposite direction.

What am I missing? A blond woman. Amanda or Lany. I

could call both of them, see if they're home. Either one is at her house, she couldn't have been here five minutes ago snatching Zach.

Removing her phone and the sheet of telephone numbers from her bag, she dialed Lany. The machine came on. *So Lany's still in the running.*

She gulped air through her mouth, then punched up the second number. Amanda answered. Cassidy suddenly remembered the older woman's reaction at hearing about the threats against Zach. *She knows something. You have to make her tell you.*

"This is Cassidy." Her scalp tingled. Needles prickled in her chest. "Zach's been kidnapped! I don't know what to do! The person who's got Zach—they're going to kill him. I have to find him right away! Please, Amanda, you've got to help me." Her mouth was dry, her voice scratchy and weak. "Don't let another person die because of Barbara!"

A long silence. Finally Amanda said, "I don't know what to do."

"Do what's right."

She sighed. "This may not mean anything. It probably doesn't. But after I left Oak Park, Pete got in trouble for sending an email threat to a computer teacher at the high school."

"Pete?" Cassidy blinked. "Email? Back then?"

"The father of the family Pete was staying with was a teacher at IIT. He let Pete and his son go online at the university."

"Amanda, thank you so much."

"But I'm sure it's just a coincidence. Pete wouldn't send email threats now. He'd never do anything to hurt anybody."

You didn't think so either. She thanked Amanda again and clicked off. *Coincidence? Not hardly. Not when Pete's one of our four main suspects.*

But Tess said he was such a good kid. Why would a good kid send an email threat? Maybe because his borderline sister had a grudge against the teacher and talked him into it. And maybe that's what's happening now. Lany got Pete to send the e-cards, then she took it from there. He might not even know about the kidnapping.

And if he doesn't know, if he's not involved, it could be he really wouldn't want to see his sister commit murder.

She dialed Pete's number.

"Cassidy . . ." His voice wary. "What can I do for you?"

She told him about Zach's disappearance. "I think you sent the e-cards and Lany's the kidnapper. Did you know what she was up to? Are you aware that she's made two previous attempts on Zach's life?" *Don't tell him about Charles or Howard. Let him think he can stop her before she kills anyone.*

"You can't be certain anybody took Zach. Maybe he just got pissed and left."

"I know Zach. He didn't walk out of there on his own."

"I don't believe you. You're making this up to get me to talk."

"Shall I send an Oak Park police detective to your door to explain that the kidnapping's real?"

"Have you notified the police yet?"

"That's my next call."

A moment of silence. "If you don't tell the cops, I think I can help—if the kidnapping's real, which I still don't believe it is."

"What are you offering?"

A black Camaro stopped in front of the restaurant door and started honking. Cassidy put her left hand over her ear and hurried away from the noise.

"If she really does have him, I think I know where she'd go. I'll drive out there and get her to release him."

Oh god. Pete knows where Zach is. I'll be able to find him.
Cassidy said, "You have to take me with you."

"That wouldn't work. She'd go crazy if she saw you there. I'd never be able to handle her."

"Pete, you have two options. You can take me to where Zach is, or I'll tell the cops you know and they'll come get it out of you." *Which'd probably be the best choice. But not the one he's going to pick. Or I would either.*

"Shit! This is a mistake. I know it is." A long pause. "Okay, tell me where you are and I'll come pick you up."

She gave him the address. "How long till you get here?"

"About half an hour."

Twenty-five minutes later she called Detective Wharton, told him about the kidnapping, and asked him to put out an APB on the Toyota. He said he'd meet her at the restaurant. She told him she'd received a better offer. He threatened to take out a warrant on her for obstruction of justice. She didn't believe him.

Pete, his large frame filling the driver's seat of his SUV, pulled up at the corner and she climbed into the car.

He looked over at her, his broad face haggard. "You better buckle up. We've got a long ride ahead."

"Where are we going?"

"My grandmother's house. It's on the chain of lakes, a couple of hours from here. I inherited it when she died."

"What makes you think Lany'd go there?"

"She's got a key. She likes to hang out there. It's remote." He shook his head. "I can't think of any other place she could take him."

A green pickup with a tall, brightly colored child's playhouse in the bed stopped suddenly in front of them. Pete slammed on the brakes.

When they were moving again, he said, "I still think you're wrong about the kidnapping."

"Why is it so hard for you to believe?"

He glanced at her, his face embarrassed. "She's gotten me to do this before. Three or four times. But she never tried to hurt anybody. I just sent the threats and that was the end of it. So why would she do something so extreme now?"

"She's escalating. You know she's pretty disturbed?" He nodded. "People who are sick like this usually keep getting worse." *And besides, I have the honor of being at the top of her hit parade of Most Hated People.*

They drove south on Des Plaines Avenue past a McDonald's, a yellow brick apartment building, and the Forest Park police station.

"Pete, you seem like a reasonable person. It's hard for me to understand how she could get you to do something like this."

"I hate talking about it." He scowled at Cassidy. "I feel like such a sap. I mean, I can hardly believe it myself. But she'd go into these rages. She'd yell and scream and hit me. And if that didn't work, she'd stop talking to me. Besides, I always thought it was harmless. That nobody'd really get hurt."

Being scared witless and intimidated and having your privacy invaded isn't getting hurt? Denial is a truly amazing thing.

Two hours later as they were crunching along a gravel road that circled the lake, Cassidy spotted the Toyota. It was parked in front of a clapboard cottage, the backside of the house extending over the lake. Hope bubbled inside her.

"So you were right," Pete said in a flat voice. He parked his SUV beside the Toyota. "You have to stay in the car. I don't want her to know you're here."

Cassidy was frantic to get inside. *But maybe Pete would do better if I'm not there. No, can't trust him to stand up to her. She's been pulling his strings too long. Besides, Zach and I make a killer tag team.*

She leveled her gaze at Pete. "I'm not staying behind."

"She's going to have a fit."

"I don't care if she breathes flames out her mouth and blows smoke out her nostrils. All I care about is getting my husband back."

He sighed. "Okay, come on."

As she followed Pete into a wide hallway, she heard Zach's voice from some far corner. *He's alive! Oh god, he's alive!* She felt suddenly buoyant, her feet barely touching the ground. Peering ahead, she saw a stairway leading down to a softly lit room, its far wall composed of small-paned windows that overlooked the lake.

Pete, taking off ahead of her, went down into the lower level room. "My god!" he said, "this is beyond belief!"

"What are you doing here?" A woman's piercing voice. Familiar, but not Lany's.

32.

Dynamite

Cassidy emerged from the stairwell. Her mouth fell open. Hair rose on the back of her neck. Seated across from her was Joanne. She wore a low-necked, clingy white dress. Strapped to her midsection were sticks of dynamite, a black button attached to a leather harness above her left breast.

Dynamite? Fashion plate Joanne in that ugly harness? No question —she's way over the edge.

Zach, seated on a sofa against the east wall, jumped to his feet. "Shit!" he said to Cassidy. "Why couldn't you just call the police?"

Joanne, rising from a sofa perpendicular to Zach's, screamed at Pete, "What do you mean bringing her here? This isn't part of the plan."

Pete appeared to shrivel under her attack. "Oh God, what have I done?"

Cassidy raced over to throw her arms around Zach. He hugged her tightly, then stepped back, gripped her shoulders, and said in a low voice, "You have to leave. Right now. Just get out of here."

"I won't go without you."

His face clouded with pain. "Dammit, Cass, don't do this to me."

"You won't go without him?" Joanne mimicked nastily. "You think you get to decide? Well, you don't. I'm in control here. Now I get to decide who goes and who stays, who lives and who dies." She seemed to burn with an inner fire, her brown eyes feverishly bright, patches of red on her cheeks and neck.

Pete took a step toward Joanne. Running a hand over his face, he said, "What a fool I've been, all these years, giving into you."

"Stay where you are." She brought her hand up close to the button. Pete stopped in his tracks.

"Joanne, I don't understand," Cassidy said. "What have I ever done to you?"

"Kevin. You took Kevin away. I had him first, then he married you. I got him back, then you took him away again. Not because he loved you. He never loved anyone but me. He only stayed with you out of pity."

"What?" Cassidy reared back in surprise. "You had an affair with Kevin? But what does that have to do with Barbara?"

Pete took another step. He started to speak, couldn't seem to get the words out, cleared his throat and started again. "Let's sit down. We should all sit down and try to solve the problem. Find some way to clear this up so nobody gets hurt."

Joanne laughed shrilly. "Of course somebody's going to get hurt. That's the whole *point*." She smiled a bright, demented smile. "Everyone's going to get hurt but Cass'll be hurt the most. That's the reason I did all this. So she'd find out what it's like to lose the man you love to another woman. Not quite the same as what she did to me, but still, she'll know that Zach and I died together—that we're linked for all eternity—while she's left alone with her guilt and her pain."

Zach shifted his weight. "But you want Cass alive, right?"

"Yes, of course. She has to suffer the way I did."

"Then why not have your good old lackey, Pete, carry her out?"

Cassidy looked at Pete. With his large, muscular frame and big shoulders, there was no question that he could overpower her. His expression had turned dark and angry. *At Joanne? Or Zach for nailing him.*

Joanne's glittering eyes darted from face to face. "But I planned to do it at the stroke of midnight. If they leave now, they'll have time to go to the police." She clapped her hands. "I know," she said to Cassidy, "I'll keep you here until just before twelve, then have Pete take you out. So let's sit down and make ourselves comfortable, shall we?" She waved at two Windsor chairs standing about twenty feet away from her on the opposite side of the large family room.

Cassidy clutched Zach's arm.

"You better do it," he whispered.

"Now, Cass, did you forget what I said already?" Joanne laughed again. "I get to decide. So, you go sit in that chair." She pointed at one of the Windsors. Cassidy crossed the room, hung her jacket on the back of the chair, and lowered herself stiffly onto the wooden seat. Zach sat also. Joanne, aglow with triumph, continued to stand between the old rounded sofa she'd been sitting on and a scarred walnut coffee table.

She's as borderline as they come. So sensitive to rejection that her husband's leaving set off all this craziness. Full of rage, can't let go of anything, completely distorted images of Kevin and me.

Joanne spoke to Pete, who'd continued edging closer while her attention was fixed on the other two. "You have to sit down too," she said in a motherly tone.

"How could you do this to me?" Pete's huge hands balled into fists. "All these years I've always been there, always loved you. Let you talk me into anything. Good old reliable Pete, the person you could always go to when everything else fell apart."

"I'm not doing this to *you*, Pete. I'm doing it to Cass. I care for you, I do. But you knew from the beginning that Kevin was the only one I'd ever really love."

"I'm not talking about love. I'm talking about using me as part of your scheme to kill an innocent person. You swore nobody'd get hurt."

"But I had to." Her voice turned childlike. "After my husband left and Kevin said we couldn't get back together, all I could think of was making Cassidy pay. I kept seeing Zach die—a car crash, an explosion, a bullet in his brain—and Cass crying over his grave." She glanced at Cassidy. "You called that an obsessive thought disorder, didn't you?"

Obsessive thinking. When she couldn't stop ruminating over the hatred she felt toward her lover's wife. Oh shit! That story she told you in therapy. The married lover—KC—it was Kevin.

"I'm not going to let you do this, Joanne." Pete took another step forward.

"You know you have to do what I say." She moved her hand toward the button. "Now be a good boy and go sit down."

He hesitated, then took his place in the chair next to Cassidy's, his fingers tapping out a rapid rhythm against his thigh. As soon as he was seated, Joanne eased down on the sofa again.

Desperate for a way out, Cassidy gazed at the west wall, made up almost entirely of old-fashioned, wood-framed windows, the outer darkness pierced by tiny lights.

She asked Pete, "How far are we from the lake?" *If only we could jump into it. But the windows don't open and there's no doorway out of here except the one we came through.*

"This room overhangs the water by about ten feet," he said,

his voice shaky. "I used to go diving right under the house when I was a kid."

"Stop talking," Joanne said irritably. "Nobody talks without my permission."

Zach asked, his voice lazy but his body tense, "Aren't you going to offer our guests some champagne?"

Glancing toward the walnut table, Cassidy noticed a vase of silk flowers and a bottle in a shiny black ice bucket.

"Let's see if there's enough." Joanne raised the bottle, which proved to be half full.

Cassidy looked at her watch. Half an hour till midnight. *Feel like I'm racing toward the cliff on a train with no brakes.*

"Isn't this fun?" Joanne picked up her champagne flute. "It's almost like therapy. Cass can ask questions and I get to talk about myself. Only this time, I'm the one in charge, not her. And the story I have to tell will be much less to her liking."

Cassidy's stomach churned. She squeezed her eyes shut, then looked across at Zach. He sat straight, face alert, eyes watching Joanne's every move. *Probably hoping to get close enough to grab her hands. But he won't try anything till I'm out of here. And the odds are, if he takes a single step in her direction, she'll blow them both up.*

Drawing in a breath, Cassidy shifted her gaze to Joanne. "There's one thing I'd like to ask Pete."

"Go right ahead." She smiled benevolently.

Cassidy turned toward Pete, who sat with shoulders hunched, knee jiggling. "Why did you let me go on thinking it was Lany?"

"I was still hoping you were wrong. That Zach'd just left the restaurant. That I wouldn't have to give Joanne up."

Joanne said to Cassidy, "Don't you want to hear about Kevin and me?"

"Didn't you tell me already in therapy?"

"Not all of it. Before Kevin met you, he was planning to marry me. He was just so glorious. But then you came along and he did this strange thing—he dropped me and started dating you." She shook her head, her voice becoming childlike again. "I couldn't understand it. I was so beautiful and you were so plain. Anybody could see just by looking at us that Kevin and I belonged together. Why would he leave me for you?"

Because you went into screaming fits and pounded on him?

Cassidy asked, "But what does any of this have to do with Barbara?"

"Kevin may have married you but that didn't mean he stopped loving me. He managed to hold out for over a year, then I coaxed him into seeing me again."

An affair with Joanne before *he slept with Barbara? God, he lied about everything.*

Joanne added, "He was going to divorce you, and we were going to be together. But then you killed Barbara and Kevin couldn't leave because he was afraid you'd fall apart. The day after Barbara died, he told me everything. He said we couldn't see each other anymore, and we both cried about it."

"What a crock," Zach said. "Cass didn't kill anybody. And Kevin wouldn't've stuck it out with you any more than he did with anybody else."

"It doesn't matter what you think. I know what happened."

Pete said, "Then she showed up at the cemetery and talked me into meeting her later."

"You went to Barbara's funeral?" Cassidy asked Joanne in surprise.

"I thought Kevin would be there. I wanted to see how he acted around you. But he didn't come. Then I saw Pete, and he looked as lonely and lost as I felt. We'd both been through such a terrible ordeal, I thought we could console each other. So I told him how sad I was and said we should help each other through this time of sorrow."

Pete turned toward Cassidy, deep lines cutting across his face. "At first we just clung to each other. But then she started coming up with little favors, like sending an email threat to this teacher she hated. I knew I should stay away from her, but I never could do it. Over all these years, she'd simply appear whenever she felt like it, and I'd let her suck me back in." He ran a hand over his face. "She had this way of making me feel like the king of the universe. I always knew it wouldn't last, that she'd turn around and disappear again. But it felt so good—it was such a high—I could never give it up."

That's what borderlines do. When they're good, they're very, very good. And for some men—and women as well—it's addictive.

Joanne tugged at the dynamite harness, then smoothed her skirt over her thighs. "If you have any other questions, you'd better ask them now."

Zach leaned forward, resting his arms on his legs. "I assume it was you in a blond wig who brought me that drink in the bar."

She nodded.

"So initially I was the only target, but now you've decided to take yourself out with me. Why the change of plan?"

Tilting her head, Joanne responded in a matter of fact voice, as if she thought her actions perfectly rational. "When Pete first sent the e-cards, I wasn't sure how I was going to kill you. I was hoping for a fatal crash, but that didn't happen. Then I accidentally confronted the wrong man and had to shoot him."

"You've killed somebody already?" Pete said, his voice horrified.

"Two people. But they weren't important. Anyway, once I'd killed that man who was driving your car, I started to worry that Pete would find out and go to the police. I considered killing Pete, but he's always been so good to me. And then I realized that after I'd punished Cass, there'd be no point to my life. Nothing left to live for. And so I thought, if you and I died together, it would be even worse for her."

Cassidy asked, "Why kill Howard?"

"Well, I'd been using sex to get him to do what I wanted."

Pete groaned.

"Along with money. I had to pay him too. But the problem was, he fell in love with me. So when I asked him to help me rig the dynamite, he said he wouldn't let me go through with it. That he'd find some way to stop me. I pretended to agree. I promised not to do it. Then I stabbed him."

"Oh Lord." Pete covered his face with his hands. "You are so crazy. I knew it all along. I just wouldn't admit it to myself."

"Don't you ever call me crazy!" she said, almost hissing. She drew in a breath, then continued more calmly. "Well, the time has come for a toast. Zach, you can refill our glasses, then pour champagne for our guests."

Zach topped off his glass and Joanne's, then stepped over to a tall cabinet, removed two additional flutes, and filled them also. Crossing the room, he gave one to Pete, then lifted Cassidy's hand, kissed the back of her fingers, and curled them around the remaining glass.

"Oh, isn't that sweet," Joanne said. "I'm so glad you two really love each other. It makes losing Zach just that much worse for Cass."

"Just do the damn toast so we can get them out of here," Zach said.

Joanne stood. "You go back over by the sofa."

He did as he was told.

Pete and Cassidy rose. Turning his back to Joanne, he whispered, "Do something. Create a distraction."

How? Throw my glass at her?

Joanne jabbed her finger at Pete. "You turn around and stop talking." She went to stand in the center of the room, her back against the windowed wall. "Now all of you—hold up your glasses." They did. "Here's to Cassidy spending the rest of her life in a torment of loss and longing." Joanne emptied her glass. No one else moved. "You have to drink your champagne." She raised her hand toward her chest. Cassidy and Pete took a swallow. Zach remained motionless. "I mean it, Zach." He drank too. They stood in silence, slowly sipping champagne.

If the only reason she's doing this is so I have to go on without Zach, maybe she'd give it up if she couldn't get me out of here.

No she wouldn't. She's come too far to back down now.

But if she can't get rid of me, it'd confuse her. Throw her off. Maybe give Zach a chance to grab her.

Cassidy stared at the dynamite. She didn't want to die. The thought of her physical self being blown into tiny pieces that would never be found sent her into an absolute panic.

Her feet were rooted to the floor. Mustering all her will power, she took one unsteady step, then another.

"I didn't say you could go anywhere," Joanne snapped.

Cassidy continued walking. Zach locked eyes with her. She could see from his face that he wasn't happy, but he knew her well enough to realize she wouldn't be defying Joanne without some kind of agenda.

"Get back in that chair!"

"I'm going to go stand by Zach," Cassidy said, "and the only way you can stop me is by blowing all of us up."

A stunned expression came over Joanne's face. She raised her hand, held it over the button, then let it drop.

Cassidy halted in front of Zach. "I have to stay here with you."

He stared at Cassidy a moment, then nodded. Wrapping his arm around her shoulders, he said, "She's right. You can kill all of us but you can't make Cass go on alone. If she dies with us, you haven't accomplished anything."

"I'm not letting you get away with this. You're going to die right here in this room, and Cassidy's going to watch the explosion from some place else. Pete will drag her out even if he has to go through you to do it, Zach. I own him. I've owned him for years."

Cassidy heard a low-pitched growl. Pete suddenly started charging forward. Joanne stared at him. Her hand hovered over the button. From four feet away, he threw himself at her. Together they crashed through the windowed wall.

Zach pushed Cassidy to the floor and lay on top of her.

A deafening boom, as if they were in the center of breaking thunder. A flash of light. The windows shattered inward, pieces of glass hurtling across the room. A shock wave enveloped her, her head reverberating like the inside of a bass drum.

Cassidy felt a sharp sting on her ankle. She knew that Zach, whose body covered hers, would be getting the brunt of it. *Thank god he's wearing a jacket for once.*

When glass stopped raining around them, Zach gingerly got to his feet, then helped her up. Throwing her arms around him, she buried her face in his chest, then stepped back and sucked in air.

"I can't believe we're still in one piece," she said, the ringing in her ears making her voice sound distant.

"I'm a little surprised myself."

"What happened to Pete—it's just so horrible. I can't stand to think about it."

"Then don't." He took her hand and started toward the doorway. "Let's go sit in the Toyota and call 911."

33.

Talking It Out

When Zach came through the doorway the next evening, the sun had already gone down, creating a cold, diffuse light in the bedroom. Cassidy, sitting on the bed nose-to-chin with Starshine, drank in the sight of him.

How sweet it is, just like Howie said! All of Zach's molecules packed into that sturdy body and cynical brain, right where they're supposed to be.

They'd arrived home at dawn, slept half the day, then Zach had gone into the *Post* to work with another reporter who'd been assigned to write up the explosion and deaths.

"How you doing?" Zach sat in his chair and swiveled to face her.

"I'm okay, except I hate it that we're going to be in the news again. Did you have to tell them about Barbara or were you able to skip over that part?" Cassidy scratched along the calico's jaws. The cat stretched her head back, squinted her eyes, and purred blissfully.

"Left Barbara out of it entirely. I told the other reporter it was a nutso client who blamed you for all her woes. Considering that therapists sometimes do get stalked and killed, I don't think anybody's going to dig any deeper."

Starshine, apparently considering Zach's presence an intrusion, threw Cassidy an irritated look and went to sleep at the foot of the bed.

"How's your back? You having much pain?" On their way home they'd stopped at an ER to have Zach's glass cuts attended to.

"Nah, the pills are working fine. So, what'd you do today?"

"Well, I finally called Amanda. It took me several hours to work myself up to it."

"I hope you're not feeling guilty again. 'Cause if you are, I'm going to haul you in to see a therapist, just like you threatened to do to Bryce."

"It wasn't guilt. It's just that I knew how devastated Amanda would be—losing another child, finding out what a mess Pete had gotten himself into—and I didn't want to face it."

"Don't you deal with people in crisis all the time?"

"Sometimes I do but it's never fun. Guess I was also a little nervous that she might not want to hear from me. But I needed to tell her what a hero Pete was, and it turned out she was really glad I called. Maybe someday we'll do mother-daughter things after all."

"You talk to Kevin?"

"I did, and his story was pretty much what I expected. The first time he was involved with Joanne, he came to see that she was pretty crazy, so he dropped her and moved on to me. But since he has such a short memory, he allowed himself to be seduced when she came back around that second time. And to keep her from having hysterics, he agreed to divorce me— never intending to do it. But then she got crazy again, so he used Barbara's death as an excuse to get out of it."

"It's amazing to me that he could get you to believe him when he said Barbara was the first."

"We were both still in love when he started the affair with

Joanne, so he made every effort to hide it. There were none of the telltale signs that showed up later, after our marriage had gone sour."

Zach stood and flexed his shoulders. "Well, I'm going to get a drink. You want anything?"

Earlier than usual. Well, what do you expect, considering his recent misadventures? It's a wonder he didn't start the minute he got out of bed.

"Would you do me a favor and talk through what happened last night?"

"I know *you* need to talk, but I'm different. Why should I have to handle things the same way you do?"

"It's just that I think talking is good for people."

"Rehashing a bad experience makes you remember it. Feel it. I can't see anything good about it."

"I didn't talk about Barbara's death and the feelings just kept festering. Talking gets rid of old garbage. It cleans out the emotional pipes."

"I don't know. Sounds like mumbo jumbo to me." He shook his head. "But if it'll make you happy—and on the off-chance you're right—I'll humor you. But not until I have a drink in my hand. You don't want anything?"

"Not now."

He fixed a bourbon, then settled on the bed beside her, propping pillows behind his sore back. "So, what do you want to know?"

Resting her hand on his thigh, Cassidy asked, "What did it feel like to have a crazy lady kidnap you?"

He stared into space for several seconds, probably reliving it, the part of talking he didn't like. "Right after you left to go to the restroom, Joanne appeared and sat down beside me. She opened her coat really fast, sort of like a flasher, and showed me what she was wearing. When I saw the dynamite, I was stunned. And then, right after that, immensely pissed at myself for letting down my guard. For not listening when you said it'd be safer to drink at home. Not that I wasn't sober. The instant I saw the dynamite, I got totally focused and alert." He took a long swallow.

"Then, when we were on the road—I drove, she sat beside me with her hand on the button—I just kept telling myself that at some point she'd slip up. The hard part was not getting scared. I knew that if I let myself get scared, I wouldn't be able to make the right move when the opportunity presented itself. So I kept trying to fight off the fear but I couldn't completely. Then we got to the house and she wouldn't let me near her. That's when I started to think there might not be any opportunities." He shook his head. "I thought about you, and how we'd been fighting when you left the table. And that I wouldn't get to say good-bye."

Her throat constricted.

"The worst part was when you walked in that door. My first reaction was to get seriously pissed. Then I felt something else." He stared into space again. "Hopeless maybe."

"But you didn't stay hopeless. I saw how you were watching her, waiting for your chance."

"Yeah, but I was beginning to think I wouldn't get it." Placing his arm behind her back, he squeezed her shoulder. "Well, is that enough? Can I go get my second drink now?"

She smiled warmly. "How 'bout you bring up two drinks and we sit and cuddle?"

Cassidy changed into a long lavender tee emblazoned with a deep red rose. Zach put on his robe. Sitting in bed, Cassidy leaning against his bent knees, Zach massaging her neck, they talked and listened to music. He finished his drink, then reached under her tee to wrap his hand around her breast and stroke her nipple.

"At last I'm wound down enough to make up for my previous poor performance."

"After seeing what happened to Pete and Joanne, I feel so grateful to have you here in this bed tonight." She ran her hand down Zach's leg. "God, it's good to be alive."